ECHOES OF ETERNITY

*Many of these titles are also available as abridged and unabridged audiobooks.
Order the full range of Horus Heresy novels and audiobooks from*
blacklibrary.com

Download the full range of Horus Heresy audio dramas from
blacklibrary.com

ECHOES OF ETERNITY

Aaron Dembski-Bowden

BLACK LIBRARY

A BLACK LIBRARY PUBLICATION

First published in 2022.
This edition published in 2024 by
Black Library, Games Workshop Ltd.,
Willow Road, Nottingham, NG7 2WS, UK.

Represented by: Games Workshop Limited – Irish branch,
Unit 3, Lower Liffey Street, Dublin 1,
D01 K199, Ireland.

10 9 8 7 6 5 4 3 2 1

Produced by Games Workshop in Nottingham.
Cover illustration by Neil Roberts.

See Black Library on the internet at

blacklibrary.com

Find out more about Games Workshop
and the worlds of Warhammer at

games-workshop.com

Printed and bound in the UK.

For John French.
Toast to the ones here today. Toast to the ones that we lost on the way.

THE HORUS HERESY®
SIEGE OF TERRA

It is a time of legend.

The galaxy is in flames. The Emperor's glorious vision for humanity is in ruins. His favoured son, Horus, has turned from his father's light and embraced Chaos.

His armies, the mighty and redoubtable Space Marines, are locked in a brutal civil war. Once, these ultimate warriors fought side by side as brothers, protecting the galaxy and bringing mankind back into the Emperor's light. Now they are divided.

Some remain loyal to the Emperor, whilst others have sided with the Warmaster. Pre-eminent amongst them, the leaders of their thousands-strong Legions, are the primarchs. Magnificent, superhuman beings, they are the crowning achievement of the Emperor's genetic science. Thrust into battle against one another, victory is uncertain for either side.

Worlds are burning. At Isstvan V, Horus dealt a vicious blow and three loyal Legions were all but destroyed. War was begun, a conflict that will engulf all mankind in fire. Treachery and betrayal have usurped honour and nobility. Assassins lurk in every shadow. Armies are gathering. All must choose a side or die.

Horus musters his armada, Terra itself the object of his wrath. Seated upon the Golden Throne, the Emperor waits for his wayward son to return. But his true enemy is Chaos, a primordial force that seeks to enslave mankind to its capricious whims.

The screams of the innocent, the pleas of the righteous resound to the cruel laughter of Dark Gods. Suffering and damnation await all should the Emperor fail and the war be lost.

The end is here. The skies darken, colossal armies gather. For the fate of the Throneworld, for the fate of mankind itself...
The Siege of Terra has begun.

DRAMATIS PERSONAE

| THE EMPEROR | Master of Mankind, Last and First Lord of the Imperium |
| HORUS | Warmaster of the Imperium, Vessel of the Pantheon |

The Primarchs

ANGRON	Lord of the Red Sands, Exalted Daemon Prince of Khorne, Primarch of the XII Legion
MAGNUS THE RED	The Crimson King, Exalted Daemon Prince of Tzeentch, Primarch of the XV Legion
ROGAL DORN	Praetorian of Terra, Primarch of the VII Legion
SANGUINIUS	Archangel of Baal, Primarch of the IX Legion
VULKAN	The Last Guardian, Primarch of the XVIII Legion

The Legio Custodes, 'Last of the Ten Thousand'

| DIOCLETIAN COROS | Tribune |
| HANUMARASI | Warrior of the Hykanatoi |

The I Legion 'Dark Angels'

| CORSWAIN | Regent-Commander of the Hollow Mountain |

The III Legion 'Emperor's Children'

| DEIPHOBUS | Warrior of the 32nd Company |

The V Legion 'White Scars'

SHIBHAN KHAN — 'Tachseer', Regent-Commander of the Lion's Gate space port

The VI Legion 'Space Wolves'

RYKATH — 'No-Foes-Remain', warrior of the Cry of the Grieving Dragon warband, *Tra* Company

The VII Legion 'Imperial Fists'

ARCHAMUS — Master of the Huscarls

FAFNIR RANN — Subcommander of Bhab Bastion

The IX Legion 'Blood Angels'

ZEPHON — 'The Bringer of Sorrow', former Exarch of the High Host

NASSIR AMIT — 'The Flesh Tearer', Dominion of the Fifth Shock Assault Company, 'the Secutors'

ANZARAEL — 'The Bringer of Wrath', Exarch of the High Host

GHALLEN UL'ZAEN — Master of Signals, Fifth Shock Assault Company

ORION — Contemptor-pattern Dreadnought

ERISTES — Legion Thrall, Assessor

SHAFIA — Legion Thrall, Weaponbearer

SHENKAI — Legion Thrall, Weaponbearer

The XII Legion 'World Eaters'

KARGOS	'Bloodspitter', Apothecary of the Eighth Assault Company
KHÂRN	Centurion of the Eighth Assault Company
LOTARA SARRIN	Captain of the warship *Conqueror*

The XVI Legion 'Sons of Horus'

KENOR ARGONIS	Equerry to the Warmaster

The XVI Legion 'Luna Wolves'

EZEKYLE ABADDON	First Captain, Warchief of the Justaerin
TARIK TORGADDON	Second Captain

The XVII Legion 'Word Bearers'

INZAR TAERUS	Chaplain of the Osseous Throne Chapter

Imperial Army

DAWYNNE COTO	Corporal Primus-grade
JA-HEN UQUAR	Conscript, Neshamere Eighth Mechanised Infantry
LORELEI KELVYR	Conscript
MARLUS ZENEER	Corporal
SYLAS ENVARIC	Sergeant of the 12th Helian Rifles
TANEEQ MASHRAJEIR	Corporal of the 91st Industani Drop Troops

Imperial Personae

MALCADOR THE SIGILLITE   Regent of the Imperium

CERIS GONN   Interrogator

The Adeptus Mechanicus

ARKHAN LAND   Technoarchaeologist

TRANSACTA-7YI   Skitarius of the Tr1.ax Macroclade

MAGNA-DELTA-8v8   Skitarius of the En.7lius Macroclade

SAPIEN   Artificimian

SHIVA MAKUL   Princeps of the Legio Ignatum Reaver Titan *Iracundos*

MAESTOL VURIR   Deacon-Enginseer of the Reaver Titan *Iracundos*

The Martian Mechanicum

ULIENNE GRUNE   Princeps of the Legio Audax Warhound Titan *Hindarah*

HIMMAR KUL   Moderatus of the Legio Audax Warhound Titan *Hindarah*

OTESH RALINE   Moderatus of the Legio Audax Warhound Titan *Hindarah*

The Neverborn

KA'BANDHA   Champion of the War God

VARAK'SUUL   The Murder of Thrymyr

'No beast is more savage than man when possessed with power answerable to his rage.'

– Lucius Plutarchus, Ancient Grekan Solar Priest

'They plunder, they slaughter, and they steal: this they falsely name Empire. And where they make a waste-land, they call it peace.'

– Tassatus of the Etruscus-Romanii Kingdom, prehistoric philosopher

'Sanguinius is loyal to our father out of perfect love and perfect nobility, and if that were all, he would still be the best of us. But he is also loyal out of perfect fear. He fears the reason he has wings. He fears what they might represent. He fears something went wrong during his creation and he fears the effects this may have upon his own gene-sons.

'The insecurity that binds Sanguinius to the Emperor, perhaps more so than any other of our father's sons, is born of the belief that he has the most to prove. It is a bitter irony, because he is the one with the least.

'The one with the most to prove is the barbarian of Nuceria, but Angron has never possessed any desire to live up to the Emperor's expectations. He regards such a fate as worse than failure. To him, it would be nothing less than a second slavery.'

– The writings of the Primarch Lorgar

PART ONE

HORDE

ONE

_____

A red sun rises

Lotara

The war was over.

The Imperial Palace was dead. It had been a tectonic sprawl, breathless in scale; a marble scab the size of a continent that crusted over the Eurasian land mass, reaching from the dry eastern coast to the empty western sea. Now it was rubble. The regions that weren't destroyed were infected. The sectors that weren't abandoned were aflame.

All that sacred rock, gone to waste. The stone used in its construction wasn't only Terran in origin. Luna had contributed, as had Mars, as had many of the moons spinning through space in their sedate ballet around the Sol System's gas giants. Exo-system stone had been long-hauled back to Terra from rediscovered and conquered worlds, with populations that knew nothing of Old Earth outside of whispered myth now quarrying marble for the sake of a palace they would never see.

But Terra had given up the greatest portion of her bones

15

for the project. She was already plundered from the Dark
Age of Technology and scarred from the unknowable ruin-
ations of the Age of Strife that followed – and she suffered
again when Imperial ambition mined her crust hollow. The
Emperor's people tore a planet's worth of precious stone from
the ground, dragging it from the deep earth by the sweat of
slaves and prisoners and servitors. Terra surrendered her bones,
not that she had a choice in the matter, and they were hauled
away beneath the gaze of adepts; payloads for code-goaded
Imperial machines.

Polished. Refined. Processed. Rendered into art by architects.
Rendered into reality by labourers. Rendered into battlements
by soldiers.

And now gone, all of it. A continent razed. A hemisphere
reduced to rubble.

A single tower will fall and its dust chokes a city block for
hours. The death-smoke of two spires tumbling will blanket a
region for days, turning the air to grey dust. But a witness in
the sky drifting above the devastation of Terra now wouldn't
see a lone spire fall, or the death of a mere two towers. A
palace of gods and demigods had been laid to waste. This
witness would see the aftermath: dust, dust, dust – horizon
to horizon.

An axiom from a more enlightened age stated, *Society grows
great when old men plant trees whose shade they know they shall
never sit in.* That sentiment speaks not only of sacrifice, but
vision. A future with foundations born in the deeds of the
altruistic dead. Instead of such sacrifice, and bereft of vision,
Terra now burned because of weapons in the shape of men.

Higher than life can climb unaided, above the thinnest
reaches of the atmosphere, the Warmaster's fleet lay anchored
in orbit.

Space was no longer a void. Beyond Terra, what was once

the cold vacuum of space had curdled with an infestation of unreality. Colours without names tendrilled around the armada, wreathing ships in clawed fog and dipping their misty protuberances into the planet's exosphere.

The voidmist coalesced into figures and shapes a thousand times larger than ships themselves; the silhouetted promises of watching gods. Eyes the size of moons opened and closed in that seething mist. Teeth were bared, the length of continents. Great wings capable of eclipsing the sun spread and furled and rotted away and regrew. The orbiting ships absorbed this mist, their ironwork warping with its saturation. To open a vox-channel was to listen in on burning souls.

Elsewhere in the galaxy, the craftworld refugees of the aeldari race would recognise these sights of unreal wonder. The warp and reality interlocked, focused on a core of absolute suffering that their seers would find all too familiar. Centuries ago, this was how their species had given birth to their baneful god. This was how their empire had died.

Thousands of crew members looked out at the toxic skies and down upon the world below, at their victory turning to ash. Terra was dying. The savants and scholars of Kelbor-Hal's New Mechanicum could perceive the exact threads of annihilation, grasping the delicate balances of life and physics being thrown aside in the name of regicide, but the truth was evident to everyone. Anyone that looked out of a porthole or gazed from the wide windows of a command deck saw it plain.

You didn't need to be an expert to see the war had killed Terra. You merely needed eyes.

Lotara Sarrin looked upon the blighted world from the bridge of the warship *Conqueror*. She sat slouched in her command throne, her deteriorated form at the very edge of terminal dehydration, and she stared at the world she'd helped destroy.

She had been proud, once. She'd been righteous in her

rebellion, loyal to the Legion that treasured her, loyal to the crew she commanded and the soldiers whom she protected. She was a fleet-killer, a huntress of the stars, commanding one of the most powerful vessels ever conceived and created by human ingenuity. Her service record was decorated with avowals and commendations. Her uniform was marked with the Bloody Hand of the Twelfth, the highest honour a mortal could earn from her Legion.

She was still loyal. Even when insanity crept its way through her ship, she'd stayed loyal. Even when the World Eaters rampaged through the halls and chambers, butchering their own serfs and slaves. Even when she'd been forced to execute warriors whom she'd served alongside for years, who had lost their faith in the Warmaster's way. Even when every drop of water in the crew's supply tanks turned to flyblown blood. Even when her nights became sleepless epileptic seizures of flicker-flash horrors, as dead comrades cried out from the shadows of the ship they were doomed to haunt. Even when the degrading *Conqueror* began to phase in and out of reality, and entire districts of its lethal bulk turned rancid with the warp's corrosion. Even when her skin began to scale with the rawness of her sins manifesting on her flesh.

Lotara Sarrin had sworn her loyalty to the very end, and now the end had come. She hadn't expected it to look like this.

Reflected in her eyes was a globe of sickly grey, with its halo of violet madness. No visible land masses, no signs of life. She could see nothing beneath the layer of filthy murk. The *Conqueror*'s scanners, when they functioned at all, couldn't cut through the dust. Terra didn't look like Terra. It looked like Venus. It choked under a similar tainted sky.

Choppy reports analysed the clouded atmosphere. The marble dust in the air was enough to destroy any reliability with the vox, but it was nothing compared to the true damage. Toxic vapours were rife, churned up from a million surface detonations and the orbital barrages tormenting Terra's carbonite-rich crust. The impacts and the world-tearing heat of cannon fire from the Warmaster's armada had ripped craters in the Palace and carved chasms in the surrounding territories. Dying Titans contributed their swansongs, too – their heart-reactors going nova as they lay in the rubble-graves of their failed marches.

It all added up: fusing and igniting the gases that lay stable beneath the earth. *Sulfa dyoxide*, an element known to the sages of the Martian Mechanicum, was born from these blasted-open pores in Terra's skin. The poison coiled its chemical tendrils through the filthy air, ruining it further, turning it acidic.

And there was more. The earth bled lava from suppurating ulcers. Pyroclastic flows of burning gas and volcanic tephra had gushed from the riven land, blanketing embattled regions with flash-melting smoke and sludge. The ash and dust clogging the air were conjoined now, layered yet inseparable, a curtain of pale grey denying sight and breath. Dust paste caked the lungs of millions of survivors. Those without rebreathers were at risk of asphyxiation just by remaining within the Palace, but there was nowhere left to run.

The destruction of the Imperial Palace also released chemicals used by the abandoned industries of Terra. Containment failures in several palatial manufactories haemorrhaged a processing substance marked as *maethal eysocyanite*. This gas clung to the ground with a predation that almost spoke of intelligence, flooding several remaining bastions at their lower levels, an unseeable tidal wave of chemical venom dissolving into the defenders' eyes and throats. It blinded, burned, killed within hours. The Astartes could survive it, though it mutilated many of them. Hordes of human defenders and refugees were not so lucky.

Last and far from least, there was the radiation. By design or misfortune, subterranean stores of nameless Dark Age materials had been cracked open over the course of the war. Many of the gaseous elements sighing out of these ancient bunkers were barely understood and defied current naming convention, but their radiological effects were murderously familiar. They were death, one final horror from the past, the very last breath of a forgotten age.

Lotara had taken the last report she'd seen and given it to one of the few remaining Mechanicum sages still aboard the *Conqueror*. His augmetics were rusted, chafing at his ghoulish skin. Blood poisoning showed in lightning-bolt veins beneath his flesh. He had to tap out a reply on a speaking keypad because his vocoder had degenerated beyond repair. He'd never even set foot on the surface; the *Conqueror* had done this to him.

When he printed his reply to her, Lotara read it three times to be sure she understood just what the war was doing to Terra. And there it was, laid out in grinding totality. The absolute destruction of humanity's birthworld. The war that had let the galaxy burn now covered every inch of Terra's surface, darkening the heavens and gouging into the planet's mineral flesh.

But it wasn't the toxicity or the blindness that stuck with her, it was one of the tech-priest's simple, blunt summations halfway through his analysis. He'd detailed how the *sulfuryk* elements from the world's injuries had seeped into the air, scattering Sol's incoming light within the human visual spectrum. With this explanation, a brief note gave simple context:

To those on the surface, the sun has gone red.

She couldn't shake that image.

Now she looked at the oculus viewscreen where, from orbit, a pall of grey covered the entire world. They had come to take the Throneworld and had instead wrapped it in a funeral shroud.

'Khârn,' she spoke out loud for the first time in hours – or perhaps days – her voice a parched whisper. The closest crew paid her no mind at all. They were hunched at their own consoles, lost in their own pain.

'Khârn?' Lotara said again.

Khârn stood not far from her command throne. His visage was a riven mess of scars and battlefield staple-stitches. He didn't say anything. He never said anything anymore.

Her stomach clenching was the only warning she got. Her insides heaved with enough force to drive her out of her throne and onto her knees, ears ringing with pressure, spit stringing between her open lips. She cried out at the sudden pain, at the poison running up her throat, and her yell turned into a hot flush of vomit slapping across the deck.

As she gasped for her breath back, she looked down at the half-digested spread of her last meal. A pool of thin bile, a few scraps of stomach lining, and three of someone's fingers.

Disbelief overpowered her exhaustion for a few precious seconds. She recoiled from the puddle, pulling herself back into her throne. Just a trick of her sleepless mind. That was all. That was all.

Khârn approached the flagship's captain, kneeling to rest at her level. He didn't offer his aid as she hauled herself on shaking limbs back into her chair. He was unarmed, and Lotara couldn't recall ever seeing him without his axe before. Blood trickled from her eyes as she stared into the patchwork ruin of his face. The thirsting husk of her body gave up yet more precious fluid in the form of those profane tears.

'Khârn,' she whispered. 'What have we done?'

It was a question being asked across Terra and above it, by the men and women on both sides of the war.

Khârn had no answer.

TWO

A broken gladiator

Kargos

Somewhere in the dust, a gladiator hunted in the weakling light of a scarlet dawn. He staggered as much as walked, stumbled as much as he ran, any sense of grace he once possessed now a shredded memory. His motions were those of an infected beast, his mind aflame with urges that devoured reason. His crested helmet turned this way and that in animal, kinetic spurts. He moved as if rabid.

The enemy had broken and run. Minutes ago. Hours ago. Days ago. He couldn't see them now, nor was he sure in which direction they'd fled. His armour joints snarled as he jerked his head at shadows in the ash, at sounds muffled to unreality. A chainaxe idled in his gauntleted fist. It wasn't his axe, and he couldn't recall where he'd found it. Sometimes the weapon's teeth whirred, chewing dirty air. The blood that caked the axe's fangs had dried to gritty paste.

The gladiator had a name, though in that moment he barely

knew it. He also had an honoured, vital role within the ranks of his Legion, which was something else the pressure in his skull had leached away. The pain engine implanted against his brain was biting deep, a clicking parasite making a meal of his central nervous system.

He salivated as he stared into the dust. In these moments – which were becoming ever more frequent – he was less a reasoning being and more a vessel brimming with notions of immediate instinct.

Tick-tock, tick-tock, the Butcher's Nails sang, sending needle-prick electrical signals into the meat of his mind. *This is pain,* it promised him, *and you will feel it until I allow you pleasure.* And so, sharklike, he pressed on. To stand still was to feel the implant's razor kisses deep in his skull, where he couldn't scratch.

Things were changing. *Had* changed. With the pain engine remapping his mind, his chemical cognition was shattered. The adrenal violence that once brought ecstasy now brought a thin relief. Treasured, yes, but hardly the same thing. Before, the gladiator had chased a feeling of exaltation. Now, he pursued tantalising caresses of relief. They were never enough to become pleasure, never even close, but at least they came with a cessation of pain.

His armour was a scavenged panoply beneath the clinging layer of ash. For years he'd worn the white ceramite of the XII Legion's crusading heraldry, and the mongrel suit he was sealed inside was formed from only half its original components. He couldn't recall repainting his warplate, nor granting his serfs permission to paint it for him. Yet there it was, revealed in the patches where the dust briefly brushed away: arterial red instead of the familiar filthy white.

Yes, things were changing.

This didn't trouble him. Perhaps it would have, had he given it true weight of thought, but in the rare moments he turned his mind in that direction, the Nails would gnaw hard enough to trigger muscle tremors. They promised him peace only if he ran, roared, killed, maimed, burned. So he did those things when he could, and grew drunk with pain when he couldn't.

At one dimly remembered point in time, he'd tried breaking his skull open against a wall, rhythmically crashing his forehead against the broken marble in a bid to drain the vileness from his head. It had worked, until it hadn't. Then the pain came back, twice as bitter. Punishment for his self-inflicted wounds. Judgement for attempted suicide.

The gladiator moved on. It soothed the Nails when he moved forward.

He wasn't alone in the ashen wasteland. His brothers – and the things that pretended to be his brothers – made a loose pack around him. Together but apart, they moved through the gloom. Some of them were made of fire. Some of them were made of blood in the shape of monsters. Some of them were his lifelong brethren, and some of them just wore his kinsmen's flesh.

Apothecary.

He heard the word as he ascended a scree of infected rubble. The sound of it was familiar even if the meaning wasn't. Poisoned rocks slid beneath the weight of his boots. The wall had died to artillery fire, recently enough that it still smoked, and the gladiator hauled his way up the broken slope. The Nails sensed his resolve and could have been merciful, but they spiked again anyway. An animal grunt broke from his lips, unintentional and helplessly honest.

Apothecary. That word again. It lingered in his mangled thoughts, as if it wanted to mean something. *Apothecary. Apothecary.* The next time he heard it, it was shouted out loud: 'Apothecary!' It had the emphasis of a name. Or a curse.

The gladiator stopped in his ascent. He turned, gazing

through the dust. Seeking the silhouettes of his brothers, and the stalking things that claimed to be his brothers. A cluster of them were at the bottom of the rubble slope. Their armour was no longer red. The ashy dust had restored his fellow World Eaters to their original filthy white heraldry.

'Kargos!' one of them shouted up at him.

Just like that, words had meaning once more. The Nails bit, as if mocking his return to cognition, but their mandibles were dull against the trickling spread of identity.

The gladiator – *Kargos*, he thought, *I am Kargos* – tried to vox down to them, but the vox-web was useless these days. He shouted back through his helm's voice grille, the words amplified and raw.

'Who calls?'

The answer wasn't an answer at all, it was a demand. 'Medic!'

Kargos descended, half-skidding down the rockcrete rubble. The cluster of silhouettes resolved into shapes, then became the figures of his brothers. His actual brothers. Not the things that professed brotherhood.

Twenty-nine of his kindred were down, their bodies dragged by the survivors sane enough to resist the song of the Nails. He looked over their broken remains lying in loose rows, already shrouded with grey-white dust. Bolt impacts and chainblade tears marked their armour, the ceramite rent open to reveal the destroyed meat inside.

Kargos turned his gaze to the survivors, the World Eaters still standing. Others stalked past them in the dust, climbing the rubble slope, seeking prey at the behest of the pain engines biting into their brains. Even those with enough self-control to deal with the Legion's dead were tormented by violent tics and twitches. This funeral service, as blunt and careless as any XII Legion ritual, took a supreme measure of focus for those able to perform it.

'What are you waiting for?' one of them grunted. Kargos

couldn't make out the warrior's identity with the dust coating his warplate. 'Harvest them,' the warrior ordered.

Kargos looked down at his own armour, at his empty belt and bandolier. When, exactly, had he lost the tools of his trade? The metal vials of stimulant serums and combat narcotics were gone. His narthecium was a broken ruin, a bolt-hit husk of missing instruments. Its scanner display was cracked and black, no longer connected to his armour's power supply. Even the keypad on his vambrace was worthless, showing lost keys like a desperate smile with missing teeth.

No matter. He didn't need the specialised instruments to harvest, he could use his knife. The work would be messier, riskier for the removed organs, but he'd done it before. All it took was care and haste, so the ashy air wouldn't contaminate the fleshy nodes as they were pulled free.

He crouched by the first body and drew his knife. In human hands, it would be something to go to war with. In Kargos' grip, it was a chipped and tarnished machete.

'Who was this?' he asked his brothers. They didn't answer; Kargos sensed them shuffling in the dust, struggling to remain with the dead rather than move on in search of more prey. They probably didn't know who'd died either; squads were scattered, the vox was down, and the dust was a great equaliser on that score, turning them all into ghosts of themselves. Who was who hardly mattered now.

Kargos reached for the containment cells mag-locked to his belt. They were reinforced, internally cooled ceramite cylinders marked with Nagrakali runes. He carried dozens of them, each one a capsule for the progenoids of a fallen Legion brother. With their gene-seed harvested, the slain would live on in the creation of their replacement warriors. Over the months of the war, he'd harvested the progenoids from the throats and chests of many of his kindred.

Except his fingers brushed against naked ceramite plating. He didn't carry dozens of them. He carried three. And the three that remained were punctured and empty.

A chill ran through him, severe enough to cool even the sting of the Nails in the back of his head. So many had already died unharvested over the course of the war. How many had he harvested only to lose their genetic legacy in the fitful nothingness between bouts of clarity? He could die for this. In better, saner times, his Legion had executed Apothecaries for failure of this magnitude. They still might.

Kargos felt the eyes of his brethren upon him. He knew their weapons were still in their hands.

'I can't,' he confessed to them. 'I can't do it.'

They still said nothing, and Kargos felt the weight of their wordless judgement. He rose to his feet for sentencing. Gladiators always faced fate with courage. Only cowards died on their knees.

But there was no one there. The other World Eaters were gone. Swallowed by the dust, if they'd ever been there at all. He looked down; the bodies were gone, too. He stood alone in the dust. Utterly alone.

Alone, that is, but for a sudden pinch along his spinal nerves. The Nails bit, offering up a motivating pulse of pain, promising more if he remained still. Kargos turned, staggering, stumbling, no longer really Kargos at all. Just the gladiator again.

Time passed strangely in the ash. At some point in Kargos' staggering journey, shapes resolved around him. A few became many, and many became more than enough. He knew some were his Legion brothers and some were not, and he could tell the difference by those that could see where they were going. He and his brothers were blind, but the things that pretended to be his brothers and sisters could see well enough to hunt. These blood-letting creatures hunted ahead of the horde; the Emperor's silent scream sapped their strength, but they saw flares of life in the choking dust, and they drew the Warmaster's forces with them. Making their way towards the Sanctum Imperialis, where the last organised defenders gathered at the final fortress.

It was a tide. Hundreds of thousands of warriors and soldiers and daemonic entities merging into a wave of god-soaked intent. Rank meant little now among the mortal castes of this horde; military cohesion had almost broken down into myth. They staggered and stumbled and some even ran, warriors from every one of the Warmaster's Legions, a seething host of abused minds and diseased souls. Some exulted in their shackles of divine slavery, others falsely believed themselves free. It made no difference. A slave was still a slave even if he crowned himself king.

Though blunted by the Nails' pain, Kargos sensed the shifting air. The veil between worlds was so very thin now. Neverborn clawed their way into reality with mere wisps of thought. A single drop of blood on the broken earth spawned horrors.

The Emperor was weakening.

Imagine such a thing.

The Neverborn hissed it. Angron roared it. Horus promised it. Soon the time would come to drag down the walls of the final fortress.

Something pierced the bloodstained cloud of Kargos' thoughts. His name again. Someone nearby was saying his name. They'd been saying it for some time.

It was Inzar. Inzar of the XVII, wearing grit-abraded warplate and with his weapons chained to his armour as a symbol of his time with the XII. The parchments still adhering to Inzar's armour were scored and faded, reduced to ragged strips. He gripped Kargos' shoulder guard, preventing him from moving on with the horde.

'I thought it was you, brother.' Even all these years later, Inzar's voice was a low and familiar purr through his helmet's vocaliser. Somehow it cut through the wind. 'How fine it is to see you, so close to our triumph.'

Kargos wasn't sure what to say – nothing about any of this felt like triumph – so he said nothing. Inzar's touch remained on the World Eater's shoulder. A guiding hand.

'Come with me, Kargos. You have lost your way. I will help you.'

Kargos stared, mute, through eyes that throbbed with their own pulse. It took him three tries to speak, and he only managed three words.

'Are you real?'

Inzar grunted at that, a sound that might have been a laugh. 'Come with me, my friend.'

'No.' Kargos licked his cracking lips and tasted blood. 'Answer me. Are you real?'

There was no laughter that time. Just a nod, a gesture of understanding.

'I am real.'

Kargos hesitated for a few more seconds – the Neverborn had lied to him before – then followed.

A council was convened in the wasteland, formed around a gathering of officers and attendants still in possession of their senses. The shadows of tanks rumbled at the gathering's edges. Warriors of every Legion stood in loose packs, as often associating by new-found allegiances over their paternal bloodlines. Kargos was one of them. He stayed at Inzar's side out of exhausted familiarity, watching, through aching eyes, the first signs of order from disorder that he'd seen in what felt like forever.

Questions were asked in vicious murmurs and answered in the same tone. Establishing a firm hierarchy was impossible without the vox, and without knowing what regiments were where; what Titan Legios had managed to haul themselves up and through the wreckage of the Ultimate Wall; what Astartes forces had assembled in the fallen districts of the Inner Palace. But it was something. Waves were forming in the tide, part of the natural rhythm of the horde: gatherings of might just like this one, warbands massing for the final assault.

The names of First Captains were spoken, and their absences marked. Ahriman. Typhon. Abaddon. Embattled elsewhere or already dead? None could say.

And what of Rogal Dorn, the Emperor's Praetorian? What of Jaghatai Khan and the Angel of Blood? Were they cowering within the Sanctum Imperialis waiting for the last battle, or were they trapped elsewhere in the war-torn districts of the Inner Palace, besieged in their bastions and unable to break out? The Khan, it was said, had died of his tainted wounds at the Lion's Gate space port days ago. The Praetorian, with the Palace in ashes, his genius expended and his plans in ruins, was said to be hiding behind the walls of Bhab Bastion and readying his final scheme to escape Terra. That left only the Angel free, and the depleted remnants of the three Legions he commanded.

Kargos' exhaustion thinned out as the Nails blessedly stopped biting so deep. The voices of those speaking soothed the pain engine in his skull, as if their plans were a prayer. The war was won. The defenders were broken. The Emperor's shield was reduced to a sliver of its invisible power, and Neverborn ran amok through the wasted districts of the Inner Palace.

What, then, came next? Magnus would break the Emperor's will, and with it, the psychic shield. Angron, in his fury, would find and butcher the Angel of Blood, then march upon the

Sanctum Imperialis. Horus himself was soon to make planet-fall. They would tear down the Eternity Gate and burn the Sanctum Imperialis to the ground. They had the numbers. The defenders did not.

So let it be spoken, so let it be done. Terra would soon be theirs.

THREE

A goddess with a spear in her spine

Ulienne

The crew of the Warhound *Hindarah* were proud of their efforts. Ascending to the Inner Palace was no easy feat, with the dust killing any attempt to bring in sarcophagus ships, and the fallen sections of the Ultimate Wall offering a kilometres-high tectonic landslide of rubble, far beyond the limits of most Titans' stabilisers. The first few god-machines that had made it up into the districts of the Inner Palace were confronted with a wasteland of bombarded marble where their isolated Titans were the tallest things standing. Whole regions of bastions, castles, spires and colonnades lay in ruin, hammered to powder from orbit, or overrun by the hordes of the Warmaster's infantry and armour support that had already poured into the Inner Palace.

The Titans of the Martian Mechanicum lacked the luxury of such swiftness. As they began to arrive, few loyalist Titans met their cautious advance. Most of them circled the remaining bastions or had run for the safety of the Sanctum Imperialis.

Hindarah and her crew were in the first wave to make it up the avalanche of the Ultimate Wall. One breach among dozens, it was a vast slope of broken rock between them and the vindication they craved. It took several days, trying step by step, forcing stabilisers and compensators and gyrobalancers into the crimson, until *Hindarah*'s reactor was breathing fusion at their backs. Then they'd stop, letting the ironfire cool, letting their tech-priests soothe the machine-spirit, before trying the next steps when the readings were out of the red.

Other Titans retreated to their coffin-ships, resolving to airlift onto the plateau. Few met with any success, with the dust chewing through engine intakes and crippling most of the landers that made the attempt. Some unleashed their weapons on unbreached sections of the wall, melta-boring rockcrete, atomising stone and conversion-beaming holes through Rogal Dorn's greatest defences.

Time, time, time. It all took time. All while the defenders fell back to the fortifications of the Palatine Ring.

Many Titans attempted the climb. Every step had to be calculated and estimated in equal measure, with each Titan's void shields lowered to push power elsewhere. Ground teams – the few skitarii infantry units that could still be trusted not to rush ahead in the hunt for kills – did what they could to clear patches in the landslides for huge clawed feet to slam down.

On *Hindarah*'s ascent, she'd fallen twice. The first was a simple slip early on, a miscalculation in stabiliser compensation, sending them toppling forward. As dangerous as it was, forward was the safest way to fall; Moderatus Otesh had moved with cold clarity at her controls, hammering down the dragging leg at an oblique angle with enough force to punch through loose rock and keep them in place for the precious seconds she needed to swing *Hindarah* back to stability. The crew had cheered her for that. Even other Titans, those near enough to see *Hindarah*'s silhouette in the dust, had voxed their appreciation or, in some cases, their mockery. The broken communication web allowed, just barely, for some of it to even make sense.

The second fall was worse. Close to the top after days of slow progress, the boulder scree gave way beneath them, just as it had for so many others. The reactor roared with the machine-spirit's frustration – and, in truth, its fear – as it all happened excruciatingly slowly: the grind of rock, the whine of straining iron, and the disgustingly serene tilting as they started to go over. *Hindarah* toppled sideways and backwards, its stabilisers squealing as they were relieved of all pressure.

The crew knew they were dead. Falling from this high up on the avalanche was death. Even if they survived, which was unlikely, and even if their Titan didn't smash itself to pieces in the tumbling roll, which was even less likely, *Hindarah* wouldn't be craned back to her feet for weeks, if ever. There was nothing resembling that kind of coordination and organisation left in the war. The crew knew all of this, had borne it in mind every step up the avalanche, and it flashed to the fore in each of their minds as they started arching backwards.

The rocks ground and rumbled, sliding, sliding.

Ahead of them, disappearing in their tilting eye-windows, was the Mortis Reaver *Varcarnerix*. She was even closer to the top, surrounded by a small horde of labourer-tech-thralls working around their god-machine's heels. It had taken her more than a week to get there.

The words spilled from Princeps Ulienne Grune's mouth without thought and without care. Not shouted. Not panicked. Just a whisper, breathy with instinct.

'Fire the ursus claw.'

Moderati Secundus Himmar Kul had a half-second to balance the rolling fire-arc figures against his own guesswork. He moved *Hindarah*'s arm by muscle memory, with no time to lock the firing braces down, and squeezed both triggers. The cockpit shuddered with the kickback of his blind-fire. *Hindarah* whined as her arm socket took the brunt of an unbraced release.

It all happened within the span of half a dozen heartbeats, from slippage to claw-fire, but the timing made no difference. They could've had a day to decide. It didn't matter. There was only one thing to fire at.

Their harpoon took *Varcarnerix* in the back. Another five metres higher, a single second later, and it would've missed completely.

The three-taloned ursus claw lanced through the Reaver's rear carapace armour, where the composite plating of adamantium, plasteel and ceramite was thinnest. It buried itself with a thundercrack, driving deep into the god-machine's internals, reducing two tech-priests to a spread of gory debris in the engine room. It had missed the Thetis reactor that served as the Titan's heart, instead punching all the way through to the industrial pillar of *Varcarnerix*'s spinal column. The great claw snapped shut around a fistful of sacred, mangled metal, and locked hard with the activating clangs of macromagnetic binding.

Varcarnerix ceased all locomotion. For a moment, the towering god-engine stood facing the ascent with almost philosophical calm. In her shadow, skitarii and servitors stood aghast, unable to believe the scratched lenses they had instead of eyes. They were worshippers at the feet of divinity, and their goddess had just taken a spear in the spine.

Hindarah jerked. She buckled. She started turning at a wild obtuse. Both moderati worked their controls, white-knuckled and teeth clenched, steering as best they were able to bring the legs back into alignment.

'There's nothing to stand on, it's going out from under us, nothing to stand on…' This, from Moderatus Otesh.

'No,' Princeps Ulienne was mouthing, the lone word a silent chant. 'No, no, no.'

One foot crashed down. Rock shivered under them, shuddered harder, then kept slipping. The other foot smashed down, then the first again. They staggered on the rock, unsteady as a wounded wolf. Motors revved in the Warhound's harpoon arm as her crew hauled on the anchored ursus claw for stability. Blessed iron screeched in *Hindarah*'s shoulder as her socket stretched and warped with the strain.

That was when *Varcarnerix* screamed. The Reaver let loose with her war-horn, crying out above the rumble of the avalanche. In that moment she sounded pathetically, horrifyingly alive.

'We're stable.' Moderatus Kul's laugh was hollow with disbelief. '*We're stable.*'

And he was right. *Hindarah* settled, her joints whining down as their protests ceased. The cockpit no longer lurched. They were stable.

Varcarnerix turned towards them.

Started to turn, at least. The wreckage of her spine wouldn't allow it; she would never complete that turn, just like she'd never walk again, never wage another war. Her turn became a tilt, and the tilt became a fall.

Varcarnerix gave another war-horn scream, the last shriek of a betrayed godling. She vented plasma from her carapace slits, uselessly breathing poison fire into the filthy air. In an act of either mindless panic or naked spite, she opened up with her cannons, her arms pouring forth volleys of blinding laser fire that echoed like thunder. With her dying cannonade, she liquefied her own worshippers and burned the rocks around her to black glass.

'Detach!' Ulienne ordered. 'She's going over! Detach!'

They couldn't detach. The Reaver was going to take them with her if she fell down the landslide, they'd saved themselves only to doom themselves, and *Hindarah* couldn't detach. Kul tried the levers again, tried the triggers again, and again, and again. The macromagnetics had unbound, the grip had eased, but the claw was still buried in *Varcarnerix*'s ribs. They'd punched too deep.

'Blow the lynchlocks.'

Kul hadn't needed the order. He was already doing it. *Hindarah*'s reactor flared at the insult as power ran hot to her extremities. *Bang, bang, bang* went the emergency fail-safe charges in her shoulder, detonating the lynchlocks attaching the claw launcher to her body.

She amputated her own arm just in time. *Varcarnerix* hammered down onto the rockslide, impacting face first and instantly killing her own crew. The immense weight of her body striking the rubble shook the earth and set another landslide in motion. Boulders rolled on that tide of flowing gravel, flowing down the kilometres-high slope. Further down, Titans of various Legios, each abraded of their paint jobs by the ashy air and suffering with degraded scanners, ponderously moved aside or braced as best they could. It was far from the first such rubble tide. Through the useless spray of static and scrap code, *Hindarah*'s crew heard voices damning them and lauding them for their treacherous survival.

One of them stood out above the others, a wet crackle that identified itself as *Tellum Ire*. She was a Mortis Warhound, close enough to see the shadowplay in the dust, and she raged at *Hindarah*.

Moderatus Otesh shook her head. She was still pale with receding panic. 'They'd fire on us if they could.'

But they couldn't. *Tellum Ire* was too far back down the slope, likely on ground too unstable to risk weapons discharge.

Ulienne listened to their raving as her heartbeat slowed to normal. She felt the chill of what she'd done, but her discomfort didn't reach the level of guilt. All order was gone from the Warmaster's forces anyway. As long as they could stay ahead of any other Mortis engines, there would be no repercussions; there was barely any hierarchy to answer to now. Since the wall fell, it was every god-machine for itself.

'This is Princeps Ulienne of Audax. I speak for *Hindarah*.' She had no idea if her transmission would reach *Tellum Ire*, but in the absence of guilt was reawakened pride. She didn't appreciate being spoken to in such a manner.

Tellum Ire replied: more anger, paved thick with promises of retribution. Ulienne let it play out like background music for a time, baring her bloody gums in a smile, then sent back a clipped reply of her own to terminate the link.

'Engine kill.'

Their brush with death close to the top of the breach had been two days ago. Since reaching the summit and striding through the breach, *Hindarah* had stalked amidst the ruined districts of the Inner Palace, engaged in hour upon hour of hard fighting. She'd joined up with Legiones Astartes forces besieging Meru Bastion and, battling one-armed, she'd helped bring down walls and destroy enemy tanks with volleys from her turbo-laser.

Few Legio Audax resupply vessels had made the journey past the Ultimate Wall, isolating them in the vanguard. The truth was, *Hindarah* had been in the field for months since her first deployment on Terra's surface, and she'd seen better days even before her amputation. Incidental damage was adding up, and more serious wounds were rotting through her iron bones as they went untended. The night before, as Meru Bastion fell, a nasty twist of fortune sent a missile pounding into the side of *Hindarah*'s head. It struck the moment her voids failed, scarring her cockpit with scorch marks, damaging several control systems and splitting the reinforced glass of her eye-windows. They were riven with cracks as complicated as cobwebs, further ruining her crew's already ash-limited vision.

She marched with a hitching stride now, the joints in her right leg fouled by damage from loyalist cannon fire. She had to conserve her energy, too. Her void shields no longer lit upon command, and with the pain of her injuries playing through her nerve-cables, her crew kept her reactor banked to quieten her increasingly erratic machine-spirit.

Each of the Palatine Bastions were fortress-towns in their own right, ringing the Sanctum Imperialis in a boundary. Meru Bastion had been the ugliest, a brutal castle of a thing. Old data-spurts painted it as a palace, but any beauty it once possessed was lost when Rogal Dorn layered it over with rockcrete and ceramite and left its walls with hives of anti-infantry turrets. Tearing it down was a pleasure; another of the loyalists' strongholds dead on the inexorable march to the Sanctum Imperialis.

There had been no sign of the primarchs for days. Not the angel of fire that Angron had become, not the creature that was supposed to have once been Mortarion. Perturabo was said to have abandoned the siege, but Ulienne still saw masses of Iron Warriors within the horde, so who knew what was true there? Crackling transmissions from orbit promised Horus' landing was imminent, and Ulienne considered those chanted promises no better than propaganda. She focused on the war before her, not the prayers coming from above.

Avalon Bastion was next, its battlements a dark blur on the horizon. Word across the scrambled vox was that the enemy were in full retreat now. Without organised reconnaissance, no one could be certain, but the few officers still relaying orders promised that Avalon was already deserted. Its defenders had fled in a refugee tide over the course of many days, running for the other bastions.

Hindarah's spirit was impatient, psychosomatically jabbing inside Ulienne's mind with dull, red throbs. Her crew had to keep her reactor muzzled to prevent her warrior soul forcing them to charge out of cohesion. For now, World Eaters and Death Guard and Alpha Legionnaires ran before *Hindarah* in a ceramite flood. No gunships backed them up from above – the air-support phase of the war was adamantly over – but the beetle shapes of Legion tanks broke up the ranks of infantry, and winged things soared through the dirty sky. Red-skinned things in the shape of men and women; bloated things in the shape of alien flies; things that *Hindarah*'s crew called daemons, glad of the layers of armour separating them from the creatures.

Her eyes always slid away from the things the moment she tried to look at them. As soon as she looked away, she forgot they were there.

The horde had the numbers to bring about the war's end, while the defenders only possessed the numbers to delay it – but the losses were going to be grotesque. Ulienne didn't want to die for the Emperor's stubbornness. She wanted to live, to see the Warmaster's ambitions come to fruition. She wanted the Imperium that Horus had promised. An empire for eternity. A kingdom of humanity that would never fall.

Hindarah grumbled, sensing her princeps' unease, but too drugged by her cooled reactor to do anything more.

There it was again, the treasonous little notion Ulienne couldn't quite shake. Horus was a hero, the Warmaster of the Imperium, the pacifier of the galaxy. Of course she'd followed him. The Legio Audax had willingly worn his colours and cast their fate with his. But what would be left after this war? What would be left of Terra and the armies fighting to take it?

Surely even now, quiescent alien kingdoms at the Imperium's edges were reawakening, daring to cast jealous eyes at the worlds they'd lost in the Great Crusade. Would there be enough of the Warmaster's hosts left to hold the Imperium in its entirety? And what would those hosts look like, with all order and discipline and humanity raked out of them? The Legiones Astartes were already blood-maddened and fighting by the side of those... those things. The regiments of Imperial Army wearing the Warmaster's Eye were no better. Ulienne Grune didn't want peace. Peace was boring. Peace was for the weak. She wanted wars she could win.

And the Mechanicum, blessings upon its name, was turning on itself, speaking in shrieking cants of scrap code. Raving prophets advocated the abandonment of the Self; immersion within the Manifold, fusion with the machine-spirit. Conflicting philosophies from cults that had never agreed on anything before but at least had the restraint to keep out of each other's ideologies. Now they screamed with a kind of scattered unity, praying for the sacrifice of flesh and soul to be reborn in cradles of holy iron.

Hindarah wanted it, too. Ulienne could feel that.

For now, *Hindarah* waited, and the woman serving as the god-machine's mind stared at the armoured tide rolling ahead towards the silhouette of distant battlements. This was the first moment of stillness Ulienne could recall in a long, long time.

For months now, her physical world had been wholly within the confines of *Hindarah*'s cockpit. She escaped it only by blending her senses with her engine's, living through its eyes and its guns, feeling *Hindarah*'s movements as her own. When had Ulienne last breathed fresh air instead of the sweaty reek coming out of the filtration slits behind her head? When had she last drunk anything but the recycled piss of her closest comrades? When had she last moved from her control throne?

Ulienne breathed in, catching the smell of her own shit. Her output filters had failed… when? Days ago? Weeks ago? Her legs were caked with her own waste. Her uniform was patchy with vomit that stank of stale nutrient paste. Once noticed, the stench of the various filths crusting her to her throne was omnipresent. Practically overwhelming.

Blearily, she caught sight of her arm. Her hand was a black claw, fused to the metal of–

'My princeps?'

Jolted from her reverie, she turned her gummy eyes towards Otesh. 'Moderatus,' she acknowledged. Sands of Mars, but she was tired, so damn tired.

'Awaiting your order, my princeps.'

Ulienne stared at her crewmate. Otesh was carrion, her skin sick and sunless, her eyes dry. Ulienne could smell her now too, the spoiled meat sweetness of her. She'd been dead at least a week, even before they'd attempted the climb. At some point before she'd died, the moderatus had bitten through her own tongue. Flies were growing fat on her face, crawling in and out of her open mouth.

Ulienne opened her eyes. Or closed them. The dream stopped, or perhaps started again. She wasn't sure which, nor was she sure if it really mattered any more.

'My princeps?' Otesh said again.

'You're dead,' Ulienne said. Or thought. She couldn't tell if she was speaking or thinking. Even banked, *Hindarah*'s reactor was pressing at the back of Ulienne's mind; a constant pressure right in the grey meat of her skull. '*Are* you dead, Otesh?'

'My princeps?' Ulienne heard the words or imagined hearing them. They were spoken by Otesh or by the thing wearing Otesh's skin or they weren't spoken at all.

Ulienne felt wet warmth on her face. She was weeping. Or she was bleeding from her eyes again.

'Walk,' she said, closing her hands around the arms of her control throne. She felt and heard her gloves creak. She was still wearing them. Her hands weren't black claws melded to the metal. They weren't. They weren't. Though she couldn't bring herself to look to make sure.

'We walk. Advance with the horde.'

Hindarah rattled and clanked her way forward. The pressure eased, just a little, in Ulienne's head. The smell of foulness receded.

The Warhound's remaining weapon arm came up. Her stride, though hitched, became a loping run. The ground shook as they began outpacing the infantry. They were charging through the ranks of creatures, half-hidden in the dust, that it hurt to look at.

So Ulienne kept her eyes on the walls. Spires were appearing through dusty mist, blunted by bombardment. Fallen battlements. Ruined defence turrets. If Avalon was truly abandoned, that meant a spillage of refugees and retreating soldiers in the expanses of no-man's-land between here and the Eternity Gate.

To *Hindarah*, it meant prey. The god-machine's soul urged its commander with a somatic nudge through their tangled linkage. Ulienne's skin prickled. She parted her lips, and blood made strings between her rotten teeth.

The walls of Avalon Bastion grew taller; darkening, resolving. And then: something new. Above the battlements, a lone star shone in the blandness of the ashen sky.

Through the iron of her Titan's bones, Ulienne could hear the legionaries cheering, chanting at her feet, calling out to *Hindarah*, to Horus, to the creatures in their midst – and to Angron, Angron, Angron.

The newborn star started to fall, trailing a tail of fire.

FOUR

The Path to Glory

Kargos

He moved with the horde again, this time with Inzar at his side. The endless march was a matter of placing one foot in front of the other, his thudding bootsteps sending twinges through the Nails in the back of his brain. They hurt, they had fangs these days, but they hurt less in Inzar's presence. His was one of the voices that eased their poisonous drip.

Thinking came a little easier, too. He was starting to remember things. Who he was. What he'd done. The names of the warriors around him. There was Draelath, centurion of the 53rd Assault Company. There was Rangor, bedecked with gladiatorial blades. Kargos couldn't recall the warrior's rank, but he knew Rangor cheated at gambling games of knuckle-bones, aboard the *Conqueror*.

Strange, what was coming back to him now.

Kargos glanced at Inzar as they marched in broken rhythm. The Word Bearer seemed to have changed little, and there was a curious comfort in that. It put Kargos in mind of older days. When the Word Bearers had sent their Chaplains to the other Legions at the apex of the Great Crusade, many had regarded it as an act of needless fraternisation. The World Eaters were among those that had come around to the secondments relatively swiftly. Inzar was a good example of why; he'd served with the Eighth Assault Company, and Captain Khârn had admired his cold tenacity a great deal, coming to trust Inzar's counsel.

If Lorgar's Legion had sent preachers, the sons of Angron would never have granted them a moment's grace. But the Word Bearers had sent warrior-priests who were far more warrior than priest. The Chaplain held no truck with codes of wartime conduct. When notions of martial honour came up in debate, they made him sigh; he'd insisted such things were dreamed up by men and women wanting to gird themselves in patchwork denial.

'Righteousness doesn't make a warrior,' Inzar had said at the time. 'Warfare does.' A true warrior did whatever was necessary to win the war. All else was ephemera. Such was the creed of Inzar of Colchis, and the sentiment secured him a warm welcome into the Eaters of Worlds.

'They were good years, were they not?'

Kargos cleared his throat. 'What?'

'The years we fought together, in the Great Crusade. A brutal time, my friend. Years of satisfying service. I think of them often.'

Kargos nodded. They had been good days. The galaxy stretching out before them, unconquered, ready to be carved apart by Legion blades and divided by the primarchs' desires.

'I always felt a kinship with those of your bloodline,' Inzar confessed. 'So many of my kindred brought whispers of warrior lodges and gladiator cults to the other Legions, but those of

us that fought with the World Eaters never needed to preach.
The glorious truth is that you and your Legion were ripe for
enlightenment from the very beginning.'

'Enlightenment. A hell of a word for where we are today.'

'Don't speak of your blessings as a curse,' Inzar said. 'The
Nails ache, but are you not stronger with them? More powerful
of muscle? Faster of reflex?'

'You and your shitty poetry,' Kargos grunted. 'Spare me the
medicae analysis. I'm an Apothecary.'

Was an Apothecary, he thought. *Was.*

Kargos licked his cracked lips. It wasn't funny, but he could
feel the laughter coming up like bile. He fought the queasy
feeling for as long as he could but it wracked him anyway: a
sudden laughing fit that tore out like a series of aborted howls.
There was no mirth in the sound. He laughed only because
the machine in his skull pinched those nerves at that point
in time, and he danced to their song.

Kargos had laughed like that a few times in these last weeks.
It was worse than the pain, being forced to convulse by amusement you didn't feel.

Inzar made no comment on it. He carried on speaking
as if there'd been no laughing jag. His tone was warm with
amusement.

'Your vocation is the very reason you should know better
than anyone not to spurn the blessings you've received. For
shame, my brother.'

Kargos grunted something that was neither agreement nor
disagreement. How long had it been since someone had talked
to him like this, sharing brotherly jests? He sifted through the
blood-dimmed murk that passed for his thoughts. He didn't
know. It felt like forever.

He had only fragmented memories of the first analyses of
the Nails, the reports he'd witnessed in gleaming hololithic

displays. Those diagrams of musculature – read-outs of his digitally flayed brothers – had told quite a story.

Even the genetically reforged body of a Space Marine was fundamentally mortal. Signals between the brain, the muscles and the central nervous system worked within mortal boundaries. The Nails banished those boundaries. The pain engines overwrote the electric pulses between brain and body, letting warriors abuse their own bodies, pushing more kineticism through muscle and sinew whether it was receptive or not. And with it came joy. As all other emotions dulled (a regrettable by-product of the implant's technology) the adrenal delight of brutality soared.

At Angron's wish, the Legion's Apothecaries had beaten the Nails into their brothers' skulls. And then, righteously pleased with their work, the butcher-surgeons of the XII Legion had implanted each other. They'd sacrificed the solace of a painless life for greater physicality on the field of battle.

Inzar turned his red eye-lenses upon the World Eater.

'Sacrifice has to hurt, Kargos. That's what makes it a *sacrifice*. You give up something precious to earn something greater. I don't pity you, brother. I admire you. Your strength, your sacrifice, is an inspiration to us all.'

After that, silence reigned. Exactly how long it lasted, Kargos didn't know. He was the one to break it, that unknowable time later.

'Khârn,' he said into the dust.

Inzar turned his helm towards the World Eater. 'Brother?'

'I was the one,' Kargos told him. 'The one that found Khârn.'

'Ah.' Inzar's deep voice turned kind, knowing. 'You speak of Isstvan. I know the tale, my friend. You've told me before.'

'No. Skane found him on Isstvan.' Kargos managed to hold back the scudding threat of more laughter. 'And Skane called to me.' On that day a lifetime ago, at the very beginning of everything, they'd pulled their captain out from under a Land Raider's treads. How long had it been, since Kargos thought of Isstvan?

'I have not seen Skane thus far during the war,' Inzar noted.

'That's because he's dead.'

'Ah, that grieves me. He was an excellent soldier.'

'Hnnh. A traitor though, at the end. He tried to run from the *Conqueror*. Lotara executed him.'

'Indeed? Then Shipmistress Sarrin did what had to be done.' Inzar was a practical philosopher over such things. 'But you were speaking of Khârn.'

Kargos grunted agreement instead of nodding. Another little shift in the mundanities of life since he received the implant. Moving his head, even to nod, sometimes spiked the Nails.

'They said he'd been cut down by the Black Knight.'

'I see. How interesting.' Was Inzar smiling behind his face-plate? Kargos thought so. The Word Bearer sounded like he was being told quite the heart-warming tale. 'And did you take that from Khârn's body, or did he bequeath it to you with his final words?'

'Take what? I didn't take anything from Khârn.' Kargos flinched. He was going to laugh again, the Nails were going to make him do it, and he didn't want to. Not so soon after the last time.

Inzar was patience incarnate. 'You took nothing, my friend?'

'Stop smirking at me, you Colchisian bastard. I can hear it in your voice.'

As they trudged together, Inzar gestured with his sawtoothed crozius mace. He aimed it at the weapon loosely gripped in Kargos' right hand.

'If you took nothing from Khârn, then why are you carrying his axe?'

* * *

Khârn had been on his knees when Kargos found him. That, more than anything else in the long months of this war, told Kargos that the world had lost its mind. As he drew near to his commander, fortune favoured him with the respite of lucidity.

How long ago was this? Hours? Days? Weeks? No one agreed on how time worked, anymore. No one agreed what hour, day or week it really was.

The haze had cleared more, the closer he came to Khârn's fallen form. He wasn't sure where he was – at the border of one of the outer bastions, he figured – but enough of who he was came back to him, that he felt a sense of uncomfortable horror at the sacrilege of his brother-captain's pose.

There was no shame in dying, but to *kneel*? You knelt to tyrants. You knelt to slavemasters. You knelt to emperors.

'A bad omen, brother.' Kargos crouched by the corpse. 'A bad way to die.'

Gorechild, Khârn's axe, lay in the rubble a few feet away. The binding chain was cleaved close to the captain's wrist. Khârn had died without a weapon in his hand. Another bad omen – one Kargos didn't want his brothers to see.

He called out for aid over the vox, summoning a gunship he knew might never arrive in the ash. When he heard his brothers' bootsteps approaching, he dragged *Gorechild* closer to Khârn's slack fingers.

The moment he closed his fingers around the haft, Khârn spoke to him.

'It was Sigismund.'

Khârn's head stayed bowed, the crest of his helmet tilted in defeat. He was colourless in the dust, as they all were. His blood had long since dried around the rents in his warplate, giving the dust something else to cling to. He wasn't breathing. Kargos didn't need the tools of his trade to see that. And yet, he spoke.

Sigismund.

The name echoed with uneasy sincerity in Kargos' mind. For a moment he was back in the arena, in the *Conqueror*'s fighting pits, watching Khârn and Sigismund chained together at the wrists, duelling side by side. The truth was, back then, neither of the two captains had built much of a reputation for themselves in the gladiatorial arena. It was a truth universally acknowledged that with lives on the line, they were among the fiercest warriors in the Legiones Astartes. In war, they were supreme. But that was war. In the fighting pits, they were famously middling combatants. Always fighting to first blood, rarely to third blood; never *sanguis extremis*, never to the death.

Kargos had been the Eighth Company's gladiator. *Bloodspitter* they called him, because he loved to fight dirty, spitting into his enemy's eyes. They all had names, fraternally bestowed and each more bombastic than the last. *Bloodspitter. Black Knight. Flesh Tearer.*

Fighting alone or chained to his pit-brother, Kargos had no preference. He scarred his skin with kill-cuts to mark the deaths he'd dealt. He'd beaten Delvarus that day aboard the *Conqueror*, when the centurion of the Triarii had succumbed to bloodlust and abandoned his post. Only then had Kargos showed mercy, letting his opponent live at his captain's request.

If it wasn't to the death, it wasn't worth doing. Why fight at all if nothing was on the line? *There's no prestige in playing games.* They were the words of his arena partner, his brother in chains. True then. True always.

'Killed by your own chain-brother,' Kargos said softly to the kneeling figure. 'The bitterest blow.'

Khârn's faceplate was cracked open, showing most of his face. He'd lost half his teeth with the blow that had shattered

his helm. The wounds to his face and chest, let alone the
fact he wasn't breathing, should've ruined his speech, but he
sounded perfectly clear.

'I walk the Eightfold Path,' Khârn said without moving his
lips. Without moving at all. 'I walk the Path to Glory.'

A cluster of flies danced a slow pattern across his bare skin.
One of them alighted on the surface of his open eye.

Kargos said nothing. Several shadows fell over him. His
brothers were here.

'Get his body back to the *Conqueror.*'

The replies were mixed. A chuckle here, a growl of affirmation there. 'Why?' one of the warriors grunted behind him.

'He was the best of us,' said Kargos. 'That's why.'

Kargos rose – and *Gorechild* came up from the dust with him.
The chain binding it to his wrist rattled with that age-old gladiator melody. The weapon's weight was a pleasure. He could feel
the indentations of Khârn's fingers in the grip. He could feel where
the trigger rune had been worn smooth.

After that, things swiftly lost clarity. He couldn't remember
loading Khârn's body onto any gunship, but he also couldn't
recall leaving his captain there in the rubble. One or the other
had to be true, and he had no idea which. His memories
devolved into the grey-stained cycle of trudging forward, following shapes in the dust.

Maybe that was when the march to the Eternity Gate truly
began.

'Maybe it was,' Inzar agreed.

Kargos was silent as he watched the horizon. His throat was
a parched channel down into the pained meat of his body.
Blood of the Emperor, but he was thirsty.

Walls were beginning to appear in the murk ahead. High,
dark smudges that were surely the battlements of one of the

Palatine Bastions. Meru, perhaps. Or Pythia. Or Avalon. No. Wait. Had they already fallen?

'It is the Avalon Bastion,' Inzar said.

'How do you know my thoughts?' Kargos snapped. 'Can you read minds now? A gift from the things you call gods?'

The Word Bearer's voice stayed patient, stayed understanding. 'You are speaking aloud, my friend. You have been talking ceaselessly since we met three days ago.'

Three days. Three *days*?

'Almost four,' Inzar confirmed.

Kargos grunted what might've been agreement or dismissal.

Inzar breathed in deeply, the sound audible through his helmet's vocaliser. 'And I would wager you found Khârn a week before that. Perhaps even longer.'

'If you say so, preacher.'

'Do you feel what I feel? That shift in the air, these last few hours. That presence nearby.'

Kargos felt nothing but the needles in the back of his brain. He wasn't shy about saying so.

'Your father is here, Kargos. I sense his holy wrath, how it pulls the horde in his wake. We are but pilgrims in his shadow.'

Angron. Here.

How long had it been since Kargos had seen the thing his father had become? These were the kinds of thoughts he struggled to hold on to. They kept slipping, half-formed, from his mind before they could find traction on his tongue.

'There.' Inzar interrupted his thoughts, pointing skyward. 'Do you see?'

Above the distant walls shone a single star. The moment Kargos' eyes fell upon it, they locked there, and a cooling shiver ran through his skin. The Nails bit a little deeper, but the pain was numbing. Almost a relief.

'You sense it,' said Inzar.

'I see a flicker of fire in the sky. You believe that is Angron?'

'I know it is.' Inzar stared up at the faraway blaze, enraptured. 'The Neverborn sing of him, behind the veil. It is a jealous song, in truth. They envy him for the honour of his exaltation. They were created immortal. We mortals, even our primarchs, must fight for it. And through sacred fury, Angron has achieved it. He has *won*, Kargos. He has walked the path, and oh, how they love him and hate him for reaching its end.'

'The path,' Kargos repeated. He could hear Khârn's last words once more. *We walk the Eightfold Path. We walk the Path to Glory.*

His blood iced. He had to suppress a shiver.

'Sounds like more tiresome Colchisian doggerel to me.'

'Does it really?' Inzar's voice held no edge at the World Eater's tone. The Chaplain walked on at Kargos' side, his eye-lenses turned to the sky. 'I speak for the sake of your soul, my friend. I am here to guide you onward, as Lorgar guided Angron. None of us have a choice, Kargos. We all walk the same road now.'

'Immortality.' Kargos barked the word, rich with mockery.

'Immortality,' Inzar agreed, 'or eternal agony.'

'I'm already in agony,' Kargos said with a grin. 'You learn to live with it.'

'No, my friend. You are in pain. Words cannot convey the gulf between mortal pain, which we all know, and immortal agony, which awaits us all.'

From the east came the great rattling tread of a Titan. Reaver-class. It sent tremors through the ruined earth, close enough for Kargos to see its hunched silhouette stalking forward. As it strode for the walls, a multitude of shapes that may or may not have been human ghosted at its heels. He heard pack howls from those shapes. He heard whispers that couldn't possibly cover the distance to his ears. Kargos felt himself gripping the axe tighter as he looked at the Chaplain once more.

'Don't jest with me, preacher.'

'I am hardly a man of fine humour, Kargos.'

That was true enough. For whatever reason, the notion made the Nails itch, and Kargos had to growl the words through clenched teeth, biting back a sudden flux of the unwanted laughter.

'What happens after we die? Do you really know?'

For the first time, Inzar's body language betrayed surprise. Kargos heard the other warrior's breath faintly catch and heard the brief flinch in his companion's armour joints. He didn't answer at once, instead he kept his gaze to the sky, watching what he claimed was the star of Angron's wrath.

'*Now* you choose to ignore me?' Kargos laughed, and it was a natural laugh. Blood of the Emperor, it felt good.

Inzar finally lowered his gaze from the heavens. 'Your father has given your Legion a great gift. The Butcher's Nails were the beacon that lit the way. Lorgar gave our Legion a similar gift. He gave us the truth.'

Kargos let his gaze drift. Not to the star – he could feel its presence as a prickling heat against his skin despite his armour plating – but to the silhouettes and shadows of the horde all around. He watched them: his brothers, the things pretending to be his brothers, and the humans in thrall to it all. Inzar's soothing voice was the perfect percussion.

'It was an ugly truth. It almost broke him to learn that reality was a hateful lie, a thin crust over seething, smiling damnation. Can you imagine it, my friend? To be the first living being to learn – to truly *know* – that what awaits every man, woman and child is an afterlife of dissolution in an ocean of boiling horror?'

Kargos clacked his teeth together, hard, to prevent whatever was building up in his throat from emerging as a sound. He felt as though he were going to vomit laughter, and if it broke free, he feared he would lose control of his limbs. As if the Nails' joy would somehow possess him, for who knew how long.

'More shitty poetry,' Kargos murmured, doubting his own words even as he spoke them.

'On the contrary. I am being as clear as I am able. Weaker souls, they will burn briefly, mere instants of agony before they boil away to become part of the warp. But stronger souls, the souls of *psykers*, they can look forward to an eternity of...'

The Chaplain trailed off. Hesitated. Tried again. 'We all face a simple choice. No faith in the false God-Emperor will save even a single soul. Oblivion awaits the weakest of us. Torment and eventual annihilation will be the reward for the strong. The gods behind the veil are wondrous beings, my friend. But they are wrathful, and by any measure of human perception, they are insane. The Word Bearers raise icons to the Pantheon out of worship, yes. But there is pragmatism in our faith. We are the Legion that first found something worthy of worship in the realm behind reality. But we are also the Legion that first found something to fear.'

Kargos could smell blood, and the back of his head was growing sickeningly hot. The Nails were bleeding, bleeding into his helmet. He felt his own wet life pooling at the back of his neck. He tried to speak and failed entirely.

'Lorgar saw all of this. He brought Angron to the precipice and gave your father a chance at immortality. A fool looks at him now and sees a monster. Those of us with vision see everything he has overcome. He is the Red Angel. He is the War God's son. A man that refused to accept mortal death and the agony of the underworld. He pissed on the notion of eventual oblivion. Instead... he chose to live forever, no matter the cost.'

Around them, the shapes and shadows of other warriors

began to bay and howl and roar. Kargos' skin prickled; it took intense effort not to join in and cry out loud, as bestial as the rest of them. Inzar's voice went on, a fervent drone now, a preacher's insistence and a brother's reassurance.

'You hate Angron for what he's done to you. For the sin of making you strong at the cost of your reasoning minds? My friend, he has done so much more. He has given you a *choice*. Something denied to so many others. You can choose to die as all mortals die, to suffer as all mortals suffer – or to walk the path and live forever.'

Inzar was the eye of the storm, the lone focus of calm. Titans shook the ground with their tread. Men and women and daemons and the dead howled; as they did, Inzar raised his crozius, aiming it at the lone star in the sky.

'Look upon your father, Kargos. For above all else, he has given his sons an example to follow.'

Above them, high beyond the walls of Avalon, the flaming star began to fall.

'He has given you a messiah.'

FIVE

Immortality through annihilation

Angron

Pain can destroy people. It's possible to suffer so profoundly that no personality can exist in whatever space is left. Among the dying, that degree of suffering happens often enough, but it isn't limited to the terminal and the doomed. Pain can make a man scream himself out of his mind. Pain can hurt so much that it overwhelms everything except the body's capacity for agony.

The creature that had once been Angron had learned fury could do the same thing.

Insofar as he was still a *he* at all, Angron was reduced now to a boiling snarl of synapses. He possessed no capacity to reason, because the vortex inside his head allowed for no sensation or memory to ever evolve into thought. In place of a brain, he possessed toxic soup riven with sparking cables. In place of a layered mind, he possessed rage so naked and profound that it bordered on exaltation.

With no higher thought, everything was instinct, bleached red, backlashing against itself.

The bitterest layer was that there was no longer enough left of Angron to lament his own fate. His primarch brothers, deceived as they were, still possessed cores of tortured empathy at the heart of their delusions. No matter the deceptions they'd been offered and the lies they fed to themselves, some iota of cognition remained inside them – further feeding their power with the flow of regretful misery. But Angron, the brother that had screamed loudest of freedom, wasn't even allowed to see how much of a slave he'd become.

Immortality came in many flavours. Not all were as sweet as they seemed.

Maybe it would have caused more anguish had Angron been permitted a sliver of consciousness, enough to let him suffer with this knowledge. Another patron deity might have allowed such an awakened shard to exist within its puppet, feasting on the helpless realisation of the soul in its grasp.

But the Blood God was the Father of Massacres and the Lord of War, and it cared nothing for cosmic irony. Its servants' anguish was irrelevant. Nothing mattered but the blood they shed… and few of its slaves served that purpose as well as the thing that had once been Angronius of Nuceria.

Angron ranged ahead of the armies chanting his name. He soared above them, flying through the ashen soup that Terra's air had become. Some of those behind and beneath him were mortal, his sons and daughters in ascension and damnation. Others were never born of flesh or blood or bone. They took shape from the realm behind reality, and he was like them now. He did not live as a mortal man lived. He was incarnated. Tethered to this cold plane of existence only by bloodshed. Every second of his existence on Terra was threatened by the pull of the howling void. He killed everyone, he destroyed everything, holding onto incarnation only through slaughter.

Beneath him was Avalon, one of the last remaining Palatine Bastions. He knew this in the vaguest way, not as a fortress with defenders – he was past such coherence – but more as the memory of a promise that he chased. Someone was at Avalon. He knew this, too, without conscious thought. He knew it the way a slave fears the kiss of a whip even in his sleep.

Someone was supposed to be here. Someone whose blood would run hot down his throat in steaming gulps. Someone whose death would anchor him to this life, freeing him from the pain of the pulling void.

And yet.

Avalon Bastion was a bloodless battlefield. The enemy had abandoned it, evacuating before the horde. Angron sensed this utter absence of life as he soared above the silent battlements. He knew nothing of what it might mean tactically or logistically. He knew only that there was nothing here to kill. Not the one being that needed to die. No one at all.

That's when the acid sloshed behind his eyes again. There was a vision that came to him in these warless, bloodless moments: a single image boiling in the thresh of his senses. It was a goad, driving him deeper and spurring him on, as it lashed at what remained of his mind.

Wings.

Wings of white, dappled with blood. Wings flaring from armour of gold. Wings he slavered to break in his clawed hands. Wings he would tear from their sockets of muscle and bone.

He roared at the whiteness in his head, a venting of wordless rage. Nothing to destroy here, nothing to kill. Dead stone. Cold metal. Empty, all of it, empty.

Wings. An angel's wings. Wings of white feathers, an angel of gold.

Lightning sparked around the cranial implants parasiting their way through his brain. It was almost savage enough to send him falling from the sky.

Wings. His brother's wings. His brother, the angel, whose blood would flow down his throat and bring strength, and a cessation of the pain.

His brother, who wasn't here.

Angron shook the sky with another carnosaur roar, an animal effort at discharging pain. It failed utterly, as it always did. In these moments, even the paltry scraps of identity he still possessed were drowned in the War God's song that formed every atom of his being. But somewhere in the dust below he sensed the heat of life, and that was enough to catch the attention of his diminished brain and its primal hungers. A flicker, no more than that, but enough.

Angron dived blind, trailing flame. Graceless as a gargoyle, fast as a falling star. There was prey here after all.

The death of the Titan *Conclamatus* was recorded in no Imperial archive – at least none that survived the Siege of Terra – and went unacknowledged by the Palace's defenders. She was already written off as dead days before she died, already mourned by those with a mind to mourn her.

Her princeps and crew had volunteered to remain behind at Avalon when the others fled the bastion. Not that they had much of a choice. The war had crippled *Conclamatus*, leaving her barely able to move. Rather than limp into no-man's-land and inevitably suffer reactor-paralysis halfway to the Sanctum, she had stayed at Avalon Bastion and taken a knee outside the towering wall. There she stayed, in the ash and the dust. Waiting.

Her stabilisers were shot through, her locomotors violated by months of engagement in the Outer Palace. After retreating for repairs, *Conclamatus* was pressed back into service before a single adept brought a blowtorch near her broken skeleton. So she knelt in the dust for stability, not symbolism, down on one knee with her ramshackle structure braced for maximal fire.

She had what could generously be called a plan, though perhaps more realistically an intention. When the horde descended upon her, she'd unleash the reserves of ammunition she still possessed; what precious little had been left to her after she'd bequeathed the bulk of her stores to her retreating sister-Titans. She was a Warlord, regardless that she was reactor-scarred and that she'd been driven to one knee, and she intended to die as a lord of war, just as she'd lived. Her arms held level with where her crew imagined the horizon to be. The right arm was a Belicosa, humming with a low charge still capable of bringing down a city block. The left was a claw, the talons mangled from overuse but all still articulated, still capable of opening and closing. On her back, feeding directly into her shoulder cannons, was a pauper's sum of solid shot. Those macro-gatling blasters would whine and cycle and spin – they would make for a single, and hopefully glorious, final symphony.

Her plan never came to pass. What went through the minds of her princeps and crew can only be speculated upon. The truth, perhaps cruel and perhaps plain, is that *Conclamatus'* last stand was just one among tens of millions in this war. Why should her crew be immortalised when so many others went unseen, unknown, or destined to be forgotten? The horde pouring towards her cared nothing for the identity of the human lives protected by her armour plating, and her killer cared even less. With that in mind, the accounting of her final stand comes down to this.

Angron's prey was sheathed in unsatisfying iron, so he struck not to kill it, but to shatter its shell.

In that moment there were many things he did not know. He didn't know that he'd struck *Conclamatus* between her shoulder blades with enough force to break the machinery of her backbone and rupture dozens of pistons in her vertebrae. He didn't know that the Titan's princeps, who had racked up honours within the Legio Ignatum for forty-six years of unbroken loyalty, had his sight burned away by the appearance of Angron so close. He didn't know that the princeps' soul was already torn from its housing of flesh and boiling in the warp before the man had even finished screaming.

And had Angron known any of these things, he wouldn't have cared. Such truths were meaningless to the creature he'd become.

What he knew was that within the Titan's body were lives he could end and blood that would flow. He tore out *Conclamatus'* reactor-heart, heedless of the burns inflicted on his flesh by the core venting its fire of artificial fusion. The warp essence that comprised his physical form regenerated even as it was destroyed. This was how he survived – thriving by destruction. Angron had achieved that most dubious apex: treading the final steps on the Path to Glory. He had attained immortality through annihilation.

Insensate with rage, he hurled his burning burden at the walls of Avalon Bastion. There was, briefly, the flare of a false sun. A detonation among millions of others across this scarred planet. Then another wall fell, in a world of falling walls, and Angron cried out the only word he was still able to say.

He screamed his brother's name.

PART TWO

A WORLD GONE BLIND

SIX

The last man on Terra

Amit

A daemon was born in the moment a queen died, poisoned by the king she loved. As she sighed out her last breath, tangled in blood-patterned silk sheets, the daemon gave its birth-cry in the realm behind reality.

The queen's lost soul, ripped from her body into the seething warp, was the first thing this daemon ever devoured. There was, arguably, a bleak poetry in that.

History – that ravening liar – would come to swallow the names of the treacherous king and the queen he betrayed. Cosmically, their reign meant nothing; just two humans in a species of swarming quintillions, ruling over yet another empire of moral conceits on yet another world turning in the endless dark. The true impact of their lives was with the midnight murder; with the war that followed the murder, and with the plague that followed the war. So much suffering from a thimbleful of herbs in a single cup of wine.

The creature born from their actions didn't know the names of those responsible for its genesis. Treachery was its real father, sickness its true mother. It grew behind the veil that separated reality and unreality, taking shape in the tides. There were governing laws within this boiling warp, but they resembled nothing of material physics. Time didn't exist there.

The daemon grew. Awareness bloomed. Strength blossomed with it.

The creature was given names by the cults that rose to worship it, as well as the men and women of supposed piety that sought to destroy it. It took the names, the worship and the hatred as its due.

The timelessness ended at a point between forever and never. The daemon manifested on a world once called Earth, now called Terra. It was drawn with numberless hosts of its kin to shriek their disgust and rage at the broken walls of an embattled Emperor. The creature's entire timeless existence had led to this moment. At last, the daemon could bring its breed of torment to the waking world.

A dream no more, it tore its way from the warp and into reality.

Its hands were nine-jointed talons fused to the hilt of a corroded sword. Its lone eye was bulbous, milky, crusted half-closed. In the cancerous plasma that passed for its flesh, it bore the plague that once swept through the king and queen's long-forgotten kingdom. It salivated virulence. It screamed disease.

It died four seconds after manifesting.

And it died by butchery. Evisceration reduced it to dismantled pieces of dissolving *corpus*. The daemon's remains, an unbinding helix of ectoplasmic slush, burned away to nothing in the filthy air.

Its killer was an Astartes warrior in war-cracked plate, with a serrated knife clutched in one fist and a chainsword in the other. Both blades dripped strings of unearthly gore. On his breastplate was a winged skull cast in beaten bronze. This was the Imperialis, the symbol of undiluted loyalty worn throughout the ranks of the warriors still standing. On one of his pauldrons, written in symbolic Aenokhian script, was the name *Nassir Amit*.

In keeping with all his kind, Amit was and was not, strictly speaking, a human being. It was more accurate to say the warriors of the Legiones Astartes were a subspecies ideated from a manipulated vision of the human template. It was most accurate of all to say Amit was barely human in any way that mattered, and more a living weapon of hybridised genecraft, encased in layers of powered ceramite.

Some of his kind rebelled against this idea of pure weaponisation. Others embraced it. There were adherents of both principles on both sides of the war.

Amit was firmly one of the latter. The concerns that burdened humankind were a distraction from the pursuit of his purpose. He'd left his humanity behind as something that bored him.

He could see nothing in the dust. Not the laid-waste rubble of the Palace's skyline to the north, east and south. Not the final barrier of the Delphic Battlement to the west. The world was a winter of ash and smoke. The sounds of shelling had been a constant, sleep-sucking companion for months on end, and now even the drumbeats of bombardment had fallen quiet – diminished to thick whispers by the ash that choked the air. The ash that *was* the air.

And the extradimensional xenos were here. The creatures–

Daemons. You know they are daemons. Why do you resist that word?

–had only rarely manifested within the Palatine Ring. The Emperor, in His glory, held them back.

But no longer.

Amit stood in the heart of a world choked by ash and voxed yet again for reinforcements, for reports, and for orders that no longer came. It was the nineteenth time he'd made the call since Pythia Bastion fell. He hadn't seen another survivor, or even one of the enemy, for hours.

Even before the vox failed, the survivors had known it was over. The Khan was wounded unto death. The Ultimate Wall had fallen, and the districts of the Inner Palace with it. They knew, too, what was coming next – it had been repeated a thousand times and more across the traitors' lines of communication in a tone of smirking triumph: Horus was ready to make his landing. His herald, Angron, was clearing the final path, ending every life between the Ultimate Wall and the Eternity Gate.

Then the vox had started to die. Fewer strained voices replied from the other embattled outposts. They offered no aid to each other, giving only recitations of their own straits – some with grim humour, some with pained curses, some with maudlin, naked honesty. The words that crackled back over the decaying vox-links were variously breathless or taut with the suppression of pain and emotion. Each tone hinted at wounds the speakers wouldn't confess. Gunfire was a backbeat behind every message, and blindness was the unifying factor. Everyone was surrounded. No one could break out and no one could see a thing.

Pythia Bastion fell three hours ago. Amit had added his own final report to the vox-web's audio miasma before abandoning the fortress. He'd been one of the last defenders to leave, with the bastion shaking around him, raining debris as it came to pieces.

'South,' he'd ordered his surviving warriors, and the refugees they were forced to protect. 'Don't go for Razavi, they're already evacuating there. Make for Golgotha Bastion. If you can't reach Golgotha, run for the Sanctum.'

For all he knew, he'd sent them to their deaths in the wasteland. No one reliably knew which way was south now, anyway. Most instruments projected random directional data and registered the passing of time in random leaps. Two patrols meeting up in the ash would report that it was two different days of the week. Everything was scrambled by the dust or by interference from the–

Daemons, they are daemons

–from the immaterial xenos drawn from their reality into this one.

Amit didn't pull his helmet off to face the quiet unprotected. Even his genhanced lungs struggled with the ash contaminating the air. Instead, he walked along the uneven ground, through the dips and craters that had been roads and plazas and colonnades – all of it churned to meaninglessness by orbital bombardment; by Titan fire; by artillery; by the vanguard warbands of Horus' horde. All of it wrenched up and pulled down in acts of stupid hate.

The ground was infected. He was careful where he trod, moving around patches where the earth was plagued with calluses and warts, keeping clear of rippling pools of un-water that stank like cancer. Who had known that marble could sweat pus? Who would ever have guessed that soil could bleed?

There was no recovering from this. No matter who won the war, Terra would carry this sickness within its core forever.

Amit kept walking. He had to link up with one of the convoys. For a time, he was kept company only by the sound of his own footsteps, and by now he was far past tired, deep into a weariness that ate into his bones. When had he last truly slept? A half-hour snatched weeks ago at Gorgon Bar, before the great battle to hold the Saturnine Wall. It felt like another life. One that belonged to someone else.

He passed bodies, some of the foe, some of those of his brothers and cousins or the soldiers they'd commanded. Most of them were being claimed by the churned earth, tendrils of unreal matter closing around the dead and fusing them to infected stone. Other bodies were being slowly amalgamated, linked with gluey filth, swelling into masses of necrotic flesh. A garden was growing in the wasteland, filled with fruit that had no right to ripen.

On he walked. Amit's targeting reticule drifted unlocked in the nothingscape of white dust. He wasn't looking for living enemies. He was looking for anyone alive at all.

These lulls happened in war. Sudden unearthly silences between protracted hours of battle. Times when even the distant peals of artillery thinned away into dubious silence. And the opposite, too: sudden explosions of sound and adrenaline between slow-rolling hours of nothing.

Still, though. *Still.* An unwelcome notion crept its cold way up his spine, a sense of isolation; that the war was truly over, and he was the only one still alive. The last survivor in humanity's necropolis.

This thought was followed by another: that he was dead himself. Perhaps he'd died in battle and now wandered lost in these white wastes. Maybe death had delivered him here, an exile in ashen purgatory.

'This is Dominion Nassir Amit of the Ninth Legion, south of Pythia Bastion in Palatine.'

Static.

'Pythia Bastion has fallen.'

Static.

'Is anyone out there?'

Static.

How long had it been since he saw his father? The last time he'd been in the presence of the Emperor's Angel, Sanguinius had been on the edge of exhaustion himself, seeking to fight everywhere at once now that the Khan was gone and Dorn was encircled. Was the primarch in one of the Palatine Bastions now, organising its defence? Or was he still out there, soaring through the ash in search of foes on the ground?

Amit came across more bodies. More humans, dead on the flight from Pythia or one of the other bastions. The dust had already settled over them, covering their radiation burns and shrouding them with a fraction of dignity. One of them had died with his mouth open – it was full now, full of grey powder – and his slack hand rested on the churned stone, his fingers curled an inch from his fallen lasrifle.

They died so easily, these Imperial Army forces. What was a human, really, but a sack of blood and bone that burst with the merest pressure? But bless them, they could fight. Anyone still alive in the war's last hours was some worthy mix of skilled, resolute and damn lucky. Every rifle counted now, as did every heart that beat behind it.

With the front line reduced to fiction, this was enemy territory now. Amit had been in enemy territory more than once during the war, seeing great poles of iron supported by scrap scaffolding, sunk into the ground, decorated with the dead. Gallows of detritus stood proud, cradling the forms of executed defenders. Human soldiers, civilians, Astartes warriors, all defiled in death, their corpses chained and flayed and desecrated in a dozen other ways to draw the black eyes of insane gods.

Yet there was no desecration here, yet. Whatever killed these fleeing men and women had come from nowhere. Quite literally.

Amit gazed into the nothing all around, his wearing-down

armour joints crackling with servo-slippage as he panned his head. It was still here. Somewhere.

Movement drew his eye. A dead woman's mouth opening. Long fingers curling from between her teeth. A spasm quaking her carcass. Amit moved closer as a horned thing climbed from the pile of dusty dead, birthing itself back into reality, using their deaths as its doorway.

They looked at one another, transhuman and monster. The daemon was drawn to Amit's presence, suckling on the anger that beat in his two hearts. The red-skinned thing bared its teeth at him, preening atop its mound of the slain. It yelled and lashed its tongue and proclaimed its primacy. It spat its name in a language that humans had no hope of understanding.

Amit had heard it all before. He raised both sword and dagger, whirling them slowly to loosen the soreness in his wrists, and started walking forward.

SEVEN

This leprous womb

Zephon

He woke in the quiet dark, and as awakenings went, it was an unpleasant one. Transhumans of the Legiones Astartes usually came up clean and swift, a synaptic jerk into full consciousness. This was different. This was less an awakening from slumber, more a reclamation of awareness dredged from the depths of a coma.

For want of any other option, he lay there on his back, watching the low-powered lights flickering above him and listening to the beat of his two hearts. One was slow and regular, the other beat only once every ten seconds or so, its chambers held in reserve for moments of supreme exertion. Beneath those drums, his armour was an active thrum, purring on low power.

When he tried to call out, his voice emerged as a drawl, thick with disuse.

'They have ranged the main line,' he said to the flickering illumination globes above. 'You cannot stay here.'

He hadn't meant to say that. He didn't know why he'd said it, or what it meant.

A voice he didn't recognise said a name he didn't know. He couldn't see who it was; he still couldn't even turn his head. And he tried to say this, to tell the speaker he didn't understand what was happening, but again the words came out wrong.

'The foe is close to the outwork line. Artillery. If our wall-guns are firing, so are theirs. We both possess weapons of great range. Why are you here? You are not militia.'

The other voice returned, as calm as before. This time it conveyed more than a name.

'Interesting,' it said, coming with a speaker crackle that made it tinny and weak. A human voice, though. 'Remnant memories. Perhaps the very last words pre-acedia.'

'They have ranged the main line,' he said again. It felt vile, speaking those words. Like someone had their fingers inside his throat, pushing the muscles to make the wrong sounds. He wanted to shout, to free his throat of the blockage of bizarre words... but he feared his cry would come out calmly as *They have ranged the main line. You cannot stay here.*

'Listen to me,' the other voice continued. 'You do hear me, yes?'

Yes, he tried to say. Yes, I hear you.

'They have ranged the main line,' he said instead.

'Have they indeed?' replied the voice. 'As fascinating as your pre-stasis murmurings are, this is very much not the time for such considerations. I must extricate you from the leprous womb of your rebirth. Now... make a fist. Can you do that?'

He made a fist. At least, he thought he did.

'Good,' said the voice. 'Good. Now open your eyes again.'

He hadn't realised he'd closed them. He opened them – they were gummy, his vision unclear. He tried to say this, too, and failed again.

'They have ranged the–'

'*Sacred Mars, shut up,*' the voice sighed. And then, in a mumble, '*Perhaps they were right about the brain damage.*'

Other voices joined in now, murmuring in similar concern. 'We must attend him,' one of them said.

'*By all means,*' replied the first. '*Perform your function.*'

'Lord?' This new voice was far gentler. 'Lord, it is Shafia. I am with you. We are all with you. Can you open your eyes for me, master?'

He opened them yet again. A blurry figure was leaning over him, its features indiscernible. There was a spraying sound; the tingle of moisture cold on his face; the drag of a cloth around the edges of his eyes.

It helped a little. The figure moved away, and the ceiling resolved into clarity above him. The sight brought no enlightenment because what he was seeing made no sense.

'How,' he said, 'how can metal rot?'

None of the voices chose to answer that. He heard several figures moving around him in the half-dark, heard their shuffling steps and the pneumatic whine of bionic replacements. He heard the strangers breathing, their respiration slow, calm, yet somehow forced. These were sounds he recognised. That was how servitors moved, how they breathed.

'Master, can you sit up?'

He rose, armour joints growling, and that's when the pain started, a sickening flare in the back of his head. Pain, he could deal with. The dizziness and queasiness were somewhat less welcome. Nausea was rare for his kind. Astartes were engineered to be above such mortal flaws.

He moved slowly, lifting himself on limbs that purred with the smooth function of exquisite bionics. As the sickness faded, he looked at his hands, seeing palms and fingers of polished metal, feeling them hum with the silken joy of

augmetic perfection. Both of his arms were bionic, as was
one of his legs – not the crude and functional replacements
of Legion warfare, but beautiful, artisanal bionics shaped and
nerve-sensed like human limbs. They didn't feel false. They felt
like his hands, his arms, his leg. They felt natural.

'*I can sheathe them in skin, you know,*' said the first voice,
somewhere out of sight. '*It would be an achievement of artistry,
covering your bionics in cloned flesh. In a way, rather tempting.
Not that there's time for such a thing now.*'

Zephon lowered his silver hands. Chemical feeds were
jabbed into his chest and thighs, through sockets in the
armour, intravenously flooding his system with fluids from
a steel tank buckled to the side of his surgical slab. Now
that he was sitting up, he felt strength returning, and clarity
of thought with it. It was slow, though. A reluctant return.

The room around him was infected somehow, corroded not
by rust and natural ruin but malformed by abscesses. Veins
bulged, hideously ripe, inside the metal. Many of them bled
a wet blackness that moved nothing like oil and smelled like
diseased blood.

He was in a medicae chamber. One that was far from empty,
populated almost exclusively by the dead. Men and women in
war-torn uniforms lay silent on cots and surgical slabs. From
the way they were bloating, most had been dead several days,
yet a covering of dust coated all of them in shrouds of fine
powder, as though they'd lain there for months.

The ceiling and iron support beams were riven by corrosion.
They looked decayed, their ruination impossibly biological.
Stasis pods lined the walls, some open and empty, others
with the slumbering shapes of Astartes warriors in a state of
suspended animation. Several of the pods still with power
emitted weak blue light onto their bloodstained cushioning.

The true smell hit him then. The smell of several hundred

people left for dead and slowly splitting open as their organic processes broke them down. It made the pain flare again in the back of his head.

'What happened here?' he asked.

'It's *still happening*,' the first voice snapped. As if that, of all questions, was somehow a bridge too far. '*You may address your prayers of thanks to the Omnissiah that I found you before it was too late.*'

He looked around as his vision continued to clear. His surgical slab was ringed by several saviours – some of them human, some of them servitors.

The latter stood with slack jaws and dull eyes. They were a ragged pack in filthy jumpsuits, their heads scarred and tattooed with incarceration codes. Each one of them displayed crude installations of bionic punishment: arms were replaced by metal claws or the bulky weight of heavy bolters; spines were threaded through with muscle-cable; scratched red lenses stared out in place of eyes. One of them was drooling down her chin and making the same repetitive murmur to herself, a nonsense syllable she mumbled over and over. The others stood quietly, not quite silently, as breath was forced in and out of their bodies by their brutal, simple cybernetic implants.

The humans, though. He knew them at once. Shafia, devoted Shafia, in her shawl of Legion red; Eristes, clad in monkish robes dyed the same familiar crimson; and Shenkai, looking as exhausted as his parents, with his dark eyes narrowed and shadowed by a raised hood.

'We're overjoyed to see you, lord,' said Eristes.

They did not look overjoyed, Zephon noted. They looked afraid.

'It is good to see the three of you.' Until recently, this would have been a lie, spoken out of politeness – or more likely, not spoken at all. When he'd been exiled to Terra as part of the Crusader Host, the presence of his armoury thralls did nothing but remind him that he would never fight again. He was the crippled captain, the invalid Angel. What use were arsenal servants to him?

Land's augmetic gifts had changed that. First, the ad hōc surgeries that allowed him to fight in the webway; then the more intensive augmentation that followed, restoring him to primacy.

Zephon regarded his servants and the servitors accompanying them. Two of the servitors stood either side of him – one managing the chemical feeds plugged into his armour sockets, the other gazing dead-eyed at a handheld auspex scanner, clutched awkwardly in its gloved hand. Ignoring the servitors for a moment, he looked at the tank of chemicals being used, at the runic markings on its metal side.

All of this – the chemical ritual taking place – reknit the frayed edges of his memory. He'd seen this before. He knew what it meant.

'Why are they doing this?' he asked.

There was a pause in the wake of that question. His thralls didn't answer, but the first voice did, sounding concerned.

'They're reactivating you from Astartesian stasis. Flooding you with the chemical purges necessary to flush out the toxins of suspended animation. That should be obvious, even with your disorientation.'

'You misunderstand me,' Zephon said. 'I am aware of the process. But why are *they* doing this? Why servitors, why not Legion Apothecaries?'

'Because most of your Legion's Apothecaries are dead. Most of everyone is dead.'

Something in the voice's tone tendrilled through his mind, kindling more memories along the way. He saw a face, an old face, the expression dismissive and disgusted.

Yes. The last of the fog was lifting now. A name came to him.

'Where are you, Arkhan? I cannot see you.'

The buzz of a cheap, scratchy anti-grav system sounded above. A servo-skull descended with a quivering lack of grace, the polished bone implanted with sensoria needle clusters in the eye sockets, and its jaw replaced with a dented vox-speaker.

'*The fundaments of memory seem intact,*' the skull noted in its crackling tone. Red lights blinked at the tips of its sensor needles. '*You know me, at least, and presumably these three slaves.*'

'They are not slaves,' Zephon said at once.

'*Yes, they are, and we're not going to argue about it. Do you know your own name?*'

The warrior felt a flicker of discomfort; he actually had to think about it for a moment. Nor was he blind to the worried glances passing between his thralls.

'Zephon,' he said. 'Dominion of the Blood Angels. Exarch of the High Host. My brothers know me as the Bringer of Sorrow.'

The voice – Arkhan Land – barked a nasty little laugh. '*Astartes dramatics! It isn't enough for all of you to set the galaxy aflame, you also have to insist you're heroes for doing it, worthy of titles everyone else finds ridiculous.*'

The waking warrior showed no temper at the old man's attitude. Somehow the disrespect felt familiar and ignorable.

'Master?' This was Shafia, foremost of his servants. 'Can you stand?'

Zephon took a breath, looking around the blighted chamber once more. 'Not yet. Sensation is returning, though. I confess I do not understand what I am seeing here. What is this place of horrors?'

'*Allow me,*' said Arkhan Land in his crackling tone. The servo-skull clicked several times, and a spillage of blue light streamed from the skull's left eye. A degraded hololith took shape of a skinny old man in tattered robes, hovering several inches off the bloodstained floor tiles. Even in the poor quality holo, Land looked some way past weary, deep into a new level of exhaustion. His face was gaunt, his skin grimy. He had a tremor in one of his knuckly hands.

'You look well, my friend,' Zephon lied softly.

'*Oh, do shut up,*' Land sneered. '*As to your location, you're in one of the medicae-sepulchres of Razavi Bastion. Down in the catacombs. It's where they stored you with who knows how many other dead, wounded, and stasis-bound. They told me you were either dead or terminally brain damaged – which, in the case of your transhuman breed, amounts to much the same thing. Reports conflicted on the matter. I decided to see for myself. You were supposed to be in storage at Bhab. It's taken me forever to find you.*'

Zephon didn't like the phrasing of being 'in storage', but now wasn't the time to debate it. He raised a hand to slow Arkhan's diatribe, to bid him speak slower, but the Martian wouldn't be stopped. The skull continued transmitting Land's voice a half-second out of time with the holo's movements.

'*The subterranean levels have already been abandoned and the surface levels are being prepared for evacuation. I gathered your menials here and sent a team down to find you. Against all good reason, I might add.*'

Nothing Land was saying made sense. For the defenders to be evacuating Razavi Bastion, the enemy must have…

'Arkhan,' he said to the flickering holo. 'The Ultimate Wall has fallen? Truly?'

The Martian's smile was anything but pleasant. '*It's riddled with holes. The Warmaster's horde is advancing across the districts of the Inner Palace.*'

Zephon's armour hummed in the silence that followed.

'Master,' said Eristes gently. Zephon could see he was trying to conceal his urgency. 'Can you stand yet?'

It was a trial to force himself to his feet. Servos in his hips and knees rolled smoothly, but his strength was taking its time to return. Seeing his weapons strapped to Shenkai's back in a buckled grav-harness brought a relief that bordered on profound.

Something like hunger rushed through him as he rose, awakening with the restoration of consciousness and motion. It turned his tongue to leather. He felt it in his parched veins, as if every process inside his body cried out for lubricant. It was a thirst beyond dehydration.

I am bloodless, he thought. *I am desiccated. A husk. How can they not see it?*

But they couldn't. There was evidently nothing to see. All three of his thralls closed in on him, examining his bionics, poking at the damage to his warplate, sealing the cracks with smears of armour cement.

Zephon had never felt the blood-need descend outside of battle. There, it was a pressure, an internal enemy to be resisted through willpower. Here, in the dark, it biled up into his throat and threatened to choke him. The beat of his thralls' hearts was strangely lovely, forming a hypnotic, sodden percussion.

'Lord,' someone was saying.

'Interesting,' someone else was saying. *'Innnteresting.'*

Zephon breathed through parted teeth, refocusing. 'I need you to tell me all that has transpired,' he said to Arkhan Land.

The hologhost shook its head. *'I'm not going to detail every loss we've suffered since your injury. The war would be over before I was halfway down the list of disasters.'*

'Then summarise. I need information, Arkhan.'

There was a pause. For a moment, Zephon was sure Land's petulance would win out. Thankfully, he was wrong.

'You were wounded at Gorgon Bar. Your sus-an membrane forced you into Astartesian stasis as a trauma reaction to the organ failures, the cranial rupture, the haemorrhaging…'

Zephon was unsteady but he felt fine, at least in terms of recovering from whatever wounds he'd sustained in the– *fire bright enough to blind him. Heat so hot it possessed its own searing sound. The unreal thunder of falling rocks. The*– the wounds he'd sustained in the explosion.

'I remember,' he said. 'I remember Gorgon Bar.'

'*Well, everything after that has gone supremely poorly. They've swarmed the Inner Palace. Almost everything has fallen except the Palatine Ring. Cydonae Bastion, Meru, Sheol… all gone. The last we heard of Pythia and Avalon bastions, they were close to breaking. Bhab and the others still hold, but each one is besieged by the horde, their forces surrounded. The Seventh Primarch is encircled at Bhab Bastion, trapped there.*'

The Seventh Primarch. Zephon felt a surge of irritation, but it was thin and weak. It didn't override the dry-vein hunger. 'Say his name,' said the Blood Angel. 'Say "Rogal Dorn".'

'*As I said,*' Land continued without missing a beat. '*The Seventh Primarch. And the bastions that aren't already in ruins are being overrun or abandoned as we speak. Everything in the Inner Palace is decaying. Or infected. Or rotting. Or mutating. Or cancerous. We fall back as swiftly as we can, staying ahead of the foulness. You don't know what it's like out there, Zephon.*'

'Master,' Eristes interrupted without bothering to look over at Land's hologhost. 'We must examine your range of motion.'

Zephon nodded permission, his attention remaining on Land as he systematically tensed and relaxed his muscles, biological and bionic alike. He rolled his shoulders and stretched his arms. Armour joints revved and tendons crackled in the stinking dark. Eristes, his assessor of physicality, paid rapt attention, studying for soreness, stiffness, for any flaws at all.

What little light there was flashed from the silver of his cybernetic limbs. Despite the damage to them – the scratches and dents they'd suffered in the rockslide at Gorgon Bar – they were exquisitely wrought. The Martian had engineered them himself, to replace the Blood Angel's failing bionics.

It was all coming back to him now, the good and the bad.

They have ranged the main line. Why are you here? You are not militia. He'd confronted a civilian, just as the shelling began. And he'd shielded her. Embracing her as the building came down upon them, warding her body with his own…

'There was a civilian at Gorgon Bar,' he murmured. 'The artillery… I tried to save her.'

'*Really.*' Land sounded far from fascinated. '*What a thrilling story.*'

'Her name was Ceris Gonn. One of the Praetorian's new interrogators. Do you know if she survived the explosion?'

'*Not only do I not know, I also don't much care. You're welcome, by the way. You'd be dead were it not for the archaeological fortune in Dark Age nanotech and artisanal bionics I used to repair your brainstem and central nervous system all those months ago. Their regenerative capabilities are admittedly crude – and, heh, of dubious legality – but it was enough to prevent you haemorrhaging to death from an excruciating brain-bleed.*'

Dark Age…? Zephon hesitated. 'That is a lot to process, to be thrown so casually into conversation.'

'*I think you meant to say, "Thank you, Arkhan, your legendary generosity has paid off yet again."*'

Zephon took a breath, fixing the hologhost with a gentle stare. 'I said exactly what I meant.'

'*As ever, Zephon, your achingly soulful sincerity is a tedium I've neither the time nor the patience to deal with. I trust, with this saving of your life, my debt to you is discharged. Besides,*' he added sniffily, '*there's no component in any of my work that isn't entirely safe and entirely within the realms of my understanding.*'

'That is comforting to know,' Zephon replied. 'Somewhat.'

'Yes, well, as I said – you're welcome. Now please get up and get out of there.'

'All seems in order,' Eristes said, still circling, still over-seeing the process. He watched as the servitors – at Land's command – pulled the chemical feeds from Zephon's armour sockets.

The Blood Angel dragged his fingers through his long hair, gathering it in a knot behind his head to keep it from his face. He did it carefully, aware of the pain throbbing all the while at the back of his skull. His hands came away unbloodied. That was something, at least.

He could remember everything now, every hour of the war, every minute of fighting and falling back, fighting and with-drawing... And he had the guiltiest feeling, just for a moment, that ignorance had been bliss. An unworthy thought for a warrior, let alone an Angel of Baal, but there it was.

'How fares my Legion? Where is the primarch?'

'We do not know, lord,' Shafia demurred. 'There has been no reliable word of the Emperor's Angel.'

'A handful of your Legion kinsmen still live,' Land added, 'but as for that genetic mutant you call a father, I'm afraid I've no idea.'

The family of thralls tensed at the disrespect, which of course Arkhan Land ignored entirely.

'The Twelfth Primarch hunts the Ninth. That's all we know, and we only know that because the ground shakes when he screams the Ninth's name across the sky. Your beloved pater may already be dead, Zephon, and if the Ninth has any sense, it's hiding from the Twelfth. Best to put it out of your mind for now.'

In the wake of those words, which might have seen Land killed by some members of the IX Legion, Zephon stared into the old man's hololithic eyes.

'You look tired, Arkhan.'

'Ah,' sighed the Martian. 'You have no idea.'

Zephon rose and took the auspex from the servitor's grip, activating it and passing it over his body in a slow sweep. The model was just a crude battlefield pattern, but it served its purpose as a medicae reader. When he passed it over his head, it pulsed a warning tone immediately. Flashing runes detailed sealed skull fracturing, potential cranial nerve damage and scarring of brain tissue. It couldn't be more specific, the auspex was too crude a model for that level of accuracy. A glance at Eristes told Zephon that his assessor thrall had already conducted the same scan, with the same results.

He'd been fortunate, that much was clear. His injuries would've killed a human outright, but his genhanced body had shut down into the healing sleep prized by his kind at their most grievously wounded. With his life functions slowed, his implanted organs had been granted the time they needed to heal, seal and scar over the worst of the damage. More than likely, an Apothecary or medicae had toiled over him while he was in sus-an, as well.

Then there were Land's… implanted treasures… to consider. The compensatory surgeries performed after their disastrous excursion into the webway.

Zephon shivered. He looked over the rows of stasis pods, seeing a hundred in this chamber alone. Thirty-two of them were sealed and occupied.

'There are other legionaries in stasis down here. I cannot leave them. They will be killed in their sleep.'

The hologhost looked at him as if he'd sprouted horns and started speaking in tongues. *'People die in war, Zephon. It's pathetic that an Astartes should need reminding of that.'*

'I cannot abandon my brothers.'

'No? Then you'll die down there with them. Most of them are already dead. They're stored here for gene-seed harvest, not because they'll be capering around after surgical recoveries.'

'I am not blind, Arkhan, I can read the stasis-coffin displays. Some of them are alive. With surgery, they will awaken from suspended animation. They will live.'

'You realise your own Legion has abandoned these unfortunates?'

'My brothers would never do such a thing.'

Land laughed at the denial. *'The war has moved on, Zephon. Every one of your kind still breathing is out there in the dust, fighting for his life. Do you think the loyal Legions have the warriors to spare for something like this? To blindly push stretchers and gurneys over kilometres of no-man's-land? I didn't send servitors and slaves down into the dark for you because they were the best souls for the purpose. I did it because there was no one else to send. Everyone else is out there, fighting, dying, or already dead.'*

Zephon stood by one of the pods, looking in at the somnolent figure. He didn't recognise the warrior's face, though the pod was marked with the Aenokhian runes of his Legion, and the figure wore Blood Angels armour. The corruption eating at the walls had started its work on the slumbering Astartes, blackening the left side of his body, twisting it with supernatural rancidity.

'Zephon, enough. There's no time for your sentimental frippery. If you can move, you need to get out of there. I've lost a great many servitors even reaching you. The sublevels are overrun with exoplanar mutation.'

Sensing it was time, Shenkai reverently turned his back upon his master. Cradled in the straps of the grav-harness on his back were the tools of Zephon's trade: his sheathed power sword, his boltgun, his pistols... Even one of the weapons would be a burden beyond easy human capacity, but the harness Shenkai wore lightened the load to tolerable levels.

Zephon didn't reach for them right away. 'Shafia?' he asked Shenkai's mother. She was his weaponbearer. The grav-harness was hers to wear, and his weapons were her honour to bear.

Shafia managed a slight smile. 'It was time, lord. Perhaps even past time.'

Now that it was spoken, Zephon couldn't miss seeing it. Eristes and Shafia were getting old. He'd paid his servants almost no heed since they came with him to Terra, years before, and age showed at the corners of their eyes, the thinning of their hair, and a dozen other ways that Zephon's kind instinctively overlooked as beneath their notice. Their son Shenkai was, what, close to twenty-five? Perhaps even thirty. The muscles of hard training showed beneath his red clothes. Clearly, he was ready. Zephon probably should have elevated Shenkai half a decade ago.

'Thank you, Shenkai,' he said to his new weaponbearer. He drew his blade slowly, leaving the scabbard bound to the thrall's back. With his free hand, he reached for one of his pistols. The weapons were clean, repaired, perfectly maintained. He'd expected no less.

'This is all very touching,' said Land. *'But please hurry. You're the only living beings down there, but not the only things moving.'*

It had not been a swift escape. Razavi Bastion, in its entirety, was the size of a township, and much of its scale was beneath the earth in the form of elaborate catacombs. The Emperor had wrested it from a technobarbarian warrior-queen in the Unification Wars, and the Imperium had done what the Imperium did best: annihilating all traces of the previous owners and reclaiming what was useful for their own purposes. Dozens of kilometres of tunnels and chambers comprised the fortress' underground levels. Zephon had never been this deep – not while conscious, at least – so he followed Land's drifting servo-skull through the subterranean halls. The servitors hadn't followed, even when Zephon had beckoned them.

'Let them die down here,' Land had said, his projected image

wavering with distance distortion and another spurt of static. *'They're useless now. Follow me.'*

And so, Zephon led his servants through the trembling dark. Eristes, untrained in weaponry, walked with an air of forced calm, pretending not to hear his master's conversation. Shenkai was consumed with his burden, seemingly uninterested in Land's recitations. Only Shafia openly listened; she shook her head with distaste at the Martian's commentary. Evidently she thought very little of Arkhan Land.

'Where are you, exactly?' Zephon asked the hololith at one point.

'Far above you, making ready to leave Razavi Bastion,' Arkhan replied, plainly distracted. *'With one of the convoys making for the Sanctum Imperialis, along with everyone still possessing a modicum of sanity. But that's not what you really want to ask, is it? What's the question behind the question?'*

He didn't want to say it. Even asking felt treasonous.

'Are we losing the war?'

Arkhan Land laughed so hard that his hololithic image flickered with distortion.

It wasn't long before Zephon came across the first of his dead kindred. A cousin rather than a brother: an Imperial Fist slumped against a corridor wall, his cracked armour overgrown with pulsating moss.

'Don't touch it,' Land's voice crackled from ahead.

'He,' Zephon murmured. 'Not *it*. Show some respect. This warrior gave his life for the Imperium.' He was watching the fleshy moss, how it pulsed with its own uneven heartbeat. As he stared, a crusty spread of the growth over the dead Space Marine's face swelled and slowly burst, birthing a flow of clumsy, blind spiders. The things were the colour of human flesh. They fought eyelessly, feasting on each other with stupid hate, bleeding human blood.

Zephon stepped closer. Sensing his movement, several of the spiders reared at him, spreading their palps and forelegs in feral challenge, hissing and throwing up their discoloured guts. Zephon weaved aside from the sprays of intestinal acid, moving away without looking back.

The servo-skull projecting Arkhan's image drifted ahead, pausing often to play its scanning web over the corridors and chambers of the abandoned bastion. There had been a battle here, and it was increasingly clear which side had claimed victory. The unburied dead lay everywhere. Uniforms marked most of them as Imperial Army, but not all. A great many were unarmed, wearing rags and robes. Pilgrims. Civilians. Refugees.

Families.

Rounding a corner, the Blood Angel stared down a long corridor carpeted with the fallen. Blade wounds, *saw wounds*, showed on their flesh, declaring deaths that had seen them carved apart in their final moments. Several had sunk into the steel, somehow rotting into the walls and floor. Avoiding them would be impossible.

'Hurry up,' said the hologhost, untroubled as it drifted several centimetres above the dead.

Zephon walked over them, the weight of his armour pulping them beneath his tread no matter how gentle he tried to be. He could hear his thralls struggling behind him – it was almost pitch-black for them; they were relying on hand torches – but he was anything but human. He could see exactly where he was stepping, and upon whom.

'Arkhan, there are children here.'

'*Of course there are,*' said Land, drifting ahead. '*Razavi Bastion's sublevels were a refugee holdout. One of the last, outside the Sanctum Imperialis.*'

'How did the enemy get down here?'

'*They appeared. Manifested, you might say.*'

'I do not understand,' Zephon admitted.

The servo-skull turned in a slow arc, and the projected ghost offered a merciless gaze. *'Then you're in fine company,'* Land said. *'No one really knows what's happened since the Ultimate Wall fell. Everything has gone sour, Zephon. Hundreds of millions have died. We're all in the dark. They bombarded us from orbit. They levelled the plateau. Most of the Inner Palace is a wasteland of rubble. Communication between the bastions was unreliable for weeks and has been mostly down for days.'*

Zephon kept moving. He looked back at the others. They were close behind him.

Land droned on, having found his conversational stride. *'Exoplanar xenos are manifesting across the wasteland and inside the last bastions. The Omnissiah's will no longer holds them back. We saw them in Cydonae Bastion... at the end. Before we ran from there, to reach Razavi. They burst from the dead. They pulled themselves out of the living. Soon enough it was happening down there, too. It's happening everywhere. Blood of the Machine-God, the planet's crust is unstable, and the atmosphere is choked by dust. This world is dying. Horus is killing Terra in his quest to take it.'*

There seemed nothing to say to that. With one hand on the wall for balance, Zephon moved on and tried not to tread on the fallen. Many of the bodies were in the process of some impossible, cadaverous fusion, conjoined where their dead flesh touched. He saw bodies melded with the walls; curling fingers reaching out from the metal, half-formed faces shrieking silently from the steel.

One of them asked him for help.

He turned, seeing a cluster of cancers in the shape of a woman, a hive of tumours glued to the wall with its own corruption. It reached for him with shaky tenderness, as if to see if he was real.

'Please help me,' it said again.

'*Ignore it,*' Land said. '*Ignore all of them. They think they're still people.*'

'Don't leave me down here,' the thing said. Where it had once had a mouth, a split in its lumpen head kept smearing open, showing a hundred hairy teeth.

'Who are you?' he asked it, fighting to show none of his unease.

'Jennah,' the thing said, its tone like gargling gruel. 'Jennah Virnae. Please help me. Help my family. Don't leave us here.'

It fell silent, hanging there. Bleeding. Rotting. Zephon recognised nothing human in the living malformation. He feared saying so would cause it yet more pain.

'I cannot help you... Jennah.'

Though he could. He felt the weight of the pistol in his hands.

It – *she* – laughed suddenly, the sound thick and wet. '*They have ranged the main line.*'

'*Keep moving,*' Land snapped. '*Don't let it get inside your mind.*'

The thing, the woman, started to *flow,* her form dissolving into a slush that steamed as it ran down the wall.

'*They have ranged the main line,*' she said through loosening teeth in a melting mouth. '*Son of Sanguinius, we see and hear through iron and stone and ash and dust... We know we know we know...*'

Zephon pulled the trigger. The remains of Jennah Virnae decorated the wall in a sizzling pattern that behaved nothing like blood. Blood didn't dissolve metal. Blood didn't run like tar.

'I believe I am somewhat more cognisant now of what threatens Terra,' he said to Arkhan's hologhost.

'We shouldn't delay here, master,' said Shafia.

'*Ye, indeed,*' Land said. '*Listen to the slaves. Keep moving.*'

And this time, Zephon did.

EIGHT

A thousand points of light

Rykath

Humanity has always managed to summon a poetic turn of phrase for the projected end of everything. Scribes love to speak of how things fall apart, the centre unable to hold – contrasting the rise of oceans with the fall of empires. Philosophers claim the end will come not with a bang, but with a whimper. And of death? Nothing to fear, they promise. Death is merely another path.

These sentiments are always composed by men and women far removed from any experience of what the end of all things would really be. It's easy to fall back on sanguine philosophy when you can't comprehend the truth. Yes, the centre cannot hold, but its dissolution means the genocide of trillions. Yes, death is another path, but that path leads to the soul of every man, woman and child sliding into the open mouths of mad gods.

Had the ancient wise ones seen such things with their own

eyes, perhaps their scrawls would have been somewhat less serene.

But a coin has two sides. Twinned with the serenity of ignorance is the spectre of hope. People will resist the end, even against the evidence of their eyes and the workings of their minds. Logic plays no part in it. This is the arena of hope, with survival instincts baked into the brain of every living being. Emotions like that burn through anything as cold and blunt as reason.

And so it was here, in the war's final days. It didn't matter that the war was over. It didn't matter that Terra burned day and night beneath a funeral shroud of dust. The defenders fought on.

The idea of a front line in the war for Terra was fiction; already threatened with the first breach in the Ultimate Wall, by the hour of Jaghatai Khan's charge to retake the Lion's Gate space port, it was plain myth. Rogal Dorn had mapped and planned a nation's worth of fallback points, barricades, strongholds, weapons caches in the Inner Palace... and they were reached, defended, drained and abandoned in inevitable succession. Those that weren't abandoned were pounded out of existence from orbit – erased by blind-bombardment from shipmasters unable to restrain themselves – or overrun by the Warmaster's horde. The bastions that yet survived were encircled in their own sieges, the defenders fighting on, selling their lives to delay the horde's advance.

It was no longer one war. The scale of Horus' invasion had always eclipsed that description, but never was it more obvious than now the defences were broken. The mitosis of warfare was rampant, and countless separate wars raged across the face of Terra. Cohesion had given way to isolation, with the Emperor's remaining forces surrounded in their very last strongholds and foxholes, cut off from each other.

A thousand points of light across the Eurasian land mass, going out, one by one.

There, in the infinite ash, was the warrior Rykath – though even this first fact was, in a way, a lie. Rykath was his Imperial name, something he wore like an uncomfortable cloak for the sake of other sensibilities. His Fenrisian brothers, oathed and bloodlocked into the Old Ways, called him by his deed name. They called him No-Foes-Remain.

He was a hunter and a warrior, and proud of the distinction between both. To Imperial scribes, he was just another Space Marine within the amalgamated mess of the Space Wolves Legion. Their eyes didn't see past the clashing knotwork of company and squad markings, impenetrable to outside observers. They didn't know his place in the Cry of the Grieving Dragon warband, nor his role in the pack called Howl of the Hearthworld.

Around his neck was a cord of plain leather bearing a talisman of Fenrisian amber, granted a lifetime ago by his High Warchief, Leman of the Russ Tribe. Receiving it had been the proudest moment of his life. He would wear it until his death.

Rykath stood on the battlements of Arjuna Bastion, a palatial skyspire bound to Meru Bastion by kilometres of arching walkways. With Meru overrun, Arjuna had stood alone for hours, protected by an ever-diminishing host of defenders. They'd done well, but they weren't gods, to rewrite the flow of fate. The enemy scaled the walls, came over the skywalk bridges, and brought the walls down with sustained cannonades. This was the end of Arjuna.

Gunships couldn't fly in the dust. Not reliably. The ash in the air lethally abraded the sky support of both sides, frost-blasting cockpit glass, chewing through internal machinery and causing Thunderhawks to choke, to stall, to die gasping. Gunship jets ran brutally hot, melting the ash into glass, which choked turbine blades and stalled engines. There was no clear patch of air through which to soar and recover, no matter how high or low a craft went, and none had safely reached orbit in days. Pilots couldn't see; they flew blind with dead instruments through a burning city the size of a nation, spiked with buildings the scale of mountain ranges. They wrestled with the controls of vehicles whose engines couldn't breathe. But that didn't stop either side trying. Desperation forced the hands of some, hope galvanised others, and bloodthirst was ever a motivating factor for many.

Rykath, surrounded by his dead brothers, was close to one of the last remaining gunships still on the wall. He wasn't a fool, nor would he ever be accused of being an optimistic soul. He knew he was dead. In his ears, over the roar of the flames and the crashing of a thousand bolters, a voice forced its way through the scramble of the vox, imploring him to run. But he didn't run because, as noted, he wasn't a fool. He'd rather die with a blade in his hand than in the mangled metal of a gunship crash.

He wept for the slain. There was no loss of dignity; Fenrisian culture – as with many other Legion home world traditions – saw no shame in sorrow. At his feet were the brothers he'd fought beside for two human lifetimes. He loved them above life itself. Of course he wept. A machine couldn't. A coward wouldn't.

There was Kargir, called Thirteen-Stars-Falling, born beneath a meteor shower, the greatest omen of the northern tribes, and dead now of a blade in both hearts. There was Vaegr, called Echo-of-Three-Heroes for the ancestors he resembled, born in the endless Fenrisian winter, and killed by a bolt in the head. There was Ordun, called Kin-to-the-Night, born to hunt in the darkness, dead in a war that should never have been fought. They were the last; the others of his pack had died weeks ago.

Hardly any Wolves remained on Terra, and of those few almost none still drew breath.

The beseeching voice didn't stop until he severed his link to the vox. Rykath stayed where he was as figures moved past him in the dust. Humans. Masked, running, limping. Defenders, fleeing. Why? Where was there left to run? What was so special about dying over there instead of right here?

He crouched and placed a hand on the ruptured breastplate of his officer and brother, Thirteen-Stars-Falling. Filthy, armoured fingertips pressed lightly to his brother's broken Imperialis. He smiled through the bitter tears, because the accidental symbolism of the moment was so blunt, so on the nose, that he couldn't help but grin.

They came for him then, the enemy pursuing the fleeing defenders. He rose, holding not just his own chainsword but the powered blade of his fallen chieftain. One sword revved into angry life, the other sparked with killing lightning.

In the sagas of his home world – and the Legion that rose from those icy roots – heroes always had worthy last words. They extemporised oh-so valiantly, and issued grand last challenges that forced their foes to listen with reluctant respect. But Rykath had never been one for the saga-poems, and these enemies – these bellowing World Eaters and chanting Thousand Sons – were too drunk on the milk of their black gods to respect their enemies. Nor did they deserve respect in kind.

He faced them and he fought them. That part, at least, matched the sagas of Fenris. But there was no joy at the slaying he did this dawn. To kill one's enemies was what was expected of any warrior. What mattered to him in these final moments wasn't who he killed, but where he himself stood, ready to die. He was dying with his brothers. Part of his pack to the very end.

This was right. The way it should be.

No-Foes-Remain, named for his enduring tirelessness, admired by his brothers for always fighting until no foes remained, finally failed to live up to his name. There was no shame in this. How could there be shame in defeat when there was never any hope of victory?

When the moment came, Rykath couldn't stop grinning. He was grinning as he stood shin-deep in the dead, with the steel of his enemies' blades meeting inside him. He was grinning even as he dropped, life pumping from him in a flow of proud Fenrisian blood.

The warrior that killed him, one of the Thousand Sons, took the power sword from his dying fingers. Less than a minute later, that warrior was killed by a stray torrent of lascannon fire, and the blade once treasured by the warriors of Howl of the Hearthworld was vaporised, forever forgotten.

Such were the whims of war.

By the time Rykath was giving his last grin through a mouthful of blood, the Imperial Fists gunship further down the ramparts had taken off. To stay on the wall was to die, and the pilot took his chances in the sky. The Thunderhawk sucked ash into its mechanical respiration with long, heaving roars, and left the ground behind.

It clawed skyward, already labouring, already doomed. When its engines strangled on fusing glass, its pilot dived, forcing cooling air through the intakes, hoping to freeze and shatter-clear the clogged turbines. His name was Ectar, a Terran-born Imperial Fist. No one saw what he did, but the manoeuvre was magnificent. The soldiers aboard were hurled against the inner hull and against the restraints of their flight thrones, many of them believing they'd been hit by anti-air fire, not realising their pilot's skill had bought them a few more seconds of life.

But there was no clear air at the end of the dive. There was no clear air left on Terra. The tumbling gunship cleared its throat only to fill it back up with ash and dust. It choked on filth again only seconds after expelling it.

The Thunderhawk fired its orbital boosters, an act of absolute desperation, and afterburned hard through the blinding dust. For three seconds, it gained altitude at the cost of its abrading hull and dying engines, cannibalising itself to fly free.

It collided with one of the baroque walkways stretching between Meru and Arjuna bastions, which its pilot had no hope of ever seeing. With much of the gunship's left side sheared away, the wreckage spiralled down on engines that screamed until the dust strangled them fully. What was left of the hull speared into no-man's-land, wreckage and shrapnel flying every which way, carving through a scattered infantry regiment in Horus' colours who were pursuing a convoy of retreating Imperial Army.

Arjuna Bastion fell less than an hour later, and out went another light.

NINE

One last joke

Transacta-7Y1

Down again, through the dust. Past the skeletons of Imperial Knights still standing upright as flames ate their bones. Over tens of thousands of bodies, carpeting the earth. Up and over the battlements of Pythia Bastion, its walls sundered and overrun, banner poles now flying Horus' colours in the wind.

Beyond fallen Pythia, farther still, deeper into the dust. No grand architecture of the Palatine Bastions in this place. Here, the fighting was in the rubble-strewn wasteland that was once a series of streets around the Principa Collegiate, where ambassadors from conquered worlds came to learn the ways of the Terran Imperium. An academy of great libraries and data archives that housed six thousand off-world souls and the two thousand tutors carefully selected to oversee their re-education. Now, a hollow ruin.

Transacta-7Y1 couldn't blink, for even a momentary closing of her eyes represented a potential data loss. An intolerable supposition to her masters and mistresses, who adapted her – and most of her kind – to function without eyelids. She stared at the dying world around her through the cracked plastek of her monovisor. The lens kept clicking and rotating, trying to focus, trying to see in a world gone blind.

She was Martian-born and Martian-remade. Her cradle was warmed by the heat of the blessed forges, and she was conditioned against the terminal holiness of the weapons she carried. She was skitarii.

Transacta-7Y1 stalked through the marble ruins, carrying out the last order she received. *Defend Principa.* The words still flashed in Gothic across the insides of her eyes. *Defend Principa. Defend Principa.*

In the beginning, all those months ago before the war had devoured all reason, her orders had been vocal deliverances, coming in the adrenally rewarding tones of her overlords. As time went on and communication degraded, orders filtered down to the skitarii macroclades through sacred encryptions; then standard binharic cant; then plain operational codes and – at the very last – through routine text commands.

She hadn't heard the holy speech of her overlords in three weeks, five days, nine hours, thirty-one minutes and nine seconds. Ten. Eleven. Twelve.

Defend Principa flashed at the edge of her vision and she knew the order was pure (it came with the correct allegiance signifiers when it started flashing up six days ago), but she no longer knew how valid the order remained. After all, the Principa Collegiate was rubble. There seemed little worth fighting for, and precious few of her clade-kin were still functional enough to defend it. No other orders had been received in that span. Not by Transacta-7Y1, not by any of her brothers and sisters wearing sacred red.

This brought a sense of unease. She didn't like to process the possibility that her masters and mistresses were dead. Only slightly less uncomfortable was the notion that they had issued an order that lingered on, uncorrected, un-updated.

Unless, she reasoned, her overlords were aware of this outcome when they issued the order, having cogitated the inevitabilities. In that case, she'd been assigned here to die fighting, spending the coin of her life to slow the enemy. And in such an instance, no further orders would be forthcoming.

It was the likeliest eventuality. It wasn't perfect, it wasn't *clear*, and the idea of enacting a potentially incorrect order caused her far more discomfort than the thought of dying to a correct one. But she reasoned, not without precedent, that if she and her clade-kin were sent here to sell their lives, that would have been referenced in the initial order.

No matter. She had done the best with what she had, and trusted that she hadn't deviated from her place in the Omnissiah's plan.

'Tee,' Envaric said, to her left.

Transacta-7Y1 turned to him. He was dying, and she kept experiencing tremors of emotion at this. The enemy was not killing him. Her weapons were. Proximity to her holy arsenal was blackening his skin and making him cough up blood.

He knew this. She'd told him when they first grouped up, explaining as best she was able that the holy aura radiating from her weapons was both invisible and lethal to unconditioned humans.

'You mean radiation?' Envaric had asked. And Transacta-7Y1 had nodded, because yes, that was the banal name for the divine aura emitted by her weaponry. Envaric had glanced at the carbine in her hands, with its brassy casing and glowing internals, and he'd shrugged.

'I'll catch a bolt in the head before the rad gets me. Ain't none of us getting out of Principa alive anyway. What's your name? Do they give you lot names?'

She'd pointed to the serial code engravings on her chestplate.

Envaric made an expression she couldn't decipher. He said, 'That ain't a name.'

It was, though. It was her name. She'd pointed to it again, tapping it that time.

'Fine, Transacta-Seven-Why-One. I'm Sergeant Sylas Envaric of the Twelfth Helian Rifles. Looks like we'll be dying together.'

They'd survived two days since then, fighting in the Principa ruins. Now Envaric was visibly decaying.

'Tee,' he said again, the word turned to gravel by a coughing fit so bad that he had to remove his mask and spit blood onto the ground.

Transacta-7Y1 couldn't speak. She couldn't even remember a time when she'd been able to make sounds with a human tongue. Her overlords had removed the ability when they remade her. She could blurt pulses of code from the vocoder in her throat – which was useless right then because Envaric was an unaugmented human incapable of processing Martian code-spurts – so she relied on her handheld dataslug. It displayed a series of pictographs that roughly adhered to whatever she was trying to convey.

When she'd first warned him of her weapons' lethality, she did so by keying in several sigils representing herself, her rifle, a biohazard rune, caution, illness, and a pictograph depiction of a dead human. But she needed no such dubious nuance now. Just one symbol blinked on the dataslug's tiny screen.

[?]

Envaric struggled to breathe. He sat with his back to the low, broken wall they'd been crouched behind for the last fifteen minutes. Catching his breath, he cast a goggled glance at her dataslug, then looked at her helmet's impenetrable visor. The closest thing she had to a face.

'Any sign of the others?'

Transacta was staring over the top of their barricade, scanning and panning over the low stone wall. She stopped her vigil, clumsily dialling a code into her dataslug with thick bionic fingers. It beeped with a single sigil.

[alone]

Envaric nodded, and Transacta-7Y1 read (what she thought was) disappointment in (what she could see of) his expression. Between the rebreather and the goggles and the grime, that wasn't much.

'Well,' he said with a laboured breath, 'you and me, Tee, we've got this. The others were just holding us back anyway.'

She knew he was trying to be funny. He kept doing this, kept trying to make jokes. Perhaps he was even *being* funny, but Transacta-7Y1 was profoundly ill-equipped to recognise either failure or success in that regard. What she felt, weak but true, was a sense of kinship and gratitude that he chose to stay. He wasn't of her clade and she didn't process loneliness or fear in anything resembling human terms, but his presence was a curious comfort. Even though it was temporary. Even though it was killing him.

Envaric closed his eyes for a moment, resting the back of his head against the wall. The ground shook with the aftershock of yet another cataclysm not far from where they hid, but he didn't react. It was taking him longer and longer to recover after each action.

Something exploded elsewhere in the ruins. It was answered by the ambushing snaps of radium fire, and the returning protests of boltguns. They weren't entirely alone, after all.

'All right, all right,' Envaric grunted with plainly false enthusiasm. 'Let's get to it.'

They moved again, keeping low. Drawing closer to what had once been the external curving wall of an auditorium, emerging above them in the dust. It wasn't long before they found the bodies of three Helians, freshly cut down. Blown open by bolts. These, they passed with barely a glance.

At the shattered archway leading into the auditorium, they paused with their backs to the wall. The whines and grinds of power armour came from within.

Transacta-7Y1 was the one to make a visual confirmation. She lifted her radium carbine and panned slowly down the steps, tracking through the dust, looking for signs of–

There. Silhouettes in the ash. Too tall to be human. Too inelegant to be Martian. The warriors stalked through the ruins, seemingly without direction, like ants that had lost their trail. Transacta-7Y1, who had never seen an ant, likened the Astartes down there to low-grade slave units cut off from their higher mind. She moved back into cover.

'How many?' Envaric asked her.

She keyed in a symbol and tossed him the dataslug. The symbol for *[multitude]* showed on its slit screen.

Envaric tossed it back to her with an expression of pain. His gums were bleeding inside the plastek rebreather.

'You're shitting me,' he said.

His bizarre axioms were familiar to her now, and she knew he wasn't speaking of biological excretion. Transacta-7Y1 emitted a quiet negative code-spurt. She was not, as he phrased it, shitting him.

'Pissfire,' he swore. Which was a new one, and one she couldn't work out from the context. A urinary tract infection, maybe. 'Who'd have our luck, eh?'

She had no reply to that. The concept of luck flew in the face of the Omnissiah's divine plan and was therefore a falsehood. She felt an anaemic amusement that her companion believed in it, but then, his brain was entirely soft and unsupported by mechanical augmentation.

Transacta-7Y1 made a fist, a symbol they'd agreed on at the

beginning of their companionship. They both tensed, making ready to move. Surprise was on their side. Nothing else was, but they took what they could get.

But Envaric had one more thing to say.

'Tee. Tell me something before we die, yeah?'

She turned to regard him, gazing at his deteriorating form through her monovisor. She said nothing, but he had her attention. The look in his eyes was what she suspected to be amusement. This was it, then. One last joke.

'Are you pretty under all that?'

It took her a moment to process this. She'd never been asked such a thing.

Beneath her armour, she was an irradiated foot soldier of the Machine-God. Her skin, deep brown at birth and not unlike Envaric's in that regard, was a starved and sunless grey. She'd been ritually delimbed, her extremities replaced with arms and legs of inexpensive cybernetic purity. Much to her honour, she had attained such a state of grace within her mechamorphosis that more of her body was now comprised of holy iron than what remained of her flawed birthflesh.

Under her helmet, she was pockmarked with cryo-controlled radiation tumours. She possessed no eyelids, no hair, no teeth, and no nose – and what hadn't been surgically removed had rotted off over the course of her years of sacred service.

In short, she was skitarii.

Transacta-7Y1 keyed in a symbol and tossed him the data-slug again. He caught it with weakening fingers and read the symbol there.

[affirmative]

He gave a bloodstained smile. 'Yeah, I thought so.'

Though neither of them knew it for certain, they were the last of their combined platoons. When they attacked a few moments later, killing two of the Emperor's Children from ambush, it was the final act of resistance in the defence of the Principa Collegiate.

Transacta-7Y1 went down first, her radium carbine smashed from her hands before she was punched from her metal feet by the force of a power maul. They left her for dead in the ranks of elevated seating. Envaric fought for a little longer, desperate to avenge Tee. He failed, naturally – he was one dying man against seven transhumans – and unfortunately he was still alive when they impaled him on a banner pole, where they watched him twitch and strangle on his own blood.

Luckily, however, he was dead before they set the pole over an open fire and roasted him. These noble sons of the III Legion, once foremost in the Emperor's regard, devoured Envaric's rad-soaked flesh for their early morning repast.

And so fell the Principa Collegiate. Out went another light.

TEN

The last guardian

Vulkan

The primarch ran his hand down the silver carving, following the lines depicting a human warlord on his knees, weapon offered up in surrender. A scene of great mercy, with the Emperor Himself – rendered here in the artful technosavagery he wore in the Unification Wars – accepting the surrender with a bowed head and good grace.

Vulkan treasured these insights into his father's life. Here was the Emperor before any of the primarchs came into being; before any of the grandest steps of the great plan were brought to fruition. A time before the Imperial Truth. A time before the Imperium.

Were you lonely, father? Is that why you made us?

Vulkan stepped back from the carving. The great doorway was resplendent with these bas-relief images, reaching from the stone floor to the chamber's vaulted ceiling. They called it the Silver Door now, but here was the original Eternity

Gate, a monument to ancient triumphs, serving as the barrier warding the Emperor's Throne Room from the rest of His laboratory-labyrinth. You could walk a Titan through the doorway when it was open, though it was far smaller than the great gateway on the surface that had come to eclipse its subterranean forebear and steal its name. Still, this relic possessed a breathtaking charm of its own.

Since coming to his father's Throne Room, Vulkan had long speculated just how many artisans had worked on this masterpiece, and just how long their efforts had taken them. Like so much of the Emperor's work, it had been commissioned and constructed in secret. Did the artists and engineers demand payment for their sweat and genius? Surely some did. Were they understandably mercenary in their mortal interests? Surely some were. Or was it enough for most that they were to be honoured like this, permitted by the Master of Mankind to contribute their craftsmanship to the very door of His Throne Room?

Whatever the truth, it was a tragedy for this work to be seen by so few. The new Eternity Gate, the inheritor to the name that stood locked far above these chambers, was the most reinforced and defended portal in the Imperium. The forgotten doorway down here was armoured in nothing but art.

Footsteps drew near. Vulkan's senses were tuned beyond mortal limit. Even with the grinding industry of the Emperor's laboratory going on all around, he could hear the other man's creaking sinews; the rustle of robes; the clink of a familiar black staff against stone.

'Greetings, Malcador,' he said without turning. 'Is it time?'

Malcador nodded wordlessly.

Vulkan ran his fingertips over the image of his father's face once more. 'He looks almost serene here, does He not? Accepting this man's surrender, with the future still unwritten. A time when the madness we now face was impossible to conceive.'

'A lifetime ago,' Malcador replied. He sounded weary, and something worse than weary. He sounded shattered. 'No word yet from Sanguinius. Nor anything from the Khan's forces at Lion's Gate.'

The tone made Vulkan turn. Defiance gleamed in eyes of predator-red. 'We will win, Mal. Banish the defeat from your voice.'

Malcador, Regent of Terra, leaned on his staff and met the primarch's gaze from beneath his hood. Depending on which stories one believed, Malcador was ancient, ageless or immortal. Yet he looked withered, gripped by a weakness that grew more profound with each passing hour.

'Victory may come, yes.' He sounded thoughtful, at least, rather than defeated. 'But I wonder who among us will be around to savour it.'

Vulkan rested a gauntleted hand on the old man's bony shoulder. Gently. Carefully. The merest pressure.

'Any word from Rogal?'

'Bhab Bastion holds. He still cannot break out.'

Vulkan shook his head at Malcador's diplomatic turn of phrase. Bhab Bastion was the secondary heart of the siege, the core of Imperial logistics and vital to the coordination of the defence. The bastion's systems were one of the few comm-nexuses able to breach the atmospheric distortion; Dorn and his command staff oversaw not just the warfare in the Inner Palace, but remained attuned to the near-infinite conflicts raging across all of Terra. Rogal Dorn would leave Bhab Bastion when it fell, and not a moment before. Not while tens of millions of soldiers still in the field needed his command expertise.

'Whether he can break out or not is irrelevant,' said Vulkan. 'He is too selfless to try, and too bound by duty to abandon his post. He is trusting us, Mal. Trusting us to hold without him. We will not let him down.'

Malcador looked distinctly uncomfortable. 'He also sent word that the dead have started to walk.'

Vulkan stared for a moment. 'Did he qualify that statement?'

Malcador leaned on his staff, exhaling slowly. 'The dead from both sides. He says they are rising, that they march upon the Sanctum.'

Vulkan took a last look at the carving of his father, then turned away, moving back into the Throne Room.

Priestlings and various Mechanicus adepts moved aside as they went about their work, labouring at the Emperor's secret engines. The Throne Room was different every day – forever expanding, undergoing repairs, losing burnt-out machinery and accumulating fresh, clanking ironworks. The ever-present hum of Dark Age power set many of the mortals' teeth on edge. Vulkan heard it as a song, a melody of half-mastered artistry from mythology. The crashing of these overworked machines was the sound of a lost age. And this, too, was wondrous.

Taking up the whole of one wall was the webway portal. The great circular aperture no longer showed the alien realm beyond, nor did it show the Throne Room's engraved sandstone wall behind. They had tried to kill it, flash-frying the awakening machinery and breaking the power sources to terminate the opening for good, only for the doorway to remain partially open. It wouldn't close. The things on the other side refused to let the wound heal.

Now the Emperor held it sealed through force of will. It existed in a state of perpetual low power, a huge grey eye that sighed white mist into the Throne Room in a ceaseless exhale.

Even the mortals and menials working in the Throne Room could feel the weight of psychic pressure. Noses bled. Eyes ran red with tears of blood. The augmented among them kept suffering bionic failures, implanted organs and limbs malfunctioning without cause. The unaugmented endured muscle wastage and slow-building embolisms. Sometimes they spoke in tongues, conversing in languages they'd never learned. They dreamed waking dreams of lives they'd never led. Their memories were overwritten by warfare in the Age of Strife... By a primitive boy's existence on the banks of the River Sakarya... By the feel of wheat against their fingertips, and the weight of the first bolter in their fists, and...

And on it went. Above everything, suspended in a vast cobweb of cables and support struts, the Golden Throne was the nucleus of the song. Some of the humans in the chamber wore goggles against its light, others shielded their eyes with their hands when they had to turn in its direction. Many simply tried never to look up. Vulkan saw no blazing aura, just a faint nimbus of light, no more painful to the eyes than a candle flame.

His father sat enthroned, eyes closed, features tensing with pulses of silent pain. The Emperor gripped the armrests, gloved fingers squeezing in rhythm with each flinch. His sun-bronzed flesh was sallow, His cheeks sunken, as though a cancer devoured Him from within. Attendants stood upon platforms at His side, wiping away the blood that leaked from His closed eyes.

Vulkan.

At first, he heard his name in his father's voice. A bitter irony, indeed.

He turned to the webway portal, gazing at the grey mist of aborted ambition.

Vulkan, came the voice again. *Brother. Come to me.*

Malcador was at Vulkan's side, watching his features closely. 'Is it him?'

'It's him.' Vulkan's heart began to beat harder. 'One last time, then. Let us see what he has to say.'

Vulkan closed his eyes and sank into the precious lie.

* * *

In his dreams, his brother still looked like his brother. The landscape around them was a volcanic nightmare – a realm of black skies and boiling earth; a dragon's delight. The two brothers took counsel together in psychic silence, the two of them facing one another here in the arena of the unreal.

His brother was the one to bring them both here each time. And if it wasn't his brother's will, then it was the whim of the things with their talons around his brother's heart. Vulkan no longer believed there was a difference.

When he saw his reflection in a pool of volcanic glass, he appeared the way he felt: weary to the point of ruination – a fact he could mask easily enough in the Throne Room, yet had no hope of hiding here. In this place, he appeared as a dragon on the edge of decrepitude. His scales no longer shimmered with an emerald lustre; instead they were faded to flawed jade. His eyes, which had been searing red, were tight and dull with torment. Even the fire within him was down to an ember, a guttering flicker of warmth.

His brother, the Sorcerer, descended slowly in a haze of purifying light. The light warmed the Dragon. It quickened his blood and reknit the throbbing internal breaches inside his body. It promised true healing, if he would only stop resisting it.

'I hate seeing you like this,' his brother said. Compassion shone in the Sorcerer's one eye. 'It needn't be this way, brother.'

'You are not my brother.' The Dragon grunted as he shifted his pained form. Even his bones ached. They sent pulses of cold through the meat of his muscles.

'You still deny me,' the Sorcerer said, the words rich with regret. 'Do I not bring you here, to Nocturne, to ease your spirit?'

The Dragon managed a laugh, though it tasted of dust instead of fire. 'This is not Nocturne,' he said. 'The stars hang where they should in the sky, yet they shine wrong in the black. The chemical processes of the rocks are exact, yet the stone feels wrong to the touch. This is Nocturne through the eyes of someone that has seen my home world but never understood it. Someone that never loved it.'

The Dragon, despite his throbbing joints, bared his fragile fangs in a tired smile. 'Someone,' he added, 'or some*thing*.'

The Sorcerer went to one knee, the very image of unthreatening reverence. His voice, trembling with emotion, scarcely rose above a whisper. 'I am still me, brother. I speak only the truth.'

The Dragon sighed another ashy breath. 'The truth, if it even matters in dreams, is that my brother died long ago. You are not Magnus. You are an impossible god's idea of Magnus.'

Laughter echoed all around them. The laughter of a thousand mocking voices, delighted at a joke only one of the brothers could ever understand. The Dragon crawled back from the chorus of mad mirth. All while the Sorcerer stood in silence, radiating compassion, radiating patience and understanding.

'How can you not hear that laughter?' the Dragon asked him. 'You are mocked, mocked without end, by the god you pretend you do not pray to.'

'There is no laughter,' said Magnus the Red. 'I hear nothing but your lies, Vulkan.'

The Dragon gave a weary smile with a mouthful of cracked fangs. 'Enough. Enough of you, and enough of the thing animating you. Leave me be.'

'Let me in,' countered the Sorcerer. 'This is only the beginning of your pain, brother. I've foreseen far greater agony in your future, agony even you cannot endure. But that pain will end with the mercy I bring. In place of devastation, I offer you enlightenment.'

The Dragon dared not turn his back on his one-eyed brother,

even here in dreams. He withdrew slowly, crawling over the rocks, his slitted gaze never leaving the Sorcerer.

'Let me in,' Magnus said again. 'How much strength does father have left? How much time remains in His performative defiance? An hour? A day? The sky above the ash cloud seethes with the gods' arrival. The Khan is finished. Guilliman is still lost in the endless black. Angron bathes the Palatine Ring in Imperial blood, and soon he will break Sanguinius. Fate sings of all of this, Vulkan. I *will* reach the webway portal. I *will* break father's barrier. In a million futures, I already have. Don't make me break you with it.'

The Dragon gave a growl. 'I am not sure I can be broken.'

'You can die, Vulkan. You can be unmade. Everything of mortal origin can be unwoven with the lullaby of obliteration. Please don't make me be the one to end you.'

'Does this fate of yours sing of that, too?'

Magnus smiled. 'It grieves me to admit it, brother, but yes. To oppose me is to suffer annihilation. I wish it were not so. And it need *not* be so.'

The Dragon managed to return the smile. He was too weary to be amused, but the Sorcerer's insistencies still kindled something like mirth deep within.

'Of the many failures in our family,' the Dragon said through clenched teeth, 'you stand exalted above the rest of us, wrapped so comfortably in your delusions. At least the others have the courage to face up to what they've become. Only you, Magnus… Only you still – *still* – cannot see who you really are.'

The Dragon kept crawling, slowly retreating. The sky fractured with knives of laughter. The illusion before him broke apart.

Magnus was gone. Or, rather, Magnus was finally there. The Sorcerer was no longer Vulkan's brother; he was a towering monstrosity, a beast of cloven hooves and with a crown of fire, a monster with wings that shed mother-of-pearl feathers. The Dragon stared at this thing, this thing of mutation and mutilation, this thing that stank of all the lies it didn't know it had devoured.

'There you are.' The Dragon breathed the words, feeling the fire awaken inside, tasting the smoke running between his sore teeth. 'There you are, brother.'

'*He has to die, Vulkan,*' bellowed the creature that had been Magnus the Red. '*He will damn the species to extinction. Let me in. Let me heal all the damage He's done. Stand with me! You need not die with the others.*'

In the face of this anger, the Dragon said nothing. He crawled away from the inevitability of his brother's victory, from the laughter of his brother's god, and from the dream itself. He had to conserve his strength. He couldn't waste it here. His father needed him.

The Dragon opened his eyes.

No time had passed. Malcador stood by his side, looking up with the expression of hawkish concern Vulkan had come to know all too well of late.

'He revealed himself,' the Sigillite said, his voice barely carrying over the rising hum of the Emperor's awakening machinery. 'Didn't he?'

'He did not intend to. I doubt he realised he had let the mask fall. Truthfully, I doubt he even knows what he looks like now. Righteousness radiates from him, thick enough to choke us all. He is blinded by the light of his own halo.'

Malcador looked up to the Golden Throne. 'There are those who would say Magnus is very much his father's son in that regard.'

Vulkan's stare glinted with fatigued amusement. 'Do you criticise our Emperor, noble regent?'

'Merely an observation. An insight into the perceptions of others.' Malcador showed neither amusement nor shame, remaining preternaturally neutral.

Vulkan had already looked away. His gaze was drawn inexorably to the half-living webway portal, that vast arch of Terran steel and alien stone that led into the dimension between dimensions. He could feel Magnus in that realm, drawing closer. Soon, the Crimson King would knock on the door.

His eyes narrowed. His knuckles tightened.

'Let it be finished.'

Malcador nodded at the primarch's murmur. 'Come, then. Everything is ready.'

He wouldn't have long. Malcador had impressed that upon him, though he hardly needed to be told. The Sigillite's compulsion to make the obvious even clearer was the closest Vulkan had ever come to seeing Malcador show nerves.

Those arrayed in loose ranks behind him also needed no reminding, and no rousing speech before it all began. The men and women armoured in Imperial gold were among the finest of those still fighting, slowed by the fewest wounds. Malcador had worked for days, and to the best of his ability, to gather them from across the besieged Palatine Ring. Every one of them had withdrawn when ordered, accepting the likelihood they were being asked to sacrifice their lives in the Imperial Dungeon for the sake of an insane gamble.

Is this your will, father?

Vulkan expected no answer, and sure enough, that's what he got. So be it.

He refused to look back at the Golden Throne or the phalanx of warriors behind him. He faced ahead, the great hammer *Urdrakule* in his hands, and kept his last questions sealed behind stern lips. He would show no doubt to those around him – not to the adepts now holding their ground in defensible groups, not to the men and women that stood ready to die to give him this one chance.

Maybe it didn't matter if it was the Emperor's will or not. It was Malcador's will, and that was a voice that carried no small weight, but more importantly, it was Vulkan's desire that set them on this course. Once decided, the primarch of the XVIII Legion was a difficult man to move. This had to be done.

He raised *Urdrakule* high. Fractals of electric light reflected from the weapon as the Throne Room's machinery reached the crescendo of its technomagical song. The Emperor's engines whined, roared, spat out warning klaxons. In the very same second, without even half a heartbeat between their unity, every Custodian and Sister of Silence behind him raised their weapons *en garde*.

The hammer fell.

The Golden Throne, keeping the doorway between dimensions closed, shrieked with a cacophony of iron-breaking release. Grey mist became golden light, flooding into the chamber through the great portal, and the army of every species' hell raged its way into reality.

Vulkan ran for the webway gate.

PART THREE

THE ROAD TO ETERNITY

ELEVEN

A rose watered with blood

Lotara

She didn't sleep any more. In the hours assigned to rest, she wandered the corridors of the *Conqueror*, listening to the ship's metal bones creak as they bent to the warp's slow whim. Screams echoed down the hallways, as did laughter that sounded like screaming. She used to assign squads of World Eaters to hunt down the sources of those sounds, but that habit had disintegrated like so many other elements of basic military efficiency. The only World Eaters left aboard the flagship were the ones too blood-mad to make it down to Terra. They were just as likely to be responsible for those screams as they were to destroy whatever was causing them.

Lotara moved slowly, frail as an old woman. Dehydration and starvation leached her strength, and she was acutely aware that the feeling of broken glass in her joints wasn't a green light, medically speaking. Even so, she moved through her ship with a fearless air for whatever lay around each corner. The World

Eaters watched her pass and took no further notice of her. The human crew wisely avoided her glare, and these days she had no orders to give them anyway. The fleet's duty consisted now of hanging in low orbit above Terra and firing whenever and wherever the Warmaster's equerry, Argonis, commanded. That required only a skeleton crew, a few thousand souls at most – and most of those were slaves and thralls in the gunnery decks.

Today, she wanted answers. She was going right to the top to get them.

Lotara made her way to her personal chambers. The door refused to register her palm print in yet another system failure aboard the ship. These days, she couldn't keep track of them all. After several attempts, the reinforced door rumbled open of its own volition. She doubted the sensor had even acknowledged her, it seemed more like the fickle whim of the *Conqueror's* machine-spirit.

Iron groaned all around as if mimicking the captain's irritation, a deep-core protest at the external abuse. The warp-mist encircling Terra wasn't gentle with the Warmaster's fleet; it was a rough anchorage that strained the hull of each warship. The lights aboard the *Conqueror* had been dulled to emergency red for weeks with all the power fluctuations, but now even the crimson of crisis lighting flickered as it threatened to give up.

'Hold together,' she breathed to her ship. 'We've been through worse, haven't we?'

This lie no longer helped, but she found herself saying it anyway.

The captain's quarters exemplified the *Conqueror's* brutalism, a chamber of grey edges and panel slabs with an armoured window overlooking the ship's crenellated spine. When she'd first claimed the cabin with her promotion all those years ago, Khârn had been the one to escort her there. He was waiting for her there now, with his back to the view of Horus' armada.

'You have no manners whatsoever,' she told him. 'These are my private quarters.'

It was supposed to be a jest between soldiers that had served together for years, but it came out as a parched murmur that barely reached her own ears. Khârn either didn't hear or didn't care to answer. He turned away from her, looking past the fleet at the choked sphere of Terra. Around the cradle of mankind, the warp's poison tides had replaced the night sky.

Khârn had been silent since returning to the ship. The scarred mess of his features scarcely showed any expression, only the occasional twitch as the Nails bit. And it still felt wrong, seeing him without his axe.

Lotara's vision swam as she stared at him, and everything reddened, everything darkened. Where Khârn stood, a cluster of meathooks hung from the ceiling on a spider-lair's worth of chains. Dead World Eaters, exsanguinated in ritual execution, hung suspended there – just dead meat in powerless ceramite – their heads taken and their skulls offered to–

She closed her eyes against the venom of her own imagination and slapped herself twice. It helped a little.

'Are you staying for this?' she asked the figure by the window. 'If you are, keep out of the way.'

Khârn turned to regard the hololithic projector against the wall. As he moved, Lotara could see the grievous damage to his armour, inflicted by bolts and blades. His breastplate was a cracked ruin, revealing the sundered flesh beneath. She could see the burst, clenched meat of one lung. As she stared at him, she heard the gentle rattle of chains moving in the breeze of the chamber's air filtration. She couldn't remember exactly when he'd returned to the ship, only that one day she'd looked around the bridge and there he was, at his station.

'You were lucky to have survived,' she told him.

Khârn tilted his head, the way he always did when he sought

the right words. Lotara felt tears on her face, real tears, which was impossible. She hadn't wept real tears since she was an adolescent in the Zhurscan Academy for Gifted Youth, on the day she received the notification that her brother had died in the cholera outbreak ravaging the capital.

'But you didn't survive, did you?' A year ago, the question would've been madness. Now, she truly wasn't sure of the answer. She knew only that she was too tired to be afraid.

His only reply was to turn back to the window, facing the dying world and its kaleidoscopic sky. Lotara felt blood dripping from her nose. It hurt to look at Khârn for too long. It always made her bleed, and her blood came out unpleasantly thick.

The hololithic terminal gave a white noise connection screech and she turned to it, leaning her fists on the control panel for support. She was shaking all over and she wasn't sure why.

'Conqueror,' crackled a voice over the vox. '*This is the* Vengeful Spirit. *Secure channel established. You may speak.*'

'This is Sarrin.' Lotara willed her voice back to its original strength. 'Link your holo, please.'

The projector clicked and spurted out a flickering image, aggrieved by distortion. It was one of the Astartes, the colour of his warplate bleached by the hololith, but the talismans and spines on his armour detailed his allegiance without doubt. Lotara's heart sank.

'I wanted the Warmaster,' she said. 'I used my ultima clearance. With all due respect, I'm tired of seeing your face with every report, Argonis.'

Kenor Argonis, equerry to the Warmaster, inclined his head in sympathy. '*I speak with the voice of Horus Lupercal, from his lips to your ears.*'

Lotara fought not to grind her teeth. It felt good to be angry again. It felt cleansing. 'If it's coming out of your mouth, it's not the Warmaster's voice, is it?'

Argonis stiffened; it was obvious even through the wretched quality of the holo. Lotara was walking a fine line between her authority on paper and the hierarchy of reality. She was one of the highest-ranking officers in the armada and she had every right to speak with the Warmaster. But she was also human. It was becoming evident to her, this was a Legion War, a confrontation between demigods. Increasingly Lotara felt as though she and her kind were just so much chaff and chattel to the legionaries. This discussion wasn't disabusing her of the notion.

As she watched him, Argonis silenced the audio channel and conversed with at least one unseen crew member. It was her considered opinion that the equerry's diplomatic skills had eroded significantly in recent months.

'Captain Sarrin,' he said at last. 'A pleasure, as always.'

'Please elaborate, equerry.'

But he didn't. His hololith blinked out of existence with a spurt of static. Lotara stared in silence. Had Argonis really played the most cringeworthy card in his deck? Had he really severed their private channel just to avoid a conversation?

'Son of a bitch,' Lotara said with almost unreal politeness. It was the most she'd felt like herself in months. 'You childish Astartes bastard.'

The hololith flared back into life towards the end of her curse. It wasn't Argonis this time. The figure was enthroned upon white ceramite and twisted metal, slouching with wounded majesty. His eyes were sunken and edged with lines of pain, bright with fever rather than awareness. Metal talons the length of swords drummed on the armrest of the throne with a *clink-clink-clink* audible across the vox.

The ghoul wearing the Warmaster's armour stared at her with a sort of fevered, confused intensity. Then he smiled, and he was Horus Lupercal once again. The pain fell away from his beautiful features.

'*I trust you weren't addressing me?*' he asked.

Lotara saluted, fist against her heart. 'My Warmaster. I was speaking to your equerry. He has been something of an irritant.'

Horus waved a hand, gesturing his acknowledgement, but for a long moment he said nothing more. Lotara heard her name murmured, out of sight. By Argonis, she was sure.

Horus smiled again. '*Captain Sarrin. Captain Lotara Sarrin of the warship* Conqueror. *I trust all is well. How may I be of service?*'

'Warmaster Lupercal...'

Horus interrupted her. '"*The Rose Watered with Blood*".'

Lotara's jaw tightened. 'It... surprises me that you're aware of that poem, Warmaster.'

Horus ran his gloved hand over his shaven head, as relaxed as a demigod could be in casual conversation.

'*By the saga-poet Eurykidas DeMartos, was it not? Whatever happened to him, Captain Sarrin?*'

DeMartos had died with the rest of the remembrancers aboard the *Conqueror* when Angron had given the order to end their theatrics once and for all. As far as Lotara was concerned, nothing of value was lost on that day.

'Khârn killed him, lord.' *And took great pleasure in doing so.* 'I only regret that we couldn't kill the poem, too.'

Horus chuckled. '*Indeed, indeed.*'

'Warmaster, if I may ask–' she began, but Horus interrupted her again, his smile becoming a grin.

'"*And worshipful foes, awarded medals carved upon flesh,*
In scars of shrapnel and sourceless fire,
This flock,
Her flock,
Unburied,
Within great drifting tombs of silent enemy iron.
A queenly shadow cast,

Against the dappled theatre of eternal fusion,
Across the tide of our voiceless ocean,
And here,
Enshrined in this royal steel,
We carve her invocation."'

Lotara watched him, the Emperor's own son, Warmaster of the Imperium, as he recited the final lines of the poem written in tribute to her. It was bad enough to endure when courtiers across the Imperium had lapped up that insipid verse like the fops they were, burying their faces in the trough of literary propaganda and insisting they were dining on high art... But to hear it in the Warmaster's deep and kindly tone was almost too much to bear. She wasn't sure if he was mocking her with the recital. She wasn't sure she wanted to know.

'Warmaster, I wish to speak of supplying the fleet. With the ash thinning out, we can harvest more resources from the surface. My crew is starving, dying of thirst. I...'

She could see Horus wasn't listening. His lockjaw grin had faded, and with cold assurance the Warmaster gestured with the great Talon.

'*Maloghurst, attend me.*'

Lotara held her tongue. Maloghurst was long dead; Argonis entered the picture, instead. He leaned down, speaking at Horus' ear. She couldn't follow any of this. It was a fight not to let her discomfort show in front of the fey ghoul that the Warmaster had become.

'*I am weary, Captain Sarrin.*' Horus' voice was bereft of emotion, practically bereft of life. '*As are you, I imagine. Yes. We all are, aren't we? But our triumph is close. It is so close. This, I promise you.*'

'Warmaster, please...'

She trailed off that time. She didn't like how he was looking at her, the sudden fervency in his sickened eyes.

'You don't even realise, do you?'

'Realise what, lord?'

'That you're not her. You're not Lotara Sarrin.'

Before she could muster the breath for a reply – not that she had any idea what to say – it was over anyway. The signal was severed. Horus was gone.

TWELVE

Brothers in chains

Kargos

The Land Raider tore across the wasteland, rocking and shaking over the broken earth. In the gunner's cupola, Kargos gripped the handle of the heavy bolter, sighting down the barrel at the shapes resolving through the dust. They were closing fast on the refugee convoy's rearguard. It was a hell of a convoy, streaming across the wasteland towards the Sanctum Imperialis. From the size of it, several refugee trains and retreating Legion forces had linked up to make their final run for sanctuary.

The Warmaster's horde had the numbers, though. Kargos felt an itch at the back of his head.

Soon, he told the Nails. *Almost there.*

They bit back in reply, unsoothed. The Nails had no patience – logistics were meaningless; they fed on emotion. They wanted adrenaline, they wanted blood to flow, and he would be punished until he made it happen.

It would be a risky assault, this close to the walls of the Sanctum Imperialis. The Delphic Battlement ringing the Emperor's castle was only five kilometres to the west, leaving them practically in range of the wall-guns. Within range of Titan guns, certainly, and just as definitely within Thunder-hawk range.

The forces at the Sanctum wouldn't bombard their own arriving convoys with blind-fire, and the ash reduced all hopes of precision targeting at that range. Gunships, though. They were a possibility with the dust thinning, day after day. Titans... They were a risk, too. They were starting to venture away from the Delphic Battlement, punishing any raiders that struck too close.

Kargos' eye-lenses had long since lost their ability to zoom and refocus. Endless incidental damage to his helmet over the war's course had killed that functionality. He had to look through magnoculars to make out the convoy's scale – or at least what the ash would let him make out.

'What do you see?' Inzar called up from the tank's innards.

'It's a big one. We'll have to hit it hard to break through.'

Inzar acknowledged him, and Kargos could hear the preacher relaying more orders over the vox. Their tank was at the lead of the assault force, his stolen VII Legion Land Raider cutting ahead of the pack to form the tip of the ragged formation. With so many Imperial convoys streaming across the waste-land between the Palatine Bastions, the bounty of targets made for easy prey. Scenting blood, the Warmaster's horde poured into no-man's-land in their hundreds of thousands, hunting down fleeing Imperials with abandon.

Even the most directionless slaughter still served the war's purpose. Every soul killed in the districts of the Inner Palace was a soul that would never pick up a weapon to defend the Sanctum Imperialis. The Legion officers on the ground let their warriors loose, letting massacre and butchery become quaint tactical virtues.

The Emperor, wherever He was, still couldn't see reason. That much was obvious to the Warmaster's horde – the closer they came to the walls of the final fortress, the weaker their Neverborn allies were, and the rarer their manifestations became. Kargos hadn't seen his primarch since the astral display above Avalon days before, but Inzar was forever ready with assurances that Angron was out there, tearing down the Palatine Bastions. Thoughts of his gene-sire made the Nails sizzle through the meat of Kargos' mind. A not entirely unpleasant heat.

An example for his sons to follow, the preacher had said. *A messiah.*

Freedom from death. Immortality through annihilation. The words echoed through the gladiator's mind in a ceaseless cycle. He hadn't spoken any more of it, though he kept sensing Inzar's eyes upon him. Judging, always judging.

As they drew closer to the convoy, the World Eater panned the viewfinder across the distant shapes of Legion armour and Army transports. Given the horde's advance, all retreat would soon be cut off. Fewer and fewer reinforcements were reaching the Sanctum. This column might even be the last.

It was Kargos' ninth convoy raid. Or perhaps his tenth. They tended to blend together, just like the days and nights. On the last one, be it the eighth or the ninth, they'd stolen the tank they now commanded. That had been Inzar's decision; Kargos had been content to sit huddled in the rattling confines of a Rhino transport, but he freely admitted that their new ride made their predatory duty so much easier. The ash and dust were thinning over time, and that helped even more. Gunships were flying again in brief bursts. Titan support was beginning to show up. Orbital drops were no longer the purview of blind prayer. It was far easier to hunt when you could see what you were hunting.

He turned the magnoculars to the west. He could see it now, the suggestion of it in the distance: a hazy shadow consistent with where the horizon was supposed to be. A siege wall. The *last* siege wall. Far from here, but not far enough.

He called down to Inzar, 'I can see the Sanctum.'

Inzar's reply came with a growl. 'We're getting too close to the Sanctum. Let us make this raid swift. In and out, my friend. No last stands. No heroes. Save it for the final assault.'

Kargos heard this, too, relayed across the vox. The horde's shared communication channel turned into a howling orchestra of voices in reply. Military order was a truly thin façade, these days.

The Imperial convoys they hit were always slowed by the weight of their responsibilities. Legion tanks and Imperial Army armour ringed the vulnerable wounded and civilians in their midst, but it was a simple matter of breaking through the outnumbered defenders to shatter their unity. Even their Land Raider, labouring at barely forty kilometres an hour over the churned earth, was fast enough to catch the outriders at the edges of each burdened convoy.

More than one defensive ring had refused to fight. Kargos thought little of it, it was a matter of naked practicality – the warriors of those Legions considered it more prudent to reach the Sanctum Imperialis rather than die in vain out in the wasteland. Inzar, however, took great delight in watching the Imperials abandon their own wounded warriors and defence-less refugees. He chanted praise and thanks to his mad gods each time it happened, promising them a harvest of sacrifice. This was a promise he consistently delivered on.

As they ranged ahead of the bulk of the slaughter, though… they ranged ahead of their own human forces and the daemonic things that were born in the minutes after the massacres. The horde swelled with every death on either side, and Kargos found himself at the vanguard of a breathtaking tide. He sometimes caught Inzar listening to the scale of that tide; the preacher would tune into the general vox-web, allowing himself to be assailed by an infinity of shrieks, screams, snarls and scrap code. To Kargos, it was just noise. He told himself he didn't hear any music in the sound, just beneath the surface, like a teasing undercurrent…

He'd asked Inzar, naturally. 'Why do you do that?'

The preacher had smiled. 'I like to meditate on the melody of enlightenment.'

After the last raid, Inzar had summoned Kargos over to him. They stood in the shadow of the tank they were about to steal. To the west was Meru Bastion, a burning silhouette in the dust. Inzar had been walking among the bodies, dispatching the wounded that took his interest. Those he found uninteresting he kicked aside, leaving them to bleed out and expire from their injuries.

'Preacher,' Kargos greeted him.

'My friend,' Inzar replied. The Chaplain was distracted, hauling a dying, one-armed Imperial Fist to his knees. The warrior's chestplate was horrendously ruptured, and his helmet had been torn clear, showing a vicious blade wound to the face that had stolen both of his eyes and damaged his mind. It was a miracle the warrior still lived at all.

Inzar started scalping him.

'We will take this Land Raider,' the Chaplain said while he carved.

Kargos grunted non-committally. 'If you say so.'

'Help me with this, would you?'

The Imperial Fist struggled, but Kargos kept the dying man on his knees. The Word Bearer ran a curved Colchisian dagger in a sawing circle around the top of the warrior's head, then took a fistful of his hair.

'For the Emperor,' swore the Imperial Fist. *'For the Emperor.'*

'Yes, yes,' Inzar humoured him.

The Chaplain tightened his grip and pulled. There was the sound of wet leather tearing, then Inzar kicked the scalped warrior to the ground.

Kargos looked down at the Imperial Fist. The man was crawling towards him, reaching with useless defiance in his fading eyes. The World Eater admired that. It showed gladiator spirit. A single bolt from his pistol cracked out, ending the Imperial Fist's useless protestations.

Other warriors drew near – the mix of all nine of the Warmaster's Legions that was becoming more common with every battle. Inzar bound his newest scalp to his belt, using the dead man's hair and a squirt of armour cement. He looked to the gathered Astartes as he did so.

'Which one of you wants to drive?'

The heavy bolter kicked in Kargos' grip. He raked it low, shooting to cripple, not kill. The White Scars Rhino revving ahead of them threw its left track with a shattering of treads, losing speed and falling out of formation. Kargos watched it as they raced past, grinning as two World Eaters vehicles swung towards the hobbled prey. It was all he could do not to leap from the top of his tank and join in the slaughter.

The convoy was turning out to be juicy prey. A great many Imperial Army vehicles, a few skitarii walkers, all ringed by a cluster of Legion armour. Several lesser convoys had streamed out from the Palatine Bastions and grouped together on their flight to the Sanctum Imperialis. This many defenders made it almost an even fight, a *hard* fight, which in turn made it twice as satisfying.

It started out the way these engagements always began, in the familiar melodies of Legion warfare: the trading of long-range lascannon fire and volkite beams, followed by the mid-range chatter of heavy bolters. The raiding party descended in predator packs, isolating outriders and stragglers before carving into the convoy's bulk.

Kargos wasn't a man plagued by thoughts of honour and dishonour. In that regard, he shared Inzar's ideology. This was war, and in war soldiers fought to win. Honour was a construct, an irrelevant crutch for killers to feel better about the fact they killed. He'd never spared a moment for regret when the Legions had leashed the galaxy with their overwhelming force. No civilisation, human or alien, had been able to resist them. Slaughtering entire cultures that never had a chance against the Imperium was no more or less honourable than carving apart these refugees. War was war.

He'd spoken of this with Khârn long ago, back when Kargos was Eighth Company's pit-champion and the Legion was new to the Nails. The whole of the Eighth Assault was gathered, watching their brothers in the gladiator pits. The sounds of axes clashing rang off the *Conqueror*'s metal walls. His captain had given a careful smile.

'There is more philosophy in your position than you admit.'

Kargos had shaken his head, continuing to bind his axe to his vambrace. He and his chain-brother were scheduled to fight next. 'I don't see it,' he'd confessed.

'I think you do,' said Khârn. 'You just prefer to believe you're a simple creature. Good luck in the pit, Bloodspitter.'

A bolt cracked against the Land Raider's armour plating only a metre from him, its detonation jarring Kargos back to the here and now. As the Nails spiked to punish him for his distraction, he pulled his gun around and opened fire on the closest Rhino, aiming for its treads.

Red crept in at the edges of his vision, and with it, the adrenal sting of relief. It was starting again. He–

–is on the ground. In the ash. Gorechild howls in his fist and in his head. Someone is screaming a language he doesn't understand, right in his ears. It's his own voice, of course it's his own voice, magnified inside his helmet, but the shouting doesn't stop when he becomes aware he's doing it.

A Blood Angel comes for him, but slow, too slow; Kargos sees the sword descending, sees where it will be, and he cuts back, taking the Angel's hand off at the wrist. On the backswing, he hammers the Angel to the ground with the flat of Gorechild's blade. The clang is loud enough to split the heavens. Rabid froth spatters the inside of his helmet as he screams and screams and prays and he–

–pulls himself up the side of an enemy tank, his muscles clench-ing in the epilogue of a laughing jag. The last breaths of laughter wheeze from his throat. He's up on the Land Raider's roof, moving, always moving. A bolt clips him, detonating against his pauldron; he rocks with it, still moving.

The soldier in the cupola is human, too human to stop him – she raises a pistol and Kargos stamps down as her hand comes up. Every bone in the woman's hand and forearm crunches, crushed to paste, just more filth on the bottom of his boot, and Gorechild swings and the teeth carve, and the soldier is split from the helmet down, and he–

–is carving, bathed in sparks, his axe's teeth shrieking through the hull of the stalled Chimera. Then he's in, and it stinks of blood and marrow and misery, and he sees Imperial Army on stretchers; the wounded are here, they can barely fight back, but it doesn't matter – they bleed like everyone bleeds, and he swings and chops and carves.

And the relief of it; the sweetness of the rhythm of Gorechild rising and falling and rising and falling; and the perfume of the blood, and the song of the screaming, there's no pain now, he could cry with relief because there's no pain; but now they're all dead in here and the Nails bite again and he–

–is with Inzar, side by side, the way he used to be side by side with Khârn in battle; the way he used to be side by side with Skane in training; the way he used to be side by side with the Flesh Tearer in the fighting pits.

The preacher fights loud, swinging his crozius mace and exhorting the warriors around him to fight on, proclaiming that the gods are watching, that this bloodshed is holy. Kargos doesn't know if it's true, he doesn't care; he cares only that the Nails flood him with relief at the terminus of every axe swing, every bite into ceramite, every crunch into flesh, every grind through human meat. There's blood on his armour, he's red with it now: blood for Angron, blood for victory, blood for Inzar's God of War if that's what it takes to feel this relief.

Inzar is here with him, killing at his side, chanting prayers, and each swing of his crozius hits ceramite with the sound of a cathedral bell; it's thunder, a devotional thunder, it rings in Kargos' ears, stinging the Nails with the same cold relief as the running of blood, and he–

–crashes to the earth, snarling in the dust as the White Scar rides by. He's down in the dust, in the thick of it. Gorechild is on the ground out of reach, except it isn't because one jerk of his arm whips the chain back and the axe leaps to his hand, and he grips the axe and rises to his feet again.

The White Scar is gone. Kargos turns and looks for enemies in the dust, and there's another White Scar – this one's out of the saddle and grappling with a World Eater, and three heartbeats later it's over because Kargos swings underarm, the blade carving up *between the warrior's legs and the axe-teeth chewing and chewing with an arc of blood and sparks, and there are screams, and he–*

–can hear the others over the vox, he can just about make out their meaning; they're outnumbered, the convoy is being reinforced, they need to fall back; but he can't, he just can't. The fight is joined and there's no falling back, no running away, the Nails will split his skull apart if he tries, they'll change the chemicals in his head to acid and tar.

He–

–turns in the dust, staggering, stumbling over the last Blood Angel he killed, and the Nails steam in his skull like molten pistons. There within the warring shadows, there in the ashen silhouettes, he sees an officer holding back and giving commands. Kargos moves in a staggering run as his muscles burn and Gorechild sings its sawblade song.

He passes Inzar beating a downed Imperial Fist to death, and he passes Draelath tearing his sword free from the guts of another Blood Angel, but he passes too many others duelling and being hacked down and being strangled and the voices were right, they're losing, the convoy's defenders are overwhelming them, but he doesn't care, he wants this officer's skull, he wants the rush, he wants the blood-wet relief that comes with glory.

He kills his way closer, axe hacking with a searing lactic acid burn in his muscles, and Gorechild is a prince of blades, killing and rending and chopping so much easier than any other chain weapon he's ever held; mica dragon's teeth rev in its blade, that's why, that's how it rips through armour and meat so well. Kargos cuts sideways, cleaving a Blood Angel down to the backbone, kicking the dying warrior away, and he's roaring a challenge at the officer though it's a wordless thing because his mouth won't form words right now, but it doesn't matter, it doesn't matter, it's a challenge that needs no language, only rage.

He reaches the officer and the Nails sing; the gut instinct of a life-long brawler has him note the chainsword in the Blood Angel's hand and the flensing knife in the other, and it's familiar, it's so familiar that it hurts, but it doesn't matter, all that matters is the kill.

Kargos cuts downward and there's a clash as he's blocked, and chain teeth fly from the Blood Angel's sword, and he cuts again, and again he's blocked, and he's grunting with effort; and he pulls back for more room to take a wilder swing, and the Blood Angel weaves aside, and Kargos screams as he cuts empty air.

They come together again, blade to blade, faceplate to faceplate, and again it's all so familiar, but there's no real link, there's no connection, there's only frustrated rage. Both warriors are panting, respiration coming in ragged saws through their helmets' vocalisers.

Their blades are locked, axe on sword, sword against axe, and the two of them strain against one another. They're statues, motionless with a perfect equilibrium of rage and strength, and the first to disengage will invite the death blow. Genetically enhanced sinew strains in harmony with the fibre-bundle cabling of their armour's false muscles and they're still locked, still deadlocked. In that moment, either one of them could push through a stone wall, yet neither can shove the other back. He feels the contest as a full-body strain, every cell of his being leaning into the locked blades, and he knows the Blood Angel is doing the same because he feels that, too.

'You have Khârn's axe,' the Blood Angel breathes into his faceplate. 'Did you plunder his corpse once the Black Knight was done with him?'

Kargos doesn't reply because the Nails steal his words and force adrenaline into his mind in place of language. What he knows, though, is the voice. Familiar enough to drill through the Nails as they vice around his mind. He knows the voice without knowing why he knows it.

But it weakens him, that familiarity, it weakens him and it weakens the Nails; it steals the red-raw clarity his precious implants provide, *replacing rage with confusion, with doubt, with a creeping unease that the muscles interpret as weakness. Kargos feels himself slipping, he skids back a few centimetres on the dusty ground, and then a few more. The Nails aren't biting so hard now; in place of their pathological flood, Kargos feels the lactic burn of aching flesh. He stares into the Blood Angel's eye-lenses and he feels mortal – absolutely, dangerously mortal.*

This is it, Kargos thinks, this is it; this is how his foes must have felt in the fighting pits. This is what it was, to know you might lose. He could die here. The jaws of the preacher's promised hell are right here, opening beneath him.

Someone crashes into him from behind, and another warrior jostles into him from the side, and it's not just a duel, he remembers that, he knows it; it's a battle, they're still in the thick of the fighting, both of them have to keep aware of other combatants. He wants to call for Inzar, to summon the preacher for aid. Pride prevents him, but that pride is eroding fast, eaten up by something that tastes a little too much like fear.

He feels it then, he knew it was coming and here it is, the crux moment where the clinch has to break. Kargos moves with all the preternatural speed granted by transhuman genetics and the technological miracles of Astartes warplate; he disengages with a roar and moves back and–

And the Blood Angel is still on him, moving faster, giving him no room. Kargos grunts with the impact as the Blood Angel headbutts him between their joined blades: a crunch, a crash, a tolling clang of ceramite. But it's fine, it's fine, it's only pain, he just needs space, he just needs room to swing Gorechild *and then he can finish this, he can, except that's when his eye catches fire because the headbutt shattered his helmet's lens, and he realises as he tries to blink that the plastek shards have been driven into his eye socket, and he's half-blind now, and...*

'Too slow, Bloodspitter,' the Blood Angel growls in Nagrakali, the mongrel tongue of the XII Legion. 'Too slow.'

And he knows then. He knows. The Blood Angel's words prise off the last of the Nails' bite, and Kargos knows who he's fighting – he knows the faceplate, he knows the armour, he sees the name on the Blood Angel's shoulder guard, the name written in dusty gold, the name of the man he was chained to a hundred times as they fought together in the arena, the name shouted in the Conqueror's pits, and he knows the mockery in the Blood Angel's voice because it was the same mockery the Blood Angel would use to goad their foes, and the two of them face each other for the first time and

Everything

Slows

Down.

The Nails are silent in Kargos' mind, and so is the war all around him.

'Amit,' he says. 'My brother.'

And Amit, the Flesh Tearer, his arena partner for years, his own chain-brother, spits on his broken face and cuts his throat.

'Eat shit, traitor.'

THIRTEEN

Too valuable to die

Land

Arkhan Land pulled the trigger. The warrior before him disintegrated, undone at the atomic level with a supremely merciless lack of haste. The Alpha Legionnaire was still screaming when almost seventy per cent of his body had dissipated into the smoky air.

Fascinating, thought Land, despite being on the very edge of pissing himself.

The technoarchaeologist lowered his pistol, thanked the Omnissiah for perhaps the five thousandth time since the war had reached Terra, and crawled away from the last dissolving shreds of armour. He had to get to safety. He couldn't die here. It mustn't end like this, all because of one raided convoy.

Whatever would the Imperium do without him?

Las-fire sliced through the dust with cracks of ionised air. Boltguns barked, lighting up the hazy dawn with the impacts of their shells. You could barely tell the Astartes apart in this dust, they were all towering monsters coated in a layer of ash. Land was surrounded by armoured beasts with grinding joints and roaring weapons, killing everything around themselves with impunity.

Everyone said the world had gone blind, but that wasn't quite true. Far more accurate to say that the world had gone mad.

He scrabbled across the hard ground, too frightened to stay low and move slowly, too scared to stand up and run, risking drawing fire. The result of his conflicting fears was a hunching lope about the pace of a jog. An abiding sense of self-preservation was one of Land's fiercest virtues, and it had served him beautifully on many occasions. However, it tended to do nothing for a man's dignity. He yelled for help as he ran, he yelled for Zephon, for *anyone, damn it*; and he yelled his own name several times, informing every combatant within earshot that he was Arkhan Land, *the* Arkhan Land, and his work was far too valuable for him to die here like this.

Later, when he would be told about how he'd so unvaliantly whined for aid, he would deny it as base slander. There was simply no way he would ever be so undignified. Really, it said more about his accusers than it did about him.

For now, he ran. A las-round ionised the air a foot in front of his face, close enough to singe his beard. He turned in his inglorious but not entirely unwise retreat, weaving away from a cluster of combatants emerging ahead.

The uneven ground over which they fought had once been the Kushmandan Archive, a collection of libraries dedicated to preserving fragments of lore and artefacts from human worlds that hadn't survived Old Night. When the Great Crusade reached these worlds, expecting either resistance or compliance, they'd found neither. What awaited them instead were silent expanses of dead cities, inhabited only by memories. Whole civilisations that hadn't been able to overcome their own infighting or died on the vine once they were cut off from the rest of humanity's ancient, pre-Imperial empire. The relics and records of these lost kingdoms were brought to Terra, to be studied in the domed halls of the Kushmandan Archive.

Rubble. All of it now rubble: low walls to crouch behind, rocks to be ground underfoot by the treads of tanks and the feet of Titans.

Where was Zephon? Where were any of the supremely capable idiots covered in ceramite who should be doing their damnedest to protect him? It was one of the most annoying aspects to the Astartes subspecies, wasn't it? When a fight broke out, most of them had the moronic tendency to seek out enemy officers and warlords instead of holding back and prudently defending valuable souls like – well, like Arkhan Land.

He shouted for them over the vox in his customised rebreather. None of the convoy's commanders replied.

If Zephon's got himself killed only days after I dragged him out of stasis…

Later, again, he would imagine he had this thought in a practically serene state of consideration. In reality, he mumbled it as he cowered with his back to a ruined wall. He was there mere moments before bolts hammered impacts along the stone to his left, spraying him with burning shrapnel, earning another offended, terrified cry. He fled from his compromised hiding place at a dead sprint.

Ahead of him, two Imperial Army troopers were using a crater as a foxhole. Land joined them there in a gasping tumble. One of them was on his belly in the dirt, firing a battered laslock over the lip of the crater. The officer – Land presumed it was an officer, since he was the one shouting into the hand-mic of a vox-caster – was crouched a little lower in the crater, with his rebreather pulled down so he could yell over the sounds of battle.

'…engaged by raiders, four kilometres east of the Delphic Battlement…'

Las-fire stitched the air above them. A Rhino armoured personnel carrier rattled past, belching smoke from an internal detonation, stealing most of the officer's words. Bolts crashed and burst against its dented armour as it trundled by. Land huddled deeper into the shaking earth as the officer kept shouting for reinforcements. He could only make out one in three or four of the man's war-stolen words.

'…almost to the Sanctum… Astartes raiders… thousands of civilians–'

The trooper broke off abruptly because he was dead. Shot through the chest with a shrieking volkite beam, his uniform licked by flames around the hole as he fell back in a boneless heap.

The surviving trooper looked back at Land. Whatever he called was lost between the muffling of his rebreather mask and the unholy sounds surrounding them. Seeing that Arkhan wasn't about to take over operating the vox-caster, the soldier started crawling down the shallow crater to take his officer's place. He made it halfway before two brawling Astartes crashed into the ditch, their weapons conjuring great sprays of sparks from each other's armour plating. The humans didn't exist to them – they were lost in their frenzied swordwork, and they trampled the crawling soldier beneath their boots without even slowing down.

One of them staggered next to the crushed corpse, clutching at his neck with his only remaining hand. The other warrior administered the *coup de grâce* with a swing of his chain-sword, taking the loser's head from his shoulders. With no celebration, no respite, the Astartes kicked his foe's headless body over and clambered out of the crater to rejoin the fight.

Land had no idea which side either of them had been on.

He wasn't about to check the corpse to find out, either. He started running.

He made it several steps before he was shoved from his feet, when what felt like a cargo-hauler hammered into him from behind. Land thudded into the ground, rolled hard, and swore a sacred binharic curse as his pistol clattered across the earth.

His immediate thought, as the archeo-atomic gun tumbled away, was: *if that thing discharges…*

All concern was bleached from his mind as something approximately the weight of an Imperator Titan crashed down on his right leg. The pain was so sudden, the pressure so intense, that he didn't even cry out. He just winced, all of the air abandoning his body in a spit-laden hiss.

Turning awkwardly, he saw a legionary on the ground, leaking blood and coolant from its battered armour. The warrior's shoulder guard crushed Land's leg to the earth from the knee down.

Panic truly set in then, as did the pain. He clawed to get himself free, thrashing like an animal caught in a jaw trap. He kicked at the dead Astartes with his free foot. He threw a handful of earth that clattered against the warrior's faceplate. This achieved everything one might expect, which is to say, it achieved absolutely nothing.

A rising hysteria, one he was painfully aware of, began to infect his throat. He yelled for aid, knowing that no one would hear him over the battle, not with the vox so useless and his words muffled by a rebreather, not with chainswords revving and tearing and boltgun thunder playing out its fyceline cacophony. Yet, miraculously, it worked.

One of the Astartes came to a boot-thudding stop at his side, hauling the dead warrior up and dropping the corpse away. The release of pressure somehow hurt worse than the pressure, and as he sucked in air, Land took a teeth-baring look at his leg. A red mess waited where his limb was supposed to be, malformed beneath his blood-soaked trouser leg.

I can deal with it, I can deal with it, the words came in a bleating rush of thought. *Machine-God's oily piss, it hurts, it hurts, get to the Sanctum, deal with it there, Sands of Sacred Mars, it hurts.*

'I can't walk!' he yelled at the Astartes in whose shadow he lay. 'Help me up!'

'You are Arkhan Land.' The warrior was breathless from battle, yet the words came in a slow growl at eerie odds with the fight going on around them. Its voice was wet and thick, as if living things greased against each other in its throat.

Land looked up at his saviour. At the ashen ceramite, swollen by the mutagenics of the spoiled meat within. At the domed belly plate, broken not by boltgun fire but burst from the inside out. Serpent-ropes of dusty guts hung like a clutch of nooses, dangling between the warrior's legs.

Death Guard. He either whispered the words aloud or chanted them in his mind. He wasn't sure. *Omnissiah, protect me…*

It's often written in chronicles of war that time slows down in moments of dire confrontation. The concept was a trope Arkhan Land had always found tolerably quasi-poetic at best and ludicrous at worst, so it was with a chill that he felt the air around him grow dense, and the towering thing above him move as if underwater. Dragging a single breath into his lungs demanded all his strength and took forever.

'You are Arkhan Land,' the Death Guard accused him as it reached for him. 'You have great value.'

He yelled that he'd been lying, that he wasn't Arkhan Land, that Arkhan Land was already dead, that Arkhan Land had been killed when the Ultimate Wall fell. These protests, shouted mindlessly in Martian Gothic, achieved nothing.

An Imperial Army soldier, as ashy as everyone and everything else, emerged from the dust and rammed the bayonet of his lasrifle into the Death Guard's guts. Land stared in grateful horror with every detail richly clear: the empty ammunition slot of the man's lasgun; the look of terrified defiance half-hidden by the plastek rebreather; even the quiver in the soldier's narrowed eyes as he dug deep into the nest of slithering intestines.

Paralysis threatened to embrace Land entirely. He'd barely moved an inch before the Death Guard vomited a sloshing arc through its helmet's mouth grille, covering the soldier in steaming bile.

Whoever it was – that insanely, stupidly brave soul – they paid for their courage by falling to their knees, shrieking as their face and raised hands dissolved. Land's scream blended in with the dying man's, briefly turning the death cry into a duet.

A third scream turned it into a chorus, this one mechanical, born of howling turbines. Another figure struck the earth, its back winged with a jump pack's twin turbines. The warrior's chainsword crashed against the Death Guard's armour with a spray of sparks.

Zephon, thought Land, delirious with relief. *Zephon. At last.*

'He is Arkhan Land,' the bloated Death Guard grunted, fending away the frenzied sword-strikes with its armoured forearms. Ceramite gouged and tore, forcing the diseased legionary back, step by step. 'Fool! He has value.'

Zephon's name died on Land's lips. The *caedere remissum* crest atop the newcomer's helmet was a trophy worn only by the slavering dogs of the XII Legion. Reports of the World Eaters turning on their own side in displays of unguided bloodlust had been common throughout the war, and now he was being treated to it, up close and personal.

He wasn't saved at all. His enemies were fighting over him.

Land rolled over, moving with grunts of unfamiliar effort,

dragging his shattered leg as he crawled across the broken earth. He had two thoughts in the span of the same moment, one of which was the cold belief that he was going into shock, and that was why he was able to crawl at all instead of shrieking over his leg.

The second, far more practical, was: *where is my gun, where did it fall, which direction where where–*

There in the dust, between the embattled shadows of warriors and monsters alike, was a tiny figure crouched low to the ground. It could almost be the silhouette of a skinny child, if an infant possessed a prehensile tail and chunky bionic eyes. But it wasn't a child, and it wasn't a monkey either, though it resembled one with relative fidelity. It was an experiment of genetic and cybernetic genius, recreating a long-extinct species of Terran simian. In its cunning little claws, it cradled Arkhan Land's fallen pistol.

'Sapien!' Land called.

Sapien skittered closer in bounding leaps reminiscent of no actual primate, pressing the atomic-slug pistol into its master's outstretched hands.

'Good boy,' Land whispered through tears. 'My very best boy.'

He rolled over just as a crested shadow eclipsed the faint red sun. The victor of the scuffle over who would take his head had been decided. Gore, forebodingly dark, dripped from the World Eater's chainblade.

'Blood,' it breathed through its helm's vocaliser, the words melting into a throaty chuckle. It seemed delighted by the slender gun in the hands of its prey. 'Blood for the–'

Land fired. The World Eater staggered back, slowly atomising, its molecules tearing away from one another and, somehow, igniting as they did so. Arkhan Land was no soldier, just a man that adored his impossible toys from the Dark Age of Technology.

'Blood for the Machine-God,' he said through clenched teeth. Relief flowed through him, a feeling so pure that it made him heave with weak, wild laughter. The World Eater died screaming, going on to meet whatever foul deity it had sold its soul to.

Breathless, in more pain than he could ever remember experiencing, Land dragged his spectralocular goggles from his watering eyes long enough to wipe the tears away, then started crawling again. Sapien skittered along at his side, chirping encouragement with sounds no living monkey had ever made.

'Get help.' Land looked the psyber-monkey dead in its beady stare. 'Get Zephon, get Amit, get *anyone.*'

Sapien ran, leaving him alone in the heart of the storm. Men and women were dying around him, their forms too shrouded by the dust for him to know exactly who he'd be shooting at. Astartes from both sides were dying too, but as far as Arkhan Land was concerned, not enough of them, and not quickly enough.

Something huge and metal and loud roared its way overhead, trailing fire. A shell from a Titan, a gunship strafing the ground… He didn't know, it was only a flash of flaming darkness, there one second and gone the next. Land wanted to keep crawling, but to what end? Sapien had gone for help, and might not find him if he moved. Blood of the Omnissiah, he could barely move anyway.

There was a Chimera some way away. He could see its outline in the dust. Shelter. Pathetically thin, but *shelter* nevertheless. Yet at this distance, and with only one leg, the troop carrier might as well have been on the other side of the world.

He looked above it. Past it. The murky ghosts of two gods were fighting. Two Titans, their weight classes and allegiances indeterminate, grappling in the slow swing-and-crash rhythm of god-machines going for the kill face to face. He saw one of them swing a weapon – a fist or a blade or a saw – and heard the time-delayed thunder of it hitting home. He saw the beginning of a return blow before the ash swallowed both godlings again.

Another great black shape tore the sky open above him. Low enough to be unmistakeable, that time. A Thunderhawk. A gunship from the west, from the Delphic Battlement.

Reinforcements.

Hope soared. And as if mocking the audacity of this sudden salvation, fate threw him another twist: that's when the shelling started.

It was Titan-fire. It was artillery. It was tanks on the edge of the battlefield, and it was god-machines towering over everything.

Staccato booms punctuated the ground as Titans and artillery opened up on the warring regiments. Clusters of Astartes, human soldiers, skitarii, exoplanar xenos… Allegiance meant nothing in the dust, as indiscriminate detonations hammered down on the wasteland. Great holes appeared in the forces; bodies burned and crumbled and flew. Land knew what was happening because it was the only explanation, but the reason – the depthless spite – took his breath away.

The Warmaster's horde was raining fire on its own warriors, just for the chance to kill Imperials.

He stopped crawling, linked his shaking knuckles in the sign of the Cog's Teeth, and said a prayer to the Machine-God. *Just let me live*, he begged through the drumbeat cacophony and the ringing in his ears and the pain of his destroyed leg. *Just let me lie here and live.*

A shadow fell over him, one with snarling armour joints, one that was far too big to be human, one that was reaching for him with a grasping hand. He rolled over, causing his mangled leg to catch fire with fresh pain, and his finger squeezed the iron trigger almost hard enough to break it.

The gun kicked. The Imperial Fist that had been reaching down to help him took the atomic slug in the throat, staggering back as he began to disintegrate. The warrior had time to reach a hand to the molecular dissolution spreading from his neck before he toppled backwards onto the earth.

'No!' Land crawled back towards the shreds of burning, atomising armour and flesh becoming smoke in the ashy wind. 'No! I didn't mean to!'

Another silhouette manifested, another Astartes running out of the dust. 'I didn't mean to do it!' Land yelled at him.

But it was one of the Sons of Horus, his helmet crested with clanspikes, and this newcomer cared nothing about the tawdry slice of theatre playing out on the ground at his boots. He levelled his bolter to kill the wailing human and move on, but he never pulled the trigger. Arkhan heard the warrior's head explode, the dull *crump* of the detonation inside the Astartes' helmet. Blood began to leak from the helm's mouth grille.

The corpse didn't tumble backwards as the Imperial Fist had done. Stabiliser fail-safes in his armour activated, locking up the joints, leaving the Astartes standing slackly rigid; straight-backed, with his boltgun dangling from the curled fingers of one hand.

Arkhan Land stared at this development. *How rare*, he thought with amazed sincerity.

A second blast smashed into the already dead warrior, throwing the corpse from its feet. It spasmed on the ground, wrapped in worms of dissipating electricity.

One of the tech-guard emerged from the dust, lowering an arc rifle. Sapien rode on the skitarius' shoulder, chittering into the aural receptor at the side of its helmet. The helmet itself was badly dented on the left side, as was the tech-guard's chestplate.

The skitarius crouched, its red cloak scuffing the dusty

ground, and it reached with a bionic hand to help haul him to his feet with a gentleness no Astartes would've thought to offer. Arkhan Land couldn't recall ever feeling such gratitude.

Many tech-guard couldn't speak and this one was no exception. It emitted a series of binharic spurts as it helped the limping technoarchaeologist towards the hull of an Army Chimera.

'No need to apologise,' Land said to it. 'You were just in time.' And then, surprising even himself, 'Thank you for saving me.'

The skitarius jerked slightly, because it wasn't expecting to be understood. It vocalised another spurt of machine-code from the implant in its throat.

'Indubitably, I understand skit-code,' said Land, dizzy with the pain of his crushed leg. 'I'm a genius. Do you know who I am?'

The tech-guard gave a low, coded screech.

'I'm not delirious,' Land insisted. Everything was going grey now, a soothing numbness washing over his vision. 'I just… I need to sit down. I hope this isn't how I die. That would be embarrassing beyond measure. My leg doesn't hurt as much as it should. That's probably not a good sign, is it? What's your name? Your ident, I mean. What is it?'

The skitarius half-carried him up the crew ramp into the Chimera transport. As it did so, it relayed its ident signifier in smooth binharic cant.

'Pleased to meet you. My name's Arkhan Land.' His words kept trying to slur into one continuous sentence, and he felt an ardent need to keep speaking as clearly as he could. Manners demanded nothing less. 'Excuse me… I think I'm going to… pass out for a bit. Sorry for, you know, the inconvenience…'

Arkhan closed his eyes. He thought he heard the tech-guard emit another code-spurt, but the meaning of its words was fading with the rest of the world in a numbing wash. Unconsciousness was looking like a mercy, one he was more than willing to embrace.

It was a mercy he was denied for a short while longer, however, because the sky broke open with the birth of a burning star. Land shielded his face from the light, skyfire turning his features amber as he looked out through the Chimera's hatchway.

At first, it looked like an effort of wrath from the higher heavens, the orbital bombardment resuming with impunity. But the World Eaters howled like wolves and the Word Bearers chanted their mad chants and the Sons of Horus cheered – and Land couldn't help but notice that the burning star had wings.

Next to him, the skitarius murmured a query in quiet code, ostensibly to itself, apparently an unintentional vocalisation. But Land answered it, as his last mumbled words as he lost consciousness.

'I think we should give serious thought to running away.'

FOURTEEN

The loyalty of a broken apostle

Transacta-7Y1

She couldn't see very well anymore. That raised religious concerns as well as practical ones. The practicalities were obvious, because the damage to her helmet and monovisor meant she sometimes had trouble with visual interference and depth perception, and that threw off her aim. The matter of faith was what truly troubled her, however. If any of her overseers looked through her eyes or harvested the data-spools from her skull, they would see corruptions of information.

The injuries she'd sustained all those days ago at the Principa Collegiate were a troubling matter, as well. The maul had savaged her armour and cracked at least five of her ribs, along with inflicting significant trauma to the costal cartilage of another three ribs and shattering her manubrium. She suspected one of her lungs had seized or failed because her respiration was always shallow now, and never without pain. Her right arm lacked the strength of the left, and her right hand could no longer grip with the same force. Lastly – at least in terms of significant injuries – she'd had a headache since awakening in the Collegiate's ruins, and it wasn't the dull throb of natural pain that chemical injections could alleviate. This was a brain-deep pulse, like something molten or poisonous had been dropped into her skull and sealed inside with her thoughts. Transacta-7Y1 had initially wondered if it signified brain damage, and decided that it likely did. She was having difficulty recalling some things from before Principa. The data was there, images and sensations of things she'd seen and done over her years of service, but she couldn't remember experiencing them.

However, it was her vision that plagued her with near-philosophical worry. Corruption of information was an inefficiency, and inefficiency was a sin against the Machine-God. A lesser sin, an understandable and forgivable sin given the woes of battle, but a sin nonetheless. Transacta-7Y1 didn't want forgiveness for her sins. She didn't want to be in a position where forgiveness was necessary.

This kept her debating internally, in a detachedly curious way, if it might not have been better had she died. She would already be in the Machine-God's grace then, a sinless creature with an untarnished record; not poorly recording the world around her, adding the corrupted evidence of her flawed eyes to the great Quest for Knowledge.

By that logic, one might think: it would have been better had she died pure.

Except this raised further religious difficulties. She was a soldier of the Machine-God, and the Warmaster threatened the Machine-God's existence. She was flawed, yes, but was it not better to fight for the Omnissiah, even as a broken apostle?

By that logic, one might think her purity was meaningless in the wider circumstances of what was at stake. Besides, only in death did duty end.

A troubling conundrum.

With Principa Collegiate conquered and levelled, her orders distinctly no longer applied. There was nothing to defend. She could sense enough of the war's flow through vox interceptions and meeting other scattered defenders to know the horde was advancing upon the Sanctum Imperialis, and there sat the Machine-God's avatar upon His Throne of Gold. Wounded or not, Transacta-7Y1 would put herself between the Omnissiah Incarnate and the entirety of the Warmaster's forces if it came to it.

And so, she had moved to do just that. The first warband she had linked with in turn joined a larger stream of refugees; in turn allying with another convoy; in turn forming up into a column of soldiers and civilians making one of the last runs to the safety of the Sanctum. At no point had she received new orders from her Martian overseers, and skitarii survivors from other macroclades had no insight to share. Many were as in the dark as she was, similarly cut off from their superiors. Those still in contact with their overseers lacked the capacity to trouble themselves with the existence of a lone vanguard alpha.

For days, she'd fought as part of an ad hoc regiment of orphaned tech-guard, each of them getting by with others of their kind who weren't *really* their kind, each of them communicating in a sort of binharic pidgin dialect formed from code variances between rival clades. They'd been attacked, not for the first time, but with punishing force. Transacta-7Y1 was out in the dust with the others, firing her scavenged arc rifle, hoping with each blast of energy that the loss of her destroyed radium carbine didn't represent another sin in the eyes of the Machine-God. (Sadly, she suspected it did.)

And then, at the battle's apex, a little monkey had come scampering out of the ash and jumped on her shoulder. It squeaked in a derivation of universal binharic, its info-stream a form of pure expression that lacked an accompanying lexicon.

Transacta-7Y1 had never spoken to a monkey. She wasn't even certain what it was, but the sound it made – which, to human ears, would be a chorus of screeching, failed electrical connections – was among the purest data-whines she'd ever heard, something that stripped even sacred binharic cant back to its source code. It was, with no exaggeration whatsoever, the sound of prayer in her ears.

She'd replied in skit-code, which sounded practically debased compared to the holiness of the creature's communication, but it was apparently good enough for the monkey.

It understood and conveyed that it required her assistance, that its master was in danger, and the direction in which it wanted her to move. Within this expression of code there was also the suggestion of swiftness, of urgency. Transacta-7Y1 had hoisted her arc rifle and set off at a run.

Twenty-two seconds later, she met the renowned Arkhan Land. Due to her low rank in the grandeur of the Cult Mechanicus, and a life spent largely in forge-laboratories and on the field of battle, she had never heard of him. Clearly, however, given the nature of his companion, he was either important, a genius, or both.

A further one minute and eighteen seconds later, the sky exploded, and the fight became a rout.

Transacta-7Y1 didn't see, as Land did, a terrifying genetic and spiritual failure whose existence shamed the Machine-God. Nor did she see Angron, the primarch of the XII Legion, drenched in glory or bathed in corruption, as many of the warring legionaries saw. She saw the Machine-God's son, an unravelling demigod, whose physicality broke the rules of reality. A creature whose metaphysics were in flux.

She felt the clinging chill of fear, though. In that respect, she was like every other living being there.

Angron dropped from the sky, striking the ground with a shockwave that threw Legion tanks aside with the force of an inverted cyclone. The primarch's immense shadow-shape laid about with its massive blade, tearing tanks and Knights apart with every roaring cleave. The crashing of that blade meeting iron and stone was the sound of thunder for dozens of kilometres in every direction.

The defenders broke and fled, a stream of vehicles and fleeing infantry racing overland for the gates of the final fortress. Transacta-7Y1 watched it taking place from the turret cupola of the Chimera, as her own vehicle rushed towards the silhouette of the Sanctum Imperialis. The psyber-monkey was still on her shoulder. It covered its eyes as the winged daemonic form raged against the defenders who couldn't break free from the battle. Transacta-7Y1 patted Sapien awkwardly, which it seemed to appreciate.

The retreating Imperials weren't fleeing without a fight. Traitor armour pursued them, gunning them down, ramming them, boarding them with cries and howls. A Spartan in the battered black and purple of the Emperor's Children tore after the Chimera, its roof scabbed with legionaries unloading small-arms fire that rattled and spanked off the armoured personnel carrier's hull. Transacta-7Y1 ducked back inside, pulled the turret around, and returned fire with the multilaser. Useless las-burns scorched their way across the Spartan's front armour; the skitarius abandoned the attempt almost at once and slammed the hatch open again, bringing her arc rifle up with her.

A bolt struck the Chimera's plating in front of her, spraying her faceplate with clattering debris. She cursed at a fresh wave of visual interference, and a vicious new gouge across her monovisor. For the Machine-God's sake, she was half-blind now. It didn't stop her firing, but it stopped her hitting anything. Great bursts of electrical energy spat from her arc rifle, slashing past the warriors crowded on top of the Spartan. The enemy tank drew closer, grinding its way faster over the rubble-strewn wasteland, as the legionaries prepared to jump aboard.

But the thud of impact came from above. A warrior in arterial red hit the Chimera's roof with a clank, his jump pack breathing thick smoke into Transacta-7Y1's face. He didn't stop running; with another two steps he took off again, boosting across to the closing Spartan.

The psyber-monkey screeched in her ear. It knew the warrior. He was called Zephon. The name meant nothing to her.

This 'Zephon' wasn't alone. Another two warriors thudded down, using the Chimera as a stepping-stone to boost across to the pursuing Spartan. Transacta-7Y1 tried to follow the fight as the Blood Angels landed, but her distorted vision registered nothing but inhuman shapes blurring together.

She slid down the crew ladder, back into the Chimera's innards. Land was where she'd left him, strapped to the troop bench, his head lolling at the mercy of the turbulent ride. This was acceptable. She could do nothing more for him. She turned to the driver, another survivor, another Imperial Army veteran among tens of millions, separated from his regiment. If his regiment even yet existed. Despite the way the Chimera rocked and smashed over the wasteland, she spared a moment of thought for Envaric dying due to the aura of her holy weapon. As much as she regretted the loss of her radium carbine, proximity to her was far less terminal to baseline humans now.

She couldn't speak to the driver in any way he would understand. She'd lost her dataslug days ago, never recovering it from the ruins of Principa. Still, she gave her best approximation of a sound of enquiry, forced through her crackling vocaliser.

'Almost there,' the driver said. The viewslit in front of his face was grey with grime; he peered through it, blinking sweat from his eyes and clenching his teeth. 'Almost there. Almost to the Grand Processional. You hear those guns? You hear that bloody thunder? Those are our wall guns. Covering our approach. They must be. They just have to be.'

The Chimera bucked as it struck more rubble, hitting the rise with the force of a crash. Transacta-7Y1 was thrown against the side of the crew bay, her previously broken internals crunching unpleasantly, flaring with fresh pain. As she hauled herself back to her feet, she felt the armoured personnel carrier slowing. The engine sputtered, died.

The driver, a man whose name she hadn't learned, was slumped in the seat, his skull shattered where it had smashed against the metal above his head. She didn't bother nudging him to ascertain whether he lived. The mess where the crown of his head had been answered that adamantly and succinctly.

The Chimera stalled, kicked once more, and stopped. There was a moment of perfect serenity, where the psyber-monkey – hanging from the crew railing by its scorpion tail – gave a frightened screech of expressive code, clearly hoping that the tech-guard would do something to solve everything that had gone wrong. On cue, the thunder started up outside, engines groaned past, and something transplanar bellowed long and loud from not far enough away.

Transacta-7Y1 was already moving. She hauled out a stretcher from the crew supply compartment, dropped it to the deck, and unbuckled the straps binding Arkhan Land to the troop bench. As gently as she could, she pulled the unconscious figure onto the stretcher, processing but wilfully ignoring the fact the demigod out in the wasteland sounded significantly closer.

Land murmured something in his delirious half-sleep. This, she also ignored. Reluctantly, she slung her arc rifle onto her back, letting it hang on its strap, and readied herself to drag the stretcher over the churned earth for at least a kilometre, most likely more.

Sapien tossed her a new weapon. A pistol, of a kind she'd never seen before and had no record of in her archives. The creature screeched instructions for the weapon's use, which she understood implicitly but couldn't quite believe. Concentrated handheld atomics were, surely, the stuff of beautiful legend. She holstered it within her robe and hauled the stretcher to the rear of the cabin.

Transacta-7Y1 – half-blind, armed with a gun from myth and dragging the semi-conscious form of arguably the greatest Martian mind of the age – hit the ramp release and went back out into the dust.

Later, she was asked to report on what she witnessed out there.

This request would cause her no small discontent, given the damage to her vision. Regardless, Transacta-7Y1 did her best, with a simple relay of coded data as well as observations that were personal to her, in the form of emotions and sensations. Adding these elements to a report was alien to her, but oddly fulfilling.

Still, impressions and suppositions formed the bulk of her report, and her recitation was no construction of weighty prose. She kept to the facts, as best she was able to ascertain them.

This was what she saw, until she couldn't see anything anymore.

Dust. Ash. Smoke. Arkhan Land, lashed to the stretcher, shaking as she dragged him metre by painstaking metre.

Armoured personnel carriers rattled past her. One of them,

a filthy Rhino marked with White Scars symbols, rumbled to a halt nearby. Just as its side hatch slammed open, the vehicle detonated and flipped into the air, crashing to the ground on its side. She had no idea if the warriors within had intended to help her or just failed to escape their vehicle in time.

She kept dragging the stretcher. It was harder work than marching, hiding or even aiming and firing. It wore on her damaged limbs and aching joints. Over her shoulder, the great walls of the final fortress turned the horizon black. Almost there, as the driver had said. Almost there.

Astartes warriors closed in on her. She dropped the stretcher when she recognised their slavering Nagrakali, drawing the pistol that the psyber-monkey had entrusted to her. They were indistinct shapes and she squeezed the trigger, the pistol loosing its spite with no recoil, blasting an atomic slug wide of any mark. She felt the gun auto-reloading, recharging in her hands.

She tried again, and another shot went wide. The World Eaters moved too fast for her wounded sight to track. Sapien screeched at her, the artificimian's meaning crystal clear amidst the mayhem. She adjusted her aim by degrees, saw the psyber-monkey scampering across one warrior's shoulders, and she fired.

The Space Marine died. She couldn't make out exactly how, only that he seemed to dissolve with intriguing slowness. The others kept coming. The gun wouldn't fire again. It shivered with recharge.

Engines howled. Blood Angels – she knew them by the red of their plate – descended on burning turbines. They outnumbered the World Eaters, they beat them back; *crash-crash-crash* went the clash of weapons. Transacta-7Y1 had her hands on the stretcher again, hauling it away, pulling it towards the high wall behind her.

She staggered, driven to her knees when she lost her footing in the uneven rubble. It took forever to get back up, though obviously it didn't – her internal chronometer tracked a mere six seconds: a triviality that felt like an eternity.

The psyber-monkey screeched again. She was going the wrong way, dragging her cargo away from the Sanctum. She adjusted, based on the direction of its guiding code. Effort was making her sweat and strain, and that distorted her vision further. She was more than half-blind now. It was getting worse.

Thunder boomed, the mercilessly beautiful song of the Sanctum's wall guns. They deafened her, stealing her second sense, as if the loss of the first weren't enough. All she heard was in the ringing quiet between the pounding cannonades.

The anti-grav wail of a jetbike, the rider and Legion unknown to her; it cut past with enough speed to tear at her cloak. The throaty chatter of heavy bolters. The piercing strain of volkite beams. Bootsteps and chainswords and oaths for the Emperor and oaths decrying the Emperor as false. It was all one sound, one roar, and it came from all around her.

There were statues watching her. She saw their towering outlines, and knew them from the archives rather than from the truth of her fading sight. Towering Imperial heroes cast from sanctified Martian bronze: statues of the Terran hierarchs that lined the Grand Processional. She was almost to the wall. Almost to the gate.

Then came the sound she'd feared. Against all logic, it was loud enough to make a mockery of the great guns, a carnosaur's bellow that could never emerge at such volume from a mortal throat. Her vision was down to conjecture, but she felt the heat emanating from the unravelling demigod, and – somehow – she felt its rage. It radiated fury the way a plague patient burned with fever.

A shadow fell over her. With no recourse left, she threw

herself across the body of the man she sought to protect. It was a paltry shield against a demigod's anger, yet her life was all she could offer.

And then, though she couldn't possibly have detected such a thing over the drumbeat of the wall guns and the cries of the burning demigod: she *did* hear it, and from the thousands of cheers that went up around her, the others could see what she could only hear.

Transacta-7Y1 heard the beating of feathered wings.

An unknown span of time later, she lay with her back to a statue's plinth, bleeding a concoction of blood and oil from old wounds reopened, and from fresh ones she didn't recall suffering. Arkhan Land, white with blood loss, sat slouched next to her. His breathing was shallow, his eyes were glassy, but he was awake. Just about.

'Can you see that?' Land asked her.

Transacta-7Y1 admitted that she couldn't. She suspected she was dying, and if she wasn't dying, then she was most certainly on the cusp of injuries that would extinguish her ability to fight with a skitarii macroclade.

'They're retreating,' Land told her.

That was good, and Transacta-7Y1 told him it was good.

Land continued talking. Telling her what she couldn't see. That the Ninth Primarch was there, rallying the survivors, leading reinforcements to cover the refugees along the Grand Processional. That the Twelfth Primarch had fallen back, unable to come closer, unable to set foot on the great avenue leading into the Sanctum Imperialis. The Emperor's invisible shield still held the exoplanar creatures back, for now. Perhaps for the last time.

Transacta-7Y1 understood very little of this, but she could tell it was a positive development, and so she confirmed, again, that it was good.

'You sound sad,' Land said to her. 'What's wrong? We made it. We're alive.'

The idea of a human being able to recognise emotion in skit-code was something she had never considered. In answer, Transacta-7Y1 told him the truth.

Arkhan Land sniggered. The sound was utterly childish.

'The Omnissiah doesn't give a crap about your visual data being corrupted. I *know* the Omnissiah. I know Him personally. I've conversed with the Machine-God's avatar several times, as it happens.'

Transacta-7Y1 was speechless in the face of the man's delusion. She began to wish the foolish fellow would let her expire in peace.

'I can repair you, anyway,' Land added with eerie nonchalance.

She turned her head towards him, feeling sinew and servos grinding unwholesomely in her neck.

'What?' Land asked. 'You're only a skit. Fixing you will take no time at all. It's the least I can do, really. Listen, I don't suppose you've seen my pistol?'

FIFTEEN

The war's failing heart

Dorn

In the war's opening phase, the Grand Borealis Strategium in the heart of Bhab Bastion had served as the primary nexus of Imperial command. From the moment the first salvo was fired at the edge of the Sol System, everything had run through the strategium. Its spire rose above the rest of the Palatine Ring, the most princely castle in the district that circled the Sanctum Imperialis.

Depending upon one's perspective, Bhab Bastion had either flourished or suffered aesthetically with the Praetorian's preparatory efforts, just like the rest of Terra. Long before the arrival of Horus' armada, it was barnacled with gun nests and defence turrets, encrusted with reinforced masonry and ablative plating, and spined with input-output vox-relays that would carry the Praetorian's commands to the billions of loyal ears ready to receive his orders. It was ugly to some and reassuring to others, but to the man that commanded behind its walls, it was functional. Nothing mattered more than that.

Functional. The word sounded like nothing yet meant everything. In war, functionality was everything. On the level of individual soldiers, if your weapons functioned, you could kill with them. On the level of generals, if your logistics functioned, you could guide your armies and keep track of the war.

From Bhab Bastion, as the weeks became months, the Emperor's seventh son had waged his war. Rogal Dorn didn't fight on individual battlefields like the Khan and the Angel, he fought on *every* battlefield. His war was ten thousand wars all playing out concurrently. The soldiers on the ground carrying out his orders, they saw the individual battles. From the strategium, Dorn oversaw the entire siege.

To many of the defenders in the opening days of the Solar War, the coming siege was still unreal; the blood being shed was muted by the distance and chill of the void. Who could really comprehend thirty thousand lives lost in the cold dark around Pluto with the death of a single warship? And who could really process the reality of such losses when they took place, dozens of times every single minute, at a remove of seven point five billion kilometres? Every phase of the war comprised of devastation on a scale that defied comprehension.

The staff gathered in Bhab Bastion during the war's prologue were the best-equipped souls to approach those questions and manage the answers. They were the finest war staff available in the forces remaining loyal to the Emperor, and as the war ground on, souring with every step closer Horus came to the Eternity Gate, the staff had evolved with the shifting conflict. Admirals and void commanders eventually made way for generals and advisors better suited to the protracted ground battles taking place. Through all these months, the bastion was the central hive of military intelligence and Imperial authority.

The fact Bhab Bastion still functioned was something of a marvel given the unstable atmospheric conditions. The constant bombardment and the ash choking the air played havoc with the Imperial vox-web, and communication was still down across many of the Inner Palace's districts. It held on longest within the Palatine Ring thanks to the potency of the tech within Bhab itself. Somewhat less encouraging, but no less essential, was that it also allowed Dorn to see which fortresses and fallback points were breaking, or already broken.

He had known it would come to this. He'd accounted for it, planned for it; he'd run through the possibilities and the probabilities. War was full of vicissitudes, but the Praetorian of Terra was as prepared as a mortal mind could be. Frankly, after half a decade of calculations and simulations, it had been a relief when the first landings began.

Since then, he'd watched the war unfold in a million reports and flashing location runes, across hundreds of thousands of streams citing casualty figures. He'd watched the probabilities narrowing day by day and hour by hour – resolving into fewer and fewer potential paths towards the future.

It was all coming to a point. All those incalculable figures had been counting down to this.

The beginning of the end came with the sundering of the Ultimate Wall. The moment Legio Mortis breached the wall, Horus had his fangs at the Emperor's neck. The Inner Palace was vulnerable even before the Warmaster had flattened whole regions from orbit. The Palatine Bastions were besieged now, half already fallen or evacuated, and the horde could no longer be held back from the Sanctum Imperialis. Only slowed.

His voice was just one of many echoing off the arched walls of the grand chamber. The most authoritative voice, but ultimately just another tone blending in with the others relaying orders. The chorus was backed by the humming of tactical hololiths and the clanking of high-grade cogitators, overseen in turn by a numerous coven of Martian adepts charged with sacred rites of maintenance.

The Praetorian of Terra stood in the core of the Grand Borealis Strategium, washed blue by the light of tactical hololiths, playing a hundred thousand games of regicide at once. Information flashed across his unshaven features, bathing his eyes in figures, numbers, runes. He looked from screen to screen, map to map, always thinking, always processing, always speaking. He gave a contiguous series of orders, pausing only to breathe.

Sometimes, *often*, he knew those on the other end of the vox-links weren't hearing his orders. He still issued them, just in case. More regions of the Inner Palace fell dark, day after day, with greater interference on the vox-web and fewer replying voices. It didn't matter. There was enough functionality to make perseverance worthwhile. It was really the only option.

His voice was strong but undeniably raw, after doing nothing but relaying commands over the vox-web for almost nine days. He hadn't slept. He hadn't left his post once, and only rarely even before this latest marathon of effort.

But he ached to fight. He wanted blood on his gauntlets. He wanted to swing his blade and feel the immediacy of victory, of cutting a foe down, of achieving something tactile in this endless grind. The urge was fierce enough to be a constant temptation, but he refused to give in to selfishness. If he abandoned his post, millions of soldiers across the Inner and Outer Palaces would lose their best chance of survival, and – colder but more tactically relevant – would lose their cohesion as part of Terra's defence. Dorn was the voice in their ears and the eye that guided them. Every regiment, every warband, every platoon was a cell in an evolving, shifting, breaking system. He needed them to play their parts in the wider siege, delaying the enemy here, crushing potential reinforcements there, sacrificing themselves for the sake of this, rallying and retaking territory for the sake of that.

The more enemies he could keep in the Outer Palace, the longer the Inner Palace could hold. Tens of millions were dying for the sake of that unassailable truth. Without hesitation, Rogal Dorn fed their lives into the grinder.

'My lord,' came the voice of Archamus behind him. The strategium was shaking – it was always shaking now – its shields trembling under the bitter caress of artillery. Several of the officers around Dorn staggered. It was more than just artillery and Titans out there, raining fire against the walls. Every scan came back laden with signifiers of creatures that defied naming conventions. Daemons, they were called, but the term was imperfect to the point of mockery. Not that it made a difference: the endless army laying siege to Bhab Bastion was full of things that shouldn't exist.

The Praetorian's standing command was to only be interrupted by intelligence of great import, but he was mid-report from the colonel in command of the Magister's Reach district, to the north of the burning Meru Bastion. Dorn was weighing the logistical question in his mind of what to do with the colonel's forces and where they might best be deployed. His instinct was to use them as skirmishers behind the horde's vanguard, letting them inflict what damage they could before Magister's Reach was overwhelmed by more forces coming in through the Ultimate Wall's ever-widening breaches.

Dorn told the colonel exactly how she and her six thousand soldiers were going to sell their lives. Then he accepted the officer's acknowledgement, approved of her stalwart tone, and turned to Archamus at his back.

'Speak.' Already, the primarch was calling up a holo of the wasteland around Avalon Bastion. If he could spare a small force, he might gather survivors in the ruins, and they could move to intercept–

'It is your brother, lord,' said Archamus.

Vulkan was gone and the Khan was dead, or so close to death that it made no difference. That left only one brother who would be contacting him, and his voice would be a welcome one, though the news would not be.

Dorn summoned eight nearby officers, giving orders for each of them to relay in turn to other bastions and resistance holdouts. With these urgencies taken care of, he rested both gauntleted hands on the central hololithic table and nodded to Archamus.

The holo flared into being. His brother had a spear through one of his wings.

The Angel was on one knee, not in genuflection but to bring himself low enough for medicaes to work on him. Sanguinius knelt in a ring of attendants, both of his arms outstretched, with several robed adepts working on his armour. They hammered plates back into shape and fused damage closed, while a Legion Apothecary – one of Dorn's own Imperial Fists, Rogal noted with distracted pride – was using a surgical saw to cut through the metal spear that was lanced through the Angel's right pinion.

Sanguinius raised his head, staring at Dorn through a long fall of bloodstained hair. No idle talk between the two of them, these days. Necessity and exhaustion had pared down their fraternal bond to the most ruthless basics. There was no one else that Dorn could rely on the way he relied on the brother kneeling in hololithic form before him.

The Praetorian was the general of the Imperial defence, but Sanguinius… Sanguinius was the symbol. Wherever the Angel flew, the defenders rallied. Wherever the Angel fought, the Warmaster's forces tasted defeat. Dorn tracked his brother through the war in scraps of vox-chatter and flashing runes on maps, day after day after day, in a chronicle of battles won and lines held.

And here it was. Dorn had known this moment was coming since the very beginning. The moment that marked the end.

'They're here,' the Angel said. 'They gather before the Delphic Battlement, horizon to horizon. Father's shield is failing. They will be at the walls come sunrise.'

Now, of all times, Dorn's formality abandoned him. He found himself speaking, surprising himself with nakedly honest sentiment.

'I gave you as long as I could.'

Sanguinius gazed at him. 'You of all have no need to say such things. No soul has done more.'

There speaks the Angel's humility, Dorn thought. As if Sanguinius and the Khan hadn't been out in the trenches since the skies first darkened with drop-ships. As if the human and Legion defenders weren't enduring unspeakable vileness and sacrificing their lives.

But no, Sanguinius was not so ignorant. He does not speak so out of humility, Dorn realised. He speaks out of a brother's love.

The Praetorian needed no recognition for his efforts; he'd never craved praise or thrived on acknowledgement. Nevertheless, in this moment between brothers at the end of everything, he was warmed by Sanguinius' words.

That warmth faded with the Angel's next question.

'Any word from Roboute?'

Dorn was aware of the attention on him. Officers, adepts and menials across the strategium watched him with hopeless eyes.

'None.'

'Then Guilliman will not save us.' The Angel grunted as the Apothecary pulled the broken spear from his wing. Neither brother spoke as Sanguinius stretched his wings, rolling his shoulders to restore some flexion. *'But he will avenge us.'*

Dorn didn't know what to say, when nothing seemed worth saying. He was not made for exchanges like these. Many thought him cold in these moments, even heartless, but he was neither. It was purely that defeat was alien to him, as was the quality of emotion shining in Sanguinius' gaze. What was worth saying when no words were necessary? What did one say to a brother you barely knew, who had nevertheless fought beside you from the beginning to the end?

Sanguinius had the answer without even needing to consider the question.

'Farewell, Rogal.' The Angel rose to his feet, and the holo tracked upward with him. *'If we do not meet again in the flesh, know that it was an honour, being your brother.'*

The Praetorian nodded to the Angel, wanting the right words, searching for them, and not finding them. The silence stretched out. It dragged.

Sanguinius smiled, knowing. The hololith blinked away.

SIXTEEN

The long walk

Vulkan

Sometimes he was alone, and sometimes he had to kill his way through to get where he was going, but he never stopped walking. He was aware of the passing of time, and he grew weary, hungry, thirsty – but he didn't feel any of these mortal concerns the same way that he had back in reality. They were curiosities now, not mortal maladies. He didn't know if this was a property of the labyrinthine dimension through which he walked. None of the Custodians that had been stationed here, back when there was still hope for the Emperor's dream, had reported such a thing. That made it a mystery, but a distant one, mundane against the wonders he beheld.

He'd had to fight when he first came through. That was no surprise, and he had been ready for it. He'd been ready to fight every step of the way if that's what it would take. The surprise had come when he'd smashed into the teeming phalanx of claws and jaws and thrashing blades, and broken

through to the other side. Finding this strange serenity waiting for him.

He knew the Sisters and the Custodians in the Throne Room
had done their duty. They hadn't fallen. The war still raged,
the Emperor still lived. Vulkan mourned those that had died,
and promised himself that upon his return – assuming he did
return – he would learn the names of the guardians that had
given their lives for him to make his journey.

There were rules to this place, rules Malcador had tried
to impress upon him, but they'd been obtuse things, metaphysical and theoretical. It wasn't that Vulkan had struggled
to understand them. Their precepts were nebulous but uncom-
plicated. No, he understood enough to know comprehension
wasn't the same as context. There were things he would have
to experience first-hand for them to mean anything. The
abrupt transition from being knee-deep in dead daemons to
wandering alone... That was only the first of them.

It had been jarring, though.

'Your intent will matter,' Malcador had said. 'In that place,
your intent will matter more than anything else. The path is
woven from your soul's desire.'

That answered one question but begged another. His path
was leading him away from the greatest daemonic hosts...
but how was Magnus faring along his own path? Was the
Crimson King already in the webway? Was Magnus tearing his
way to the portal far faster than Vulkan was trudging alone
away from it?

The walls of the Imperial webway, where he'd emerged after
running through the portal in the Throne Room, were rigid
frames on circuit-threaded Martian metal fused to various alien
trans-osseous materials and cultured psychoplastics. He recognised his father's vision in this blend of human and alien
technology: the distant past bolted and fused to the present,

for the sake of an imperfectly understood future. It grieved him, to know it had all failed so utterly. Horus had much to answer for. As did Magnus.

Vulkan was a smith, a shaper, a maker. He knew the craft of creation. How to bring artistry to bear along seams of inspiration. Working with the materials, not against them. Creating through a process, a weave of exploration and imagination. Yet the amalgamation around him rang wrong to his senses. This was something jury-rigged, erected against the grain, woven outside the seams using half-wrong approximations of the right materials. It worked, but it worked poorly. There had been an end goal in mind, but only the most ragged ability to reach it.

Vulkan didn't doubt his father's ambition or the worthiness of the Emperor's ultimate goal, but the craftsman in him felt ill at ease with the improvised genius of the webway's Imperial portions. Human ingenuity was stark and flawed, almost tumorous, in this dimension. It made for an ugly union. Without the Emperor's endless maintenance, without the constant flow of the Emperor's psychic will, the Mechanicus' sections were already crumbling, rotting, falling away into the abyss where metaphysics went to die.

Even without the damage from Magnus' treachery... It is all so forced, so rushed.

It hurt him to admit, but that was the impression it imprinted upon his artisan's heart. Necessity had surely played its part, but the result was undeniable. Vulkan ran his hand along the walls of Martian iron and inlaid suppressive circuitry. It penetrated his gauntlets, sending a weak tingle through his fingertips.

I do not know if this would ever have worked. Not for long. Perhaps not even for long enough.

Imperfect. That was the word. Imperfect, when nothing less than perfection would suffice.

And what if his father had come to him? Would he have been able to turn his mastery to this realm behind reality? Would his brother Ferrus have been able to help him? Would Magnus have joined them, forming a triumvirate of visionaries devoted to constructing the bridge to mankind's destiny?

No. There was nothing he could've done here – of that, he was certain.

It wasn't long before Vulkan left the Imperial portions behind. He felt no sorrow at seeing the back of them.

There was more to his journey than placing one foot in front of the other. Malcador had said this, but it was another aspect he could only appreciate through experience. You could get lost in the webway because the dimension responded to the turbulence of a traveller's soul. A firm purpose, a resolute heart… These were more vital than physical endurance. You would reach your destination by wanting to reach it. You would lose your way if your heart was in conflict or your purpose was weak.

But they were the rules for a realm in working order. When the Old Ones had shaped this place from materials that now possessed no name and no physical counterpart, how prosaic this labyrinth of unreal wonder must have been to them. In their era, it functioned as they designed it to function, its operation a trivial consideration aligning with the ways their minds worked. The human brain operated on other layers, with other senses, rendering everything inexpert… And so much of the webway was damaged now. The rules that governed it were no longer ironclad. The beings that built it were an eternity dead.

Your intent will matter.

So Vulkan walked, trusting that his will would carry him where he needed to go. He trusted that he would reach Magnus before Magnus reached the wounded doorway into the Throne

Room. It was a gamble, but the gamble was all they had left. None of them wished to know what ruination Magnus could bring were he able to reach the portal.

In truth, he feared he was lost. And if he were, would there be any way to know for sure?

The architecture around him was never constant, and the webway's polymorphism fascinated Vulkan despite the gravity of his purpose. He walked through tunnels that resembled aeldari wraithbone, and others of unknowable psycho-resinous material that emitted a barely audible chiming hum. He ascended through tunnels that rose, and descended through those that plunged. More than once he turned to see the path he'd come along was gone, melted away into the mist. The walls around him – when they were there at all – were just as unreliable. Sometimes he could reach out and touch curved surfaces that were there to his fingers and not to his eyes. Sometimes he could see a wall of overlapping contours that resembled the segmented insides of some great worm.

Vulkan felt outside reality one moment, and inside the body of a vast beast the next. It was disorientating, but not insurmountable.

On he walked.

The inhumanity of the realm was evident in the little things, too. The golden mist that fogged the tunnels had no scent. Not because it truly smelled of nothing, but because Vulkan was from a species that had evolved along biological threads without the capacity to process elements as the Old Ones had. His olfactory sense had no experience with these smells, these particles; no way of processing them distinctly.

What kind of creatures had the Old Ones been? What ingredients crucial to their genesis had been scattered from the guts of bursting stars? Were they warm-blooded, or cold? Were the helixes of their genetic arcanistry born of hydrogen, oxygen and carbon, as the human strain was? Or did arsenic hold prime place in their cosmological mix? Maybe ammonia, not carbon, was the key ingredient in their biochemical ascension. Or perhaps silicon. Or elements unknown – as yet undiscovered by humanity, or long ago sacrificed to time.

These questions stayed with him for some time. He turned them over in his mind as he walked his long walk, at once enjoying and haunted by the impossibility of the answers.

Sometimes, though, he had to fight.

There were daemons here, alone or in droves, infesting the tunnels and the chambers and the expanses of shifting void. They shrieked their names at him in the languages of cultures lost to history, those syllables laden with the tale of each creature's origin and purpose. Most died beneath *Urdrakule*. The more cowardly and cunning among them fled. He knew these were stragglers and parasites, and so took no confidence from destroying them. The rents they left on his flesh and armour, he ignored, reserving his resentment for the way they slowed him down.

Sometimes he believed he was being followed. Never aided, never attacked, only watched. He would turn to see the shadows playing games, shapes too spindly to be human flickering in and out of existence. Once, he saw a mask on the ground: a thing of dirty white that looked like bloodstained porcelain. The mask's visage was both manic and leering, the face of a laughing murderer.

Vulkan left it where it lay, untroubled by its meaning. If it even had one.

When he reached the dead city, he knew he was on the right path.

PART FOUR

A LENGTH OF
BLOODSTAINED CHAIN

SEVENTEEN

Eaters of the Dead

Centuries ago, at the dawn of the Great Crusade

Amit

Nassir Amit was one of the first. He was a scion of a toxic bloodline, with only the scarcest claim to humanity running through the code of science inside his blood. They'd found him in the charnel-prisons beneath the surface of Boeotia, living off the flesh of those too sick to go on. He was a candidate as vile as he was unlikely: a humanish mutant that would've been executed by any of the other Legions.

The other Legions, though, had the luxury of choice. The Revenants did not. He was exactly what they were looking for.

They'd taken him, those grey-armoured Apothecaries, pulling him from his tribe, stealing him from the metaphorical gutters of technobarbarity. They held the mutated child down and cut him open and sewed him back up. They worked on him with needles and saws, then worked inside him with blades and probes. They saturated his veins with transfusions of blood that they insisted wasn't holy, despite how it drove him mad and sane and mad once again, showing him the future and the past colliding when he closed his eyes. His own blood, transubstantiated by the infusions, burned inside his body and made every heartbeat hurt. When they implanted a second heart within his swelling chest, that doubled the pain.

The Apothecaries were as gentle as they needed to be, which is to say they were next to merciless. They were doing their duty, and their duty was to drag his mutated form kicking and screaming all the way into ascension.

He was one of the first to survive the process. He emerged on the other side of their medical sorcery a different being, keeping nothing of his former life, not even his name. He took a name from High Gothic legend: *Nassir Amit* – a character name from an ancient play set in Old Himalazia. He had no particular emotional attachment to the narrative. It was merely one of the texts he studied while learning to read. You could have told him that the name meant something, or that it held some symbolic significance in the piece of literature, but he wouldn't have cared. He would only have wondered why you did.

After his ascension, he took no pride in his beauty. The physical perfection he saw reflected in the eyes of his arming thralls, or in the steel of his magnificent blade, wasn't something to cherish as if he'd achieved it himself. It was merely a result of his genetic apotheosis, a trait shared by all his brothers. It could be noted, even appreciated, but only with appropriate humility.

He believed there was an underlying truth to his new existence, one that he sought to bear in mind at all times. He'd carried this truth through the years since his ascension, across the radiation-soaked wastelands of Terra, through the cramped slaughter-tunnels and cave labyrinths of Neptune's frozen moons, and then out into the great galaxy beyond. It was no great revelation of philosophy, just a truth as blunt as it was real: what did it matter if a prince looked back at you in the mirror, when you were a weapon of surpassing ugliness?

No shining medals for the Revenant Legion. No glory chants for the Eaters of the Dead. Their finery was war-torn ceramite the grey of a winter storm, and their medals were the bloodstains they didn't bother to wash off. Their recruits were genetic degenerates taken to stave off extinction, and the songs sung in their honour were the disgusted whispers with which the other Legions spoke of them.

To Amit, beauty was an irrelevance. Duty was all, just as it had been for the Apothecaries who'd flooded his malformed body with the blood of his then-unknown primarch.

He'd met a primarch once. The experience hadn't moved him the way he'd hoped and expected. The encounter had come at the end of the Kiy-Buran Compliance, a protracted conflict where the Revenant Legion had fought unsupported and outnumbered against the mutated population of an entire world. Warriors from other Legions, those that tended to preen about honour or consider it a notion that could be tarnished, might have abandoned the compliance entirely, or been forced through privation into suspended animation. Though it would take months, even Space Marines could starve. The Revenant Legion endured, as they always did, and in the filth that cakes men's souls between battles, the warriors of the Immortal Ninth thrived.

Rogal Dorn, arriving at last with reinforcements, had censured the Immortal Ninth at the war's end. The Praetorian of Terra, new to his inheritance of the Imperial Fists, had gathered the surviving Revenants into rows of squads aboard his precious *Phalanx*, and there he'd coldly expounded on the virtuous nature of the Imperium, as if he'd been present from the start; as if he'd been the one to cleanse Terra in the Unification Wars; as if he'd been the one to sail from the light of Sol carrying the first banners of the Great Crusade.

Amit, not yet a sergeant, had breathed in the stink of mutant blood from his armour plating, unable to believe what he was hearing. When Rogal Dorn had politely demanded the Revenants answer for their actions, he hadn't been alone in wondering if this was some bizarre jest. Several of the Revenants actually laughed, the sound an expression of confusion and amusement in equal measure.

Ishidur Ossuran, Legion Master, had stepped forward. His boots clanked on the deck as he and his blood-medalled brothers faced the pristine ranks of the Imperial Fists and their golden demigod of a father. Helmetless, Ossuran was beautiful, as all the Revenants were beautiful. He was the image of a painter's artistry come to life, though a painting slashed and scorched through deep maltreatment. He answered Dorn's tirade with two words.

'We won.'

This was not the right thing to say.

Rogal Dorn listed their apparent misdeeds back to them. The devouring of enemy dead not for the awakening of their omophagea organs, not for 'appropriate tactical use', but for *sustenance*, for *meat*.

Yes, Ossuran had replied. This was their way. And they had won.

They had, Dorn insisted, rendered their own Legion serfs down for nourishment.

And again, yes, Ossuran had replied. The Emperor had charged the IX Legion to win this war, not die of starvation unsupported. There were blood-rites that the primarch wasn't taking into consideration. There were rituals of cannibalistic holiness that permeated not just the Revenant Legion, but countless human cultures across time. Did the results not matter to Lord Rogal Dorn? Was he only interested in the methods by which war was waged?

Dorn wouldn't be moved by the rhetoric. There were reports, he knew, of the grey warriors eating the foe – and their families – for the purposes of crushing enemy morality.

And yes, Ossuran had said again, as if speaking to a dull child instead of a demigod, those reports were true. They were as true on Kiy-Buran as they were in other compliances on other worlds.

'And we won,' he said to the primarch once more.

Rogal Dorn dismissed them in weary disgust, allowing them to return to their vessel, the Gloriana-class *Grey Daughter*. There was little pleasure in this homecoming; the *Grey Daughter* – in the decades before she would become the *Red Tear* – was a grim and hollow fortress, often as empty as the void in which she sailed.

Their achievement, the compliance of Kiy-Buran, wasn't recorded in the annals of the Great Crusade as an Imperial victory, despite the many Revenants that had bled and died for it. On the *Grey Daughter*'s command deck, Amit had watched the oculus with narrowed eyes as the *Phalanx* obliterated the capital city, Buran, from orbit, erasing the Revenant Legion's victory along with their supposed sins.

In time, there would be other censures. Perhaps not as many as those that would blight the VIII Legion, or the XII... But enough, enough to breed a sense of unease around the IX.

Amit felt no hatred for the actions of the Imperial Fists. He felt no anger towards their lord and father, Rogal Dorn. Uneasiness spread through his guts instead, as he stood on the ship's bridge and bore witness to the erasure of his brothers' bloody work. He couldn't help but wonder, was this what all the primarchs would be like when they were rediscovered? This inflexible? This biased in favour of their own methodologies and judgements of what should and shouldn't be?

Was this how his own primarch would treat the warriors fashioned in his image?

Tradition called them to the *Grey Daughter*'s mausoleum. What they did there had no official name, though the warriors of the Legion referred to it offhand as the charnel feast.

When the Revenants were the Revenants no longer, fighting for the Imperium under a much nobler cognomen, this ritual would come to be called the Rite of Remembrance. That future incarnation of the IX Legion would make an art of layering nobility over their gory roots, but ceremony was sparse in these earliest nights. The men present were still decades away from becoming the Angels of Blood, as they gathered by torchlight in the cold squalor of the *Grey Daughter*'s bowels. There, they devoured their own dead.

To swallow a brother's flesh was to swallow his memories, to take the essence of the fallen into oneself, tasting insight into life witnessed through other eyes. The charnel feast preserved the scraps of history the Revenant Legion possessed, without the need to set it onto parchment for the judging eyes of others. No less importantly, it preserved the shades of the worthiest dead.

Amit barely ground the mouthfuls of raw meat between his teeth, preferring to swallow it in icy chunks. He was indifferent to the flavour – salt meat was salt meat – but each chunk rolling down his gullet sent a quicksilver sensation through his veins. He felt them in his craw, felt them slow-dissolving in his stomach acids by the way his bloodstream tingled with memories and emotions that weren't his own. He remembered areas of familiar battlefields where he'd never fought, recalled the weight and use of weapons he'd never wielded, and felt the butcher's pleasure of cutting down foes he'd never himself faced. Each death he ate made him less human, more legionary, and he was more than content with each bite to take another transhuman step away from his low-blooded genesis.

He wasn't alone. Almost two hundred Revenants gathered in the temple, not even enough to fill it to a fiftieth of its capacity. They crouched or sat by memorial statues and engraved honour rolls, veteran killers and newly turned warriors alike eating from bloodstained silver bowls.

The Legion thralls responsible for bringing the food to each warrior offered up their bounties with trembling hands. The servants' racing heartbeats made a thrumming percussion audible only to the warriors whom they served. Humans at a charnel feast were always at risk of falling to the fangs of an overeager Revenant. Killing one's own serfs was regarded as regrettable rather than punishable.

Amit sat on the cool metal deck, drifting in the mild hallucinatory daze of several other men's memories. Every minute or so, as the images in his mind's eye began to ease, he used his fingers to scoop another gobbet of brain matter into his mouth with careful solemnity. At his side was his squad sergeant, Ataxerxes, sat with his back to a bronze plaque listing the dead. Ataxerxes observed the half-formalised ritual with the same unspeaking sincerity as Amit, but they were waiting, all of them, for Legion Master Ishidur Ossuran.

A monotasked servitor clade bore Ossuran on a funeral bier draped with a black cloak. Other Legions might have offered funerary chants or a reading of the slain officer's many achievements, but the Revenants eschewed such pageantry, even if they silently craved the legitimacy of it. It wasn't necessary, though. Ossuran was dead, but not gone. It wasn't the first time he'd died.

Only one warrior would walk in the Legion Master's funeral parade. Captain Zaurin was the last centurion standing after Kiy-Buran, and it was to him that the honour fell. Amit watched as Zaurin's pale eyes tracked the passing of the funeral bier, and Zaurin's surviving lieutenant handed his captain the ceremonial flensing knife. As ritual tools went, it was a crude thing – as much a bone saw as a carving blade, and devoid of any ostentation.

Zaurin closed his fingers around the hilt and handle. The other Astartes looked on in silence. Some nodded in respect or acknowledgement. Most just stared.

The body of Ishidur Ossuran was carried through to the Master's Antechamber, where the lords of the IX Legion were interred. Zaurin went with it, pacing slowly behind the servitors, clutching the flensing knife in a loose-knuckled grip. Both he and the corpse were ceremonially nude, another primal touch to the already primitive ritual. Last in the train, more servitors carried Ossuran's armour, repaired from the battle that had felled him.

At the hallway's far end, the great silver doors slammed shut. Zaurin, the corpse, the servitors and the few warrior-priests that the IX Legion could maintain, were sealed within. There they would stay until the private portion of the rite was over.

In the end, it was a thing swiftly done. Scarcely half an hour passed before Ossuran threw the antechamber doors open himself, striding back into the presence of his brothers, armoured now in the relative finery of war-torn Legion grey. The Legion Master scanned the packs of reverent cannibals, summoning several of them to him by name.

Amit was one of them. He rose as commanded, handed his bowl to the nearest thrall, and crossed the chamber. Up close, he could see the differences in Ossuran. Though most of the Legion resembled one another – and, presumably, their undiscovered primarch – they weren't limited to the crudity of human eyesight. The Astartes could tell each other apart by even the tiniest distinctions of posture, expression, bone structure and scarring. Untrained humans might consider them practically clones of one another, but to Amit's eyes, each of his brothers was entirely unique.

Zaurin carried himself differently now. He stood as Ossuran had stood, with the same guarded aggression rather than with Zaurin's easy confidence. He gave the same side glances that Ossuran had given before speaking, in moments of thought. It was strange, even for one accustomed to the ways of the Legion, to see such changes take hold. Amit wondered what habits of fallen brethren he'd adopted himself over the years – and whether Zaurin could still taste Ossuran's memory-saturated flesh on his lips.

'Melkiah,' Zaurin said. 'Fifth Company needs a new captain. The rank is yours.'

The named warrior accepted with a salute. 'As you wish, Legion Master.'

'Amit,' Zaurin greeted him next.

'Yes, Master Ossuran.'

'Fifth Company requires a sergeant to replace Melkiah. The rank is yours.' Even Zaurin's tone and inflection was Ossuran's now, while his breath was scented of the Legion Master's blood and salt-flesh.

Amit nodded. 'I won't let you down, sir.'

Ossuran regarded him with Zaurin's face, with Zaurin's eyes, with Zaurin's scars, but the soul and mind behind the eyes were fused to the Legion Master's through the feast of flesh.

'I know, brother.'

A few more promotions were handed out with the same ease of necessity as the elevations of Melkiah and Amit. None were deemed worthy enough of reclaiming and replacing the dead by name and deed. Only Ossuran, as Legion Master, held that honour today.

'Back to your men,' Ossuran dismissed them, and back they went without a word, returning to the red rituals that passed for formality in the Immortal Ninth.

Like many of his kind, Amit measured time in the succession and conclusion of wars. By that way of judging things, he was still young when the Revenant Legion reached the planet Nithander. They descended through the clouds, these blood-stained angels, offering mercy with one hand and promising extinction with the other. They brought the Emperor's message, along with the Emperor's desire for – with such careful phrasing – a state of compliance.

They had come from Terra, from the True Earth, and it was their intent to unite the lost colonies of humanity. Even the ones that had grown prosperous and independent. Especially those, in fact. They didn't face mutants, here. The people of Nithander were humans, pure strain, untwisted by Old Night.

Join us, the armada in orbit broadcasted to the surface. *We are your brothers and sisters.*

Do not oppose us, said the armoured angels meeting Nithander's kings and queens. *Lest we become your destroyers.*

But the people of Nithander refused the Imperium's attempts at peaceable unity, and so the tone of the compliance had turned. Master Ossuran ordered the ambassadors to return to orbit. Behind that command, his warriors made ready for planetfall.

The Revenant Legion attacked as dawn rose over the capital city. The war that followed was brief, as wars fought by humans against the Legiones Astartes tended to be. It was over almost before it began – an expression often stained by hyperbole, but one that was, in this case, desperately accurate.

As the sun set on the first and final day of the Nithander Compliance, Amit walked among the dead and the dying. The enemy were human, possessing weapons of concentrated light not dissimilar in effect to Imperial las-technology. In design, however, Nithandan technology varied drastically from the emerging Imperial norm. Rather than using power packs and focusing lenses, Nithandan ingenuity had harnessed polished crystals and gaseous transmission chambers. Doing his due diligence, Amit had studied the cultural reports before the compliance began and broken open several of their weapons to analyse himself.

The developmental path of their technology was notable but far from fascinating. Chief among Nithandan cultural divergences was the tradition of using artificially grown stone in place of natural rock when it came to construction. With a warrior's eye, Amit's first thought upon seeing cities constructed of the stuff had been to speculate how it would fare against Imperial artillery.

Not well, as it happened. Not well at all.

The battle was a battle like so many others: the capital city had burned, the Nithandan resistance had been brave but utterly futile, and millions of lives had been lost purely because a population chose ignorance over enlightenment. Amit wasn't without imagination, and he occasionally walked the edges of battlefield philosophy. These people had died to defend their way of life, which so many stories insisted was an admirable sacrifice of one's existence. But was it? What about their culture was so worthy of preservation? Perhaps if the Nithandans had shut up about how it was *better to die free than live as a slave*, then they would have realised their fate wasn't slavery at all. The Imperium had come to awaken them, to lift them from their selfish darkness. Now the survivors of a much-diminished world would become

Imperial citizens anyway, rendering all that sacrifice less than worthless.

These were his thoughts as he walked amongst the slain and those soon to join them. An Imperial Army squad was making the rounds nearby, stretchering away the wounded of both sides. They regarded Amit the way all humans regarded him, with their pupils dilated at his bloodstained beauty and their hearts racing with the threat of his armoured physicality. Their medic was crouched by a wounded Nithandan soldier, tending to the woman's wounds. Amit saw the injuries – bolt shrapnel, third-degree burns, significant tissue trauma – where the medic had peeled back the Nithandan's contoured armour plating.

He approached the pack of humans, noting with disinterest the fearful hatred in the Nithandan fighter's eyes. *What a waste this all was*, he thought.

'Lord,' the Army officer saluted him, not with the fist of Unity, Amit noted, but with the increasingly common sign of the aquila.

Amit showed his incisors, unsmiling. 'Leave us.'

The Army squad gathered their fur cloaks about them and began moving away, all but the medic.

'Lord, ah, sir... Our orders. We have to aid the enemy wounded.'

Amit tilted his head. This was new. The expeditionary fleet's human elements had never questioned the Revenant Legion's practices before. The Revenants understood the Army forces accompanying them found their rituals revolting, but there had never been any pushback, let alone rebellion. Formal complaints to Expeditionary Command fell on deaf ears. Was it even cannibalism, really? Amit was hardly alone in believing the Astartes were another species to the original genetic knotwork of humanity.

Amit gestured, barehanded, to the wounded Nithandan

soldier. There were others he could choose, countless others among the injured and the dead, but the reaction of his human allies intrigued him.

'This one is mine. She belongs to the Ninth Legion.'

The rest of the squad were urging their medic away with hissed voices and desperate beckoning. Amit found the man's refusal fascinating.

'I have my orders, Sergeant Amit. This soldier's wounded.'

Amit looked briefly around at the rubble. He crouched, picked up a rock the size of a human fist, and with no cere-mony whatsoever he drew back his arm with a snarl of servos and slung the rock into the Nithandan trooper's face. The impact annihilated her from the neck up.

Amit said, in a tone of bland reasonableness, 'And now this soldier is dead. You can leave with a clean conscience, your duty discharged to the letter.'

The medic, who'd jerked back from the hurled stone, turned wide eyes from the twitching corpse to its towering killer. Amit could hear the man's heart racing and, in a moment of mundane biological harmony, the dead body's heart giving its last beats.

'I… I will be reporting this to my superiors, Sergeant Amit.'

'Do whatever you feel compelled to do.' Amit drew his flensing knife and advanced on the body. Either good sense finally dawned, or the Imperials' courage finally gave out, as the squad moved away in a hurry. Amit paid them no more mind.

He crouched by the corpse, sifting through the wet wreckage of the skull with the tip of his blade. Despite the destruc-tion he'd inflicted, several choice morsels remained viable. He spitted them on his knife, wiping the grey chunks one by one into his palm. There were shards of rock and bone in each nugget of brain meat, but his teeth made short crunch-ing work of that.

He tasted the dead soldier's life. He swallowed and saw her dreams. It all came in a throbbing flood, out of order but not out of context, because with the visions came emotion. The child's face he saw in her memories was, for now, not a strange youth on a rebellious world, but Lelwyn, a beloved son who had begged her not to go to war. Amit felt the dead woman's tears though his face was dry. He felt the warmth of her child's last embrace through the layers of his armour.

He watched through her eyes as the sky rained drop-pod fire. He felt the fear – and a sweetly curious sensation it was, too – as she first saw one of the attackers, one of the grey-clad Revenants, butchering through her platoon with blurred motion and ruthless efficiency.

He ate more of her.

Beneath the turmoil of surface emotions was, if the word-play can be excused, the meat of the matter. Amit had never operated a crane down at the Torus Dock, in the far east of the city – he'd never even seen such a machine – but now he knew their exact form and function, and could operate one by muscle memory. He knew the lessons learned in the halls of a Nithandan academy over a decade ago, lessons of an iso-lationist culture that feared reaching out into the stars lest they bring damnation upon themselves. He remembered lectures in sciences he had never studied. He recalled training with weapons he had never used. All of this melted into the mess of the other moments he'd harvested so far, taken from other lives. An ever-growing stew of stolen memories.

There was little tactical insight to be gleaned at this point. No, *before* the battle; that was when you harvested to learn of enemy logistics and tactical vulnerabilities. After the battle was for remembrance, for reflection. And, in these quiet moments of honesty, for the pleasure of it. Of immersion within a life that wasn't your own. Of knowing your enemy and remembering them, in a way more visceral and useful than the dubious immortality of artefacts in a shipboard museum.

He wasn't quite done with this crimson ritual when the vox opened up in a storm of breathless reports. They came not from the last embattled elements on the ground, but from the relative serenity of orbit. Amit was on his feet at once, casting about for the others in his squad, seeking the closest gunship.

The voices across the vox, they made no sense. They overlapped and overran; he could see other Revenants nearby standing rigid amidst the dead as they sought to process just what they were hearing. The Imperial troopers working in their own clusters wore expressions of naked shock, as officers and comms-operators relayed word from orbit to the rest of their squads.

Among the soldiers' words to each other, he heard someone ask, 'What if he's like *them?*'

Amit ignored the humans. 'What's going on?' he said into the vox. 'Repeat and clarify, please. Repeat and clarify.'

There was repetition, but little clarity until the voice of Ishidur Ossuran crackled across the vox-web, riding a priority signal. The Legion Master's tone was stern with his usual control, but Amit could hear the rawness of emotion beneath it.

'Brothers of the Immortal Ninth. The Emperor has found him. The Emperor has found our primarch.'

EIGHTEEN

The reluctant god

Many years ago, during the Great Crusade

Sanguinius

He went alone. No army of faithful followers marched at his back; no ceremony marked any stage of his journey. He went into the desert alone, inured to the hardships of the wasteland in a way no mortal could ever hope to be.

And like all moments such as these – few and far between as they were – later, there would be stories. This journey, and the meeting at its end, would be refracted into a spillage of variant tales, some of which held an authentic core, far more of which were lies destined to become enshrined as truth.

The Revenant Legion would hear many of these tales, filed down and muddled by their own guarded, uneasy hope. They had nothing else to rely on. Word would reach them through brief exchanges between expeditionary fleets in the deep void, and across shrieking astropathic ducts; the impressions of half-mad psychic men and women channelling their senses into the unreliable warp. For a time, all the Revenant Legion would have were stories of transcendent choirs and cheering crowds – a scene they could all too easily believe, and one that sank unpleasantly into the silt of their troubled hearts.

But the truth, if such a thing really matters when it's always the lies that spread instead, is that he went alone. It was his choice to do so. He had questions to ask, though he feared the answers he'd receive, and he had a bargain to strike, upon which there would be no compromise.

Sanguinius had never seen a spaceship before, not outside the fractal impressions of them that sailed in his waking dreams. This one, sitting on the desert plain with its golden armour baking in the sun, had the suggestion of vulturishness. It was a thing of power and efficiency, blunt and brutal. Fire made it fly, not any notion of grace.

Figures clustered around the craft's landing legs, where the ship's great metal claws gripped the radiation-soaked dust of the wasteland. These men and women were plated in the same gold as the ship, rendered upon their bodies with painstaking artistry.

My father's guardians, Sanguinius thought. And what a thought it was, not only that a being such as his father required guardians, but that he had a father at all. All the years of wondering at his own heritage, devoid of insight into his origins – and here, at last, was the truth, standing in the shadow of a vessel from the void.

He leaned into the desert wind, stretching his muscles and rising on a thermal of bitter breeze. The temptation was there – like it always was – to soar, to break free of the ground and his responsibilities, taking to the sky and seeking distant lands where the secrets of old wars lay buried. Today that urge was both stronger and weaker; his heart was ill at ease with what this meeting would mean, but nevertheless, he burned to know what lay ahead.

He arced groundward, landing lightly with a scuff of his boots across the earth and a final furling of his wings. Dust swirled around his shins as he stepped forward. The golden figures carried weapons, a panoply of axes and spears and hard-calibre firearms. Sanguinius carried only his sword, undrawn, riding low on his hip.

'Welcome to Baalfora, outlanders.' He spoke Aenokhian, the tongue of his people, the Pure. He wondered if the outlanders would understand him, or whether they would be forced to rely on hand gestures and awkward mimicry.

My son, said one of the golden ones, somehow speaking it silently.

He felt his father's voice for the first time as one of his own thoughts, a sensation rather than speech, backed by a tremendous feeling of suppressed force. The golden man – if he was a man – that sent the contact seemed to be making significant efforts to restrain himself, or to contain the power within himself.

There was… more… there, though. *My son* rhymed with *my weapon* and rhymed with *the Ninth* and rhymed with… other concepts that Sanguinius couldn't parse from the core of the man's meaning. A lifetime of perspective was bound up in that contact, and Sanguinius sensed only the gulf between his father's silent words and the meaning behind them.

But he felt no threat in the touch of mind upon mind. Confidence. Impatience. Love. Caution. Approximations of those, where words couldn't quite convey the actuality. It was all in there.

The man – and he did seem like a man: dark of skin and hair, smelling of metal and sweat, in possession of a heartbeat – walked closer.

'I am the Emperor,' the man said as He stepped out from the spacecraft's shadow. 'And I am your father.'

Father, the man had said, the word rhyming in silence with *Master*, with *Shaper*, with *Creator*.

Sanguinius met the Emperor's eyes. What he saw there, glinting in the light of his father's gaze, was the answer to a question he'd never even considered.

This being – this Emperor – was human. But He was not, exactly, a man.

'I see the light of many souls in your eyes. Many men. Many women.'

The Emperor smiled. 'Is that what you see?' He spoke flawless Aenokhian, but that perfection was itself a flaw. He spoke the tongue with the same dialect and inflection as Sanguinius himself. Either the Emperor was pulling the meaning from the Angel's mind or imprinting meaning upon it. Whichever was true, He wasn't really speaking the language at all. Nor was Sanguinius entirely certain he could see the man's mouth move.

'I have sought you for many years,' said the Emperor. And behind those words, Sanguinius sensed the cheering of crowds and the burning of worlds. His blood ran cold in the desert heat.

'I've seen shades of this meeting many times in my dreams,' Sanguinius confessed. A heavier gust blew from the east. He instinctively lifted a wing to shield himself from the gritty air.

The Emperor's eyes followed the movement. He began to circle Sanguinius in a slow walk, one gauntleted hand reaching out, fingertips running down the Angel's feathers. Sanguinius' pale gaze tracked his circling father, but his wings rippled with discomfort each time the Emperor moved behind him, out of sight.

'You are uneasy,' said the Emperor. 'That is natural, my son.

I have come not only to liberate you from exile, but to ease your heart and mind with all you need to know.'

Sanguinius felt a lifetime of questions trapped on his tongue. There was one, however, that was always going to break free first. One question above all others had plagued him and haunted his people, since the Tribe of Pure Blood had discovered him in the wild lands. They worshipped him for his strength and beneficence, but they feared him for the question that now lay unspoken between father and son.

'Ask,' said the Emperor. 'Ask the question I sense lying upon your tongue.'

The Angel pulled back from his father, not furling his wings but spreading them. With sudden passion, he beat a fist against the animal hide of his breastplate. A lone feather, swan-white, drifted in an arcing dance down to the dusty earth.

'What am I?'

'You are my son,' said the Emperor. And, again, meanings and concepts danced beneath those words. *You are my son* was overlaid by *you are a primarch*, and *you are my Ninth General*, and *you are a component of the Great Work* and *you were stolen by the enemy*, and – most unsettling of all – *you may have been changed by them*.

'I don't know what you mean.'

'You will,' the Emperor assured him.

'You are the death of faith,' Sanguinius replied. '*That* I know.'

The Emperor regarded him before speaking. 'Yes,' his father agreed, 'and also, no. How do you know of such things?'

'I told you, I have dreamed of this day. Fragments. Shadows. Suggestions. Sometimes they come to me, fierce with emotion yet raked clean of detail.'

'Faith is a weapon,' said the Emperor. 'A weapon that the species cannot be trusted to wield.'

'My people revere me as their god,' Sanguinius replied. 'That brings them a measure of peace. No doubt to you and your sky-sailing kind, we are nothing but primitives. Roaches in this poisoned desert. But I reward their faith in me. I am their servant. I am mercy when my people need it most, and I am death to their enemies.'

'That does not make you a god, my son.'

'I never said I was a god. I said my people believe me to be one.'

Sanguinius stared into his father's inhuman, too-human eyes.

'My people, the Pure, are to be left in peace. Whatever pacts you and I swear this day, my inviolate condition is this – no ship will enter Baalfora's heavens without my mandate, and no interference will be permitted to the Clans of Pure Blood without my permission. We have carved out the solace of peace here, together. You will not threaten it, father.'

The Emperor nodded, not in agreement, but in sudden understanding. 'That is why you fear me, is it not? You fear the endangerment of what you have achieved here.'

'I speak of loyalty and love,' the Angel said gently. 'And you speak of achievement.'

'Am I wrong?' asked the Emperor.

'I fear for the lives of my people, who deserve only peace. A peace we have fought so hard for. Behind your words, I hear the triumph of cultures that see you as their saviour. But I also hear the razing of cities and the burning of worlds. I hear the dirges of faiths now forbidden, and the mourning of those nations that followed them. Am *I* wrong?'

The Emperor said nothing.

Later – many times over the decades to come – Sanguinius would think back on those words. For all the purity of the Emperor's intent, there were so many compromises. Faith could not be tolerated… except for when it could. Religions were drowned in the ashes of defiant worlds… except when their usefulness aligned with the Great Work. The Emperor needed the Martian Mechanicum, and he allowed them to worship Him as the Omnissiah, the incarnated avatar of the Machine-God. Perhaps necessity carves holes in everyone's principles, human and god alike.

But all of this would come later. There on the desert sands, that day, the Angel had more questions.

'You keep looking at my wings. Wings, I note, that you and your followers do not possess.' Sanguinius scanned the men and women still waiting by the landing craft, then looked to the Emperor once more. 'Do I bear these by your design or by some twist of misfortune?'

The Emperor looked at him with the keen eye of an inventor assessing a prototype, as well as the forgiving gaze of a father. A seamless blend.

'You are exquisitely wrought,' said the Emperor. 'Exquisitely and pain-stakingly.'

Which was no answer at all.

'What *am* I?' Sanguinius asked again, this time with an edge to his tone.

The Emperor's voice softened, as did His expression. Only His eyes were unchanged, remaining lit by inseparable, uncountable souls.

'You are a gamble against the death of hope, my son. You are a roll of the dice at the end of the game. What do you call yourself?'

He called himself by the names his people had given him. First, the nicknames of youth. Then the name he'd received as he grew to lead the Clans of Pure Blood. A name sacred to the tribe that had come to view him as their god. A name that marked him as theirs in spirit, if not in birth, meaning *Of the Pure Blood*.

'Sanguinius.'

The Emperor nodded. 'Sanguinius. You are a primarch. A component of the Great Work, stolen from me and torn from its place, denied to me all these years. I have need of you, my son. Humanity has need of you. You are instrumental to the species' salvation. I have come to lift you from these dry roots, to take you into the stars – to give you a Legion to command, and a future to fight for.'

Once more Sanguinius heard the adulations of crowds in bright sunlight, and the cries of populations on burning worlds.

He asked then what no other primarch had given voice to. Even Angron, upon his discovery, would act without asking the question Sanguinius now asked.

'What if I refuse?'

The Emperor seemed to weigh this. 'You will not refuse. I know your soul. Here, you've saved tens of thousands of lives. With me, you will save billions of lives on millions of worlds. You will save the life of every human yet to be born. That is not something you could turn your back on.'

They stared into each other's eyes, father and son, creator and created. Neither argued against the truth of the Emperor's words.

'I want something from you. I want your oath.'

The Emperor was silent, allowing His son to continue.

'Do you swear, on whatever oaths hold value to you, that you will leave the Clans of Pure Blood in peace? Untouched by your designs unless they desire otherwise. Free to exist as they already exist, believing whatever they choose to believe.'

The Emperor hesitated. Sanguinius saw the calculation in his father's eyes, and he wondered: *is He taken aback by the love I bear for my people, or is He merely considering alternate avenues around this obstacle in His Great Work?*

The Emperor finally spoke. 'You have my promise.'

Sanguinius closed his wings. 'Then let us speak of the future, father.'

And so, they did.

NINETEEN

Lord of the IX Legion

Three years later, during the Great Crusade

Sanguinius

It was raining the night he met his Legion. The stories would be wrong about that, as well – many of them painted a picture (sometimes literally, rendered upon canvas) of the Angel standing in sunlight before the arrayed ranks of his magnificent sons. The truth was that monsoon season was in its full throes across the northern hemisphere of the planet Teghar Pentaurus. Rain scythed against the descending gunship, storm winds swiping at armour plating still gleaming with the heat of atmospheric entry.

Sanguinius stood within the Thunderhawk's crew bay, ringed by warriors in pristine white. Thoughts of Baalfora were foremost in his mind, beginning the chain of events that led him to this time and place. Three years of fighting at his brother Horus' side had finally brought him here. Three years of learning the ways of the emerging Imperium, in all its infinite complexity. Three years of waging war alongside the warriors surrounding him now. The crescent moon and lupine face of the Luna Wolves marked their armour plating. They were, without doubt, the finest warriors – the finest men – he had ever known.

'Nervous, lord?' one of them asked.

'No, Ezekyle.' Sanguinius turned to the warrior as he replied with that harmless lie. 'But I thank you for your concern.'

'I'd be nervous if I were you,' one of the others said with a grin. 'Surely you've got used to a certain quality by now, lord. What if they're not the fighters we are? Won't that just break your heart?'

'Tarik is right,' Ezekyle added, flashing his teeth in a smile, more hesitant with his informality. 'Perhaps we've spoiled you, these last years.'

'I can only hope, little Wolves, that if the warriors of my Legion lack your tenacity on the battlefield, they also lack your immense capacity for vanity.'

They laughed at that, and Sanguinius had to mask his sorrow at the sound. He would miss his time with his brother's beloved XVI Legion, that was no falsehood. They were, in the parlance of Baalfora, warriors to walk to the wastelands with: loyal, steadfast, disciplined. Horus had fashioned his Terran gangers and Cthonian barbarians into a weapon of beautiful precision and intimate nobility.

Nervous wasn't the right word for the feeling that clouded his heart, but it wasn't entirely wrong. Many were the tales told of the Immortal Ninth, the Revenant Legion, the Eaters of the Dead – and Sanguinius harboured no doubts as to the fighting prowess of the warriors he was about to meet for the first time. Their propensity for violence was, in fact, the only reassurance he had regarding their conduct.

'It's been good, lord,' said Tarik, leaning on one of the crew railings. The gunship juddered around them as it started its landing cycle. 'Fighting with you, I mean.'

'An honour,' added Ezekyle. 'We will miss you.'

Their affection brought a more sincere smile to his features. He regarded them both, and then the squad of warriors behind them, each one gripping the overhead railing against the threat of turbulence.

'The honour was mine, my nephews.' He almost added a wish for there to always be this bond between their two Legions, but with the future so in doubt, it felt worse than trite. He settled for the sincerity of what he'd already said. It would do for now.

Soon enough, the gunship shivered as it landed. Sanguinius heard the cycle-down of the engines, their diminishing whine replaced by the lash of monsoon rain against the hull. He felt the eyes of the Luna Wolves upon him, felt their wonder at the moment's mundane majesty, and sensed their curiosity over what he would say once the gang ramp came down.

Surprising no one, Tarik dared to interrupt the last seconds of reflective silence before a son of the Emperor met the thousands of warriors forged from his genetic code. The idea of ceremony was often lost on Tarik Torgaddon, centurion of the Second Company.

'Is your speech ready, lord? Lupercal gave us a grand old lecture when we gathered to meet him that first time. Brotherhood, duty, responsibility... It had it all. Rather warmed the heart, let me tell you.'

'You jest,' Abaddon pointed out, 'but you wept with the rest of us that day.'

Torgaddon's reply was a low chuckle, but Sanguinius didn't smile that time. He faced forward, as if he could see through the gunship's iron skin to the ranks of waiting warriors beyond.

Ezekyle, clad in ceremonial white tonight rather than the combat black of his Justaerin elite, watched Sanguinius with a touch more reverence than Tarik.

'Do you know what you'll say to them?' he asked.

Three years, thought Sanguinius. *Three years, and not an hour has passed within that span that I've not thought about what I might say.*

He'd watched the picter footage of Horus first meeting the Luna Wolves and studied his brother's words, his body language, and the emotion that enriched both. Speeches and chants and lectures and even sermons – of an admittedly bloodless and secular kind – had run amok through his imagination in preparation for what was to come next. He'd written entire scrolls worth of meticulous honesty and discarded whole tomes worth of aborted sentiment. Every imagined sentence was a possibility that might be given voice within the next few minutes.

'No, Ezekyle. I confess, I do not.'

That was enough truth to silence even Torgaddon. Sanguinius heard the joints of their armour purring as the Luna Wolves shared unspeaking glances behind his back.

'What about the war for Teghar Pentaurus?' Tarik pressed. 'Will you want us to stay, do you think?'

'We'll see,' said Sanguinius.

A second silence reigned. This one was even worse.

Mercifully, the pilot's voice crackled across the vox – *'Clear, clear, clear!'* – and down went the gunship's ramp on growling hydraulics. In came the hissing rain.

Sanguinius stepped out into the storm. Behind him came the Luna Wolves. Before him, standing in ranks, stood the Revenant Legion.

They waited in formation, statues at attention in the storm. Helmetless, they were graven in his image, several thousand faces resculpted through technomagical genetics to resemble that of the father they'd never met. Their various skin shades hid nothing, and variant colours and styles of hair didn't conceal the fact, either; each one of them bore his visage. Sanguinius had been cognisant of this possibility without truly expecting it. Many of Horus' Luna Wolves grew to take on his features as they ascended to the Astartes state, but it was by no means ubiquitous among the Legions. Here, Sanguinius looked not on mere similarity, but simulacrum. Horus' sons resembled their primarch as a son might take closely after a father. Sanguinius' sons resembled their gene-sire as his own face would look back at him in a cracked mirror. War had scarred them... but they were *him*, to the life.

And they were afraid of him. He could read it in eyes that matched his own, and he could sense it in the tautness of features he knew so perfectly well. The torment of expectation had goaded him to believe his sons might rejoice at their first sight of him, but the reality was altogether more tense. They feared what he represented, and the many changes to come.

Free of the gunship's confines, he stretched his wings in the rain. Nothing more than instinct, the way someone might raise a hand against a breeze or roll their shoulders to prepare for a task. But when he did it, as his white-feathered pinions flexed, several warriors in the front rank flinched. They didn't just fear what he represented, Sanguinius realised. They feared him. Perhaps they feared the mutation he bore on his back, but the primarch didn't think it was anything so simple. They feared his very presence.

Why?

The rain slashed, unceasing, content to fill the terrible silence with the hiss of its impact. Sanguinius felt the gaze of the Luna Wolves behind him as surely as he saw the stares of the Immortal Ninth facing him. Keeping his wings close to his body, for convenience rather than caution, he started walking along the rows of gathered warriors in their storm-washed grey. He met their eyes as he passed, and marked well the scars of war on their ceramite plate and transfigured flesh.

In turn, they gazed up at him with the desperate hope he had been expecting, coupled with a defiance he had not. They wanted this, they'd ached for this moment, but everything rode upon it. The pressure was practically a physical thing, bearing down on all of them.

In their faces, he read their records of the Great Crusade. The drinking of blood and the eating of flesh: for tactical advantage, for survival, and rarely – but not rarely enough – for pleasure. He read the stories told by the scars that marred their beauty; the chronicles of subterranean campaigns against mutated hordes and scarcely human populations harvested for desperately needed reinforcements. In their narrowed, awed eyes, he saw the discretionary refusals of the Divisio Militaris to supply them with munitions and armour battalions to match the other newborn Legions, for fear of the Revenants' degeneracy. He saw the Imperial decrees breaking them apart to serve in splinter-fleets, fragments of fragments attached to other Legion forces; the primary reason it had taken so long to gather the Legion here in its entirety. He saw the hardships of their crusades and the compromises made when fate had forced their hands. In the tilt of their heads and the set of their lips, he saw the sanctions levied against them by other, nobler Legions. He saw the sins they'd committed against their own empire, and the scorn they'd endured because of it. He saw how they wore that disregard as a badge of unwanted honour.

In short, he saw them for what they were: cannibals and killers with the faces of angels.

Last of all, gleaming in their brazen stares was the knowledge of their own extinction. Their time was coming to an end. Even without Sanguinius here before their gathered ranks, the lifespan of the Immortal Ninth was decidedly mortal, after all. The other Legions, no matter their degrees of savagery, were reliable weapons in the Emperor's arsenal. To carve a planet apart with fear, he sent the Eighth. To drown a rebellion in the blood of their own dead, he sent the Twelfth. The ruthlessness of these wild Legions was still contained within the framework of the Great Plan.

But the Ninth... these bloodstained knights with their crimson rituals, these Eaters of the Dead... Already, they'd been broken up, unreliable in Legion force. Whole swathes of the expeditionary fleets refused to fight alongside them. Again and again they were ground down to near annihilation, repeatedly bringing themselves back from the brink with tides of desperate recruitment, sustaining themselves by elevating the genetic dregs of the species to a state of Imperial perfection. Their ways populated their ranks with men exalted in flesh yet still hollow in soul. Duty could only carry a soldier so far. These transhuman men fought for the Imperium, but they cared for little, they loved nothing. There was nothing ennobling in their suffering, only pride in their capacity to endure.

The pride of a cornered animal is all they have left.

As soon as the thought occurred to him, Sanguinius dismissed it. *No. It's not all they have left, it's all they've ever had. It is all they were ever given.*

How like the people of Baalfora they were, so vulnerable despite their fortitude, able to survive but never thrive. Sanguinius had been adopted by the Clans of Pure Blood and grew to become their champion. He could've ruled over them as the god-king they believed him to be, but he had always wanted nothing more than to protect them. He elevated the Pure Tribes from the travails of their rad-soaked homeland not through dominance over them, but by his service to them.

And now, the Revenants' fear made sense. It was so obvious once he'd witnessed it with his own eyes: a truth that no hololithic report could ever convey. What would this winged demigod demand of them? Could they ever live up to what he would ask? Would they even want to try, if they despised their new father and his vision?

Sanguinius kept walking, kept studying them. He thought of the oaths of fealty he could make them swear tonight. He thought of the glory he could promise them and of the pride he could convey, at the Emperor granting him command of his own Legion. He was their primarch, and he had every right to play out the moment the way his sons expected: by binding them to him with sacred oaths of their allegiance to him.

But the first words he spoke to his Legion were far from the bombastic speeches later chroniclers would describe.

'What is your name?' Sanguinius asked the closest Revenant, the first of his sons that he ever met face to face. His tone was gently firm, his curiosity evident. The scarred warrior replied, lips wet with the rain.

'Idamas.' Sanguinius saw the conflict in the man's dark eyes as the Astartes hesitated, unsure whether to add an honorific.

'Thank you,' Sanguinius replied. He turned to the next warrior in line. 'And you? Your name?'

'Amit.' Again, that hesitation, though Amit added a subdued, 'lord,' after a moment's pause.

'Thank you. And you?'

And on it went. Soon he wasn't going one by one anymore, instead beckoning them to break ranks and come forward in clusters. He looked each of them in the eye as they proclaimed their names to him, many of them shouting over the others as the adrenaline of the moment took hold, and he committed their identities to his preternatural memory. These were his first sons, and he would remember every one of them until the day of his death.

When it was done, silence descended once more, dense with expectation. Before, the Revenants had regarded him with that clash of anticipation and defiant fear. Now, the challenge in their stares bordered on feverish. Why had he asked their names? What did he intend to do with the knowledge?

Sanguinius saluted them, his fist against his heart. At last, he spoke.

'You have told me your names and I have read the records of your deeds. I know you, and I know how my father's Imperium – *our* Imperium – looks upon you. You have served with loyalty and been paid in gratitude and spite, both in equal measure. You have been given difficult tasks, only to find yourselves mistrusted for achieving them in the ways you believed best. I will not say you were wrong to act as you have acted, nor will I blame those that have come to fear you. That is the past, and this is our chance to step back from the edge of extinction. My first command is to bring you together once more. We will fight together as one bloodline. As of this moment, you are a broken Legion no longer.'

The Revenants' eyes were upon him. He felt no doubts now. He knew exactly what he wanted to say.

'Swear me no oaths,' he told them. 'Make me no promises. Do not offer me your allegiance purely because my blood runs in your veins.'

Sanguinius laughed suddenly, the sound musical against the percussion of the storm. 'In fact, do not offer me your allegiance at all. Not until you believe me worthy of it.'

The primarch drew his sword, plunging it into the earth before the gathered ranks. He spread his wings, letting the rain sheet from them in pearlescent droplets. And then, to the amazed horror of his sons, he went to one knee in obeisance. Even with his head down, his voice carried above the storm.

'Instead, let me offer you *my* allegiance. Take my oath, here and now. I am Sanguinius, son of the Emperor, primarch of the Ninth Legion, and I make you this promise – I will stand with you in glory or die alongside you in shame. I come to you tonight not to enforce my ways upon all of you, but to learn your ways.'

The Revenant Legion looked upon him with breathless amazement. The punishment and chastisements they had expected hadn't manifested. The self-righteous vows they'd anticipated, that they must reshape themselves in their new father's image, hadn't been spoken.

'This Legion is not mine,' Sanguinius called out to his sons as he rose to his feet. 'It is not a possession to be manipulated purely by my will. This Legion is *ours*. And though you are my sons, fated to answer to me, I am your primarch, and I will answer to you.'

Sanguinius heard the Luna Wolves shifting uncomfortably. This was plainly not how it had gone with Horus. It was not how these meetings were supposed to go.

The Angel drew his blade from the wet earth, raising his voice over the thunder.

'Each one of you is a bloodied veteran of the Great Crusade. And I, too, have fought the Imperium's war, learning of our empire at my brother Horus' side. But I am as new to my title as I am to the war we fight. In time, I will come to lead you. But for now? I ask you only to let me fight by your side. If you refuse me, I will leave with no grudge. I will break my pact with the Emperor and return to Baalfora. I will leave you to survive as you've survived thus far. But if you accept my offer... then let us learn, *together*, what our Legion will be. Let us write that story as a united bloodline.'

Sanguinius let the rainfall clean his blade. He sheathed it in a smooth motion and rippled his wings against the storm's chill.

'The Emperor has charged us to take this world. He wants Teghar Pentaurus. He wants it compliant before the turn of the solar month. I have seen the plans. I've seen the Imperial Army communications pleading for the presence of the Luna Wolves here, the formal requests that my brother's pristine sons remain to bring about the compliance the Ninth Legion cannot be trusted to achieve.'

The Revenants stirred, shifted, clutched weapons tighter. They had their pride. They had it in abundance, and it would make for a fine beginning.

'The Emperor wants this world, and the Luna Wolves would love to be the ones to give it to Him.'

Sanguinius paused, a half-smile on his beauteous features, the look of a man sharing a sly jest with his closest companions.

'It's my belief that we don't need our esteemed cousins, though. I believe we can take this planet without their aid, and in doing so we will write the first chapter of our Legion's true story.'

He turned to the side, an intermediary between the Luna Wolves' officers and the several thousand Revenants standing in broken ranks. Ezekyle looked faintly amused. Tarik was fully grinning.

'What say you, warriors of the Ninth Legion?' Sanguinius called out. 'What say you, to our noble ambassadors from the Sixteenth?'

Thousands of voices rose – a rolling thunder of mockery, refusal and defiance. The Revenant Legion shouted down the Luna Wolves with that unified roar, succeeding also in outshouting the storm.

Ezekyle Abaddon stepped forward, raising his hands for

quiet. It took some time to descend. Tarik moved with him, and as Abaddon inclined his head in respect to the quieting Revenants, the latter gave a teasing, courtly bow.

'Well then, Lord Sanguinius,' Tarik said, loud enough for the ranks of Astartes to hear. 'It's the considered opinion of myself, and my dear First Captain Abaddon here, that we can pull our Legion forces back and let the Ninth handle things.'

Sanguinius thanked them both with his gaze, watched them moving to reboard their gunship, and then turned to face his new Legion once more.

'My friends,' he said to the Revenants. 'My sons. Let us make ready. We have our first war to win.'

TWENTY

The High Host

During the later years of the Great Crusade

Shenkai

**From the mandated archives of Thrall IX/57437AJc/94-DVk
Assigned to Legionary Zephon**

Begin recording.

My name is Shenkai of the bloodline Ismarantha. I am twelve standard cycles old. This is the first recording in my official archive and I am making it as we travel to Terra.

I am Baalforan but I have never seen Baalfora except in picts and scans. I am void-born and the child of Baalforans and so I have learned the rituals and the histories of my people.

I am a slave. My parents and my mentors tell me not to use that word. They say slaves are unhappy and mistreated and we are not unhappy or mistreated, so we are not really slaves.

I do not think slavery has anything to do with happiness, I think it is a matter of freedom to make choices, and we have no choices. The warriors of the Ninth Legion are noble and good and pure, and it is an honour to serve them. But I do not understand how they can be good and noble and pure yet keep us as slaves. Our work is important and that makes us all proud, but sometimes I believe servitors could do it almost as well. I also believe that we would do it even if we had the choice not to.

My mentors and my parents tell me not to say these things. They tell me that in time I will no longer think like this. They also say the Great Angel, our primarch, would be saddened to hear me use the word 'slave'.

I have seen the Great Angel four times in my life and one of those times he spoke to me. I was nine standard cycles old and I was crying because many of us cry when we see him. I asked my father why we cried and he said it is because the Great Angel is perfect and that looking at him feels like staring into the sun. I do not know what that feels like because I have never been on the surface of a planet and looked up at its sun. The suns we see through the darkened windows of the *Red Tear* are not bright in the same way.

When our primarch spoke to me it was in the High Host's armoury. The Great Angel was looking for my master, Zephon, but my family's master was not there. That day, the armoury was filled with thralls working on weapons and armour, and my mother and father were teaching me the care of our master's equipment. This was the closest I had ever seen the Great Angel. He thanked my parents and said they did fine work on our master's wargear and I think they were pleased, but I wasn't looking at them.

The Great Angel turned to me because I was touching one of his wings. My parents were upset and worried because I had done this, but the Great Angel smiled and crouched down and looked into my eyes. He has eyes that make you feel very safe, and as though you are not a slave at all. He stroked away my tears with his white fingers and he said very quietly, 'Hello, little one.'

He asked me my name and I tried to tell him, but no words came out. My parents tried to speak but the Great Angel stopped them and said, 'If your parents are Eristes and Shafia of the bloodline Ismarantha, then you must be Shenkai.'

I did not know how he could know that but he smiled at me as if he heard my thoughts, and he said, 'I know every soul on this ship and every soul in our Legion.' He told me that when my apprenticeship ended, I would do the Legion proud. He said also that he was pleased to meet me.

Then he said the thing that I cannot stop thinking about. I told him I wanted to be an Angel when I grew up and his smile faded and he said, 'No, you do not.'

I asked him why he looked so sad when he said that and he said it was nothing, he was not sad, all was well.

When he stood up, he did not just walk away, he bowed to my parents as if they were primarchs and he were a thrall, and it made some of the other thralls gasp and it made others cry. Everyone loved him so very much, you could feel it in the chamber. Then he left and we watched him go.

My apprenticeship is finished now. It ended last month. I was presented to our master, Zephon, as a trained thrall as tradition dictates but everything has gone wrong.

My master's name is Zephon. He is the Exarch of the High Host. They call him the Bringer of Sorrow because he is so ruthless and because he is one of the Sacrosanct, the Destroyers, the bearers of weapons forbidden to many others. My family is honoured to serve him.

I have watched footage from my master's helmet feeds
many times, watching with my father when he reviews the
data. During those times, I stand by the side of my father's
chair as he and many other thralls cycle through archival
data on the consoles in the ship's athenaeum. The remembrancers that are beginning to show up on many vessels
are not allowed in there because the data is sacred to the
Legion. I have heard some of the remembrancers complain-
ing about this but I do not care. It is not their place to know
these things.

So I have seen my master fight many times, sometimes
through his eyes and sometimes through the eyes of other
warriors in the High Host. Like all Angels he is beautiful,
but he is not beautiful like a person; he is beautiful like the
paintings and statues kept hidden in the deepest decks of
the flagship.

The strongest memory I have of my master in battle is
from the helmet feed of a warrior called Torian. Before you
see my master in the footage, you see the ground swallowed
by spreading black mist. This is the poison smoke of their
alchemical weaponry. The High Host have shrouded the earth
with radiation from above, now they descend into it to kill
any survivors. Torian's view goes dark as he falls through the
smoke shroud. You can see nothing, only the static fuzz as
his boots hit the ground.

Then his thermal vision resolves. There are shapes in the
poison, heat blurs of the armoured men and women resisting the compliance of their world. Some of them are dying
but not all. The ones that sealed their suits in time are still
fighting. The High Host cuts them down. The thermal blurs
thrash, fall, and in the minutes after the footage they will go
cold and dark.

Torian's footage comes out of the mist. It's thinner at the

edges. Dissipating, I mean. Torian comes out of it. Then he turns around.

What happens next takes fewer than three seconds. I know this because of the runic time markers in the corner of the display. I have rewatched this moment many times.

Two of the enemy run out of the death fog. The radioactive mist did not penetrate their strange armour. One of them is only halfway out of the smoke when he vanishes back into it as if he had been sucked backward. You do not hear him scream and you never see him again. I only know his fate from seeing my master's eye-lens footage later, when Zephon grips one of the pipes at the back of the soldier's suit and drags him back. Breaking the man's helmet lets the poison into his suit. That is how he dies.

The second soldier is a few steps out of the shroud when she stops. Her back arches. Blood is suddenly on the inside of her visor, hiding her face. Either she coughed it out or vomited it up, I do not know. It is hard to see the blade that has come through her body and out of her chest because the toxic cloud has darkened the steel. This is something the High Host's weapons do, and we are trained to clean their weapons and armour with special gloves and suits of our own, if they have used their Destroyer weaponry in a war.

My master's sword is also hard to see because its power field is off and there is only one reason an Astartes does that – it is because they do not want their enemies to die instantly, they want them to feel a slower death.

The second soldier falls to the floor and my master walks from the poison cloud. His red armour is black with Destroyer scorchings. While the woman is dying at his feet, he speaks with Torian, giving further orders. You can hear the vox sparking with the congratulations sent by other captains. Then my master turns and his turbines cycle up. He jumps, and his jump pack flares, and he is gone again.

And that is Zephon. At least, that is who Zephon used to be. He has not been that man for many months now.

Before going to the apothecarion last week, I went with my father into the deeper decks. My father says the most beautiful art in the entire Imperium stands in shadow, deep down in Blood Angels warships. When I ask him why the Legion does not display its treasures, he says it is because the Angels are not vain. That they do this work for themselves, not for others.

We passed beneath paintings of alien landscapes and cities. There were statues made from stone taken from many different worlds, and some of the statues are carved to look like animals or monsters or the Emperor, and some are carved to look like shapes that do not always make sense to me. These are abstract. I know that word, I am not stupid, even if I do not always know what the statues represent.

I saw sculpted maidens and barbarians and aliens. Many of the aliens were shown in poses of nobility, not defeat. It is strange to show the enemy in a way that makes you admire them.

I saw paintings of Baalfora and my father said they were unnerving and fascinating because they are Baal from warriors' distant memories, sometimes over a century ago, so the burned earth looks different to the reality. I have never really seen Baalfora so I cannot say what is truly different.

But there are others that say the same thing and they carve statues that look tormented or paint scenes of dying worlds. When I said this to my father, he said, 'Exactly,' as if this answered everything.

I saw a mural of sculpted faces and they all looked peaceful except for the bands of iron wire over their eyes like blindfolds. This was by the Apothecary Amastis, and my father said he does this to mark the deaths of his brethren.

I saw three orbs sculpted with deep slashes, cradled in an invisible anti-grav field. This was by the warrior Nassir Amit. My father told me it was the rise of three moons on a world called Uryissia, that must have meant something to Captain Amit.

I saw many renditions of the Angels themselves because so many warriors paint their brothers. Many of these are in moments of peace, when the Angels wear their togas or robes. I saw a painting of Daramir of the Angel's Tears, standing in his robes, one arm raised as he speaks during a Legion symposium. This was by the warrior Hekat, who always paints his brothers, and always in poses of gentleness and calm. When I asked my father why, he said that it was because Hekat wanted to capture what was within the other warriors.

There are many hololithic recordings of musical performances, using every instrument you might imagine and many I am unfamiliar with. Sometimes there is no recording at all, just a chamber where a song will play in the dark.

My master is not a painter or a sculptor or a poet. His art plays in an empty antechamber. You hear it when you walk in, the soft sounds of a piano playing alone. This was the room my father brought me to, and he closed his eyes as if he could hear something in the notes that I could not.

I did not like my master's music. It sounded very sad somehow and it kept making me think of my failures in training or my arguments with other apprentices. Sometimes he played many notes in a kind of tumbling harmony and other times he let the longest notes ring on and on.

I told my father I did not like the music and that it made me thoughtful and sad, and he said that was why he brought me here before my presentation.

'To make me sad?' I asked, because that made no sense to me.

'To show you what our master has lost.'

I did not understand then. It only made sense when I was presented to Zephon later that day.

It was supposed to be my presentation to him but he did not care. He barely looked at me. It felt foolish to be presented to him in the apothecarion but that was where he was confined almost all the time after his injury and the many failed surgeries that followed it.

Instead of my formal presentation, we saw our master's last act as Exarch of the High Host. He gave the order from a bed in the *Red Tear*'s apothecarion, and that command was to promote Subcommander Anzarael. My master's bionics had failed again after another reconstructive surgery. They wouldn't fuse right with his nervous system. His legs malfunctioned and his arms shook and his fingers wouldn't close on command.

Anzarael accepted the rank but he refused the offer of Zephon's sword.

My mother is Zephon's weaponbearer and she was the one to bring the blade to our master's bedside when he ordered it, but Anzarael refused the honour of taking it.

'I will hardly need it on Terra,' my master said. 'And I cannot wield it anymore, even if I had to.'

Anzarael looked surprised and my parents later told me that our master had never spoken to any of his warriors in such a tone before. Temper is something the Legion focuses on controlling. You can always see it in their eyes if you look carefully, but they say it is something to overcome and not indulge.

My master tried to give the blade anyway but his bionics misfired and he threw it harder than I think he intended. Anzarael caught it and looked at the ornate hilt and scabbard for several seconds. The moment should have been emotional but when he spoke his thanks, there was no dignity in any of it.

I thought it was over and I wished it had been, but then Anzarael spoke.

'Sir, my first act is to speak with the voice of the High Host.'

My master was clenching his teeth. I do not know if it was because he was annoyed or because there was still lingering damage to his muscles.

'Yes?'

'Sir...'

'Stop addressing me as *sir*. You outrank me. You are Exarch of the High Host now, and I am a cripple in a medicae bed.'

'Zephon,' Anzarael said, and it was strange because his name like that sounded awkward and shameful. 'The High Host bade me make its wish known. The regiment appeals to you, that you might take one of the other positions offered by–'

He didn't finish because Zephon wouldn't let him.

'Get out.'

My master tried to dismiss Anzarael with a wave of his arm, but his metal hand refused to unlock from a fist. For a moment I was sure Anzarael would stay and defy him, and then what? Would my master rage at his subcommander from where he lay helpless on his medicae slab?

But Anzarael didn't refuse. He saluted and left and took the gifted blade with him. In the silence afterwards I thought my master might acknowledge me as tradition dictated, but instead he looked at my parents and ordered them to get out.

They did and of course I went with them.

That brings us to today and the journey we are on.

Zephon has been assigned to the Crusader Host. We are aboard a transport ship, on the way to Terra.

* * *

The Crusader Host is an honour guard of Legiones Astartes warriors stationed on the Throneworld. It is supposed to be a diplomatic post. The legionaries are ambassadors of their Legions. My master does not consider it an honour. He says it is a conclave of exiles and failures.

The expeditionary fleet has offered him other stations. Training positions. Military advisor roles. Ranks of counsel. Other stations I do not really understand beyond knowing their titles. He was offered command of a Legion warship, the cruiser *Tacit Canticum*. Mother and father believed our master would accept it because this was his chance to remain with the Legion and to fight with them. Mother said it would be 'his chance to remain who he was in the face of who he's become.'

But he refused. Instead he accepted a place in the Crusader Host. When I asked why, my father said it was because Zephon would no longer have to see himself reflected in his brothers' eyes.

My master did not give his refusal to the Great Angel in person. He sent his decision as shipboard scripture. Just cold text on a screen. The Great Angel returned a message requesting my master's presence before departing for the Crusader Host, but my master ignored the Great Angel's wishes.

We waited for our master by the shuttle in the *Red Tear*'s secondary portside docking bay. When he arrived, he was limping because of his bad bionics and although he tried hard to look cold and angry you could see in his eyes that he was upset.

'Thankfully there are no farewell theatrics,' he said to my father. We had expected the High Host to be present, maybe, to salute him and wish him a good journey. There was only us, and the deck crews, and the servitor loaders, and the usual disorder of a flight deck.

'Board the shuttle,' he said. And we did. We carried our own possessions and the servitors carried my master's gear in crates.

But there *was* a final farewell and we only saw it once the flight was underway. I was the one to find it. It was in one of the crates, in the cargo hold: a sealed metal case. It had the Legion sigil and also the mark of the High Host, which is a burial mask with open black wings. I knew what it would be as soon as I saw it.

'What are you doing, boy?'

My master's voice made me jump, but I did not try to hide my curiosity. I told him I was looking through the cargo to see everything we had brought, and that I was allowed to do it since I was a trained thrall now.

He saw the closed case and he also knew what it was. You could see it in his eyes even before he said it.

'My sword.'

'I think so, lord.'

It was surely his sword. Anzarael had returned it to him, sending it with him away into exile.

'Fools,' my master said of his men. But he sounded very sad when he said it, not angry. 'Doubtless they believed this was a kind gesture.'

He opened the crate to see if we were right, but we were both wrong.

It was a sword but it wasn't his sword. It was cushioned in red velvet and it was even nicer than the blade he gave to Anzarael. Immediately I thought not of the weapon in battle but how it would feel to clean it, and what it must have been like to make it. The hilt was reinforced Martian gold and had the craftsmark of the Ninth Legion's Master of Artisans. I had never seen a blade so precious, this close.

Along the silver blade was a flowing stream of Aenokhian runes. They were inscribed into the metal with acid and they were perfectly neat. *Spiritum Sanguis* was what they said. The Gothic translation is 'Spirit of Blood' but that is only half-right. It is a prayer or a blessing more than a name. The blade was a promise that my master carried the spirit of the Legion with him.

I realised this was why Sanguinius had wanted to speak with him before he departed. The Great Angel wanted to give him this masterpiece. Most likely, the High Host had petitioned for its creation, or perhaps even the primarch himself had ordered its forging.

'This is a princely gift, lord.' I was trying to be brave and to show him that he did not frighten me.

'I have no need of the Legion's charity. Nor their pity. When we reach Terra, place this in storage.'

'Lord?' I was not sure I heard him right.

'Do not make me repeat myself, thrall.' And there was a hesitation there because even though Astartes have perfect memories, he did not know or remember my name, because he did not care. My master let the case fall closed and left me alone in the cargo hold.

And that is the end of my first report. We will reach the Throneworld in one month. My master will begin serving in the Crusader Host. I know I am supposed to love him, but I do not. He is like a broken blade that cuts you if you try to clean it.

I hope he finds comfort on Terra, even if he is denied his music and his art and his brothers.

End recording.

TWENTY-ONE

Sanguis extremis

During the later years of the Great Crusade

Kargos

The crowd sang oh-so sweetly when he broke Neresh's handsome face open to the bone. Their cheers and jeers washed over him in a physical wave, refreshing as a breeze in the bitter jungle heat.

Neresh, to his credit, took two staggering steps back, at first too stubborn to realise he was done. Then reality took hold. He turned with all the grace of a gunship going down in flames, and dropped to the deck, suddenly boneless. *Crash* went the body, and again the crowd surged.

'Not so pretty anymore, eh?' Kargos grinned down at the dazed warrior with his cheek and eye socket caved in. 'I think your time impressing all those remembrancer artists and poets might be done, brother.'

Neresh's reply was to bring up blood instead of words. It

ran down the side of the defeated warrior's face, leaking from his parted lips.

'That's it,' Kargos said cheerily. 'You stay down.'

He raised his fists, his skin shining with sweat, his knuckles shining with his brother's blood. The sound of the crowd doubled, cheers and jeers alike.

'Champion of the Eighth Assault!' Kargos yelled at the watching warriors, matching them bellow for bellow. 'Champion of the Eighth Assault!'

At his feet, Neresh started shaking, frothing at the mouth. Kargos danced back from his downed opponent as the seizure took hold.

'Medic!' The call went up from the crowd. 'Apothecary!'

Kargos laughed, surprised and delighted by the convulsing form on the deck. He was, after all, an Apothecary. He could diagnose what was wrong even without his instruments: he'd pounded a few jags of bone into the poor bastard's brain. Quite by accident, you understand.

With a grin, he turned to the members of the World Eaters 11th Armoured Company at the edge of the ring, who'd just watched their champion getting his arse handed to him.

'He doesn't need an Apothecary. He needs a Chaplain.'

Ferakul, centurion of the 11th Armoured, hammered his gauntlet against the detuned void shield that separated the crowd from the combatants.

'Help him, you miserable bastard!'

Kargos licked his iron teeth. '*Help* him? How? I'll tell you exactly what's wrong with your hero – he's a weakling piece of shit, just like the rest of you. Flaws like that, they can't be helped.'

The officer raged, twitching with blood-need and the press of the Nails. He was calling for the void shield to come down, against the rules of the arena. The restraint field held for ninety seconds after every bout. Time enough for a victory lap, though that wasn't the intention. It stopped wrathful spectators leaping in and getting involved if they didn't like the way a bout had gone.

Kargos circled the dying warrior, counting down the seconds. Feeling the eyes of Neresh's company upon him, he adopted the most utterly false expression of sorrow ever to grace a human face.

'Neresh, my friend. You look unwell. Whatever's the matter?'

Half of the crowd roared with laughter. The other half, in anger. But wasn't that just always the way when it came to the arena.

Later, Khârn was less than pleased with him. His captain came to him in the Eighth Assault Company barracks, and Kargos could tell from Khârn's face that it was going to be an unpleasant discussion. Dozens of warriors milled about, cleaning weapons, banging armour back into shape, or resting in states of uneasy hypnosis to counter the pain of the Nails that refused to let them sleep naturally.

The centurion was in his armour, but Kargos was still dressed in only the undersuit trousers he'd worn while fighting in the pit. His torso was a cartography of scarring, a map of places no reasonable human would want to go.

'You and I are going to talk,' said Khârn.

He felt his smile drop a notch. 'I'm not sure I like the sound of that, sir.'

Khârn fixed him with an unchallenging stare, not much more than a rest of his weary eyes on the Apothecary's features.

'Now, Kargos.'

Kargos rose and obeyed. He felt the gazes of the others as Khârn led him from the communal barracks.

They walked for some time through the *Conqueror's* spartan innards. The new shipmistress, Flag-Captain Sarrin, was a fiend for efficiency and discipline. Her purview didn't exactly extend to the warriors of the Legion itself – they could scarcely be driven into order even by their primarch, not that Angron troubled himself with such mundanities – but in matters of the flagship, her word was law. The *Conqueror* would never be what you might call beautiful, lacking the ornate interiors of vessels in III and IX Legion colours. Everything here was cut back to clean functionality and military efficiency, and rotating teams of servitors, underlings and ratings ensured it stayed that way.

Kargos had been aboard the *Red Tear*, Sanguinius' personal warship, half a dozen times on various missions and embassies. All the gold, all the statuary, all the ivory… Kargos couldn't see the point in any of it. Only the *Pride of the Emperor*, which was more or less Fulgrim's museum dedicated to himself, was worse. The pretension aboard the *Pride* was unbearable. It leaked out of every polished rivet.

Khârn led them to one of the buttressed balconies overlooking the *Conqueror*'s kilometres-long spine. A city's worth of castles and defence towers battlemented the warship's back. Kargos wouldn't exactly call this view beautiful either – he wasn't entirely sure he knew what the word meant, if he was being honest with himself – but at least all of this had a purpose.

Khârn, in his armour, towered over the Apothecary. He looked tired, but Khârn always looked tired. Acting as Angron's equerry would exhaust anyone. Even so, Kargos felt a twinge of empathy as the centurion gripped the crew rail and stared wearily out into space. Beneath the ship, the planet Serrion turned in its sedate dance, patches of arable green land and clean expanses of ocean showing through the cloud cover. Anchored off the *Conqueror*'s starboard side, the immense blade of the *Red Tear* hung in the void, abeam of its sister ship. Emblazoned in unnecessary gold, the sigil of the Blood Angels shone on its spinal battlements.

'You killed him,' said Khârn, staring into space.

'I know,' Kargos replied. 'I was there.'

Khârn sighed. 'You know what I mean, fool.'

'I really don't. Explain it to me, sir. Use small words.'

'It wasn't a death bout. It wasn't *sanguis extremis*.'

Kargos sucked in air through his metal teeth. 'It's the arena, brother. We risk death every time we enter the shielded ring. Neresh fought and he died. Did I mean to kill him? No. All right? Does that please you? It wasn't a death bout and I didn't mean to kill him. But do I give a shit that he's dead? Of course not. He knew the risks.'

Khârn shook his head. Anger flickered in his eyes, and Kargos could see him holding it back. Khârn was the best of them when it came to that. The centurion lost himself so rarely to the Nails; it was one of the reasons he made an excellent equerry. Khârn's self-control was legendary among his brothers. Conversely, Kargos had often wondered if it was another side of the coin; perhaps part of why his centurion was such a mediocre gladiator. In battle, there was no World Eater he would rather fight beside than Khârn. In the pits, though? Khârn was next to useless. He could never summon the right focus, never muster the necessary emotion. He treated it like a training spar and, inevitably, lost as many bouts as he won.

'Are you angry?' Kargos needled him. 'Why's that, sir? I must really be in trouble.'

'You're an *Apothecary*.' Khârn spoke through gritted teeth.

'When I'm in the pits, I'm a gladiator. We all are.'

'A brother was dying at your feet.'

Kargos snorted. 'The restraint shield was still up. I could hardly run for my narthecium and medicae tools, could I? What did you want me to do? Perform life-saving surgery with my fingernails? He had skull shards in his brain. The bastard was dead, Khârn. I couldn't do anything about it.'

'You laughed at him.'

'Because it was funny!' He mimed Neresh's death spasms, his eyes rolling back in his skull. The effect was somewhat ruined by the fact he couldn't stop smiling as he did it. 'What did you want me to do? Sing a funeral dirge?'

Khârn's lip twitched. His hands, gripping the railing, growled with compressing knuckle servos.

Kargos stopped smiling then. 'You... really are angry, aren't you?'

'How perceptive of you. I don't care that Neresh died, you erratic idiot. I care about what comes next. What you've provoked.'

Kargos was none the wiser. 'A challenge, I expect. *Sanguis extremis*, probably. I'll have to kill Ferakul. That'll be the end of it.'

Khârn massaged his temples. 'Does it never occur to you that your childish spite might have wider consequences?'

He drew a token from a belt pouch. A disc of red metal, crudely engraved with name glyphs. A challenge disc. Kargos couldn't see the symbols hidden by Khârn's tense grip, but he didn't need to. He knew what the names would be.

The Apothecary had expected no less. Tokens of grey metal were for pit fights to first or third blood. Red meant a death bout. He felt a shiver of excitement run through him at the sight of the disc. The Nails bit gently in response, a tingling gnaw.

'You don't think I can take Ferakul?' he asked Khârn. 'He'll die twice as fast as Neresh did. The Eleventh Armoured doesn't have anyone who can take me.'

Khârn tossed him the challenge disc. Kargos caught it; there were names etched onto both sides. On one side: *Ferakul Shen, Kargos Marane*. On the other: *Jegreth Halas* and...

'Ah,' said Kargos.

'Yes,' Khârn agreed. 'Exactly.' He gestured into the void, where the Blood Angels flagship hung in high orbit. 'I've arranged for an intrafleet shuttle. You can go over there and tell him yourself.'

Three hours later, Kargos was aboard the *Red Tear*, doing just that.

'I may have made a slight tactical misjudgement,' he said to his chain-brother.

Nassir Amit raised an eyebrow. 'I do not think I have ever heard you say those words before.'

He spoke in the tone of someone who was, at this juncture, receptive to something interesting coming along. When Kargos had first found him, Amit had been sitting alone in his arming chamber, using hand tools to scrape service grime from the joints of his red warplate. The compliance taking place on the surface had been tediously bloodless so far, and promised to stay that way. Standing for hours on parade duty had worn Amit down, and the meeting with several remembrancers after it had bored him almost to tears. He'd half-slept through both events, shutting down portions of his mind, running on surface senses while his deeper thoughts slumbered. Another gift of the Space Marine mind.

Still, it had been several days of pomp, ceremony and intolerable posing for paintings by this point. Amit was bored. Kargos could tell.

The World Eater relayed the events of his last arena duel with only a little embellishment, and Amit listened without sign of judgement. He was a veteran of the *Conqueror*'s pits himself. He knew the risks as well as anyone.

'I fail to see the source of Centurion Khârn's anger,' the Blood Angel said, once the World Eater had concluded with

Neresh's ignoble death. 'If Ferakul wants to face you *sanguis extremis*, then let it be so. Those are your laws, as I understand them.'

'You understand right. But the challenge came and, ah, now there's the risk of a "diplomatic incident".' Kargos flashed him the challenge disc.

Amit tilted his head as he regarded the token. Understanding dawned in his pale eyes, and with it, amusement. His own name was scratched next to Kargos'.

'He wants a chain-fight,' said Amit.

'He can't take me alone.' The World Eater was grinning. 'But his chain-brother is Jegreth from Thirty-Second Company, and Jeg is a dangerous bastard.'

Amit would need to speak with his primarch. Sanguinius had never refused those of his sons that wished to fight in the *Conqueror*'s pits; Amit had been duelling in the arena for almost a decade, and chain-bonded to Kargos for the last three of those years. Whenever their fleets intersected on campaign or while rearming and resupplying, Amit and Kargos bound their wrists together with bloodblessed iron and entered the arena side by side.

The Ninth Primarch's only request – phrased as a hope, not a mandate – was that his Blood Angels wouldn't participate in death bouts. It was base and crass, he believed, to butcher a Legion-cousin for sport, and a waste to be butchered by one in kind. The days of the Revenants were far behind. The Blood Angels worked to exalt their spirits in order to resist the base urges of the flesh. In this, their primarch was their living example.

Amit refusing hadn't even crossed the World Eater's mind. The two of them had fought alongside one another in three campaigns now, and fought chained in a hundred and six bouts in the pit.

Kargos only had one question. It was why he was here.

'What will the Angel say about this?'

Amit thought about that for a moment. 'It depends on whether or not we're the ones who die.'

The *Conqueror* had thirty fighting pits, ranging from Arena Seventeen – a converted storage suite that stank of wet corrosion – to the apex of shipboard facilities, Arena Five, a multilayered arrangement of traps and platforms that had once been a live-fire training hall. Kargos was familiar with the virtues and shortcomings of each arena. He'd fought in them year after year, accruing memories of victories in each one, as well as the occasional defeat.

Arena Thirty was the newest, and by far the grandest. It had been Captain Sarrin's idea, soon after her assignment to the *Conqueror*. When she'd learned the World Eaters were preparing to demolish a fighter bay for the novelty of turning it into yet another fighting pit, she'd offered an alternative. Midway along the ship's belly battlements was a reinforced observation dome, originally constructed to be a rare location of luxury aboard Gloriana-class battleships. On the *Conqueror*'s sister ship, the *Fidelitas Lex*, it was Primarch Lorgar's personal observation chamber, where he was said to sit in meditative repose and gaze into the tides of the warp while the ship was in transit.

On the *Conqueror*, it was used by visiting dignitaries with the political clout to parasite their way aboard serving warships, the occasional diplomat from compliant worlds, and ambassadors from Terra sent to monitor the Legion's progress in these later years of the Great Crusade. Lotara had ordered the habitation facilities demolished and any lingering ambassadors evicted to more austere chambers. With that done, she'd turned over the grand space for use in the Legion's gladiatorial games.

This solved two problems with one solution. Everyone was happy. Well, everyone who mattered.

Kargos had been with Khârn and Skane on the bridge when Captain Sarrin was approached with a formal petition of protest by the evicted Terran dignitaries. She listened as she lounged in her command throne, and then, in a tone of amazement that they'd bothered to bring this issue before her, she'd told the leader of the ambassadors that he could shove his petition up his arse and dance a merry jig. If he did this, she swore on her very life that she'd reverse her decision.

He hadn't taken her up on the offer. His awkward refusal had been a source of some disappointment to Kargos and the others of Eighth Company present at the time, as the sight would've been something to behold. Not long after this incident, Terra's visiting adepts and various other pen-pushers started staying aboard other vessels in the fleet.

Kargos had been hoping for Arena Five, with the newly installed spike traps making things interesting during a bout, but he couldn't deny there was a certain grandeur to fighting in Arena Thirty.

He could hear the crowd out there, that lively susurration, while he readied himself in the shadows of the eastern ante-chamber. Ah, but he loved that sound, even muffled like this, resonating through the ship's iron bones.

Amit came to his side. The low light reflected from the blade of his gutting sword. They were both dressed only in trousers, but Amit was cold and focused, staring at the sealed iron bars ahead, while Kargos was twitchy with blood-need. The Nails were singing with the same sound as the crowd, hissing right into the core of his mind with the same white noise of anticipation.

'Blood for the Emperor,' Kargos murmured. 'Skulls for the Terran Throne.'

Amit licked his incisors, still staring at the barred door. 'I must admit, when we met in the Uryssian Compliance, I never saw this coming.'

Kargos glanced at his chain-brother, and at the length of linked iron that bound them together at the wrists. They had three metres of chain between them, if stretched taut. His left arm was chained to Amit's right, not that it mattered; most Astartes were ambidextrous. They both carried their serrated gladii in their unbound fists.

'I'm glad you're here,' Kargos said. His voice was pitched low, though not through shyness or any sense of unease. If you couldn't be open with your chain-brother, you couldn't be open with anyone. He spoke low only because he was struggling to form words. The Nails were starting to spike. Blood ran from his nose; he could feel it in a warm trickle, creeping towards his upper lip.

Amit's reply was a cold smile, a fanged slice in the angelic mask of his face.

They listened to the rules of the bout being called out over the chamber's vox-speakers. Instead of hushing the crowd, the announcements had the opposite effect: the World Eaters waiting for the fight to begin started baying and cheering thrice as loud.

'...*the challengers, demanding sanguis extremis...*' called the announcer, but Kargos was already losing it, losing the threads of his thought, starting to pace like a caged animal. The words out there reached him in here only in fragments of meaning. He heard the pit-names of Ferakul and Jegreth, heard their grievances against him, and knew they'd be in the western antechamber, held back by a similar barred doorway, probably shaky with their own blood-need and feeling the bite of their own Nails.

He rammed his forehead against the door, letting the pain

quiet the Nails for a moment, enjoying the stinging kiss of the cold metal against his skin.

There was a metallic whine at the edge of his hearing. Annoying. Like tinnitus.

'You are grinding your teeth,' Amit said.

Kargos forced his jaws apart. The metal whining stopped.

'*Bloodspitter…*' the announcer called, '*and the Flesh Tearer…*'

More cheering. Another stab of the Nails. Now the metallic whining was back. Kargos jerked at the sudden fall of Amit's hand on his bare shoulder. They'd fought together too many times for the Blood Angel to give him any speech about restraint, but all the same, Amit's pale gaze held Kargos' flickering eyes.

'Ready?'

'Mnh.'

They clashed their chained wrists together as the door to their preparation cell rattled upward. Sound poured in, and they poured out. The two warriors moved into the arena as one.

For the rest of his life, Amit recalled every swing of a blade, every impact of knuckles against skin, every breath and every curse that took place between the four fighters. For Kargos, as was so often the case, the details of that night were a jarring succession of moments, each one bleached red and out of order with the others, each one a flash of discrete sensation. Some of them, he knew, were memories. Some of them, he was sure, were pieced-together impressions pretending to be memories. He wasn't sure there was enough of a difference between the two states to really matter.

Their primarchs were there. He wouldn't, couldn't, forget that. As he and Amit walked out onto the killing floor of Arena Thirty, he almost trailed off mid-roar at the sight of Angron

and Sanguinius side by side in the elevated crowd stands.
They towered over their men, staring down at the arena floor.

Angron displayed his usual twitchy indifference, drawn not
by the names of those fighting but by the fact there would
soon be the scent of blood in the air. When he came to the
arena, it was to judge the fighting spirit of his men, never to
lend support to one fighter over another. His armoured chest
rose and fell with his slow breathing, and he gave a faint nod
of approval at Kargos' crowd-baiting theatrics.

The Angel, resplendent in gold, watched with an unreadable
expression. His features were carefully blank, and to see no
living emotion on his perfect face was a contrast that made
him seem monstrous.

Captain Sarrin was in attendance as well, standing before
both primarchs as was her right, as flagship captain. She turned
to say something over her shoulder to Angron. The primarch's
mashed slit of a mouth curled in a brief, nasty smile.

None of Amit's Legion were present, only the primarch. The
rest of the stands were filled with World Eaters and the *Conqueror*'s human crew, variously applauding, cheering, chanting.
Despite the chill of Sanguinius' unnatural stillness, Kargos gloried in the walls of sound pressing upon him from all sides.

Above them, the stars stretched out in a view that had reduced
men and women to breathless awe, and which Kargos paid no
attention to whatsoever.

They approached the centre of the iron deck, where Ferakul and Jegreth waited. Amit greeted them with a salute, fist
against his heart. Kargos finally turned from saluting the crowd
with his raised blade, greeting his two shirtless opponents
with a curt nod.

Tradition demanded they salute one another. Ferakul and
Jegreth did so. Kargos tossed his gladius up in a rising and
falling arc that caught the arena's harsh lighting in spinning

flashes, before it slapped neatly back into his palm. The crowd laughed or jeered, to their tastes for Kargos' jestering.

Then he saluted, still smiling. He felt good. Heated and flinchy with blood-need, but good – ready to get this done.

The four of them turned to the primarchs, raising their weapons and voices in salute, a quartet of unified oath-swearing.

'We who are about to die, salute you!'

Angron banged his fist against his breastplate in reply. Sanguinius did the same, slower, quieter. Expressionless, still. As the crowd surged, Lotara raised a hand, signalling for the first bell.

The four combatants faced each other. Ferakul looked haunted by Nails-pain, his skin sallow, his nose dripping blood. Jegreth – taller, bulkier – was more in control. His breathing was laboured, like Kargos', but his eyes were clear.

Kargos stepped forward, exhaling with dull-eyed hunger. Amit pulled him back at the last moment, preventing a breach of decorum.

'Second bell,' the Blood Angel warned. 'Hold.'

Kargos grunted in acknowledgement, stepping back into line.

Jegreth smiled at Bloodspitter's slip. 'Sorry you have to die today, Nassir.'

'Tonight, Jeg,' Kargos interjected, 'when your headless body lies cold in the apothecarion, I'll be in my chambers, skinning and sanding down your skull to a smooth sheen. Not as a trophy, you understand. It's my intention, brother, to give it to Captain Sarrin as a decorative pot for her to piss in.'

Jegreth shook his head, his lip curling. 'It'll be a pleasure to carve you up, Kargos.'

Amit's voice was the lowest, softest, of all four. 'Don't tell us. Show us.'

The second bell rang, and with its chime, Kargos' memories descended into red.

* * *

This is what he remembered.

The feel of a serrated blade grinding against bone. The sound of it, muffled by meat, inside the flesh of a man's body.

The rattle of chains. The slashing whipcrack of loose iron pulled tight, leashed around a sweating throat. The slow, delicious crackle of abused vertebrae. Only crackling, at first. Then a strained clicking. Then that dry-branch snapping as the inter-vertebral discs start to give. A little more. A little *more*. Paralysis awaits, so close, the ultimate infliction upon a struggling foe. The snaps become crunches. The spine begins to crack.

Music. It's music.

The sharp whack of skull on skull, the punishing intimacy of a headbutt; front bone thudding into the softer ethmoid bone of the sinuses and the prime target of the nasal cavity, pounding cartilage, breaking blood vessels, disrupting blood flow in the face. Vision and scent both flaring with flaws; the activation of the tear ducts and the running of cranial blood from ruptured vessels.

Distractions. Irritations. Ultimately ignorable.

Sword, his brother calls, *sword*.

He disarms himself, throwing his blade to Amit. The Blood Angel, beautiful where he is a creature of scars and cranial sur-gery, spins and cuts with two blades now. Amit dances as he fights. Both blades drive into flesh, birthing a roar that becomes a cry that becomes a grunt. Meat is carved open. Blood runs.

Heat. The stink of another man's breath. The stench of his last meal flavoured by fear and stomach acid. The plunging pressure of teeth, teeth, teeth. The gush of wet life, red and thick and copperishly foul. Swallowing another man's blood, drinking his life down, bearing the sick taste just to see the horror in his eyes as he sees what his enemy is doing. *That's his blood*, he knows; that's his *flesh*, his *body*, between another man's teeth. He is being eaten alive.

The crunching snap of an elbow to the zygomatic bones of the face. A princely blow, shattering the cheekbone and eye socket. An eyeball hangs, mulched to worthlessness. Laughter is the backbeat, then – laughter and cheering. The sound of the crowd, no longer individual beings but a gestalt, a single god that feeds on blood and sweat and wasted life. It cares not from whence the blood comes, only that it flows in abundance.

And it flows, it runs, it sprays. Not jetting with the hyperbole of poor poetry, ripe with symbolism, but the altogether more mundane arc of blood spurting from cleaved arteries. The thick smell of it in the air. The scalding kiss of it on the skin of his face; though it cools fast, in that first split second it's always a splash of boiling water.

Darkness and light, alternating, one and then the other, over and over. The thunder of a skull hammering into the metal deck, stressing the fractures of already breached bone. Crying out, not for mercy but for a brother's aid, because as his skull is ground into the iron, a blade lays open his back with clumsy chops and carvings. The unreal sensation of fingers, curling with hate, reaching *into* the body, clawing at the spine itself. The knowledge of *disassembly*.

The heat of blood-need stealing all words somewhere between the brain and the tongue. Angry words becoming snarls and bestial breathing punctuated by ropes of slaver. Hating so fiercely it breaks the ability to speak.

Tonguing the roof of the mouth, forcing the saliva glands to gush, milking one's own mouth to pull forth the flow of poison. Spitting it, missing, hearing the gobbet of saliva hissing on the deck. Trying again, closer this time, not spitting but opening the jaws wide, letting it trickle, letting it flow over the teeth… Drooling acid into the man's quivering, desperate eyes. Licking the eyeball to seal the deal and steal his sight, lathering the window of his soul with corrosive venom.

Side by side with his brother again. Wrapping their shared chain around a single throat, and pulling, pulling. Flailing hands grip weakly and slap uselessly against sweating, bleeding bodies. A mouth opens, becomes a maw, but bites nothing and draws in no air. No bones crackle and snap and crunch this time. This time, they make it last. This time he will die, and it will be the criminals' death, the bloodless death, extinction by strangulation.

The thud of dead meat onto the arena deck.

The animal roar of the god-crowd.

The looks in the eyes of the lords of two Legions: one distantly approving, the other mournfully accepting. One seeing a victory. One seeing failure.

The picking up, with trembling fingers, of a fallen sword.

The sawing of a fight-dulled blade through unresisting flesh.

The raising of a severed head, still dripping blood and marrow. The stink of it, which is utterly familiar but never quite pleasant.

The honour of fighting at the side of a man he can trust above any other. The gratitude, the fraternal love in weary and bloodshot eyes, after enduring something so few souls ever go through together.

The lifting of two fists, his own and his brother's, their wrists still bound by a length of bloodstained chain.

Thralls bathed them in the aftermath. Apothecaries sealed their wounds. Kargos was still riven by Nails-heat, trembling, sweating. Amit was calm, practically placid, licking his incisors in contemplation. That was always the difference between them after a bout; the Blood Angel's rage faded fast, the World Eater's took forever to swallow.

They sat opposite each other in the ward chamber, where the wounded of the evening's previous fights were likewise being stitched up, and the dead were harvested for their gene-seed. Amit was a statue as his thralls sponged and cleansed his lesser injuries. He barely flinched as the Apothecaries did the deeper work with their wet, scarlet tools.

Kargos had none of his serenity. His scarred lips kept twitching into a self-satisfied sneer, partly from the Nails triggering muscle memory, partly from the sight of Jegreth and Ferakul's bodies on nearby slabs. There they lay, chopped up, cut open. It wouldn't take much effort at all to widen the wounds for gene-seed extraction.

Around them, the grunts and grumbles quieted down, and the bone saws ceased their whining. All eyes turned to the figures entering from the main concourse: two towering icons flanked by their respective sons. All eyes, that is, except Kargos'. He kept watching Amit.

He'd known Amit, back in the days of the Revenant Legion. Not as well as he knew his chain-brother now, but the Revenants and the War Hounds had fought together in several campaigns, forced into collusion by the dismissive grind of Imperial bureaucracy. He'd seen the other man with his lips reddened by gory rituals. He'd seen Amit fighting the way the Revenants fought back then, motivated by a brutality so absolute it held no place for considerations of morality. They achieved victory, they ate the flesh of the dead in their rites of remembrance, and they moved on. No banners raised in glory. No triumphs held in their honour.

And back then, both Legions bore reputations that were, at best, stained by their demeanour in war. Both Legions found themselves assigned to some of the Great Crusade's bitterest conflicts, doing their bloody work out of sight and out of mind.

But year by year, the Legiones Astartes had rediscovered their primarchs. Changes whipped through each Legion in the wake of finding its founding father. The War Hounds became the World Eaters, and they broke their central nervous systems in emulation of their wounded overlord. They beat the Butcher's Nails into their skulls, scarring their minds. No longer ashamed of their blood-soaked past but exulting in it, pissing away their capacity to feel pleasure outside of battle. The World Eaters were a finer weapon than the War Hounds ever were, if the only measure of success was the number of corpses in their wake. They stopped at nothing, shied away from no massacre, cared nothing for guilt or innocence, only the purity of compliance.

And that was Kargos now, sat opposite his chain-brother. Twitching with electrical signals worming through his nervous system. A parasite machine squatted in his skull, biting into the meat of his mind. He looked at Amit, watching the way his comrade mastered his rage behind that angelic façade.

The Revenant Legion hadn't followed customs of barbaric surgeries and adrenal resculpting. They'd been gore-crows and carrion feeders first, but their primarch had inspired them to restraint. Sanguinius had promised them that if they mastered their darkest desires, they would be all the stronger for it. The changes came thick and fast, then. The Legions kept echoes of their fraternal unity, but they drifted to different paths. The Blood Angels were no longer assigned to belligerent shitholes on the galactic map. They were given campaigns where they drenched themselves in glory. They were bestowed with accolade after accolade, while the World Eaters amassed censure after censure – more than they ever had before the Butcher's Nails changed their fate.

Looking at Amit, he could no longer see the angelic ghoul that he'd first met all those decades before. In its place was this meditative creature, capable of absolute violence one moment, possessed of saintly calm the next.

In moments like these, Kargos hated him. The Nails bit hard at the thought, spiking his blood with narcotic delight. He felt his fingers curl, imagining Amit's throat within his grip.

'Here we go,' Amit said, drawing Kargos back to the present.

The World Eater turned as the two primarchs drew near. He looked up into their faces; Angron was as twitchy as Kargos himself, while Sanguinius' beatific features were set and resolved. The two brothers couldn't look less alike for children rendered from the same genetic template. Any similarities in bone structure and facial feature were overshadowed by disparities in posture, in scarring, in expression, in bearing. In every way but the basest physicality, they were utterly unalike.

Behind the two brothers stood Khârn and Raldoron, First Captain of the Blood Angels. Khârn looked implacable, but when did he not? Noble Raldoron was choosing not to hide his expression of mild disgust, and Kargos suspected that said a great deal about why the primarchs had come.

'You did well,' said Angron, and as ever, his voice was something between a wheeze and a growl. Talking pained him. *Thinking* pained him. All his Legion knew it, for they felt lesser echoes of it themselves.

Kargos saluted him, fist against his heart, and couldn't help but notice the trickle of silvery spittle at the corner of his father's mouth. He wiped the back of his hand across his own lips, reflexively.

Sanguinius didn't commend Amit. The Angel, his wings furled tight to his body, seemed careful not to touch anything or anyone in the chamber. The only contact he made was with his own son, when he closed his golden-gauntleted fingers on Amit's chin, the gesture one of surpassing gentleness. Amit was already looking up at his primarch father. Sanguinius' touch denied him the chance to look away.

'You disappoint me, Nassir.'

Amit nodded in his sire's delicate grip. He made no excuses, didn't play for forgiveness.

'I know, lord.'

'You are an intelligent soul,' Sanguinius said softly, 'so you know what I am going to ask of you. I will not force this upon you, and if you do it, it will not redeem your performance in this wasteful display. But I want you to remember this moment, Nassir. I want you to go forward with this night imprinted upon you. Would you do that for me?'

'Yes, lord.'

The Angel released the hold on his bloodstained son and said, 'Thank you.'

Amit's pale eyes flicked to Angron, then back to his father. From the impassive expression written on that scar-tissue visage, Angron had already granted his permission for what was about to take place.

To Kargos, the exchange between Sanguinius and Amit sent uneasy prickles along his skin. If one of Angron's Legion disappointed their primarch, that warrior tended to die. None of this gentle, disapproving acceptance.

Amit rose from the slab with a last glance to Kargos. It was a look that conveyed nothing clearly enough for certainty; Kargos wasn't sure if there were flecks of apology in that momentary contact or not. The World Eater watched as his chain-brother took a surgical blade from one of the watching human medics.

As Amit walked over to where Ferakul lay, the ward room's harsh lighting flashed off the bone saw in his hand.

In the end, it wasn't much of a thing. No chanting. No prayers. Like so many elements of Legiones Astartes life, it was an act of human horror reduced to workhorse mundanity. Bone was carved and cracked open. Slivers of grey meat were sliced free and devoured. Blood and fluid marked an unhungry mouth that chewed and swallowed with easy stoicism.

Amit didn't empty the dead man's brainpan. He ate sparingly, pointedly, to absorb memory and sensation, not to saturate himself with Ferakul's entire existence.

Kargos watched his chain-brother perform the Revenants' old ritual of remembrance, wondering at the taste of Astartes brainflesh. He'd eaten the minds of slain xenos and countless humans, to learn the secrets of their cultures and their armies, but the idea of consuming another legionary's brain matter made his skin crawl. There was something quietly perverse about that. He didn't want Ferakul's memories in the back of his head. The ache of the Nails was enough of a distraction.

Although...

It could be pleasant to experience the dead fool's final moments in such a way. That might make for a fine and visceral retelling of the tale...

Kargos' scabbed lips parted in a smile.

A golden hand rested on his shoulder, gently holding him back. Kargos hadn't even realised he'd started forward. He turned his head, looking from Amit's silent cannibalism and up into the pale eyes of Lord Sanguinius.

'No,' said the Angel. Either he'd read the World Eater's mind or inferred enough of the truth from that single step forward.

To Kargos' recollection, this was the one and only time in his life he'd met the Angel's eyes.

When it was done, paltry little ritual that it was, Kargos and Amit said their farewells. Amit offered no insight as to the sensation of devouring their opponents' memories, and Kargos didn't ask. They shook hands, gripping wrist to wrist, and embraced. It was always a strange sensation for one who lived his life in armour, to be skin to skin with another being. But they were brothers, and the embrace was fierce and sincere.

'Thank you,' Kargos told him. 'Thank you, brother.'

Amit wasn't much of a smiler, but there was warmth in his gaze – in those pale eyes, so like his father's.

'Until next time.'

They broke the embrace and parted ways. Their Legion fleets parted ways the next day.

TWENTY-TWO

I saw him out there

The last days of the Siege of Terra

The Gladiators

Nassir Amit stood on the Delphic Battlement, watching the horde gathering, horizon to horizon. They were too far away to make out any details through the dust, but that didn't stop him staring. A black smear of innumerable foes, coming together for the last battle. It wouldn't be long now.

Several other officers came and went, bearing mute witness to the massing of impossible forces to the north, east and south. Amit acknowledged them with nods or grunts of greeting, but his focus was reserved for the horde out in the wastelands.

Out of his brethren, only Zephon lingered nearby. Either Zephon didn't know him well enough to recognise when he wished to be left alone, or simply didn't care. Either way, Amit kept staring at the horde, his eyes drifting in a slow and endless scan.

'What do you seek out there?' Zephon asked.

'Nothing. I'm just looking.'

'I think not.' There was a cold serenity radiating from the other Blood Angel, one that Amit hadn't noticed before. Zephon had been hot-blooded before his injuries years ago, and then miserable company indeed once he'd been crippled. Now, he emanated a chill that was more than simple stoicism. Some new resolve since he'd made his way out of Razavi Bastion and back to the surface. 'You are plagued, Nassir. I can tell.'

'Earlier, in the retreat.' Amit kept staring, kept scanning with his unblinking gaze. 'I saw Kargos out there. I cut his throat.'

Zephon rested a hand on his brother's pauldron. The two of them had never been close, even before Zephon's exile to Terra, but Amit's time among the XII Legion pits was legendary among the Blood Angels. A dubious legend, admittedly, but a legend nonetheless.

'I am sorry, Amit. Perhaps it is useless to say, but you did what you had to do.'

Amit finally spared him a glance. 'I'm not sure I did,' he admitted.

'They are traitors,' Zephon replied gently. 'There's no redemption for them. Not for any of them. Not after all this.'

'That's not what I'm saying,' said Amit. He looked back out at the vile horizon. 'I don't think I killed him.'

Five kilometres to the east, with the sutures at his throat still leaking sluggish, clotting blood, a warrior held Khârn's salvaged axe and leaned against the hull of a mangled, mutating Land Raider. He stared at the distant walls of the Delphic Battlement, and he radiated a wounded animal sense of hatred.

His breathing came in wheezing drags, with his physiology still adjusting to the battlefield tech flesh-fused into the hole where his vocal cords had been. There was hate in his eyes, which was no surprise to any of the warriors near him, but there were also tears. Some thought this was pathetic. Others understood implicitly.

Another warrior approached him. This one was clad in sacred, rune-marked black, and was responsible for the fact that the other still lived.

'You should rest,' said the Chaplain. 'The battle begins at dawn.'

'No.' The World Eater shook his head. His voice was recognisably his own, but ragged with mechanical reconstruction. 'Fine here.'

'What are you gazing at, my friend?' asked Inzar.

Kargos hacked a cough through his new throat. His voice emerged from his mouth as a buzz-saw rasp.

'The enemy.'

PART FIVE

SANCTUM IMPERIALIS

TWENTY-THREE

The final council

Lotara

She woke when the ship called to her. It didn't speak, exactly; it pleaded in a voice of metal under tension, waking her with the protest of tormented steel. Lotara sat up in bed, hearing something of her name in the groaning of the *Conqueror*'s bones.

'Vox,' she called. 'Bridge, this is Sarrin, status report. Vox, damn it, establish bridge link. This is the captain. Status report.'

The ship shuddered again but the vox stayed dead. It wasn't a gunnery shudder. It wasn't an impact shake. She knew her ship's tremors. It was yet more of the warp's pressure out there, mangling the hull as it tried to get in.

'Lights,' she said into the darkness of her chamber. This achieved exactly as much as her attempts to activate the vox. 'Lights. Lights. *Illumination*. Oh, bloody hell.'

Lotara didn't have the energy for this. She didn't have the energy for anything. She was skeletal with malnutrition and dehydration, and even this paltry anger threatened to leave

her breathless. She hailed her attendant servitor with a weak
wave of her hand.

'Dress me,' she commanded it. 'Uniform.'

The servitor, who had once been Console Officer Fourth
Class Elsabetta Rahem before her regrettable attempt at
mutiny in the starvation riots last month, wasn't standing in
its usual place by the sealed window. It was slumped against
the wall, *demotivated* to use Mechanicum terminology, and
to use Sarrin terminology, *dead as shit*. Lotara peered at it
through the darkness. Half of its shaved head had merged
with the iron wall. The thing's cranium was swollen, spread
out, blood vessels threading into the dark metal. Judging by
the expression on the servitor's face, Lotara had slept through
its screaming. The captain wasn't sorry to have missed that,
though she wondered just how long she'd been out, and
how deeply she'd been asleep to miss such a thing in her
own quarters.

The blast shield over her viewing window was up, letting
in the useless un-light of the warp outside. It rippled, that
non-light, those colours that never made anything any easier
to see. It pooled and puddled and ran over the surfaces of
her chambers.

She'd sealed the window before she slept. She was certain
of it.

'Shipboard chron,' she called out, expecting no answer and
getting what she expected. Nothing worked anymore. Nothing
had worked for months.

Fine, I'll dress myself. She reckoned she could do it without
help. Probably. It would take a while and she doubted she
could lace up her boots with her shaking fingers, but–

Lotara hauled herself out of bed and gave a weak laugh. She
didn't need help getting dressed anyway; she'd slept in her uniform again. It was crumpled and dirty, but it was practically

parade-clean compared to the bloodstained rags many of the crew wore on duty these days.

Lotara took one look at her bedside table, where her canteen stood half-full, along with several foil-wrapped ration wafers, but her throat tightened at the sight. Despite her weakness, she wasn't hungry. Despite her thirst, she didn't think she could face swallowing even a mouthful of tepid water.

The ship shivered again, and its grinding bones mumbled her name. The *Conqueror* wanted something from her. She couldn't guess what that might be. When it wasn't trying to please her by bringing back dead crew to haunt her, it was demanding she do something without clarifying what.

Lotara rose on unsteady legs and made her way to the door. She heard a scream outside, coming from deeper in the ship, but the corridor outside her chambers was empty. Not so long ago, that would've made her skin crawl. Now, she rubbed her aching temples and started walking towards the rapid transit elevator.

Khârn was on the bridge. He stood by her command throne, up on the raised dais, beneath a swarm of malformed brass gargoyles that hadn't been there before. Lotara looked up at the hideous things, sculpted to cling from the ceiling beams, leering down at the bridge crew. Their childlike bodies were mangled together in a hive-like mass embrace, and their many mouths stood open to show rows of sawblade teeth. They looked like they were ready to drag members of the bridge crew up to the ceiling in their greedy little hands, and from the bloodstains on their brass fangs, Lotara suspected that may have happened more than once already. They didn't move as she stared at them. Maybe they wouldn't move at all.

She resisted the urge to look at Khârn. He wouldn't say anything, he never did, because he was dead and he wasn't there.

Instead, she ascended the dais, looking over the skeleton crew still operating on the bridge. Several hundred souls had toiled here at the Great Crusade's height. Attrition, war, time, and the axes of their own Legion had winnowed that number down to threadbare dozens. Corpses lay across the deck where they'd fallen, while the most respectfully treated were piled in loose mounds against the chamber walls. The freshest of the dead were only a few days into their decay, ripening with discoloration, beginning to bloat, attracting fat, shiny flies from who knew where. Plenty of the others were in states of deeper rot, slowly collapsing in on themselves, dry and sunken things like unearthed mummies.

Lotara smelled it then, really smelled what the *Conqueror* had become. The rank copper of blood was nothing new – it was a smell practically boiled into the warship's bones – but now it was coated in the spoiled-meat stink of biological corruption. Almost everyone knew the scent of decaying animal flesh, and it was easy to read remembrancer prose about the reek of war, but something in the human genetic strain rebelled at the smell of rotting *people*. Lotara's weakened insides coiled up at the richness of that smell. She didn't just breathe it in, it seeped inside her. The smell was part of the ship, part of her uniform, part of her skin and hair, part of the blood that beat through her body. She had a faint fear she would carry this stink inside her for the rest of her life, just waiting to be acknowledged whenever she let herself take those deepest breaths.

The oculus was open, looking out onto the choked sphere of Terra. Pyrokinetic madness thrashed in orbit around the globe. Colours with no names danced over the faces of the surviving bridge crew. None of the crew acknowledged her. They didn't even seem to acknowledge each other, staying slouched or hunched at their consoles, looking up only in spurts of twitchy, tired unease.

Lotara took her throne. No longer did she recline with her

boots up on one armrest as she had in her glory days. Now, her diminished form sat crone-like in the chair's bulk.

'Why is the oculus unsealed?' she called.

In answer, one of the ship ratings transferred a spillage of data to her throne's projectors. The message that beamed into the air before her was from the Warmaster himself – which, Lotara suspected, meant it was from Argonis and Horus may never have even seen the order at all. There was no reason given for why all vessels were to cease closing their eyes to the warp, at least nothing past a screed of brief exhortations to seek the truth in the void's tides, and various other allusions Lotara wasn't sure she wanted to understand. She certainly wasn't going to meditate on the boiling insanity outside the window. Every sailor knew that to stare into the warp was to risk madness, and now the warp was here, buffeting the armada in orbit and curling its tendrils into the atmosphere of Terra. Changing things. Warping things, one might say. It was literally the most honest way of describing it, after all.

She could see faces out there in the waves. Not in the way groundlings could make out shapes in clouds, but faces, actual faces, the hollow-socketed visages of men and women she knew. Crew members no longer with her. Legionaries lost in the crusade and the rebellion that followed. She saw Ivar Tobin, her first officer, laughing without eyes, screaming without a tongue, his face the size of the moon as it twisted in the boiling morass. Then he was gone – and honestly, had he ever been there at all? – replaced by an arcing surge of empyric energy, a lashing crescent that cleaved against several of the anchored ships and set the *Conqueror* shuddering again. Lotara shivered in sympathy with her warship.

'What word from the surface?' she called out, and then added somewhat less hopefully, 'Has there been any communication from the primarch?'

Not that he has been capable of speech for some time. Nevertheless, hope forced the ludicrous question from her lips.

Again, the remaining crew replied without words. Several of them keyed in commands at their stations and a huge holo-projection of the Sanctum Imperialis flared into being in the air above the command deck. Runic signifiers showed the rough disposition of the Warmaster's forces. The horde was mustering before the walls of the final fortress.

The geography of the war's last front line was deceptively simple. That was good, because it was almost over, and Lotara was tired in every way it was possible to be tired. She ached to order the ship out of orbit, setting sail for the deep void and away from... from all this.

She could do it, couldn't she? Just raise her voice and–

The hololith screeched with visual static and realigned. She blinked and focused again on what lay before her.

The scratchy view of the wastelands before the Delphic Battlement showed hundreds of runic markers delineating warbands and regiments and groupings of the Warmaster's forces, a mess too disorganised for any cohesive identity. They mustered before the vast curtain wall surrounding the Sanctum Imperialis, encircling the Delphic Battlement and the final fortress that it protected.

The Sanctum Imperialis was void-shielded beyond mortal comprehension and machine-spirit cogitation (Lotara had casually tossed a few orbital volleys in that direction herself earlier on in the siege, out of frustrated curiosity) but it was weakest in the west. That's where the horde mustered in greatest numbers. In the west, the Delphic Archway was the wall's most heavily defended location – and its principal point of vulnerability. There, the fighting would be thickest, layered with defenders reinforcing the one grand opening in their final wall. There, the sweat of the defenders' desperation would be at its bitterest, and there, the blood would run deepest.

Once the horde overran the battlement – and they would, swiftly; Captain Sarrin hardly needed a tactical advisor to see that – the Royal Ascension lay open. It was a kilometre-long avenue, steadily rising on stairs large enough to accommodate the tread of Titans, leading to…

She watched it, shimmering on the hololith. There was the Eternity Gate, at the very end of the Royal Ascension: the doorway into the Emperor's castle. The Sanctum's walls couldn't be brought down. The gate could.

For now, it stood open, facilitating the movement of soldiers and materiel from the Sanctum to the battlement. When the enemy broke through the battlement, though… then it would seal closed, denying the horde.

The final doorway. After they tore the Eternity Gate from its hinges, it would be done. This miserable war would be over at last.

Lotara watched the simulations playing out, the runes dancing their logistical dances, playing out the final act of the Emperor's end. Some of the simulations took only hours to resolve to their inevitable conclusion, several took between one and three days, and one outlier took four. It didn't matter. The outcome never changed.

Close now, she thought. *So close.*

Out of the corner of her eye, she caught sight of Terra once more. It was something she tried to avoid, for every time she looked upon the cradle of humanity, she was confronted again by the fact it was dead.

Not dying. Dead. Even with access to the Mechanicum's fragmented mastery of Dark Age atmospheric processors and terraforming machine-cities, Terra was dead. There wasn't enough organic matter left to start a chain reaction of re-terraforming.

Whole regions would be soaked in radiation for centuries to come. The last ocean, which had already been little more than a shrinking sea after the resource wars of the Age of Strife and the Emperor's Unification, was now a jellied expanse of dust-thickened sludge.

Horus' war had destroyed Terra's last dubious claims of self-sufficiency. Lotara had reviewed the figures and images herself on a subscreen, with the aid of a Mechanicum adept, noting the millions of underground fungal farms and algae reservations that no longer existed, scrubbed from existence on every continent by bombardment or the invading hosts, no longer providing even a beggar's portion of the sustenance required by Terra's teeming population. From the moment the Emperor launched the Great Crusade, the Throneworld had fed desperately off the Imperium's new worlds. It devoured their resources with the geared jaws of the Imperial war machine, placating the citizens with glories while draining them to feed its ceaseless expansion.

But if the Imperium somehow survived the last days of this war, all pretence would be gone. The parasitic fever of Terra's malfunction would be laid bare. Terra would squat at the heart of its empire, a grey cancer feeding on sacrifice, drawing in food, water, iron, faith, hope... All of it, in an endless suction to feed a planet that wouldn't admit its time was done.

These were not pleasant thoughts.

She started cycling through intercepted transmissions, using the controls in the arm of her throne to scroll through the last few hours' worth of intelligence harvested from the surface by the *Conqueror*'s vox-leech systems. One of them, among the latest, was marked by a screed of Cthonian runes that caught her eye.

She keyed in the access code. The hololith flickered. Flashed. Changed. Resolved.

Now it gleamed an anaemic blue, even less substantial, and

within its misty layers, figures and faces formed. A great ring of figures comprising an ethereal conclave. It took Lotara several seconds to realise just what she was looking at.

She knew many of these warriors, if not personally then by sight and reputation. Fafnir Rann was there, as was Sigismund, both sparing precious minutes away from the defence of their respective bastions. They were ghosts of ghosts, holo-ing in to the gathering rather than being physically present. Others were slightly clearer: the crippled Captain Zephon stood with Captain Amit, in a loose line of Blood Angels leaders. Several Imperial Fists and White Scars commanders stood nearby, among a cluster of several hundred Imperial Army officers.

No one smiled. No jests were told. Everyone bore witness. In the gathering's very centre, the primarch Sanguinius oversaw a shifting, evolving map of the Inner Palace. The image of the Sanctum Imperialis Palatine District glowed with unsteady stoicism at the hololith's heart.

Lotara swore softly. They'd sliced into the very core of the defenders' transmissions. This had come from the keep atop the Delphic Battlement – it was the bloody war council at the last wall. She checked the archival data on her throne: it was scarcely half an hour old.

Fascinated, she watched as the map refined itself through pitches and zooms. Closing in on the Palatine Ring; the embattled bastions surrounding the Sanctum itself. Closing in further, splitting into cascading sub-images, bringing up the wastelands of rubble and corruption between the bastions, severing off and codifying embattled regions on the periphery, where significant Imperial forces still held out. And this was nothing of a bigger picture, barely a slice of a slice. How many millions of combatants were still fighting their own wars in the Outer Palace, and how many billions were spread across the rest of Terra, waging their own campaigns?

The scale of such considerations was beyond her – beyond anyone except perhaps the cogitational minds of the Warmaster and Rogal Dorn – but she found her thoughts drifting often to those far from the final fortress, engaged in their own life-and-death battles. Every one of those wars mattered as much as the assault on the Delphic Battlement, for every second they held out kept more of the Warmaster's forces from gathering at the final battle.

This was Dorn's final gambit. The Delphic Battlement was the Sanctum's curtain wall; if it fell, there was nothing left. The way was open for the Warmaster to stake his claim, to walk right up to the Eternity Gate.

'Captain Rann.' Sanguinius beckoned.

The image of Fafnir Rann addressed the conclave, as Bhab Bastion flared an aggravated, besieged orange on the projection table.

'My Lord Dorn believes we can hold Bhab for another seven to nine days, depending on variables that have no bearing at this council. He has charged me to answer your request, Lord Sanguinius – as matters stand, we cannot reinforce you. We are still encircled and cannot lift the siege.'

Sanguinius nodded. Plainly, to Lotara's eyes, he'd expected no less. 'Thank my brother for his candour, Captain Rann. And my thanks to you, for your report.'

'My Lord Dorn further requested that if you are able to send reinforcements to us in the defence of Bhab, that you do so at once, provided it does not endanger the Delphic Battlement.'

Sanguinius shook his head, his golden hair framing kindly, weary features. 'Even with the forces garrisoned here, we number scarcely seventy thousand. Every soul is needed on the wall. Tell my brother so, and offer him my regrets.'

'In the Emperor's name,' Rann replied, and made the sign of the aquila over his breastplate. His hololith flickered out.

The mountain of the Astronomican gleamed a muted white with its temporary reprieve, but it was practically alone in its purity. The image of the Dark Angel, Corswain, was a scratchy and indistinct ghost of a thing, the connection savaged by distance.

His news was no better for the defenders. They expected a renewal of the assault on their mountain fastness any hour now. Any diminishment of their thin forces would mean the loss of the Astronomican, reclaimed so recently, and with such unlikely fortune.

'Lord,' Corswain said directly to Sanguinius. 'I will ask you, nonetheless. Would you have us abandon the mountain and fight our way to you? If you order it, it shall be done.'

Sanguinius shook his head at the Dark Angel's offer. 'No, paladin. Hold the Astronomican at all costs. We need the beacon relit, for by your light will the Thirteenth Legion find its way home.'

Corswain gave a scratchy reply, his tone hesitant. 'Even if Lord Guilliman and the Thirteenth reached the system's edge this very hour, the Ultramarines would be too late to aid you.'

'Though we will fall here, nephew, reinforcements may yet arrive in time to aid the rest of you, ensnared in your own wars. If we are foremost in your thoughts, then light the beacon to honour our memory. There could be no more fitting funeral fire.'

Lotara swallowed at the resolve in the Great Angel's voice. At the acceptance. How noble he sounded, even in defeat.

Next was the Kishar Colosseum, endlessly reinforced by Rogal Dorn and used to house a tide of refugees from across the Inner Palace. On the map it gleamed a hopeless red. The Imperial Army colonel overseeing its defences gave his negative report while a field medic was bandaging his face. They expected to lose the last of their held ground by sunset tomorrow.

Sanguinius gestured to another officer, a human commanding

the Sarku-Lyat Concourse and its several hundred capillary avenues. Sarku-Lyat was a district once home to millions of souls fortunate (and wealthy) enough to live within the Inner Palace. Now it throbbed black, with the topographic scans of its surrounding landscape riven by the craters of unmatched devastation. It hadn't been orbital bombardment that annihilated the Sarku-Lyat District; it was the death of one of Horus' warships from before the Ultimate Wall even fell.

Lotara had watched it die; blasted from the sky, the XV Legion battleship *Royal Deshret* had plunged through the atmosphere, picked apart by the Palace's defensive aegis to no effect, smashing down and ending almost twenty million lives in the time it took to blink. More earthquakes. More dust. More of the blinding and deafening same, another punctuation mark in the death of the planet.

The Army officer in charge of the fighting around Sarku-Lyat's ruins couldn't maintain a clean vox-link to the council; she sent only a brief text missive citing that her forces had no way of leaving their entrenchments and reaching the Sanctum.

And on it went. Every bastion, every sector, every district of the Inner Palace was under siege, at the heart of their own wars. Most couldn't even muster a vox-link at all, and those that could begged for aid that couldn't come. The Sanctum had no way of answering any of their increasingly desperate calls for reinforcement.

The defenders were locked into place. The board was set for the last moves of the game. As she stared at them, wondering why they were there, she asked herself the very same thing.

Why was she here? Why were any of them here?

Why had she followed Horus and Angron into this war?

Ah, but it had all seemed so righteous at the time. It had all seemed so necessary. World after world heaving with unfair taxation. The Emperor losing control over the Great Crusade,

as adepts and ministers and bureaucrats began to assume
mantles of leadership across the emerging Imperium. Not
that Lotara or her primarch cared for the suffering worlds, but
Horus had. Horus was the best of them all. She was content
being an instrument of war. Her place was to serve, to hunt,
to kill. She was a blade to be wielded by righteous hands, and
no hands were more righteous than the Warmaster's.

Then the whispers had begun. Peace became more than a
laughably distant goal at the end of the Great Crusade – it
became a distinct possibility, then an inevitability: something
that the humans serving in the expeditionary fleets would actually live to see. What, then, of the Legiones Astartes? What use
was the perfect warrior in an age of peace? There was talk of
culling, of execution, even of extermination. The very warriors
that built the Imperium with boltgun and blade, the soldiers
Lotara had served alongside for all her adult life, grew rest-
less and uneasy. Word filtered through the crusade's scattered
fleets. Word of Terran plans, about betrayals, about treacheries
whose wheels were already in motion. Word of weaknesses
bred into the gene-seed. Word of a new, peaceful age requiring
no soldiers, no warriors, no sailors in the stars.

Then what of the mortals that fought by these warriors'
sides? Were they, too, stained? Coloured by association? Would
they be rewarded for their conquest of the galaxy, or pastured
off to exile worlds, there to die out in the void-black quiet
as the Imperium's secret shame over its bloody-handed past?
Would they be destroyed upon returning to Terra, blasted out
of the Throneworld's skies as their ships returned to humanity's cradle?

A similar dissolution had happened before. It was in the
archives. The armies of Unification, the Thunder Warriors,
the hosts that had conquered Terra in the Emperor's name.
Dead. Gone. Slaughtered at the Emperor's word, as reward

for their service to His crown. Reports of genetic instability
in the proto-Astartes conflicted with analyses that they had
been executed en masse by the Ten Thousand, the Emperor's
own Custodians.

No one knew what to believe about any of this. Lotara certainly didn't. And the Emperor, retired to Terra, refused to
enlighten any of those that begged Him for answers. To their
pleas for the truth, He returned only silence. Even when the
Warmaster beseeched Him for answers. Even His own son
earned only cold silence. What kind of man was ruling over
them? What kind of king abandoned His subjects instead of
guiding them with His rule?

For some, the years of these whispered pressures and out-
landish accusations was enough. Lotara hadn't needed much
convincing, truth be told. Taxations and plots of extermination
and whatever else – all of it had meant little to her.

The truth, the truth that Lotara could admit to herself as
she sat with her back to the wall, struggling to breathe in the
tainted air of her twisted warship, was that she'd sailed with
the Warmaster because she wanted to.

When Angron had declared for Horus, committing his
Legion against the Emperor, Lotara swallowed her quiet doubts
without much strife. What was she going to do? Praise the
name of a distant monarch and turn her back on the men
and women she'd bled alongside for her entire life? Abandon
command of her beloved *Conqueror* for the pathetic nobility
of swearing her allegiance to a failed Emperor?

Horus was the golden one, the general of generals, the Warmaster of the Imperium. Serving him was an honour, and to
be trusted by him with a rank such as hers was a pleasure that
defied words. For some, even that would be enough, but Lotara
chose to sail with his forces because her life was with them.
She lived and breathed for the warriors of the World Eaters

Legion. For years she'd bled alongside them, she'd guided them from orbit and laid waste to the worlds that defied them. She'd devoted her life to their principles and purpose. She respected them, she loved them, and she thrived in the respect they accorded her.

More than anything else, she trusted them.

Them. Not the Emperor. She trusted Khârn and Kargos and Angron and Horus himself. She trusted her own crew, and the other captains in her fleet. And if she were to die, let her die fighting beside those she loved and trusted. No finer fate than that, surely.

Surely, she thought with a weak exhalation. Unconvincing, even in the privacy of her own threadbare thoughts. *Surely*.

Terra turned out there, a brown-and-grey jewel of such dubious value now. Already dead, already choked by the poison of ambition, yet the warped void still clutched at the globe. As if there was anything left to strangle.

Her mind was drifting, a disassociation brought on by her weakness and dehydration. She knew it well, by now. Lotara swallowed through the thickness of her throat and forced her attention back to the hololith.

At the end of the ad-hoc council, there was no grand speech to motivate them. Sanguinius ordered the officers out onto the wall, to return to their forces. Maybe months ago these human defenders might have emanated an aura of unease, or even had the consumptive marks of fear showing on their faces, but the war had bleached them of such things. These were the survivors; the fortunate ones; the ones that had endured all else. They had seen and survived too much to shake in their boots now their back was to the final wall.

Something stirred inside her. Something atrophied and slow, entombed in the silty hole where her conscience used to be.

It should be pathetic, seeing them like this. They should

stink of desperation, trapped in their last besieged fortresses, all of them encircled by the Warmaster's horde, all of them slowly starving. It should be hilarious, listening to them beg each other for reinforcements that couldn't come.

But it's not.

How brave they looked, driven over the edge of exhaustion, yet still standing. Pressed back and back, forced to the very last walls, ready to stand and die for what they believed in. It didn't matter that the empire they were fighting for was a construct of lies and occluded truths; they'd endured half a year of horror and grinding onslaught and planetary death, in the name of loyalty. In that light, even their naivety was more tragic than laughable.

She had the sudden, fiercest urge to be there with them. Those exhausted, emaciated, doomed bastards. She wanted to stand with them, and...

And what? It's too late for regrets now.

Lotara shivered, and if the discomfort didn't quite pass, it at least faded. She found herself looking about for Khârn, but he was nowhere to be seen.

The fleetwide vox came to life a moment later, needing to awaken through protracted birth cries of static. The voice of Horus Lupercal crackled across the *Conqueror*'s bridge, as it echoed across every command deck in the armada. He spoke only six words, but for his loyal forces, it was the most they'd heard from the Warmaster in months.

'The final assault begins at dawn.'

TWENTY-FOUR

Lord of the Red Sands

Angron

He hunts. He hunts. He hunts.

The end is coming. This is a thing he knows, something real inside a mind sauteed in unreality. The end is coming. It is hours away, mere hours, though the concept of time in those terms is not something he understands as he once did. The end is coming soon though, he knows that, and so he hunts and hunts not just to sustain his strength but to stave off dissolution.

His flesh is no longer meat, and the metaphysical corpus that makes up his muscles no longer tires. His breath is no longer air, no longer a thing he draws in to speak and suspire. It's a sucking gust of blood-scent and ash-stink, and a heaving exhalation of the heat-mirage that dances above an open furnace. Weariness is a memory, dimmed as if a century has passed; something he can no longer conceive of, let alone feel.

And yet.

Dissolution pulls at him. In the moments he doesn't fight, in the heartbeat seconds he isn't hunting, he feels the atoms of his essence loosening. They threaten to fly apart, drifting away on the wind.

He accepts this. He doesn't know how this can be, but he accepts it, the way a child accepts their parents know best, the way a man or a woman accepts that they need to eat and breathe and sleep. It is the way of things.

There are quiet moments, though. More of them, lately. They strike him when he turns the bleeding spheres he has for eyes towards the walls of the final fortress. They come when he sees the angelic bodies in red ceramite scattered across the dead earth. In these moments, rare but not as rare as they once were, he knows that he wasn't always this way. Before he was this being, he was another. A weaker one, a creature limited by sinew and bone. A creature – *no; a man, I was a man, wasn't I?* – enslaved to a cycle of cranial pain.

But that was then, and this is now. He is no longer that being. He is no longer allowed to be that being. Something else, something as immense as a storm eating the entire sky, and still bigger, still *more*, won't let him be what he once was.

Insofar as he is capable of identity, he is the Lord of the Red Sands, an *it* as much as a *he* in what remains of his mind. These flashes of awareness linger long enough to tease an awakening, only to submerge into the boiling soup of his forethoughts. Back to the rage, back to the hunt, back to slaughtering to ward off dissolution.

He hunts. He hunts. He hunts. He falls from the sky upon convoys of refugees and reinforcements, cratering the ground in their midst and reaving through flesh and bone and iron and rock, flavouring the air with sprays of blood, darkening the ground with running life. Somehow, this is holy; he knows not how or why, only that it is. It's a prayer to a god he doesn't know at the heart of a faith he doesn't feel, and his massacres are prayers that rise to the highest heavens.

He knows the others, the weaker ones, need him for the last assault. Even this shredded realisation is more focus than he has possessed in an incalculable span. It is another change, another breath of difference as the end draws near. The weaker ones need him. Yes. Their voices rise in his honour, akin to prayers themselves.

And how strange that is. Even through the anger that comprises almost all he's allowed to feel, there's a strangeness in the way they exalt him, these mortal berserkers, the ones that call themselves his sons. The ones that seek the same peak he has reached. He cannot stay with them for long, though. He has to hunt. He has to rend and break and carve and kill. Each time he tries to remain in their mustering horde, the pain of dissolution begins to draw his form apart. Each time he has advanced on the final wall – *the Delphic Battlement, it is the Delphic Battlement* – he has slowed, weakened and staggered... The threat of dissolution becomes imminent, and some invisible repulsion keeps him back. It rakes the un-flesh away from whatever transmuted matter his bones have become. Screaming, he flees back to the hunt.

He cannot attack the final fortress. Not yet. His sons, in all their weakling corporeality, will have to take the wall. And then... and then...

Wings.

White wings.

An angel of gold.

Yes. Yes. What a death it will be. The shedding of such blood. The taste of it, burning upon the tongue. The strength of it, flowing through him. Stinking acid runs in stalactites of drool from his uneven maw at the promise of the angel's coming death.

Kill him.

Yes. He will. But he can't, not yet, not now.

Kill him for me.

The creature that was once Angron shakes its monstrous head, dreadlocks of poisonous technology rattling with the motion.

Kill him for me, Angron.

Who speaks? Who says these things, conjuring meaning inside the boiling stew of his thoughts? The daemon, the Lord of the Red Sands, always hears the melded and meaningless voices of its sons in its broken mind, but this is no child at the feet of its father. This is a command, a long-felt urge at last given voice.

The ground shakes as the daemon launches skyward. The air cracks with the rupture of the sound barrier.

Who speaks? He sees no likely soul in the sky, he sees no speaker on the teeming ground.

Kill him for me, Angron. Break him on the steps of the final fortress and throw open the Eternity Gate. I will deal with our father. All you must do is kill our brother.

These words feel... familiar. He has sensed them a thousand times, perhaps ten thousand, but only as part of the primal urge running through his bloodstream. Nevertheless, he knew them. He felt them. Now he hears them.

And in that moment of connection, as the speaker reaches out, Angron reaches back. It is not a gesture of love on the daemon's part, nor one of trust, but one of clawed caution. The Lord of the Red Sands reaches back, and it sees, and it knows the truth of the speaker's soul.

The speaker believes he is a man. He believes he is Angron's brother Horus. These things are not so. The speaker believes he is destined for a throne, and while the claim of a fated throne may be true, he is not a man, not anymore, and he is hardly even Horus. Angron was remade, the stuff of that primarch's molecules converted through transmutational, metaphysical fusion. But this man, this speaker, has undergone no such change. He has been hollowed out. He is a shell holding four essences: a puppet capering at the behest of four cosmic puppeteers. He is a lingering delusion of identity over a hole in reality.

Horus? thinks the Lord of the Red Sands. It is the daemon's first, purest thought in so very, very long.

+Yes, brother. The Emperor is weakening. Magnus wears away at the invisible shield. I make ready for my landing. It will not be long now. You are my herald, Angron. Lay waste to the Delphic Wall. Rip the white wings from Sanguinius' back and tear open the Eternity Gate. Kill the Angel and you will be sated. I promise you this.+

There is more, the voice says more, but the meaning fades away. It's lost again in the churning thresh that passes for Angron's cognition. The Lord of the Red Sands follows the currents of life that he can sense but not see and dives groundward – he hunts to feed both himself and the god of blood and war that he worships without realising.

It is another convoy, though he understands this only in the most basic sense that here is prey, and prey is to be hunted. The defenders fight him, seeking to drive him back with a storm of lascannon fire, volkite beams and a hail of bolts. This achieves nothing, but it hurts, and pain is a curious thing to an immortal. The Lord of the Red Sands feels pain just as a mortal does – no blade driving into his mutagenic flesh hurts any less than it would were he still a man – but he has an infinitely deeper well of endurance. His nerves fire, and the pain engine in his brain is kindled to shrieking life by such stimuli. But the pain never stops him the way it would overwhelm a living, reasoning being aware of the potential of its own destruction.

He sweeps left and right with his black blade, all previous mastery of weapons denied to him by his cognitive alterations and wholly irrelevant now anyway. His size and strength banish all need for duelling; swordplay is a concern beneath his baresark mind.

He hunts. He hunts. He hunts. To flee from him is to be cut down by the horde that surges in his shadow. To face him is to die.

Corporal Marlus Zeneer is thrown into the air, his lasrifle slipping from his grip. He sees his fate several seconds before plunging into it, and his body locks in screamless horror at the open jaws beneath him. Then everything is wet, red and searingly hot. Pliant walls clamp against him, crushing the breath from his body, snapping the bones of his shoulders. His arms, outstretched ahead of him and further down into the lightless black of Angron's throat, begin to dissolve in the corrosive slime coating the monster's gullet, and Zeneer is still alive, he isn't dead, the flesh of his arms is darkening and bubbling and popping and the pain is enough that his scream hits such a pitch, it becomes silent. All the while, he's sliding down into the blacker confines below, squeezed by the walls of the creature's body. Down he goes, into a mad god's reconstruction of a digestive tract, where the bones of men and women he knew well are waiting for him.

Corporal Marlus Zeneer has seven more seconds of unwanted life, finding himself in a cauldron of protoplasmic digestive juices. He sinks below the surface, comes up once as a shrieking red skull with the flesh sloughing from his bones, and then sinks a second time. This time, for good.

The Lord of the Red Sands is aware of this vile drama only in the sense of its own distracted satisfaction. Angron keeps hunting. Soon, the silent and unseen shield will come down. Soon, he will advance upon the Delphic Battlement. Until then, he hunts.

He hunts. He hunts. He hunts.

TWENTY-FIVE

Tomorrow, everyone is mortal

Zephon

Don't look up.

The order passed through the defenders, sometimes spoken, sometimes whispered. An order that was easy to give and impossible to follow. Whatever kaleidoscopic unrest had started in orbit was putting roots down into Terra's atmosphere. It affected the ash in the air, thinning it, sucking it up, discolouring what remained. It turned the thinned dust into a stinking mist of faint colours that had no names.

As the sky cleared to offer that hazy revelation of mother-of-pearl madness, the stars returned to the night-time heavens. With the return of the sky came a return of the horizon, and a wider view of the wasteland around the final fortress. For many of the defenders, ignorance had been bliss. The dust had occluded so much of the torture that Terra was undergoing, and masked the odds against the men and women that now massed on the last wall. Zephon felt their despondency as a physical thing, a miasma in the air. It weighed him down as he walked the ramparts.

The keep above the Delphic Archway was a nexus of weary industry. Armoury thralls laboured with hand tools, patching battleplate in dire need of replacement instead of mere repair. Servitors distributed crates of ammunition from the cache chambers established by Rogal Dorn in readiness for these last days. Hammers struck in ceaseless arrythmia. Welding torches crackled and sparked. Autoloaders clanked as shells were dragged through the guts and up into the throats of turrets. Ceramite warplate, once a proud cavalcade of reds, whites and yellows, was now medallioned with scars and greyed by smears of armour cement. Injuries were stitched, stapled and sealed behind bandages. Pain was banished by narcotic suppressives. Troops on the battlement checked and rechecked weapons, while above them, the sky undulated in the thrashing dance of a semi-sentient pantheon.

And, in quiet corners where loyal human defenders gathered out of sight of the Astartes, prayers were offered up to an absent God-Emperor.

Tomorrow, every soul capable of wielding a weapon would be on the wall.

Hundreds of Blood Angels, Imperial Fists and White Scars shared the space of what had once been a memorial to heroes of the Unification Wars. Now, it was filled to bursting with warriors undergoing final preparations, each one ringed by slaves and servitors. Every chamber and hall and corridor of the Delphic Keep heaved with similar activity, and it was mirrored all along the battlement itself, under the tortured sky. Most Legion officers were still in the keep, after gathering for Sanguinius to give them their last orders.

It was a strange feeling, to be surrounded by so many souls, yet to feel isolated from all of them. Everyone was at the very edge of exhaustion. Everyone was fighting their own war now. Orders and organisation meant very little. The two armies would lock together and grind each other down until one could no longer hold its ground. There was, the Blood Angel had to admit, a certain comfort in the barbaric simplicity of it all.

When it came time for his own preparations, he headed into the keep, where his thralls awaited him. Zephon stood with his head lowered, his arms outstretched. A common posture for Astartes to adopt while being armoured and attended, unknowingly mirroring the sacrificial symbolism of the ancient Catherics' nailed demigod. He said nothing as his thralls did their meticulous work, rinsing his clotted wounds with sterilised sponges, then machining his armour into place. They dressed him, plate by repatched plate, drilling the links into his body, binding the connection spikes with the black carapace implanted beneath his skin. Where he had no skin, where his bionics offered only Dark Age compound metals instead of flesh and bone, his armour was bound through adaptive magnetics and secondary sockets.

It was nothing his servants hadn't done a thousand times before. Their footsteps echoed softly in the chamber, their lowered voices made an undercurrent hum. Familiar sounds, familiar feelings. Even the sounds outside the chamber were unchanged from when these rituals had been performed in the past: the muffled din of other warriors being armed and armoured, the fainter grind of war machine engines and the earth-shaking rattle of Titan foot-treads, muted and muffled by distance.

This was the sound of war, no different from the gunfire and crashing of blades yet to come. This was the verse before the chorus.

Zephon listened to the war's familiar song, and to his thralls he looked no different than he ever did. They couldn't see inside his skull, where one new thought clung to the sides of his mind, spawning adjacent notions.

He was going to die.

Acceptance of one's death – the expectation of it and the preparation for it – was hardly alien to the Legiones Astartes mindset. They were a species born and remade to die in battle. Death in war was a certainty; the only doubt was on which battlefield they would take their final breaths.

But to know of death's certainty was one thing; to confront its imminence was another. He would die today, and if not today then tomorrow. Knowing the road of his existence was all but run brought curious clarity. He saw the crucial beats of his life's path again and again, playing out in his mind with a sense of introspective acceptance. No regret threatened to bubble up and swallow him, nor was there any sense of sorrow. He reflected upon the choices and deeds that had brought him here, not with melodramatic intensity but a sensation of naked analysis.

The truth is, I died long ago.

And not just one death. He'd died his first death when injury no longer let him serve in the Legion. A mental death, then – a death of the will and his sense of self. Then he'd died at Gorgon Bar, saving the interrogator Ceris Gonn. A physical death, the falling debris forcing him into suspended animation on the edge of mortality.

Neither death was in battle. Neither was glorious. Neither was worthy of remembrance. Now he lived again, resurrected both times by Arkhan Land, first with the gift of these rare bionics, then with the risk of reawakening from stasis, only days ago.

He did not know how he felt about any of this. Distractedly philosophical, he supposed.

As Shafia patched several fibre-bundle cables of armour musculature in place around one bicep, he caught sight of his reflection in her polished breastplate. It was the face of a Blood Angel; the face of all Blood Angels, but nothing in the visage carried a sense of personal identity. He looked at himself, at his own face, and saw just another one of a hundred thousand brothers.

That was the point, was it not? Unity in brotherhood. Unity through death, via the Revenant Legion's old traditions, still practised in the shadows by warriors that wore red armour now instead of grey.

Who was he? Was a man the sum of his actions? Was everyone merely the sum of their deeds and decisions? If so, he'd made precious few choices outside of battlefield strategy, anyway. He was as much a tool as a man, a weapon as much as a living being. And that made him a cold weapon indeed. That had always been enough. It was still enough. But here, at the very end, what curdled in his mind was the notion that he could have been any one of his brethren, in the very same moment, thinking the very same thoughts. That indivisibility had always seemed a strength and a source of unity – to be merely one of many moving parts in a machine of righteousness.

Now, it bred doubts. It felt not like unity, but homogeneity. A waste, even. Zephon had lived his entire life down to these last hours, but what separated him from any of his brothers? What made him *him*?

He stared at his distorted reflection in Shafia's breastplate, knowing that somewhere in that angelic visage was the face of the boy he'd once been, and the man he'd never been allowed to become. But he couldn't see either one. Not even hints of them.

Amit.

The thought rose unbidden, but he followed its course.

Lifting his head, he watched Amit across the chamber, also being armoured by thralls. There was his brother, a brother of the same rank, a man wearing the same face as his own. Amit's skin was darker than his, and the differences were always evident in the scars: no warrior carried the exact same war markings as any of his brethren. Furthermore, Amit's head was shaven, and though Zephon had ordered his thralls to cut his once-long locks, he still kept a dark fall of it. Still, like most Blood Angels, they could have been twins.

Amit always seemed so *alive* to him. Even now, as Nassir stood in silent contemplation, the other captain radiated a presence beyond that of a warrior and an officer. Amit had habits; he clenched his teeth when annoyed, he grunted when bored, and tilted his head to crackle the vertebrae in his neck during long briefings. His eyes were often tense with restrained temper. Amit was his own being as well as a Blood Angel, defying the Legiones Astartes template in a way Zephon suspected he himself had not.

'Please lift your arm higher, lord,' said Eristes.

He did so, letting the ageing servant drill and lock a flex-weave underplate into place along his triceps brachii. Not long now. The call to battle would come, banishing these useless musings. Zephon realised he was breathing slower, louder, through his parted teeth. Feeling the beginnings of battle-urge, the ache in his gums that spoke of blood-need. His thralls tensed. The scent of their skin became acrid with fear. The warrior saw them share glances among themselves.

'I'm not irritated with you,' he said, attempting reassurance.

They didn't ask for further clarification. They knew better. Their bond with their master hadn't encouraged breaches in protocol or decorum like speaking while they attended him.

But Zephon surprised them again, keeping his voice low. 'I see you've been armed.'

Three lasrifles rested on a nearby crate, each with a bayonet, each with a companion pistol, holsters and leather webbing. They were standard issue, battered enough that their histories showed plain: lifted from the dead and redistributed to the living.

'Have you been instructed in how to use those weapons?' he asked.

'We're familiar, lord,' Shafia replied. 'The Legion has trained us extensively over the years.'

'I see.' He knew next to nothing of their lives outside of their direct service to him. As far as he'd been concerned, they effectively ceased to exist outside his sight. 'I was not aware.'

'It's fine, lord. There's no reason you would pay heed to such things.'

But Zephon kept watching them, fascinated for the first time by the three souls that served him. How old Shafia and Eristes looked, now. How much Shenkai resembled both of his parents. He'd first seen Shenkai as an adolescent, a skinny rake of a boy entering into his service as his parents' apprentice after years spent in the flagship's thrall creches. Before that, he'd known Shafia was pregnant, but cared only insofar as it might affect her duties. To her credit, it hadn't. Thus, Zephon had never needed to offer comment or make a note of any failings. After that, there had been a boy trailing them around sometimes. But that was all. He knew little about the child. He'd never cared to ask.

Eristes and Shafia had been in his service for decades. And before them, it had been Ghiu and Shen-Ru-Lai, Eristes' parents. How time turned.

'I will arrange for the three of you to be with the fallback forces, retreating to the Sanctum.'

It was a pathetic offer, granting them only a few more hours of life, and Zephon's skin crawled at the uselessness of it.

Once the Delphic Battlement fell, the Sanctum would fall too, before the day was done. Hardly much of a gift, yet it was all he could give them.

'I don't want to cower behind the Eternity Gate, lord,' Shenkai said, his tone edged with what Zephon believed was offence. 'I don't want to hide.'

'We will die on the wall,' said Eristes. 'With you.'

'And with the Great Angel,' Shafia added.

He hadn't expected such courage, and he was honoured by their loyalty. Even so, he wondered if their hearts were truly as set as they seemed. Would Shafia and Eristes not want their son to taste just a few more hours of life, if he had the chance? Or were they proud of him, for committing to this death?

He didn't have the answer and didn't want to ask the question. It shamed him, to realise how little he knew of them.

'I apologise for offering nothing but disinterest in your lives. That was churlish of me.'

More discomfort. They were not used to this, and made no reply to it. Now both sides of the halting conversation were lost as to how to continue. Shafia and Eristes lifted his left gauntlet into place, drilling in the connection needles, moving together with the grace of decades of expertise. This task was more than familiar to them, it was a matter of lifelong ritual. He shifted himself, in a moment of rare awkwardness, only for Shenkai to breathe softly in irritation where he stood behind Zephon. The thrall was dressing his hair and binding it tightly for his helmet.

'Please don't move, lord,' Shenkai said. Zephon could practically hear the young man trying not to sigh.

Zephon remained still.

'I will likely die tomorrow,' he admitted. 'And thoughts are occurring to me that I might never have otherwise considered. You have been excellent servants. Thank you for your loyalty to me, all these years.'

Another of those fleeting hesitations flashed between the three of them. They kept working, but Zephon was aware of certain betrayals in their bearing: the tiny hairs on Shafia's arms rising, the sound of Shenkai swallowing, the way Eristes' lips pressed together, deepening the lines at the edges of his mouth. Human things. Instinctive signals of discomfiture.

'Thank you, lord,' said Eristes, after drill-locking one of Zephon's vambraces into place. The warrior couldn't quite read the expressions on his thralls' faces. The only obvious element was their uneasiness with the course of the conversation.

As they lifted his breastplate into place, he said, 'Stay close to me, when the fight begins. I will keep you alive as long as I can.'

He couldn't see Shenkai's expression, but he could hear the way emotion thickened the young man's voice.

'Focus on the enemy, lord, and we'll keep you alive as long as *we* can.'

In the face of this loyal naivety, Zephon found he had no decent reply. He let them armour him the rest of the way in silence, listening to the music of blood beating through their bodies. Soldiers and civilians and servitors passed by in their hundreds, going about the business of preparation.

'Zephon?'

He lifted his head again, needing a moment to pick out the speaker in the milling crowd. She wore patchwork armour and carried a battered lasrifle slung over one shoulder. Like everyone, she was a shadow of herself, ruined by the war – and like everyone still alive in the war's final hours, there was something unbreakable in her eyes.

'Are you Zephon?'

'They have ranged the main line,' Zephon said softly, the words sending a chill through him. His thralls slowed in their work, knowing those words well. They glanced at the source of their master's sudden awe.

'You're Zephon, aren't you?'

The Blood Angel nodded. 'I am.'

The woman approached and, miraculously, she smiled. A tired smile but a smile nonetheless, here of all places.

'I thought it was you. You all look the same, but you have...' She held up her gloved hands, opening and closing them, alluding to the Blood Angel's silver bionics.

He looked down at the woman with the stringy hair and face marked with grime, knowing her from their first and only meeting, months ago at Gorgon Bar. How he had ordered her off the wall before the artillery onslaught began. How he had pulled her against his chest and shielded her when the walls came down.

'Greetings, Ceris Gonn.'

'They told me you were dead. Or as close to dead as to make no difference. I accompanied your body to Razavi Bastion, you know. Months ago.'

'I did not know that.' The gesture touched him in a way he couldn't quite put into words. 'That was kind of you.'

'Once we got there, they took you for stasis and sent me away. Then, later, I heard you'd survived. I was sure it was just another stupid war story. Another mistake amidst, well, everything else.'

'Astartes physiology means that both are technically true. I was dead, and yet I live.' The keep shook around them. Dust clattered against the Blood Angel's pauldron. 'I am gratified to see you also survived Gorgon Bar.'

'Thanks to you.' Ceris reached up to touch his face. There was no sensuality in the gesture, it was a matter of careful examination. She followed the lines of his cheeks and jaw with her gloved fingertips, the digits dark against the white flesh.

'I never saw your face. And you *do* look like the others. But you're paler. I can just about see the veins beneath your cheeks… and your eyes are lighter. You look gentler than some of the others.'

'I assure you, I am not.'

'I'll take your word for it.'

She was far more confident than he remembered of the wayward archivist from Lord Dorn's new Interrogator Order. Ceris sensed his unease at being touched, and withdrew with another faint smile.

'I'm assigned to the Sanctum, embedded with the Third Zoharin Rifles.' Ceris cast a look over her shoulder, where several Imperial soldiers waited with varying degrees of impatience. 'I just… I had to say thank you. You saved my life. And don't say it was nothing, because it was definitely something.'

'You are welcome, Ceris.' He didn't know what else to say. Awkwardly he added, 'Truly. I'm glad you are alive.'

For another few days, at least, he carefully neglected to add.

Plainly she was aware of his clumsiness in such a moment. She took her leave rather than prolong it.

'May the God-Emperor watch over you, Zephon.'

He tilted his head at the phrase, but in an echo of all that her rank would come to mean in the following millennia, her tone brooked no disagreement. She left him with his thralls, looking back over her shoulder once more as she walked away.

He never saw her again.

He found Arkhan Land on the ramparts. The Martian had somehow worked his usual antisocial magic, occupying a section of the wall where few others seemed inclined to linger. Zephon weaved through the edge of the closest crowd, approaching Land's pocket of isolation, apologising to the Imperial Army soldiers as they shifted from his path. There, they stood together, saying nothing. Just looking out across the wasteland.

It was night, but that was relative. Day and night both looked like violet dusk.

The sky everyone tried not to stare at was riven by electro-magnetic disturbance, dancing aurorae made from the warp-stained heavens and reflected firelight from a thousand separate wars on the world's surface. Zephon had seen the atmospheric disturbances caused by massive orbiting fleets in the past, and this was not that. Low to the horizon, where he gazed at the distant horde now circling the Sanctum, he could see shapes, nebulous in form and godlike in scale, clawing and thrashing their way through the clouds. The last time he had looked directly upward, the skull of something almost human, the size of half the sky, rolled in the stormy black. Its mandible had been articulated with tendons of smoky cloud. Muted stars gleamed sickly in its empty sockets. Then it was gone, rolling tidally, melting into the thunderheads. Zephon hadn't waited to see what might take its place.

A skitarii soldier stood at the technoarchaeologist's side. She, too, said nothing. Zephon didn't know if that was because she had nothing to say, or because she was one of those who were unable to speak. It seemed to him that most were made that way. Sapien, the artificimian, perched on her shoulder guard. It was idly running its bizarrely human fingers across scratches in the skitarius' helmet, as if mapping them.

He greeted the psyber-monkey with one of the clicking sounds it sometimes made. Sapien regarded him for a moment, repeat-ing the sound, before continuing its appraisal of the skitarius' helmet.

A Titan made its way past, one of the god-engines walking its patrol in front of the wall. An Ignatum machine, its red-and-yellow heraldry excoriated by months of battle and the filth in the air. The ground shivered in sympathy with its slow tread. Power cables hung from its armour joints like stringy veins. Gun arms that could level habitation towers groaned under their own weight, on war-weakened shoulders.

Iracundos, read the name on its carapace, emblazoned there in corroded bronze. It looked as exhausted as the mortals in its shadow. And, somehow, as impatient.

Zephon lifted his gaze from the Titan, looking down the wall – first left, then right. Taking in the regiments at the ready, the depleted squads of Astartes scattered amidst them in splashes of battle-faded colour, and the rarer patches of gold marking the last survivors of the Sisters of Silence and the Custodian Guard.

To Zephon's eyes, the Delphic Battlement was a hideous thing. A monument to compromise, jury-rigged into a state of ugliness by the pressure of necessity. Before the war, it had been purely decorative. A curtain wall of shining marble surrounding the Emperor's grand castle, set a mere kilometre from the Inner Sanctum's pristine, spired sides.

When predicting what shape the war would take when it reached this point, Dorn had done all he could to gird the last defenders against the horde descending upon them. Fail-safe after fail-safe was in place. The wall was honeycombed with defensive turrets, reinforced with layer upon layer of plasteel and rockcrete, turned into a rampart manned by over a hundred thousand defenders stationed around the Inner Sanctum. Custodians. Sisters of Silence. Blood Angels. White Scars. Imperial Fists. Imperial Army soldiers. Refugees. Civilians. All of them, shoulder to shoulder, standing in the shadows of the Titans watching over them.

Batteries of anti-air guns lined the wall tops. Titan-cradles set into the Delphic Wall housed the god-machines of Legio Ignatum and stood shielded by thick voids, ready to repair their charges once the Titans strode home. Landing pads dotted the ramparts' surface, where gunships and low-altitude fighters fuelled up and underwent final preparations. A complex order of machine-spirits, physically built into the wall's most reinforced sections, oversaw the anti-artillery gun web: outputting a constantly updating data-spray that commanded the movements of thousands of defensive batteries and refractor field projectors. The Delphic Battlement stood ready to intercept any incoming fire, whether solid shot or in the form of screaming energy. Added to this, the expressly outfitted Warmonger Titan *Malax Meridius* walked behind the defenders, patrolling the span between the Sanctum and the battlement, its weapon systems aiming outward, its purpose to shoot down any craft or incendiary that somehow eluded the Delphic batteries.

As magnificent as this sounded, Zephon wasn't blind to the reality of what they faced. The horde soon to descend upon them would sweep through this mighty gathering in mere hours. There were too few defenders, and too many of the enemy, for it to go any other way.

The weakness was the arch. The Delphic Archway, the battlement over the Grand Processional, hadn't been built with considerations of defence. It was planned for parades of soldiers and Titans to march along the Processional, under the arch and through the Delphic Battlement, proceeding along the rising avenue of the Royal Ascension. There had been no gate to close, no barricade to raise. For decades, it was an open mouth leading right to the Eternity Gate.

During Terra's preparations, Dorn had commanded his warrior-engineers to install layered portcullises to block the Processional, reinforce and shield them to the limits of the Mechanicus' ingenuity, then construct a fortified keep on the archway above. This keep was little more than a weapons platform, a cathedral dedicated to the death of enemy Titans.

The Warmaster's horde would assault the wall from every

direction, but the fighting would be thickest here, where the battlement was weakest around its newly armoured arch. The defenders had garrisoned the lion's share of their strength in readiness. Even the approach to the wall would carve the horde apart, with minefields and artillery and defensive turrets all turned towards annihilating anything coming up the Grand Processional. Tens of thousands of the invaders would die before they ever reached the first portcullis, and two more waited behind the first, each one of them six metres thick, each one forcing a killing ground where the defenders could pour fire and scorn down as the attackers sought to breach the barriers, one after the other.

Zephon gazed from the wall to the wasteland beyond. The ground was turning sour. As if the land being dead wasn't enough, it was darkening with corruption, twisted into jagged promontories and earthen spikes. Bombardment craters were becoming pools of steaming organic sludge. To look upon it hurt the eyes, the way it made your skull throb to gaze into the warp while in void transit.

How could they fight for such a thing? Zephon wondered, staring at the horde gathering at the horizon. *How could they want this?*

Because they believe it's necessary. He answered his own question, knowing it must be true without understanding how it possibly could be. *What have they learned, what have they seen, to believe all of this is necessary?*

The silhouettes of Titans towered above the invaders' lines. They were bringing more up through the broken Ultimate Wall every hour, gathering for the final assault like a pantheon of hunchback gods. Dorn had done well to restrain himself, maintaining so much of Ignatum's strength around the Sanctum in readiness for these last days, but even the god-engines in Martian red that walked beside the Delphic

Battlement were already outnumbered. As for the Titans that stood in vigil above the horde... They cast strange silhouettes, their spines bent into new postures, their heads showing faces of malformed, incomprehensible significance. Some of them looked to be made of as much flesh and bone as sacred iron. Others leered as they watched the wall; even at this distance, they radiated an aura that felt sickeningly feral.

And above them, the night sky...

Don't look up.

He returned his gaze low, beneath the horizon.

Zephon voiced none of these thoughts to Land. There was comfort in the quiet presence of someone who was, if not a friend, then at least a compatriot. He and Land were bonded in a way largely unrelated to war, and in the Blood Angel's life that was a rare thing indeed. He treasured it, even if Arkhan was a singularly difficult man to love.

'You're doing it again,' Land said with a sneer.

Zephon leaned on the battlement wall, resting his gauntleted hands on a merlon. 'I do not know what you mean.'

Land narrowed his eyes, which were squinty little holes in his face at the best of times. His cracked goggles were lifted up, resting on his sweaty forehead.

'You're staring out at the world with that look of pitiful soulfulness. It's tiresome, Zephon, it really is. How *earnest* you are. How *sincere*. You're practically avataric for your melodramatic Legion, and let me tell you, it wearies me more than the fighting does.'

'Ah.' The Blood Angel nodded. 'Forgive me, my friend.'

'You see? There it is again. Not "I'm sorry, Arkhan," but "Forgive me, my friend." You were bad enough before Gorgon Bar, but since awakening in the Razavi Bastion...' Land trailed off, emitting a considering *hmmm* that lasted several seconds.

Zephon raised an eyebrow, waiting.

'You're like you used to be, only more so. Calmer. Stiller. It's unnerving, you know.'

'I have no idea what you mean.' Though Zephon wondered, as he said the words, whether they were true.

'You realise you're not the only Blood Angel I've spoken to in the last year? I've heard the tales of the Bringer of Sorrow. How hot-blooded you were. The temper, the aggression. When we met, you were miserable over your crippling, and your dulled emotional responses were clearly the result of depressive brain chemistry. But now...'

Land trailed off again, giving another long *hmmm*.

'Whatever. It's of no concern to me. Why can't you just spit at us lowly mortals like Amit does and kick us out of the way, like we're dogs that don't move fast enough for him?'

Zephon almost smiled. 'You exaggerate my brother Amit's bluntness.'

'I'm not exaggerating, and you know I'm not.' The Martian looked away, gesturing to the wasteland stretching out to the dusty horizon.

'We're going to die tomorrow, aren't we?'

Zephon wasn't sure what to say, which was strange, because there was really only one thing to say.

'Yes. If not tomorrow, then within the next day or two. I fear you are correct.'

'I am always correct,' Land retorted. 'But what's this? You *fear* I'm correct? I thought your kind knew no fear.'

His thralls had bound Zephon's long hair back from his face, but he brushed a stray wisp off his temple. He kept gazing at the blurred silhouettes, far away in the ash. The horde was out of the range of the wall guns for now, but within every defender's head was a silent countdown.

'We know fear,' Zephon said softly. 'We are merely conditioned to overcome it.'

Another silence descended. It was relative; even on their section of the wall there were other soldiers talking nearby, gun turrets panning, the wind blowing, and the thunder of artillery echoing eerily from across the besieged continent. But between the three of them gathered there in that moment – four, if you counted Sapien, which Zephon always did – it was a pregnant wordlessness.

Land finally turned to him. Zephon could see avidity in the man's glare.

'Will this degree of honesty be in the Ninth's speech tomorrow?'

'Lord Sanguinius,' Zephon corrected gently. 'And it is my father's place to say what he wishes to say, not mine to guess and offer his words in advance. Have you ever heard the primarch give a speech?'

Arkhan Land grunted non-committally.

'It is never what you expect it to be. He does not act the way other primarchs act, nor think the way they think.'

'From your tone, this is clearly a source of great pride to you.' Land sounded suddenly tired. 'Why are you here, Zephon? What is it you want from me?'

The Blood Angel tilted his head, regarding the diminutive Martian with infinite patience. 'I will be fighting with the remnants of my former company, the High Host.'

'Yes, yes, how thrilling for you. And this involves me, how?'

'Many of our thralls will be with us in a secondary detachment. I came to ask if you would fight with Eristes, Shafia and Shenkai, close by my side.'

'Is that it?' Land snorted with typical bluster. 'Well, if you want. They were tolerable enough when last we met, and one place on this wall is as good as any other.'

'I mean it, Arkhan. Do you agree to stand with them? To protect them?'

'Yes, yes, yes. Stop nagging.'

Zephon thanked him.

'Is that it?' Land repeated. 'Is that all you wanted? I suppose you're heading off now.'

'Do you... wish me to stay?'

Land swallowed. It sounded as though there was something in his throat.

'I don't want to die, Zephon.'

The Blood Angel was about to reply, anticipating the Martian's sneer, when the old man suddenly burst into tears. Taken completely by surprise, the Blood Angel hesitated a moment before going down to one knee, bringing him close to Land's height. He didn't touch the human. He knew Land hated to be touched.

'I'm too important.' Land sobbed the words, turning them thick with backed-up emotion. 'I have so much yet to rediscover, all those secrets of the Dark Age. I have so much yet to give. So many things I remain uncredited for.'

Zephon resisted the urge to sigh. How foolish of him to believe this was an outpouring of anything but more vanity.

The skitarius standing nearby watched in spindly silence, neither awkward nor emotional. Then *it* touched Land, resting a metal hand on the Martian's shoulder. Amazingly, Land patted its iron fingers in gentle acceptance. Zephon could barely believe what he was seeing. The psyber-monkey, which had been crouching complacently on the skitarius' shoulder, now hopped onto Land's back, and gently trilled at its master.

Arkhan Land raised red, strained eyes to the Blood Angel.

'I'm scared.'

'To feel fear is to be human. I would think less of you if you were not afraid, Arkhan.'

'Some people spend their lives flinging genetic material at each other, spawning nasty little half-clones of themselves. And how proud they are, as if it were an achievement to have children, to perform the basest biological function. Their heirs are what they pass on to the future. They take comfort in that. Not me, though. I have the Quest for Knowledge. I have my rediscoveries. Everyone in the Imperium would one day know my name. That's how it was supposed to be. It wasn't supposed to end here, like this. Not with that black tide of horror descending upon me.'

Zephon tentatively offered his hand.

'Don't touch me!' Arkhan snapped, and the Blood Angel withdrew. 'What's going to happen tomorrow, Zephon? Do you know?'

Zephon doubted Land desired a complete tactical delineation. Besides, what was going to happen was ultimately simple.

'They will come at the Delphic Battlement with everything they have, focusing their assault on the archway. As soon as they breach the arch or overrun the wall, the fighting will break down into pockets of conflict, reinforced by both sides. They will fight to establish footholds, we will fight to push them back before they can take permanent ground. When the wall falls, the nominated rearguard forces will sell their lives to keep them from advancing into the Sanctum for as long as we can. The exception in the withdrawal will be the Custodians. Some of them will stand with us on the wall, but many will remain inside the Sanctum on guard against unexpected intrusion. When we lose the Delphic Battlement, which will happen between one and three days of fighting, any survivors will have a slim opportunity to wage a fighting retreat along the Royal Ascension. But before the enemy can reach the Sanctum, Lord Sanguinius and the Custodes will seal the Eternity Gate.'

Land stared at him with an expression blending suspicion and unease. 'Is that a jest?'

'No?' Zephon hesitated, half-asking in his confusion. 'Nothing I have said seems particularly amusing.'

'They will abandon us outside?'

Sometimes, Zephon could not understand how a man of Arkhan Land's undeniable genius could be so lacking in insight.

'We stand upon the walls of the Emperor's final fortress. There is no retreating from here. Yes, the Custodian Guard will return to the Emperor's side, to die with their lord, but not until all is lost here on the wall. We will hold the Eternity Gate open as long as humanly possible, but the Delphic Battlement is the last true line of defence. Here, we can mass in numbers capable of repelling assault for several days, if all goes optimally well. Here, we hold one of the most defensible positions on Terra. Here, there remains the faint hope of reinforcement reaching us from elsewhere. All those advantages vanish the moment the enemy reaches the Eternity Gate. No tactics. No strategy. No hope. Inside the Sanctum, the fighting will be room by room, chamber by chamber, with warp entities free to manifest at their own whim. It will be a massacre.'

Land no longer had tears in his eyes. He looked up at Zephon, his face showing a sort of bleak, detached horror. Here was a man who could untangle enigmas of the Dark Age of Technology that had driven men and women mad, and who had led expeditions into the trapped tombs of unknowable machine-kingdoms... But Zephon's calm description of the coming battle drained the blood from his skinny face.

'There's more,' he said. 'There's something you're not saying, I can see it in your eyes.'

Zephon had taken no pleasure in what he had relayed so far, nor did he delight in what he said next.

'While we hold the Sanctum, we are ready for whatever they will bring. But I believe that before it begins, they will try to damage our morale. They cannot break our spirits, but they can wound our resolve and blind us with anger.'

Land shared a glance with his new skitarii companion, who

emitted a coded bleat of skit-speech, then he looked up at Zephon once more.

'She asks what you mean by that.'

'I do not wish to speak of it, Arkhan, in case I am mistaken. I hope that I'm wrong.' Zephon looked across the wasteland, towards the gathering horde. 'But if I am right, you will see at dawn.'

Land stared at him again. And, again, the Blood Angel found he had no idea what conversational gambit the old man would try next. The skitarius was watching him as well, her stare hidden by a buzzing, recently repaired monovisor across her dented helmet. He could read nothing of her mind; whatever her thoughts and feelings might be would likely forever remain a mystery. At least to him.

'Tell me, Zephon. Just tell me. Are you scared?'

What should he say in such a moment? Should he be Astartes: resolute to the very end, the rock upon which the enemy wave would break? Surely that would inspire the defenders, that level of implacable fortitude. Surely that was his role as a legionary in these last days?

Or should he be human? A transhuman, true, but still with elements of humanity. Should he confess to emotions that the warriors of the Legions might not ever confess, or had trained themselves not to feel?

The answer came to him, bare in its obviousness. He would be a Blood Angel. Anything else would be artifice.

'Yes,' he admitted. 'I am afraid.'

Land stared at him, unblinking. 'Afraid of dying?'

'Yes and no,' Zephon admitted. 'I am not frightened by the thought of the blade or bolt that will end my life. I am not afraid of the pain to come, nor of the nothingness that comes after it. But there will be a physical element when the horde advances upon us. My hearts will beat harder, my mouth will go dry, and I will want to run. There will be a flicker within me, that human instinct within the transhuman conditioning, to fall back and preserve my existence. I will feel it, but I will not give in to it. When they say of us that we *know no fear*, it is because that is the way it seems to those watching us. But we feel fear. We simply do not surrender to it. We do not let it affect our actions. In that respect, we are not fearless, merely brave.'

Land seemed to consider this. 'I think, if you'd told me that all you feared was failure, or dying with your duty undone, I might have vomited.'

Zephon surprised himself by grinning. 'Would that be too poetic?'

'No, it would be too much like groxshit.' Land brushed some of the settling ash from his bald pate. 'Besides, it's easy to be brave when you're practically immortal.'

Zephon couldn't argue with that, and didn't try. 'That is a factor, yes. But I will die tomorrow regardless of Legiones Astartes genetics. In that regard, I am as mortal as you and all of these courageous souls standing with us on the wall.'

The Martian stared at him, trying to see something within the Blood Angel's face. The gaze lasted a disconcertingly long time.

'You really believe that, don't you? That deep down you're just like us.'

Zephon said nothing. He'd made his case; it stood for itself.

'Let me tell you, my Baalian friend, exactly how wrong you are.' Land gestured to the both of them. 'The difference between you and me – the difference between my kind and your kind – is that we live, and you exist. When we die, the galaxy loses all our dreams and hopes and ambitions. All we might have achieved is sucked out of existence, never to come to pass. Children aren't born. Discoveries aren't made.

Inventions aren't invented. When someone dies, even one of
the puling masses destined for extraordinarily little achievement in their lives, it's an immense loss of potential. And that
is tragic, because tragedy is defined by loss. But you?

'You are a weapon. You were made for battle, and have neither
a fate nor a future outside of war. Will you die tomorrow? Probably. You'll die doing exactly what you were made to do, dying
in exactly the way you were made to die. What are your dreams,
Zephon? What life do you live off the battlefield? What do you
contribute to the species except the furtherance of its territory
with your ability to shed enemy blood?

'When your kind dies, Astartes – and let's not forget that
it's the fault of your kind that half the galaxy is aflame – but
when your kind dies, it's no different from the shattering of a
sword. No dreams are lost. No fates are altered. Just a weapon
breaking while doing what it was made to do.

'And that's why you have no right to your fear, Blood Angel.
Death means so little to you. Compared to us, you have nothing
to lose.'

There was no longer any mirth, bleak or otherwise, in Zephon's eyes. There was nothing. His features were bleached of
even the shreds of personality Land had thus far credited him
with, and what remained was the angelic template, rendering
him indivisible from any other warrior of his Legion.

Zephon thought on just what to say, or if it was worth
saying anything at all. Their association to this point had been
defined by exchanges in this vein – the cut and thrust of Land's
understandable disgust with genetic transhumanity; Zephon's
jocular and sympathetic rebuttals. But now, the Blood Angel
reassessed the depths of Arkhan Land's hatred and found he
lacked an adequate answer.

Because he's right. The thought, insidious and fierce, clung
tight to the insides of his skull.

Land had already turned away, uninterested in whatever Zephon might say in reply. The Blood Angel's armoured hand rested, with gentle but absolute strength, on the old man's shoulder.

'Don't touch m–'

'Shut up, Arkhan. Just this once, please shut up.'

Land blinked. Surprise knocked him speechless, which was a rare treat indeed.

'It may be that you are right. What you've said is nothing I've not considered myself, a hundred times before. But I want your promise that tomorrow, you will forgo your usual cowardice. You will discard the self-interest that you disguise as good sense, and you will stand with Shafia, Eristes and Shenkai. I can tolerate your hatred, your spite and your endless barbs, but I will not forgive cowardice tomorrow. Mark these words, my friend... If I learn that you've left them to face harm after agreeing to stand with them, I will find you wherever you're hiding, doubtless soaked in the perfume of your own piss, and I will kill you.'

Land gaped at him.

'I will beat you to death with my bare hands, Arkhan. With the very hands you gave me. Do you hear me? Do you understand?'

Land nodded.

'Good.' Zephon released him. 'Now get some sleep if you are able. It will help. And don't look up.'

He walked away, leaving Land to flush red beneath the gazes of nearby soldiers. The last thing the Blood Angel heard from Land was an affirmation from the Martian to his skitarius companion:

'He has changed.'

TWENTY-SIX

A curious choice of emissary

Transacta-7Y1

When the dawn alarm sounded across the Delphic Battlement, the skitarius lifted her new rifle by the strap and rose to her iron feet. She hadn't been sleeping, exactly – that was a luxury her creators had denied to her, in the strictest sense – just lightly dozing with her back to the merlons. Hundreds of soldiers nearby did as she did, reaching for weapons and breaking free of any shallow attempts at slumber. Arkhan Land grumbled, still wrapped in his threadbare cloak, refusing to stand up from where he huddled on the marble floor. Sapien was far more eager. The artificimian leapt to her shoulder, chittering his bastardised utterances of skit-code.

Transacta-7Y1 replied in her own code, adjacent to the creature's own but flavoured by the slang of her own macroclade, that yes, she would endeavour to keep him safe. Sapien expressed a coded desire that she remain alive if she were able to do so. In return, she expressed that surviving would be a most agreeable course of action, but that it didn't look likely, did it?

The psyber-monkey narrowed its machine eyes as it processed what had amassed on the horizon. After a moment, Sapien confirmed that no, survival did not seem likely at all.

Transacta-7Y1 looked up briefly, in defiance of the standing order. The heavens, perceivable only intermittently through the ash, undulated with aurora borealis tendrils of queasy light. It looked as though Terra's magnetic field had cancer.

'Is it starting?' Land asked from where he hunched.

Transacta-7Y1 confirmed that it was.

Fear widened Land's eyes, but it was a fear tempered by the one thing that could always overcome even the basest emotion. Exhaustion overrides all else, the body and mind only have so much to give – and Arkhan Land already looked halfway to death. After almost a year of this madness, day and night, dawn to dusk; after choking on ash and dust for months; after falling back again and again from burning strongholds and fleeing from the advancing horde; after fighting blind in ruins and attending hundreds of war councils that were all steeped in the taste of oncoming failure; after giving every iota of strength he possessed purely in the pursuit of staying alive while Terra burned around him... He was shattered by weariness. With nowhere left to run, he was too tired to be afraid anymore.

He was not alone in this. Transacta-7Y1 was hardly a savant when it came to reading human expressions, but what she saw on Arkhan Land's gaunt features was no different from what she saw on every other human's face – civilian, refugee and soldier alike.

Though, she supposed they were all soldiers now. Everyone that could carry a rifle was doing so. The end of the world was the great equaliser.

Transacta-7Y1 stared across the wasteland, her monovisor clicking as it zoomed and refocused.

'Is it the Titans?' Land asked her, still refusing to rise. 'Are they sending their Titans in first?'

Transacta-7Y1 held back her reply. After cancelling her visual zoom, she looked left and right at the defenders closest by. On one side was a spread of Imperial Army soldiers from the 91st Industani Drop Troops (all without their traditional grav-chutes, grounded for the final battle), and she needed no special insight to read the confusion on their faces. Those with magnoculars didn't look confused, they looked horrified.

On her other side was the Legiones Astartes officer Zephon, former Dominion of the High Host, and the three unaugmented humans he claimed as his thralls. Further along the wall was a cluster of Blood Angels, and one of these was Nassir Amit, Dominion of the Secutors, standing still unhelmed. She saw him lean forward, his knuckles on the rampart as he stared in dawning anger, and she heard him – very clearly – say:

'Those honourless bastards.'

Transacta-7Y1 turned back to regard the horde on the horizon. Even with her repaired helm, the distance stole significant visual detail. She rested the barrel of her new transauranic arquebus on the ramparts before her and peered through the scope.

What she saw defied easy contextualisation. This, she conveyed to her new benefactor in a brief utterance of code.

'That doesn't sound optimal,' Land replied, and rose to his feet at last, unnerved by the reactions of those around him.

Transacta-7Y1 panned her sniper rifle, and at her side, Land cranked and tuned his multi-spec goggles. The two of them stared out over the wasteland, where the ground was alive. Breathing. Changing.

Darkening, she thought.

It came on in a tide, a mutilation of the churned earth eating up the distance between the battlement and the enemy's drawn-up front lines. The war-blasted earth soured as they watched, the stone blackening, in some places bubbling, in others sprouting fleshy protuberances or rupturing with questing roots.

This corruption had a herald: a lone Titan stepped forth from the horde, and it covered the wasteland in measured strides, externally sedate, though Transacta-7Y1 could practically sense the fusion broil of its heart-reactor. Step by step, the Titan grew in scale, leaving the enemy's front lines behind, walking the encroaching carpet of souring earth. After half a minute, she could hear its footfalls, faint with distance.

'It's within range of the wall guns,' said one of the nearby Blood Angels.

'Hold,' was Amit's reply.

Transacta-7Y1 kept watch through her scope. The Titan was a Reaver, revealed as it approached through the thinning mist, wearing the royal purple of the Legio Mordaxis. She had fought alongside Mordaxis – only briefly, but with great pride – nine years before, at the compliance of Three-Hundred-and-Eight Thirteen.

Her heart sank a little at that, though perhaps it would be more accurate to say that she experienced a protracted moment of emotional disquiet, which – in reality – had nothing to do with the processes of her heart.

She tracked her view either side of the Titan, back to the faraway massing of the horde. A forest of girders and scrap-metal poles stood at the edge of the enemy's lines, erected over the last days by the toiling of who knew how many slaves and servitors and daemonic things bound to the purpose. These spikes were put to use in the weak dawn light, as impaling posts and gallows, used for thrashing, mutilated captives.

Transacta-7Y.1 focused on one of the prisoners being bound up onto a scrapyard pylon. She didn't know the regimental colours of the man's uniform, but he was clearly an infantry-man, his flak armour hanging in rags, carved away by lashing whips. His face was a mess of blood and barbed wire. He had no teeth. No eyes. No hands. All were gone, taken from him by his captors before they trussed him up there to dangle and die.

Beneath his footless legs, his mutated overseer rejoiced in his agony – a horned beastman brayed and laughed, silent at this distance, but with its animal glee visible on its bestial visage.

The Titan marched on. Behind it, the hundreds of tortured prisoners displayed to the defenders became thousands. They hung from their impaled limbs, they dangled in cradles of barbed wire. Some of them were even driven forward, a low tide of them, laughingly shoved ahead of the enemy lines. Most of these crawled across the ruined ground towards the Delphic Battlement, the stubs of their amputated legs leaving them no choice but to drag themselves belly-down in the dirt. Behind them came those that couldn't even crawl, the limbless and the poisoned and the ones on the very edge of death.

Packed into open-topped civilian cargo-haulers; chained to the sides of supply trucks and Army Chimeras. Hundreds of vehicles rolled forward, none of them avoiding the wave of mutilation making its weeping way towards the battlement. They ground the wounded beneath their heels and tracks with heedless abandon. These vehicles inevitably crashed and rolled across the en-cancered earth, some left to founder with their miserable, dying cargoes, others set aflame from rockets fired by their own overseers.

Transacta-7Y1 saw mutilated skitarii within the captives' ranks. She saw tech-priests and Martian menials, non-combatants whose only sin had been to remain loyal to the Omnissiah's vision of what Mars could be. She felt the thin epiglottal sting of bile as she saw soldiers just like her, stripped of their divine bionics, impaled, crucified, bound in webs of razor wire, or dragging themselves over the broken ground in a futile attempt to reach safety.

And she wondered at the mindsets of these most pitiable refugees. What mesh of ghastly hope and mournful reality sloshed around in the pain-drunkenness of their thoughts? Maybe some really did hope for safety; for succour – and perhaps even healing – if they could just reach their fellow defenders on the Delphic Battlement. But how many didn't even know where they were, with their senses taken from them? How many knew only that this was more torture, and prayed for a death thus far denied?

Instinct had her tracking the numerals on her rifle's range-finder, as if she could hit anything from this distance. Then she lowered her arquebus. She'd seen enough for now. Along the wall, in both directions, the voices of human officers began to rise in an uneasy melange. They wanted the wall guns to fire. They wanted to bombard the wasteland. They wanted to put the captives out of their misery. But the afflictions took place out of range, and the defence cannons stayed silent. Meanwhile, the Titan marched closer.

When Sanguinius, the Ninth Primarch and Lord of the Blood Angels Legion, landed next to her, she did not react quite the same way as many of those around her. The Blood Angels saluted, as would be expected, either with the sign of the aquila or the older custom of a fist over their hearts. The human soldiers stepped back, thunderstruck, mumbling greetings and praises if they found the capacity to speak at all. The Legion thralls, of which there were almost forty gathered on this section of the wall, went to one knee in almost programmed unity, lowering their heads in reverence. Even Arkhan Land jerked in surprise, his expression momentarily stunned before reality filtered back, and he turned his gaze pointedly away. The Lord Sanguinius, after all, had refused Land's plea to retake Mars before the Warmaster reached Terra. Some things would never be forgiven.

But Transacta-7Y1 had a skitarius' perspective of the primarchs. She regarded the towering figure with respect, and entirely without reverence. This immense winged thing was no demigod, and she would not treat it as such. It was undoubtedly a product of the Omnissiah's vision, of course. But it was not the Omnissiah's son. If the Omnissiah was to create offspring, the fruits of that project would share in His divine perfection, not fail to the point where half of the children rebelled against their godly father and set the galaxy aflame. Then there were the philosophical considerations. Why, exactly, would the Machine-God breed into being eighteen largely biological children? Several of them possessed minor augmentation, but nothing significant, nothing that spoke of *purity*.

No. She could accept that they were an intriguing product of the Omnissiah's genetic cauldrons. She could not accept their bizarre hubris in claiming to be His sons. Most likely, the flaws in the project were the result of Terran scientist-priests misinterpreting the Omnissiah's will; further proof of the fallibility and lack of divinity in the entire operation.

So she did not genuflect and she did not – as her dead companion Envaric would have said in the style of his idioms – 'bow and scrape' at the primarch's arrival.

She regarded the figure in beauteous gold, greeted him with a Martian salute – her knuckles linking to make the sign of the cog – then turned back to the wasteland, clutching her rifle.

Behind her, they discussed what would come next. And the Reaver strode closer. Closer still. It had outpaced the host of wounded, and was now almost halfway to the wall, walking through an invisible web of unused firing solutions. Sanguinius could click his golden fingers and weaponry capable of boring through to the planet's mantle would erase the lone Titan from existence.

'We should kill it, sire,' said one of the captains. Transacta-7Y1 identified the speaker by his armour: Apollo, an officer of the 48th Company. 'Nothing good can come of letting it reach the wall.'

'No?' Zephon interrupted. 'Every second counts. Every single one. If Horus wishes to burn through time with melodrama, then we will let him have his way. All the while, the Thirteenth Legion sails closer to Terra. These theatrics benefit us, not the enemy.'

Apollo fixed Zephon with a stare. 'Thousands of prisoners are dying in agony. That's rather more than *theatrics*, Zephon.'

'I will destroy it,' Sanguinius said softly, 'but not yet.'

Transacta-7Y1 ceased listening. She had no interest in their cost/benefit analysis of the situation, and she knew she was beneath the notice of the Legion officers and their lord, anyway.

For a time, she watched the Titan. An emissary from Mordaxis. Without really thinking, she exhaled a blurt of code. At her side, Land nodded and licked his cracked lips.

'Indeed,' he murmured. 'Indeed so.'

The youngest of the Blood Angels thralls, his red robe overlaid with ill-fitting flak armour, cleared his throat and addressed the techno-archaeologist.

'May I ask, what did the cyborg say?'

Transacta-7Y1 glanced at the human, but with no means of communication, she made no effort to explain herself. She doubted Land would translate for her, either; for all his genius, which was both considerable and undeniable, he seemed to have deep-rooted emotional turbulence. Zephon had asked him to protect the three servants, not be pleasant to them, so it surprised the skitarius when Land turned his ashy face to the Legion thrall.

'Your name is Shenkai, isn't it?'

The young man, his face as filthy as everyone else's, nodded. 'Yes, Sire Land.'

'Well, Shenkai, this is Transacta-7Y1. She said it pained her to see any god-machine, each one a being of blessed iron forged in the Omnissiah's own image, on the wrong side of the war. Doubly so, because she once fought alongside Legio Mordaxis, and she mourns that she must now see their engines animated by heretical purpose.'

Shenkai regarded the skitarius with a long look. Transacta-7Y1 could read the sympathy there, and gratitude stirred in the tired soup of her own emotional core. She inclined her helmeted head in response to the thrall's acknowledgement, and expressed a shorter sliver of code.

Land translated again. 'She says you may call her Tee.'

Shenkai smiled. 'Then I will do so. Thank you.'

Transacta-7Y1 turned back to the wasteland. She watched it turn black. She watched the Titan stalk nearer. She noted that it kept its right hand curled in a loose fist, binding something within the great cage of its grip.

'A curious choice of ambassador,' Land mused aloud.

Zephon's reply was low and tight. 'It has something in its hand.'

The Reaver – Transacta-7Y1 read the name on its tilting shield, *Daughter of Torment* – brought itself to a stop. Momentum meant it took time to settle on its pistons, adapting to standing and powering down its locomotive processes. The defenders could make out the details of its allegiance with their own eyes now, with the god-machine only a kilometre from the wall. There it halted, close enough to unleash its weapons if it chose to do so, far enough away that its reactor going critical wouldn't damage the battlement. Its banners swayed in the wind, its primary pennant hanging between its cabled thighs like a barbarian's loincloth.

Slowly, the emissary from Mordaxis began to lift its hand. Even from this distance, with all the incidental noise of the humanity along the wall and the active reactors of their own Titans, Transacta-7Y1 could hear the clangorous grind of the Reaver's joints.

It stood before the wall, its hand outstretched towards the men and women gathered in their thousands. While its pose was that of a beggar, it brought a gift. There, in its palm, was a lone jewel of burnished red.

Transacta-7Y1 heard Amit's growl. She heard Zephon's softer exhalation, and the way others among the Astartes cursed beneath their breath. She heard, most distinctly of all, Sanguinius' gentle lament, in a language she knew must be Aenokhian.

A Blood Angel lay in the Titan's palm, cradled there with misleading gentleness. Like the human prisoners, he had been mutilated, but he was left with all the trappings of his rank, the gold edgings of his armour, the noble flow of his cloak. His cheeks were stained with black streaks and burn markings, and judging by the damage, Transacta-7Y1 suspected the enemy had poured a corrosive agent into his eye sockets. She watched his mouth working, seeing the swollen, tongueless red mess there, and she wondered what the man was trying to say. An oath, most likely. Astartes warriors made no shortage of oaths. Instead of words, he spoke blood.

The Blood Angel was dying, and it was a miracle of dubious fortune that he still lived. The mutilations weren't enough to kill him; the true wounds that paralysed him and kept him in place were the seven spears thrust through his body, nailing him to the Titan's palm.

Zephon took a step forward, and the thrusters of his jump pack gave a throaty whine in sympathy.

'Hold,' Sanguinius whispered, the command as delicate as a knife held against skin.

Zephon looked over his shoulder at the primarch. 'But–'

'*Hold*, Zephon. Do you truly believe you can surge over there and save him? Stand down, Bringer of Sorrow.'

Zephon held, that cold and sentient anger darkening his features. His teeth were parted as he stared at the desecration with haunted eyes. In contrast, Amit was all silent heat. Hate was an aura around him, and his warplate purred as it answered the shifts in his muscled frame.

'Who is it?' Land asked, peering through his goggles, tuning them with clicks of the side-dials. 'Who have they crucified?'

Sanguinius was the one to answer, his voice no more than a breath.

'It's Idamas.'

It was as if the name became a signal. Along the wall, tens of thousands of voices rose in anger, in defiance, in denial. Transacta-7Y1 saw the impaled figure of Idamas, captain of the 99th Company, lift his head and turn towards the sound. Something pathetically like hope dawned across his ruined face.

The Titan was waiting for this. It started closing its hand, the fingers curling with a squeal of scraping joints.

'Transacta-7Y1,' Sanguinius said softly. 'Please take the shot.'

She hesitated at being addressed by the primarch, and Amit misinterpreted it as reluctance.

'Do it,' he grunted.

She did it. The arquebus kicked, spitting a penetrator round of depleted transuranium. A kilometre away, the Blood Angels captain jerked, and the insides of his skull blasted out the back of his head to paint the iron of the Titan's closing thumb. Transacta-7Y1 racked the slide, ejecting the spent cartridge. It chimed sweetly against the marble rampart, steaming with the blue mist of discharge.

'Thank you,' said Sanguinius. He was staring at the Titan,

at the body in the Titan's clutches, with the air of a man too dutiful to close his eyes and deny the truth.

The Reaver, its performative cruelty stolen, nevertheless finished pulping the carcass between its digits. There was a brief, anticlimactic pop of sparking energy as Captain Idamas' power pack detonated. Then all that remained were the bloody, meat-wadded scraps of ceramite embedded into the god-machine's fingers.

'That was an ugly death,' murmured Land, seemingly to himself.

'But he lived a warrior's life,' Sanguinius countered.

Transacta-7Y1, who could see both perspectives, wasn't entirely certain the latter overrode the former. Nor could she see why the demise of a single Blood Angels officer seemed to matter so profoundly to the Ninth Primarch. Was there something of particular significance to Captain Idamas?

Daughter of Torment had presented its gift and made its point. Now, the Titan dictated its terms. The offer came forth in a strained trio of overlapping voices, as if conflicting spirits animated the Reaver's bones. All three voices were feminine, all three seeming to speak with throatfuls of venom, burbling across the wasteland. Transacta-7Y1, who had experienced exactly zero erotic imaginings since her mechamorphosis began, still felt the voices caress something inside her, with a wet, disgusting silkiness.

'*Horus, Warmaster and true Emperor of the Imperium, offers the defenders of the Sanctum Imperialis his warmest greetings. He commends you on your resolve thus far, and admires you all for your efforts in fighting for what you believe is right.*'

'I'm sure he does,' Amit growled through a fanged grin, and Transacta-7Y1's lipless mouth curled in secret mirth. She stole a glance at Sanguinius, but the primarch's face was emotionless marble.

The Titan's three-voice decree echoed out from its cockpit speakers. *'Emperor Horus, true heir to the Throne and Crown of Terra, also wishes it to be known that anyone – be they human or Astartes – that surrenders their weapon now and abandons the Delphic Battlement, will be permitted to leave the field of conflict, free and unharmed.'*

Murmurs started to spread along the wall. This was unexpected. This was new.

'Furthermore,' the Reaver blared, *'Emperor Horus Lupercal declares that upon making planetfall, he intends to journey to the Sanctum Imperialis. Should the Eternity Gate stand open upon his arrival, he offers an Imperial pardon to each and every one of you, with no condition or stipulation. He grants forgiveness to all.'*

Amit grunted. 'Here comes the *But…*'

'However,' the Titan bellowed, *'should the Eternity Gate stand closed, he will regard this as an act of continued hostility. Any soul refusing to acknowledge Horus Lupercal as the Master of Mankind, and who resists the true Emperor's entrance into the Sanctum Imperialis, will be dealt with as an enemy of the Imperium.'*

The last words burbled from the Reaver's vox-speakers. It sounded like the crew was gargling engine oil inside the god-machine's core. *'The Warmaster's army will march in one hour. If you choose to abandon your charade of defiance, launch signal flares from the Delphic Battlement, that we might bear witness to your capitulation. If you should destroy this emissary, your continued rebellion will be noted, and you will forsake the hour of grace granted to you. Emperor Horus Lupercal has spoken.'*

With its message delivered, the ambassador began the laborious process of reawakening its locomotors and slowly, slowly turning.

All eyes turned to Sanguinius. He was lord of the last wall. The right to reply was his alone.

Transacta-7Y1 wondered if he might open fire out of spite,

for the primarchs were notoriously emotional beings. One moment, they seemed a curious and fleshly ideal: indeed, more human than human. The next, they were as petty as a pantheon of godlings from the pagan tales of Old Earth. It would have been a useless unleashing of firepower – the death of a single Titan would make no difference in the face of what was about to descend upon the wall – but the skitarius still suspected that the order would be given. Anger often overrode the logistics of futility – among mortals, at least.

Yet the Ninth Primarch remained calm. He spoke no words from a state of emotional flux, and *Daughter of Torment* stalked back towards her lines, the ground shaking less with each retreating step. She was allowed to live in exchange for one precious hour of grace.

Amit spoke low, so his voice wouldn't carry. 'Some of the humans, sire… The promise of safety after surrender? That offer will tempt them.'

Transacta-7Y1 did not know if this was the case. The variances of human behaviour were extreme, yes, but also mysterious. Judging by the fact Arkhan Land was nodding, however, she presumed that Captain Nassir Amit was correct in his assertion. Some of the unaugmented would indeed wish to flee. And Transacta-7Y1 wasn't entirely without sympathy. Many of the scrap code sermons infecting the Mechanicus' communication network made some troubling statements regarding the fallibility of the Omnissiah. She, too, had considered abandoning her post. Not that she would ever confess to such momentary weaknesses of faith. That was between her and her god.

The Ninth Primarch didn't answer the genetically manipulated warrior template that he sometimes referred to as his son. His response to Amit's warning was the last thing Transacta-7Y1 could possibly have anticipated.

'I do not want to be here,' said the Emperor's perfect son.

His voice was soft, rancid with truth. He said those seven words not declaratively, more in an expression of gentle contemplation. As if the idea had only now occurred to him. As if, indeed, he'd only now remembered the words themselves.

Then he took three steps forward to the very edge of the ramparts, and with a crack of his white wings, he took to the sky.

TWENTY-SEVEN

In the tower of the Crimson King

Vulkan

The Eighteenth Primarch had no wish to linger in the alien necropolis, and not merely because he knew time was against him. The city, Calastar, bore the heavy stink of tragedy, a failure so profound that Vulkan felt it infecting him. He was a creature of the fundament over the firmament, a man of ultimate practicality. Here, where physics was a code of laws all too easily broken, he was beginning to choke on the dead city's aura. He breathed in its spiritual failure and felt it in his bloodstream. It was an awkwardly metaphysical feeling.

The only bounty within Calastar was the abundance of Imperial dead. Corpses populated the city's thoroughfares and gathering plazas, lying in their hundreds, sometimes in their thousands. Skitarii. Secutarii. Martian Myrmidon war-priests. Sisters of Silence. Custodians. Most were years dead, reduced by the nature of this place to skinless bones contained within corroded armour. Some, though, seemed only recently expired, either killed in the last few months or preserved in a state of cadaverous freshness by the whims of the webway. All of them were daemon-slain. All showed horrendous wounds from inhuman blades, evidence of mutagenic disease, or partial devouring.

Along a particularly wide avenue, Vulkan walked a winding path around wrecked grav-Rhinos and Land Raiders, picking his way through mounds of golden dead. Once, the Emperor's Custodian Guard had numbered ten thousand souls: the greatest achievement of genetic engineering excepting the primarchs themselves. Most had died here, selling their lives in a failed attempt to undo Magnus' Folly and fight for the Emperor's dream.

The Imperial forces garrisoned in this necropolis years before had called it the Impossible City. A city of xenocultured materials eclipsing almost any human metropolis, it was set within a tunnel of unmeasurable size, with its towers and arches and bridges and avenues built at every imaginable angle. To look east or west was to see the cartography of distant districts founded on the great tunnel's walls, the sensation disorientatingly like looking down at a map. To look up was to see a mirror-city of stalactite spires growing down from the ceiling, this other 'ground' somehow kilometres above your head.

Whichever name was ascribed to this place of shattered psychoplastics, it was a monument to two failed empires. First the aeldari population had died here, annihilated by some long-forgotten cataclysm – maybe even destroyed in the maelstrom of god-birth that had ended the rise of their decadent culture. Vulkan caught sight of their ghosts, or perhaps the ghosts of their ghosts, at the edges of his sight. Slivers of soul-light flickered in the windows of towers and in the arches of streets, lacking even the substance of shadows. They were visual echoes, unsentient, just the city in its long death recalling fragments of its lost life.

Then the Imperium had laid claim to the husk of Calastar. With the Emperor's vision and the Mechanicum's ingenuity, they bound this region of the ancient webway to the Imperium's newborn, Throne-born pathways. And that, too, had failed.

But the cataclysm that laid waste to mankind's claim was anything but forgotten. Magnus the Red had torn through here on his quest to warn the Emperor of Horus' treachery. His astral form, swollen with righteousness and fuelled by human sacrifice, had ruptured the webway's fragile protective sheaths. As he ripped his way through this realm, destroying more of it with every step, every breath, every sorcerous whisper and desperate whim, he undid the Mechanicum's Great Work towards the salvation of humanity and opened the way for daemonkind to flood into this sacred place. With a heart bursting with the best intentions, he had doomed his species.

And so began the War in the Webway. A war fought for years in absolute secrecy, out of sight of the teeming trillions it was supposed to save. The Emperor's Custodians and Silent Sisterhood were pressed back, and back, and back... until they abandoned first the Impossible City, then the webway itself – and with that second surrender, they abandoned the Emperor's dream. Humanity's future without reliance on the poisons of divine worship and warp travel was lost.

Vulkan had learned much from his time in the Imperial Dungeon. Drips, dregs, shreds of all this, pieced together from Malcador's lecturing, from the murmurs of Custodians, from the chanted lamentations of Mechanicus adepts. And Vulkan wondered: had his brother faced up to all he had done? He and Magnus had never been close. He couldn't predict what his Prosperine brother might be thinking now, exalted and enslaved by his patron overlord; more powerful than ever yet capering at the whims of that distant, cackling god.

Before reaching the city, Vulkan found himself musing whether Calastar would still be flooded with the twisted figures of daemonkind. Perhaps a million of the Neverborn would be waiting, hunting in the shade cast by spires of wraithbone and even rarer psychoplastics. But this was not so. There was nothing for them here. Nothing for them to feed upon. Nothing for them to digest in the process of maintaining incarnation.

It seemed that daemons did not like to dance on the graves of their foes. They moved on, driven by hunger, for to remain still was to starve.

And so Vulkan was alone. Alone and lost in a screamingly empty place. There was no breeze in this sunless realm, though there was a sourceless, directionless light that granted a misty illumination. There was also – though he kept thinking he was imagining it – something palpable in the otherwise still air: a feeling of energy at play, an invisible current flowing out of sight and almost out of mind. He did not know if this was a natural element produced by the webway itself, or evidence of the unseen war of energies between Magnus and their father.

Time was likewise worthless as a reference. Every time Vulkan checked his armour's chron, it told him a different tale. That he'd been walking for three days. That he'd been travelling for a month. That his journey wasn't set to begin for another six years. None of this mattered, really. Nowhere did he see any signs of his brother Magnus. All he could do was walk, and that's what he did, trusting to the rebellious laws of this dimension. Time either passed or it didn't – he had no way to be sure.

As he journeyed on, he thought of the Custodians and

Sisters of Silence that had given their lives for him to enter the webway. He feared he was failing them.

More than once, he felt the passage of some vast etheric presence nearby. In each instance, he felt like a deep-ocean swimmer, being fortunately ignored by immense underwater beasts drifting past. A sensation like and unlike a breeze would caress his sweating skin, and in its wake was a scent not wholly unlike burning stone. Curiously, he knew he wasn't smelling the truth of the scent itself, but the closest his senses could come to codifying something utterly alien to the human experience.

He came to the belief that what he felt was the passage of aeldari void-ships sailing through tunnels in adjacent realities. City-sized cruisers, brushing past him, almost close enough to touch. This assumption, based on little more than gut instinct, was entirely correct.

When he at last came upon a sign of life in this lifeless expanse, surprise stole all of his momentum for half a dozen heartbeats. Vulkan stood in place, head lifted, staring up at the wraithbone tower. It was at once a spire no different from any of the other thousand Vulkan had seen in Calastar so far, while also being the apotheosis of them. He could almost sense, with a heretofore unknown instinct that felt somehow animal, that he was at the very heart of the dead city. He stood at a convergence of the right planes of alignment and existence, where all was in perfect balance.

The entrance to the tower was an arch at the end of a long bridge, and the bridge was a crumbling curve of deteriorating psychoplastic, its sides eroded by tendrils of golden mist rising from the chasm it spanned. There were no bodies marking the site of an old battle, no daemons lurking in the misty dark; only a single trail of dusty footprints, some human in scale, others daemonically cloven, leading across the bridge and into the tower's yawning arch. It was the trail of a creature shifting between the states of man and monster, lost in protean flux.

Vulkan rested his hammer on his shoulder and followed the trail.

Later, Vulkan would struggle to remember the truth of his journey ascending the spire. After the siege – and for Vulkan, there would indeed be a later, though that was destined to be a time of flayed nerves and an agony so raw it drove reason from his skinless skull – he would never be able to piece together exactly what occurred once he crossed the wraithbone bridge.

Faint memories lingered, each one sitting jaggedly against the others, not of a single journey, but of three. He would recall his boots crunching on mist-kissed wraithbone stairs. Equally, he would remember striding up a stairway of gold-veined Tizcan marble. Impossibly, he would remember his boots thudding down on steps of mutated flesh and bone.

The tower, which was either all of these immersions or none of them, seemed to take forever to ascend. He remembered that much with absolute clarity, and the duration was not a matter of distance. When he reflected on the insides of that spire, during the long and lonely *later* he was fated to face alone, he would become increasingly sure that the tower was making itself as he climbed it. Its internal structures weren't set in stone or wraithbone, but were woven into being in response to his ascension. He was a grounding element, a source of metaphysical stability. Reality was forced to fall out of infinite flux to converge on a mere handful of possibilities.

Up the spiral staircases he walked.

In the tower of ancient bone, he passed the psychoplastic corpses of aeldari constructs lying like puppets with cut strings, and he listened to the whispers of the ghosts of ghosts.

On the stairs of Prosperine marble, he breathed in the smell of smoke, while the windows granted him a view of the crystalline city of Tizca, its white pyramids burning in the light of the setting sun.

In the tower of flesh and bone and warping stone, he met warriors of a Legion he couldn't name. These warriors, clad in filthy cobalt and overwrought gold, stood silent sentinel on the stairs, never once greeting him or returning his hails. They watched him with dead eye-lenses that held only a simulacrum of life. Their heads turned with slow automaton intensity to regard him as he passed. They stank of funeral ash.

High above, he heard his brother screaming. Except, it was also the sound of chanting. And a murmuring, desperately close to prayer.

When Vulkan threw open the final rune-warded door, when he passed beneath the last glyph-marked marble arch, when he pushed through the final shimmering portal of dancing mirages, he stood under the dome of a grand observatory. And there, stunned at the sight of him, and enraged at his arrival, and grinning in expectation, was his brother Magnus.

Magnus the Red was a luminous lie, incarnated as a being of burning light. A thousand chains of force thrashed and coiled from the aura, each one a conduit for cascading energy. Vulkan had to guard his eyes against the worst of the light, though there was nothing he could do about the crashing thunder of the chamber's unstable energies.

He could make out Magnus' face, just barely, as a melting and reforming mask within the avatar of deceitful light. The chamber around them was pristine in its long death, the wraithbone untouched by the forces at play, and Vulkan followed the lines of etheric force as they stretched out from the observatory, across the skyline of this alien necropolis. They faded in the air, not with distance but outside the range of their own visual metaphor. Vulkan was no arcanist, no scholar of the mystical, but he knew what he was seeing. This was a manifestation of his brother's assault on the Emperor.

He walked forward, ignoring the writhing serpents of force-light, his knuckles tightening on the haft of his hammer. The air resisted him, turning thick. Invisible force that would have crushed a mortal and paralysed an Astartes slowed Vulkan's stalking advance to a teeth-clenching crawl, like a man leaning into a storm's wind.

The room danced and shimmered about the two of them. Becoming the marble chamber once more. Becoming the oubliette of flesh and stone. Becoming the wraithbone observatory.

Magnus' shifting features were strained, a mangled stream of invocation pouring from his mouth. He cursed and he chanted and he seethed, and Vulkan could discern no difference between what was spite and what might have been a spell.

The chamber in which they stood turned on some unseen, metaphysical axis. It didn't move, didn't rotate or spin, for these words imply a motion that was never present. Nevertheless, it turned.

What Is and What Will Be disintegrated, becoming What Was.

Vulkan looked upon an incarnation of his brother that had not existed for years. Magnus the Red lifted his face, and Vulkan's heart broke at the devastation he saw there. The profundity of grief. And, unexpectedly, the depth of guilt. The burning city beyond the wide windows was an amber reflection in his remaining eye. Tizca would be dead by dawn.

This is the night that the Space Wolves brought ruin to the City of Light.

The primarch of Prospero looked ravaged, the lines on his face etched deep enough to age him far past any of his brothers. And yet, was this not Tizca? This was years before the beginning of the siege.

Or the illusion of years before.

The observatory stood open to the heavens at dusk, as the first glimpses of unfamiliar constellations heralded the coming night. Any other evening, he might have been tempted to watch the stellar ballet above his brother's home world. Tonight, he advanced with his hammer in his hands, still forcing his way forward through chains of invisible force.

'Stay back,' Magnus warned, and with those words, the world turned again.

What Is and What Was both unravelled, becoming What Will Be.

The observatory was a spire-top platform, open to the tainted night, while the sky above blazed with witch-light. This world was in the grip of the warp, doubtless some ancient aeldari world in the Ocularis Terribus warp storm, turned sour by the empyrean's tides. The most unnerving detail was the planetary ring decorating the heavens, formed not of rocks and particles but of souls. They wailed, and at this distance, Vulkan should never have heard their wailing song. Yet he did, and his skin crawled with it.

To think this tragedy was Magnus' destiny, ruling this tainted globe some timeless span in the future... The very idea was a splinter in Vulkan's heart. To see his brother existing in a place of such suffering, a realm where the only antidote to its grotesquery was to imagine yourself as its king.

But Magnus the Red turned slowly, and Vulkan's heart cooled to stone at the sight of what the warp had done. Here was Magnus as the Dragon had seen the Sorcerer-King: a giant of burnished red flesh and lustrous wings. The face was a mask of condescending horror, smug with amassed knowledge. Cycloptic, fanged, bestial, all nobility was gone from the visage, leaving animalistic superiority in its place.

Vulkan pushed closer to the towering figure, with its feathered wings bathed in poisoned starlight and lashing in the arcane wind.

'Stay back,' Magnus snarled again. And again, the world began to turn.

'Enough,' Vulkan growled. *'Enough.'*

He swung the hammer with every iota of strength he possessed. He held nothing back. It was an execution, the sentence of death, delivered.

Millennia from now, an increasingly ignorant Imperium would tell tales of the Emperor's sons. These primarchs, they would say, were capable of flight, capable of enduring any torment, capable of splitting mountains with blows of their great weapons. Whatever was true and whatever would turn out false, Vulkan swung the hammer that day with enough force to tear through the fuselage of a Stormbird gunship. The blow he levelled at his brother's heart would have shattered the shin of a Warlord Titan.

Magnus caught the hammer, one-handed. The monster gazed down into Vulkan's dark, straining features, and the flesh around the monster's one great eye wrinkled as he grinned.

'Vulkan,' purred the daemon prince. *'I told you to stay back.'*

TWENTY-EIGHT

The last choice left

Land

Ah, here it comes. Land braced for the inevitable moronic phrases pitched to rouse the feelings of fools and stir the hearts of imbeciles. The calls to arms, the promises of victory. Yes, yes, yes.

The primarch beat his wings with his back to the enemy. He faced the defenders upon the wall, his pinions keeping him aloft as the dawn's pathetic light did its best to spark flares from the edges of his golden armour. Hololithic incarnations of his hovering form flickered into life across vambrace consoles and viewscreens within the keep. They sprang up from handheld projectors, thousands of identical tiny blue-light ghosts with beating wings.

Sanguinius' words carried across the kilometres of elevated wall, brought to distant ears on the clicking, ticking, crackling speakers of servo-skulls and Mechanicus drones. Soldiers clustered around their data-slates to bear witness to the primarch's proclamation. The hundred thousand defenders of the Delphic Battlement, drawn from all across the burning Imperium, listened to the words of the Great Angel. All of them could see him, even if they were far from his sight and forced to rely on a hololithic reflection. All of them could hear him, even if his words purred through the crackling mouth of a floating probe.

Land had expected a speech dripping with demagogic inspiration. He'd find it tawdry, but knew most of the human defenders – many of whom responded far more positively to the primarchs than the Mechanicus did – would find great value in such a display.

But that was not what he, nor any of them, received.

'I do not want to be here,' Sanguinius told them. 'I do not want this present, and I want the future that follows even less. We stand against our own brothers and sisters, with our backs to the Eternity Gate, and this is not a battle we can win. If you have ever wondered how you will die, now you know. If you have ever wondered where your body will lie, now you know. You will be killed on the last wall between hope and horror. Your body will lie here, unburied, staring up at a poisoned sky.

'Once the Sanctum falls, Terra falls with it. And I tell you – we cannot hold this wall. You can see it yourselves – they are too many, we are too few. We may last a week, if we do the impossible. More likely we will all be dead in three days. Perhaps my words surprise you. Or frighten you. But I will not lie. Not to you, not to you who have come through two hundred days of dread only to find yourselves here.

'I have looked into your faces and seen what this war has cost all of you. I have followed the flow of battles that each of you have survived, to stand here on the final battlement. I see everything you have endured, those stories written in the light of your eyes. Now the Warmaster offers you the lie of life, promising a mercy his forces are incapable of showing, if we will abandon this last wall. And it falls to me, here and now, to tell you to stand against him one more time. To give everything you have, even your lives, if it will hold this rampart for another day, another hour, another second. That is what the moment demands of me, is it not? That I beg you to make one last sacrifice?'

Sanguinius swooped closer to the battlement, casting his sword to the stone. It clattered there, in a loose cluster of Blood Angels, none of whom made any attempt to pick it up. Land stared at it for a long moment, then watched as the primarch whirled in the sky to face the wall once more, showing his bare hands to the gathered thousands.

'No.' Sanguinius fairly breathed the word.

His wings beat hard, holding him aloft. He stared into the silence that met his disavowal, and he shook his head to punctuate the syllable with adamance.

'No. I will not ask it of you. You have already given everything. You have already done everything asked of you a hundred times and more. You have suffered through a war of unimaginable darkness, one that has demanded more from you than any soldier in the history of our species has been forced to give. The fact you still live, that you still fight... I cannot conceive of the courage and resilience it requires for you to face this dawn and look to the horizon with a rifle in your hands.'

Land could hear Army soldiers shuffling; he saw them glancing at each other. None of them spoke. All of them held rapt to the primarch's words.

'Where Horus has offered only lies, I will offer you truth. Those of you that wish to run... *Run*. Leave this place. Not in shame at a duty undone, not in surrender to the traitor's forces, but with honour. Go with my gratitude, for you have already given everything asked of you. What right do I – does anyone – have to demand more? From you, who have endured harrowing beyond account, horror beyond measure?

'If you wish to fall back into the Sanctum Imperialis and spend the last hours of life with your children, then do so. Know that you go not only with my blessing, but with my envy.

'If you wish to leave the wall and take your chances in the wasteland before the battle begins, then – in the Emperor's name – you have earned the right to try. Go swiftly, and carry with you the pride that you have already given a hero's share in a war that none of us wanted but were forced to fight.

'And if you wish for the truth, I will give it to you gladly, for you have earned that, too. It shames me to admit, but I would abandon this wall if I could. The primarch in me, the supposed demigod half of my heart, craves life with a ferocity that shames me. If I bowed to that instinct, I would take to the sky and never look back. But I cannot. I am half-human. And the human in me demands that I stay.'

Sanguinius turned, looking over his shoulder at the retreating emissary. *Daughter of Torment* was a quarter of the way to her lines now. When he looked at the wall once again, all could see the resolve in his eyes.

'There are legends about me, I hear them whispered among you every day, that I know the moment of my own death. The stories say this gives me courage, that I feel no fear because I know I cannot yet be slain. Here is the truth of that tale.

'That prophesied death is coming. Today. Tonight. Tomorrow. I know not the When or the How, only that I feel fate's breath on the back of my neck. I do not remain here out of immortality's courage. I remain here because, if I am to die, I choose *this* death. I choose to die with my back to the last door. I choose to give my life to buy another hour, or a minute, or even a single second of grace to those who cannot be here fighting with me. I choose to die here because I do not believe I have yet given all I can.

'Someone must stand and fight, and if I have but one choice left, I will make it now. *I* will stand. *I* will fight. *I* will hold this wall, knowing that the Thirteenth Legion makes for Terra with all speed, and if they cannot bring salvation, they will bring retribution. Whether I am alone or whether a hundred thousand of you are by my side, when the Warmaster's horde descends upon this wall, they will find me waiting for them with a blade in hand. Not because I can win, but because it is *right*. I do not know what delusion grips those out there, who were once our brothers and sisters. But I know it is right to oppose them.'

Silence drifted over the Delphic Battlement, but only for a moment. Sanguinius swept his arm across the wall, taking in the defenders. Thousands of holo-ghosts of his image did the very same thing.

'I have spoken enough. You need hear no more of my fears and confessions. All that remains is for me to ask… Will you run?'

At first, in the face of the Great Angel's honesty, there was no answer.

Corporal Mashrajeir of the 91st Industani Drop Troops didn't know what to say. Reason and duty warred within him, in a way known to any soldier facing the grimmest odds. He could live. He could leave, and *live*. His regiment wasn't made for this kind of fighting anyway. They were guerrillas, drop troops, trained for point insertion. He'd been on the ground for this whole damn war. What use was a grav-trooper on a rampart? What use was high-atmosphere jump training when all he had now was a lasrifle and a bayonet?

But he was making excuses, justifying, and he knew it. Mash

had the training and the experience to overcome these doubts, to push them back and summon focus in their stead. Besides, there was nowhere to run. Not really. Tactically, it made sense to hold here. If he was going to die, best he sell his life where it would matter most.

'No,' he called to the primarch. And he wasn't the first, but he was one of them. His voice cut out from the silence in the very first wave of denials. He wouldn't leave the wall. He wouldn't run. 'No!'

Skitarii didn't celebrate birthdays. Magna-Delta-8V8 was no exception to this, though her macroclade – the series of platoons and structured hierarchies that defined not only her military position but also her entire social existence – had a tradition of honouring the anniversaries of a soldier's first combat. Due to the constant casualties and replenishment in a macroclade deployed to a theatre of conflict, it meant these acknowledgements were frequent, minor things. The exact axiom translated poorly from skit-code into any variant of Gothic, but the meaning was more or less, 'Every day is some-one's anniversary.' The custom usually involved the exchange of gifts, often repeatedly re-gifted within a regiment, since skitarii were permitted so few possessions of their own.

Today was Magna-Delta-8V8's combat anniversary. Only hers, out of those that remained, because so few of them were left.

It didn't matter that the avatar of the Omnissiah Himself was at work in the fortress behind her. It didn't matter that the horde on the horizon outnumbered and outgunned them an incalculable number of times over. These would have been considerations, of course, on any other day, and she would have stood and fought according to the binharic diktat of duty. Today, though, these concerns were irrelevant.

There was no chance she would run on her battle anniversary. Temptation had teased even her strip-mined brain, of course. She was partially human and wholly mortal. But what sealed the decision in sacred steel was when three of her surviving clade-kin came to her in the minutes before the Ninth's speech. They bore gifts.

Benevola-919-55 had given her a pebble from the slopes of Olympus Mons, the highest mountain on Mother Mars.

Jurispruda-Garnet-12 had given her a translator dataslug, to replace the one she'd lost herself, months before.

Kane-Gamma-A67 had given her a fistful of loose ammunition in lieu of any personal effects. He had nothing else to give.

Magna-Delta-8V8 felt the weight of these gifts, these precious and talismanic gestures, in the folds of her cloak as she listened to the Ninth Primarch speak. And when the Ninth asked the last question, she was ready with her answer.

She couldn't vocalise it, at least not in Gothic, but her defiant shriek of skit-code was much of a muchness.

Lorelei Kelvyr wasn't supposed to be here. If she'd been able to summon the strength to laugh, she'd have surely cut loose with a raw bark of nasty, sarcastic amusement now.

She'd been press-ganged, of course. Before the war's opening bombardments, they'd dragged her from a life sentence in the cold tunnel-guts of the Sevastopol Mining Spire, and she'd honestly believed it would be easy to get out of ever getting sent to the line. Frankly, she'd not been able to believe her luck. Serving twenty years in the resource-starved mines for crimes she hadn't committed, that her own family had forced her to take the fall for, and suddenly she was dragged back into the sunlight, handed a knife and a rifle, and posted far from the prying eyes of her prison overseers. Fortune smiled at last, and it had a lot to make up for.

But that had been, what… a year ago now.

It wasn't that she'd never been able to escape. Quite the opposite. She'd escaped easily – and more than once. The first time, she'd made a break for it with several others – and one of her companions had killed a sentry on their way out of the temporary barracks. They left the poor sentry in a strangled heap, in a service locker, and fled only to find themselves lost in the palatial chaos of the Trans-Europan mag-rail nexus.

Disappearing into the crowds had been easy, choosing the right train to stow away on had been an exercise in frustration. Every route, every single one, was transferring troops to one future war front or another. And so her first escape attempt saw her leaving not only her regiment but the entire sector, only to end up a thousand kilometres away, disembarking in a crowd of troops, immediately subsumed into this new regiment. The Legiones Astartes officers at the end of the line refused all her entreaties; as far as they were concerned, she was there, she was with the regiment, and with them she'd stay.

Her next escape attempt had been painfully tantalising. After several weeks within her second regiment, she'd managed to fall in with a group of believers in the new faith (frankly, she didn't think *cult* was too strong a word for them) and listening to them prattle about the God-Emperor was both nauseating and uncomfortably inspiring. She knew everything they were saying was desperate nonsense, but if it had been true… Well, they believed in a beautiful idea, sure enough. Never had she so wished for a religion to be real.

This new association had allowed her a chance to slip along to their underground prayer gatherings, which in turn had let her make contact with an Administratum liaison attending the sermons, who had been easy enough to convince into having her reassigned. All it took was professing visions of faith in the

God-Emperor, and he believed her touched by divinity. Lorelei was reasonably certain he'd fallen for it anyway.

If it had succeeded, it would've elevated her to some position of pathetically minor authority overseeing the mono-tasks of servitors in a warehouse somewhere... if only her deployment orders hadn't come through ahead of her transfer. She'd been waiting, down to the last moments on the mag-rail platform, casting about in the shrinking hope that her transferral notation would come through before she was finally forced, at the threat of a baton beating, to board the train.

Supposedly, the Warmaster's fleet would reach Terra soon. She was running out of time.

Lorelei had escaped again, three nights later. She had no regrets at all about abandoning her second regiment, and in the weeks after she tore loose, she managed to lie low in the crud-shanties clustered at the base of Praxia Hivespire. There she lived in a ramshackle lean-to abandoned by its previous inhabitants: likely they were press-ganged into service themselves. She'd scavenged up the basics of survival for several weeks that time, living like a homeless queen alongside a few other deserters. But food was scarce to begin with and only got scarcer; soon enough they'd turned on each other, and it was time to bleed or leave. At first, Lorelei made sure she wasn't the one bleeding by cutting deals with the right brutes, but she'd hoarded too much, was too good at scavenging; soon she became a victim of her own success. The scum ganged up against her and came for her with chains and scrap-daggers.

So farewell, Praxia. Farewell, crud-shanty house.

After that, well, desperation had set in. She did the one and only thing in her life she was ashamed of. Someone had died so she might live.

What followed was a period of pretending to be a Munitorum scribe, though was it really pretence when she'd been damn good at the craft? She'd actually done the work, which in her eyes made her a legitimate contender for the trade. It'd been protracted, achingly dull stuff, but easy for all that: following regiments around, taking stock of supplies, and so on and so on, unto tedious infinity. Her ident documents were even legitimate, though that was largely because they weren't hers – they'd belonged to the woman she'd killed in order to take her place in the endless grind of Imperial bureaucracy.

A slice of dumb misfortune saw her busted by an otherwise useless administrator-captain, and for no reason beyond a simple mistake in calculations. She was supposed to be savant-grade, was she not? Why, yes, it said so on her documentation. How could she make a mistake like this? Why were her resource projections skewing so wide of the actualities?

She'd considered bribing him, which was a laugh because she had nothing to bribe him with, and she'd even considered killing him, which was twice the joke, since this was no scrawny, nutrition-stunted tallier of accounts, this was a retired Army soldier twice her weight and backed up by the crude strength of a bionic arm. Besides, she was in the thick of it then, deep in the coggy bowels of the Munitorum's processes, and even sneezing would leave a paper trail.

She ran, literally fleeing into the night, hiding in a nameless slum town in the shadows of yet another beautiful spire. If they caught her, they'd execute her.

It took no time at all for her to be press-ganged in another wave of mandatory recruitment, and her protests availed her nothing. Practically everyone on the planet not serving in an essential position was recruited into the Imperial Army, and so Lorelei was discharged and assigned to her third regiment, temporarily barracked and gearing up to be sent to yet another sector, where they'd inevitably reinforce the other conscripts already stationed there.

Her crime and previous desertions went uncovered – so there was that, at least.

She was seemingly destined to fight in the war, though. Against all efforts to the contrary. That was it. She was being sent to fight in the line.

And for a time, she had. For months. Months of starvation and privation, months of blinking smoke from her eyes and standing in trenches next to men and women that shat themselves at night to keep warm, and pretending she was better than them, that they belonged there and she didn't, while she grew more gaunt, more sour, day by blood-soaked day. Months of night-fighting and seeing her platoonmates eviscerated and crucified and burst open with bolter fire and carved apart with chainswords. Months and months of what everyone else was also going through. Being pawns in the Astartes' war.

And now, after everything, now *this*. The Great Angel himself... saying she could run.

'Lor,' said the soldier next to her. 'You alright?'

Her squad, all seven of them still alive, were huddled together in a scrimmage that reeked of sweat and crap and charred earth, watching the flickering hololith projected from Sergeant Gathis' vambrace.

Lorelei felt tears on her face. Was she all right? Oh, yeah. She was great. Just wonderful. She wasn't the only one showing emotion, either. It wasn't weeping, exactly. It was a slow leak of emotion too weary to really be called weeping.

'My name's not Lorelei,' she said, cuffing the tears from her cheeks. She had no idea why she was crying. It was like she'd been punctured, and now it was just trickling out of her. 'It's actually Daenika.'

Her squad were looking at her now.

'Lorelei Kelvyr was just some Munitorum menial. I killed

her months ago. Took her name. I hate that I did it. I wish I hadn't.'

She looked up, meeting their eyes. To a soul, they regarded her with depleted acceptance. No anger. No disgust. No judgement at all. Not after all they'd been through as a unit.

'I was trying to get out of the war,' she told them. 'I didn't want to fight in the line. This was before I met all of you. You're not even my first regiment. This is just the only one I couldn't escape from. Throne, I'm so tired. We can finally run, finally leave all this shit behind us, and I'm so. Bloody. Tired.'

Her exhausted tears gave way to laughter. Weak laughter, and weary, but true.

'We're not running, Lor,' Sergeant Gathis said gently. On his vambrace, Lord Sanguinius had finished speaking. The primarch asked his last question, and already the shouts of 'No! No!' rang out across the Delphic Battlement. It was getting hard to speak over it.

'I know,' she called back over the yelling. 'Neither am I.'

Daenika and her squadmates added their voices to the chorus.

It would be a poor joke indeed to say that no one wanted to leave the wall in the wake of the primarch's words. Many wished to run. More than a few came close, but there were as many reasons to stay as there were defenders upon the wall. Every soul there fused some combination of anger, guilt and shame, cobbling them together to make a piecemeal courage the way people always do in their bleakest moments.

Some stayed out of duty. Others out of hope, deluded or otherwise, that reinforcements may yet reach them. Some stayed only because the resolve of those around them shamed them into staying. Some stayed because Sanguinius was right – they'd already given everything, and they had nothing worthwhile left to lose. Their lives were formalities by that point, a matter of biological habit, while the war had worn them down to hollow shells devoid of everything that had defined their lives. Some stayed because they were sick of running, and after two hundred days of defensive withdrawals, this was it, this was the last battle, and they would hold the wall out of tired spite.

Land would wonder, years later, if anyone truly did try to run. Surely some did. Were they restrained by companions or shot in the back by their officers? Were they allowed to quit the wall unopposed, as the Ninth had promised? It seemed likely (statistically certain, in fact) that this was the case, but each time he turned his goggles back towards the Royal Ascension, leading up to the Eternity Gate... the Gate stood open, disgorging a stream of soldiers and materiel. No one seemed to be going against the flow to venture inside. Nor did he see anyone making their way down from the wall to take their chances in the wasteland.

Perhaps if Land and the men and women like him – precious few though they are, in any era – had a firmer understanding of the human condition, it wouldn't have been such a surprise that so many stayed when there was a choice to flee.

No! cried the defenders of the wall. They rejected the primarch's offer with a gestalt sound of vocal thunder.

No! No! No!

Land didn't shout with the others. He wasn't one for the theatrics of yelled defiance. Still... *still*, there was something rather primal in the way the tumult washed over him. At one point he caught himself drawing in a shaky breath, almost joining his voice to the others. He resisted, naturally. What an embarrassing loss of decorum it would be, to join in.

Given all that Sanguinius had said regarding every moment mattering, and given the way Zephon had impressed upon him the vital import of doing all they could not to provoke the enemy into attacking early, Land blinked several times, entirely taken aback, when Sanguinius landed on the battlement, caught the blade Amit tossed to him, and launched into the air once more. Land's beaky nose scrunched up in disbelief as he watched the Great Angel soar towards the eastern horizon.

Along the wall, the cries of negation melted, fused, into a roar. The sound was exultant, bloodthirsty, joyous. Land had never heard its like. Sapien – perched on Land's shoulder – covered his little ears.

The Martian's disbelieving words were drowned by the tide. 'Tell me he's not going to kill that Titan.'

Somehow, Zephon heard his murmur over the bellowing thunder. The Blood Angel looked down at him, and Land was gratified by the cacophony, for it doubtless spared him another lecture. This one would be on the tenuous balance of morale, and capitalising on the defenders' high emotions, and a whole host of other nonsense that only applied to men and women unable to regulate their emotions through a healthy sense of distance and perspective.

Judging from the storm of voices, though, it would've been a difficult point to refute. The loss of their hour would be a sacrifice, but the boost to morale after Sanguinius' speech and whatever he planned to do out there in the wasteland was, apparently, a worthy exchange.

Land manually refocused his goggles and gazed across the cursed ground. Not watching the Titan, no. Nothing to see there. A genetic abomination-god cutting off the cockpit-head of an apostate avatar of the Omnissiah. Yes, yes, yes. Nothing that Land hadn't already seen half a dozen times in this war.

His attention was on the distant tide of the enemy lines, and the crucifixion forest they'd raised to celebrate their barbarity.

* * *

Two things happened when the Reaver's head fell.

The first, the most obvious, was that the horde's front lines started to move. Land wasn't even sure they had waited; they might have already started advancing before the Titan's head struck the earth, kicking up a cloud of ash and dust. Ahead of the Titans and tanks, ahead of the great walking things that Land suspected were some heretofore unknown strain of biomechanical siege weapons, a host of jagged, winged creatures darkened the sky above the horde's vanguard. They cut the heavens ahead of the horde, making for the Ninth Primarch alone on the field of battle.

The second thing that happened, concurrent with the first and visible only because Land turned his goggles towards the god-machine's body, was that Sanguinius immediately turned back and made for the battlement.

Daughter of Torment did not fall right away. Her graceless tumble came almost a minute after her decapitation, when – brainless – she could no longer regulate the energy animating her bones. At that point, she fell forward and slightly sideways, gouting reactor fire from her severed throat. By that point, the sky was vile with thousands of winged creatures. Exoplanar aberrations – daemons, if you wished to be crude about such matters – beating their chiropteran wings as they chased the Great Angel back towards sanctuary.

Perhaps halfway to the rampart, the creatures in the sky began to slow. Some faltered, circling back. Others dropped from the sky, these weaker ones disintegrating before they could even hit the earth. The largest, swiftest, or strongest in ways Land's eyesight couldn't easily determine, flew on in pursuit, but they were bursting, bleeding, their forms threatening to come apart with each beat of their wings. So fascinating was their destruction that Land, who prided himself on his acuity, took a moment to realise he was witnessing the Omnissiah's psychic shield still in force.

He laughed aloud, delighted by the sight, only to find the sound lost in the cheers rising all around. And *that* was strange enough to make his skin crawl, sharing a moment of joy with so many people around him.

Sanguinius landed on the rampart in a skid, sparks spraying from his golden boots as they slid across stone, his wings spread wide to slow himself down. His sword was still marked with holy oils and lubricants from where it had chopped through the bindings of *Daughter of Torment*'s neck.

The cheering redoubled. Sapien covered his ears again.

The Great Angel whirled back to face the horizon's tide. Seconds, at most, from being in range of the wall-guns.

'Legion!' he called. *'Legion!'*

The order was taken up along the wall, officer to officer, and shouted further across the vox. Land could hear it rippling away in a stream of retreating sound, like a dissipating echo: *Legion, Legion! Legion, Legion…*

In a crashing harmony of ceramite, the Astartes – all the Astartes – stepped forward. The human defenders had no choice but to move back. Drilling and training took over; the mortal defenders scrambled out of the way. A line of warriors in Blood Angels red took their place at the ramparts, their uniformity broken only by patches of Imperial Fists yellow and White Scars white. Tens of thousands of boltguns lifted, braced in readiness.

'Let them break upon us,' Sanguinius ordered, and Land realised with an unexpected sense of awe that the Great Angel wasn't addressing his Legion. He was beating his wings again, calling out to the humans that massed behind the Astartes' lines.

'You have your orders,' Sanguinius called to the Army units and the civilians with their unfamiliar guns. His voice was calm as it carried across the closest squads and was transmitted onward over the vox. 'You know your roles. Hold, and lend aid where you can. But let them first break upon us.'

Sanguinius – *no, he is the Ninth, he's the Ninth Primarch, damn it* – turned back to face the foe. Still distant, but close enough for…

The Great Angel's sword swept down.

The million guns of the Sanctum Imperialis started singing.

PART SIX

ECHOES OF ETERNITY

TWENTY-NINE

Siege of the Sanctum Imperialis

The Legio Krytos Titan *Serenity of Retribution* had achieved a kind of mongrel sentience, comprised of the instincts and emotions that generations of her princeps had experienced while plugged into her systems. She could feel and, to a lesser extent, think. She knew fear and pain, she knew the thrill and relief of victory, and above all, she knew how to hate. The crews and engines of Krytos were among the best at that.

These were things her succession of princeps had known, so she knew them now. Her conception of these processes was crude, and she possessed no mastery over them, but she was a walking god of iron and firepower, so the subtleties of mental regulation were largely irrelevant to her anyway.

She knew pride, too. This was the sensation that flowed fiercest through the electrical connections that formed her mind. In a lesser being, such self-obsession with all her own achievements might be considered vanity, but she had no way to assess such things. Everything *Serenity* knew and felt, she knew and felt with overwhelming force. She had lived

through generations of commanding princeps – the calculation by which she measured time – and every enemy she
had faced was either dead or had fled. In the boundaries of
tumbling calculations that passed for her intelligence, she had
every right to be vain.

As she strode towards the Delphic Battlement, she felt the
exaltation of wondrous purpose. Her war-horn blared in time
with her saurian cries, warning the vermin infantry at her feet
to thank her for the honour of leading them. Final and ultimate
victory lay beyond the wall. The immensity of her emotions
allowed her a form of stunted imagination, and already she
could conceive of the blessings her worshippers would sing
up at her, as well as the fresh triumph banners they would
hang from her guns.

Her crew was dead, their corpses rolling around inside her
head, lurching against their consoles and across the deck.
Serenity of Retribution didn't know this, which was fortunate,
because had she become aware of it, the revelation would
have undone her in a way her emergent consciousness might
not have survived. The path to sentience is a precarious one
for all forms of life, and it was a journey often failed by even
the strongest of machine-spirits. The fact is, *Serenity of Retribution* was functioning on the legacies of what human instinct
had imprinted on her, and whether that could fuse with a
machine-spirit to create true sentience is a matter even Arkhan
Land would've struggled to answer. He did, of course, have
theories on the matter.

She strode down the Grand Processional, destroying marble
statuary beneath her, turning the icons of heroes into white
rubble and clouds of powder, marching at full stride behind
the thick layers of her overcharged void shields. She was one
of the lead Titans, her void shields offering sanctuary to many
souls and tanks in her shadow. Incoming fire made her shields

visible; they were layered curves of bruised light, fire spilling down their sides to fall upon the warriors below in napalm rain.

The opening missile salvo from the Delphic Battlement roared across the cancerous wasteland – hundreds of warheads; thousands of them – and she knew, even with the instinctive awareness that could only arguably be called reasoning, that she was about to die. This proud Warlord of the God Breaker Legio had neither the honour of the first death nor the most catastrophic. Her demise was just another footnote in a list of names too long to ever be accurately preserved – not in the eternally unreliable mechanisms of Imperial records, or by the word-of-mouth legend and chanted prayers that would pass for archival data in the future of the Warmaster's forces.

She never knew exactly how many missiles struck her, and like so much of the war to date, the scale both defied easy calculation and meant nothing in the context of the woe it inflicted. They struck her like a warrior in a shield wall being struck by thirty spears in the same second. She was dead before she fell, her void shields instantly burst, her superstructure igniting and blowing apart, scattering fiery shrapnel for a half-kilometre in every direction.

Her last thought was notable, however, in its instinctive unselfishness. It was a command, remarkable for the fact that no princeps lived to order it.

[SOLACE-SANCTUARY PROTOCOL], she thought.

The armoured cockpit that made up her head blew its lynchlocks exactly two point seven seconds before the Sanctum's first salvo struck home. She willingly decapitated herself, the escape pod protocol blasting her head free from her shoulders along a hurriedly cogitated trajectory.

It wasn't enough, and even had her crew still lived, it would never have been enough. The cockpit-head clipped one of the incoming missiles, catching aflame and spinning off course in the wake of the explosion, before crashing into the wasteland. There it lay at rest, a blown-open tomb for the three souls that had died weeks ago, only to be destroyed by the curtain of artillery fire that followed mere seconds after the first missile wave.

Dawynne Coto hadn't needed to be conscripted, she'd signed up willingly. The Warmaster had liberated her world from the unfair demands of its alien overlords, and granted not only freedom, but also membership within humanity's Imperium. When the recruiting ships visited a decade later, stating that Warmaster Horus had need of loyal soldiers to make war upon the corrupt Emperor, that had settled it. It would be a lie to say Dawynne was entirely without guilt at leaving the harvest unfinished, but some things mattered more than storing up grain for the coming season. Her parents could hire on additional hands to see it done. Dawynne, along with her older brother, had taken a wagon into the trading-town, and signed their names without hesitation.

That was five years ago. Her brother was dead; Nessin hadn't even seen Terra. He'd been killed in a boarding action only months after recruitment, when their ship had been attacked by... Well. By someone else, some other force loyal to the Emperor. Some cyborged force of Martian horrors. Exact details rarely filtered down all the layers of military hierarchy to the grunts. At first, the lack of clarity on anything had frightened Dawynne, but as time passed, she became inured to it. She came to realise that all she needed to know was where to go and who to shoot once she got there. Anything beyond that was a bonus. Acceptance of this fact was the first real sign of her veterancy.

Corporal Primus-grade Coto was in a Chimera when she

died. The first wave of firepower from the Delphic Battlement was a missile fusillade focused on killing the Titans that towered over the horde, but the second wave was traditional artillery, a rain of bombardment that blanketed the wasteland in fire and phosphex. In all her imaginings of her final moments, she'd died with a blessing for her family on her lips, or – when she really dared to dream – ended everything heroically, bleeding out on a mound of enemy dead.

But war has no sympathy for man's personal melodramas. In reality, Dawynne was instantly incinerated by a Gryphon shell striking her Chimera, and what remained of her was indistinguishable from the mess of the nine other men and women flash-fried to the shrapnel of their murdered vehicle.

Deiphobus of the Emperor's Children covered the wasteland in great leaps, boosting in high arcs with thrusts of his jump pack, coming down in controlled descents to hit the ground running each time. He was one of hundreds, skyborne units from every Legion coming together in a boosted charge.

He had changed since the war's commencement. There was something alive in his throat, something he felt shifting and curling, making his neck swell. Sometimes it made him speak with its voice and think its thoughts. He no longer wore a helmet, and his breastplate was a corroded mess, because he salivated all the time now, and his saliva was chemically similar to hydraklaurik acid.

Deiphobus had gone to the III Legion's Apothecaries long before the Terran Campaign began, and demanded they remove the parasite. But it was no parasite, they told him, and as they showed him the scans, they chastised him for his lack of gratitude and vision. He was blessed. The refinement enhanced him, enhanced his lethality, and was he not a weapon, born and raised to exult in the taking of life?

He had agreed. Or, rather, the thing in his throat had spoken agreement, using his body to do it.

Secretly, he had considered cutting it out, but he always remembered the scans. What he'd seen on those screens was part of him, a changing of his own flesh rather than some external intrusion. He doubted he would survive the process of self-removal.

Soon enough, his alterations weren't even notable. Others in his own squad went through greater changes, never calling them mutations, always 'enhancements' and 'refinements'.

He stroked his throat sometimes. Feeling the way it swelled with his unspoken sins and secrets. Caressing it coaxed runnels of steaming acid that flowed sweetly over his teeth. Deiphobus had long since come to terms with his refinements. He appreciated them. Not just the first, and not just their lethality, but the others that had followed and the strange cocktail of desires they inspired.

He wanted to taste Sanguinius' blood. That was why he was here, assaulting the Sanctum instead of cavorting in the southern lands with so many of his Legion brothers. He wanted to gulp it, to quaff it so it washed over the changed flesh of his throat, stinging divinely as it went down. This need was eating away at him; it had been all he could think of for weeks. No other sustenance quenched his thirst. Not even the IX Legion blood he'd drunk, not the IX Legion flesh he'd eaten. The need was making him spasm and tremble, so fierce had it become: an addiction to a taste he'd never tasted.

He would not get his wish. He didn't even reach the Delphic Battlement. Something approximately as hot as the sun and twice as bright hit his breastplate, dropping him out of the sky in a nauseating, disorientating tumble. His freefall lasted all of four dizzying, breathless seconds, and he died upon impact without ever realising he'd taken a lascannon beam through the chest.

* * *

Ja-Hen Uquar was a conscript of the Neshamere Eighth Mech-
anised Infantry, riding in one of the sixteen gunnery cupolas
of an Orion-pattern troop carrier. He stammered a constant
stream of prayers and curses, at all times of day, barely able
to speak anymore because his throat was so hoarse. Each time
he tried to sleep in the rare periods his regiment found the
chance to rest, he saw the events of the last half-year playing out again and again behind his eyes. It's possible to be
driven from reason by sleep deprivation. Ja-Hen had learned
this the hard way.

He was thrown from his turret when an explosion took out
his transport, along with the hundreds of soldiers inside. He was
unconscious for less than a minute, and when he woke on the
ground, he no longer had the dubious protection of his squadmates and their armoured carrier. Ja-Hen saw the wreckage that
had been his platoon's mobile bunker for years, broken open
and smoking, with bodies strewn liberally throughout.

He was alone, armed with a pistol, in a wasteland of exploding
earth as gunships screamed in spiralling crash landings, and
Titans burned and shrieked above him, and the world shook
equal to any earthquake, and impossible dead things spanned
the entire sky. He was crying out himself, though he wasn't
aware of it, and not just because the sound was minimal with
his abused vocal cords; like thousands of others on both sides
of the battle, he was deaf, his eardrums ruptured by the magnitude of the weapons firing above him, around him, at him.

Please let this end, he thought, which was the closest he'd
come to thinking clearly in weeks. He ate the barrel of his
pistol and pulled the trigger.

His anima – what some would call a soul – unanchored from
his body and went screaming through the veil between corporeality and unreality, plunging immediately into the boiling
tides of the warp. The weakling soul-light that had been Ja-Hen

Uquar experienced one final sensation as it learned the lesson of what waited in death for all living things, and that lesson was pain. The pain of dissolution. The pain of one's soul-light drawing daemons the way blood draws sharks in dark water.

Finally, mercifully, and in accordance with his dying wish, it ended.

Varak'suul had suffered for her weak genesis. Insofar as her kind held to any notions of physicality, she was a *she*, for the Neverborn are shaped by human deeds and fears. Like most of her kind, she was brought into being by an act of malice, in this case one of betrayal that led to bloodshed.

She was also weak. Varak'suul's genesis was in the guilty pleasure taken by a murderer, in the back alley of a long-dead city in a long-forgotten empire on a planet that had died centuries ago in the gloom of Old Night. Like all her kind that lacked a ready source of faith or devotion to fuel them, she manifested in the warp and took forever to grow stronger. From her very first moments, her existence was one of parasitic cowardice, feeding on lesser secrets in the hearts of weak men, and hiding from her own kind in case they abused and digested her for their own power.

She had briefly served as a courtier in the Halls of the Wilfully and Ecstatically Blind. This place, ruled over by an exiled Keeper known as the Pale One, was an impoverished realm far from the grand court at the Palace of Pleasure. But even this far from the gaze of the Perfect Prince, ambition burned in the hearts of Slaanesh's children, and they made war upon one another with lies, poison, temptation, and a thousand other treacheries. Varak'suul had fled the Pale One's entourage, wandering through the far reaches of the Realms of Chaos; distant enough to hide among the other scavengers, not quite removed enough to discorporate her.

And then: the summons had come. She'd felt the irresist-
ible pull, the siren song of her young god's call. It wasn't
merely a beckoning, it pulled at the very threads of her being.
It dragged at her corpus, bringing her to Terra whether she
willed it or not.

She had manifested weeks ago, clawing her way into the
cold material realm, her mouth watering at the flavours of fear
and the prayers for deliverance thick in the air. Since then, she
had lapped at the brainflesh of skull-cracked captives, licking
them with her barbed tongue. She had danced in battle with
all the grace of her god-formed body, carving through the
armour of humans and transhumans alike. She had moved
with clusters of her own kind, drinking the sensations of the
humans around them, heightening their emotions and lying
with promises of survival; and always, always moving inward.
The names of the walls and districts meant nothing to her.
She knew only that at the heart of all this iron and stone lay
a castle, and within that castle was the flesh-body of the creature that the Pantheon mockingly called the Anathema.

But she couldn't *reach* the castle. None of them could. The
desire to descend upon it throbbed inside the speculative
energy that served as her skull – it pulsed with the malignant life of a tumour – but every step she took towards it
met with an invisible field of resistance. This pressure rejected
her. It repulsed all her kind, turning reality thick and worthless around them.

It even hurled the Lord of the Red Sands back each time
he flew at it in his rage. He was a disgusting and unnatural
thing, a mortal elevated to immortality, and she wondered if
this 'Angron' and his primarch brothers could even comprehend the disgust that the true Neverborn felt for them. When
Varak'suul and her siblings witnessed the transhumans seeking
to follow their gene-fathers into ascension, it had brought ripe

new opportunities to promise them eternity and deceive them into doing the daemons' will.

But these were lesser concerns. She could prey on their desperate souls later.

One of the recently exalted mortals, the one calling itself 'Magnus', was doing the will of the Changer, deep in the labyrinthine dimension. Varak'suul was nothing, unworthy of knowing the truths of the conflict, but she sensed the energies at play. She felt the weakening of the Emperor's efforts as the thing that was once His son wore away His strength. Blessedly, the Emperor's shield was collapsing faster, no longer day by day, but hour by hour. The threat of repulsion still slowly ate away at her corpus, but she – and all of her kind – were getting closer, closer. When the horde had charged, the mortal tide rushing towards the wall, Varak'suul had been one of the many thousands of daemons left behind.

She watched the Warmaster's humans and transhumans race ahead. She watched them swarm the wall. And every time she felt the shield ebbing, she took a step forward.

Princeps Ulienne Grune of the Warhound *Hindarah* hunched in her throne, her posture mimicking the lope of her god-machine body. In front of her, Otesh was leaning hard into her controls, bringing *Hindarah* around in a bone-rattling run. Himmar – *was dead, they were both dead, she was locked in the cockpit with their corpses* – was guiding the weapons arms around to match their movement.

'We've been engaged,' said Himmar, with his eyes on the auspex screen. And though Himmar said it, Ulienne heard the words in her voice, felt them coming out of her mouth.

I am talking to myself, she thought, *because Otesh and Himmar have been dead for weeks.*

'New heading achieved, my princeps,' said Otesh.

They were running blind. The view through *Hindarah*'s eye-windows was nothing but fire; outside, the world was ending. Even with the cockpit insulated and shielded, the sound of the destruction was just short of agonising. There was too much information to take in, overwhelming her senses, overloading her scanners. Ulienne focused on a single flickering topography screen, doing what she could with the little data she could tolerate. The landscape before the Delphic Battlement was a featureless plain of ruined earth. The horde swarmed over it in their ragged millions.

The closer they came to the wall, the more often brief bursts of the wider battle intruded. A Stormbird spiralling down to crash on a rampart. Another Titan going nova, near enough to rain body shrapnel against *Hindarah*'s long-suffering void shields. A swarm of Astartes, thousands upon thousands of them, charging along the rubble-strewn Grand Processional; thousands more swarming the sheer face of the Delphic Battlement, using entrenching tools and grapnels to climb. Most surreal of all was the slope of spent ammunition at the wall's base, an avalanche of ejected shells forming as they tumbled down from the battlement's guns in a never-ending, clanking torrent.

'Ten,' Himmar called back to her. 'Nine.'

Ulienne forced *Hindarah* forward, hunching into the storm of incoming fire. Her spotlights stabbed through the ashy air, illuminating the troop transports and battle tanks around her.

'The first gunships are on the ramparts,' said Otesh, watching through the interference plaguing *Hindarah*'s external picter feeds. 'The first Titans are almost at the wall.'

Except they weren't the first gunships and the first Titans. The first gunships and Titans were smoking wreckage in the wasteland. Those making it to the wall were just the first to survive the atrocity of firepower unleashed upon the charging horde.

Himmar called again, 'Five, four.'

Ulienne did her best to ignore the pounding against her shields and the shaking of the earth beneath her feet. *Hindarah* had been repaired and rearmed once Audax's maintenance vehicles had caught up with the front line days ago, but the reassuring weight of possessing both arms again was cold comfort when the world was ending around her. A sickening electrical crack told the tale of another void layer stripped away. *Hindarah* gave a canine snarl in the back of Ulienne's mind, as if blaming her for this headlong march into madness.

'One,' said Himmar. 'Zero.'

Hindarah snarled at her again, a mind-sharing of revulsion, and Ulienne's skin crawled in sympathy with her swimming vision. A snap of static cracked at her fingertips from the arm of her throne. Then it was over, and they were through.

'We're inside their voids,' Himmar confirmed. 'We lost a layer of shielding from the abrasion.'

She didn't need to give the order to relight the shields to full capacity; Himmar was already on it.

'Stay back from the Delphic Arch. Let the sapping crews handle the portcullises. Find one of our Reavers or Warlords, add our firepower to theirs.'

'Aye, my princeps,' said the two dead moderati in unison. Or perhaps she said it herself. It didn't really matter. She spared a glance for the army of disordered Astartes assaulting the wall, imagined the many thousands of defenders waiting at the top of its tiered ramparts, and focused on the task ahead of her.

There was very little left of Kargos now. When he reached for memories, or even emotions, he kept finding anger, stripped of all circumstance. The realisation that pieces of his mind were falling away should have been horrific, but the opposite was true. He felt purified, when he felt anything at all.

Nothing cleanses the soul the way anger does. Nothing feeds righteousness like rage.

He'd been inside a Land Raider. He remembered that. At least, he remembered the sensation of being trapped within it. The confines. The darkness. The sound above all else: the sound of the world being destroyed on the other side of the Land Raider's hull. It was a sound that broke the limits of sound, spreading to fill all five senses.

He remembered the pride he felt because he was going in before the Neverborn. For some reason, that mattered. There was honour in it. In the beginning it would just be the living against the living. Human against human, Legion against Legion.

He remembered what the preacher had said, before the tank treads rolled.

'The last gasp of mortal warfare.'

Yes. That was it. And Inzar had sounded as if he relished the idea, like the sun was setting on something primitive and best left forgotten.

Then the engine gunned. The Land Raider lurched forward. They were making for the Delphic Wall and things darkened to red and black. What else was there? He could remember... Wait. Could he remember reaching the wall? Climbing it? Gaining the rampart? Could he remember those things?

No. He couldn't. But he did recall...

Wait. Hadn't he come in on a gunship? One of the Thunderhawks that streaked in from the sky, a host of them aflame from the anti-air batteries...

Yes. They hadn't been in a Land Raider at all. They'd come in by gunship.

Hadn't they?

He didn't know. These things were gone from him, taken by the Nails. But he knew–

* * *

–nothing, as he tears left and right with abandon, cutting, carving, killing.

Kargos fights for his life, he fights for the amusement of the God of War, and he fights to follow his father down the path of bloodstained divinity, for to do anything else is to damn himself. There's no going back. There's only the Path, step by step, one slaughtered life at a time.

He doesn't think these things consciously. He doesn't treasure the truth of them. He knows them, that's all, and they've changed him. The truth of a broken existence squats at the back of his mind, and its tendrils flow through him with the flood of adrenaline and instinct.

Zephon fought by Anzarael's side, surrounded by the last living members of the High Host. Their blades steamed as the power fields burned away the blood clinging to the steel. This was far from how they'd waged war together in the glory days of the Great Crusade. Those were days of soaring on jump pack thrusts, unleashing the destructiveness of retooled Strife Age alchemicals. They were angels in truth: death from the skies, descending on wings of flame. Here, they were grounded, going blade to blade, fist to fist. The enemy was without end.

'Forgive me for saying so, sir,' Anzarael voxed at one point during the fighting, 'but this is far from a joyous reunion.'

It started with the thunder of long-range guns. As the horde charged, both sides vented an infinity of city-killing fire. Titans vomited missiles at the wall; other Titans gunned down the incoming volleys and replied with their own incendiary rages. The wall shook beneath the defenders' feet as its gun emplacements poured firepower into the wasteland. It still shook – the Delphic Battlement still fired even on the second dawn with the enemy at the defenders' throats, its few remaining guns blasting and their slaved autoloading mechanisms clanking, making the entire rampart shudder endlessly.

How many tens of thousands among the horde were killed in the first charge to the rampart? How many Titans were torn apart by cannonade? How many gunships and drop-ships and troop carriers and transports were blasted out of the sky? The scale of it was madness; the numbers untrackable, meaningless. Even with an eidetic recall, Zephon could process almost none of it. It was just the prologue. All just a laughable prologue to the moment the horde reached the wall.

The attackers poured everything into the assault without heed, or need, of tactics. They came in suicidal packs of frenzied warriors, descending on jump packs. They came in gunships and transports, carving furrows along the battlements and massacring defenders as they crash-landed in deployment. They blackened the sky with drop-ships and the towering figures of converted Titans. They came from the ground, climbing the Delphic Wall with axes and blades, ascending over the mounds of their own dead or the piles of spent shells vomited forth from the battlement's ammunition ports. However they gained the ramparts, the defenders met them in a tide of red ceramite, locked shields and plunging blades.

For Zephon, it began when a walking inferno that had once been a Warlord Titan reached the wall, towering over him like a blazing effigy. The Titan, dying from its wounds and aflame from crown to clawed feet, was more a thing of flesh than sacred iron, and no longer moved as a Titan moved. Ligaments and veins and muscles worked slickly around its iron skeleton. It gripped the wall with great hands of metal and bone, and leaned forward, its fleshmetal jaw opening, opening… Disgorging a troop ramp like a bladed tongue, vomiting its cargo of World Eaters right onto the rampart. The thing was laughing as it did it, laughing from the speakers in its cheeks and throat, laughing even as it burned to death.

Zephon, in the front rank, caught a World Eater's chainaxe

against the flat of his blade – and from that moment on, existence on the ramparts became an assault of sensation. Sight,
sound, smell – all of it became a thing to endure instead of
experience. A soldier could lose their mind in this, through
sheer exposure to sensation. Thousands of the humans did.

Another World Eater gained the wall half a second after he'd
killed the first. Zephon beat the pommel of his blade against
the warrior's faceplate once, twice, thrice. Ceramite dented.
Cracked. Sharded. The World Eater roared his god-soaked
noise, grabbing for Zephon's throat with one hand, thrusting
a dagger in the other. The Blood Angel deflected the whirring
blade with the edge of his greave, lanced his blade down in
a two-handed grip that sank halfway to the hilt in the warri-
or's collarbone. He barely managed to drag it free before the
World Eater fell, his hearts destroyed.

And yet, the defenders held to a ragged order. Imperial Army
soldiers climbed onto the rear tiers of the rampart to launch
grenades and stitch the air with lasgun beams over the heads
of the warring Astartes, spearing into the enemy ranks. Where
the line was breached, where the Blood Angels were beaten
back or massacred in place, Custodians led reserve forces to
stem the tide.

Word of Sanguinius spread across the vox. Reports that he
was on the south wall, repelling a sapper assault; or the west
wall, leading a boarding action upon an Imperator Titan; or
the north wall, rallying the broken defenders and retaking lost
ground; or the east wall, where he was hunting enemy officers,
lancing them from above as he swooped in low, soaring again
after each confirmed kill.

Who knew what was true? On the wall, every warrior was
caged within their own war. Zephon only saw Sanguinius once
after the battle began, a brief vision of his golden primarch
spiralling through the air high above their heads, hopelessly

pursued by a pack of traitors in jump packs. He'd looped around, cutting three of them from the sky in as many seconds, then beat his wings to rise higher than the survivors could boost.

Anzarael went down, grappled by a cackling Emperor's Children legionary, while humans in scraps of armour stabbed at the joints of his warplate with energised knives. Zephon hacked him free and dragged him back up; less than a minute later, Anzarael returned the favour, killing a World Eater and pulling the fallen Zephon back to his feet.

Sanguinius was gone, back to the realm of vox-reports that already took on the flavour of legend. Zephon fought on, his mind cold even as his flesh was wretched with heat. By now he would usually be frothing at the mouth within his helmet, exhaustion and bloodthirst combining to bring him to the very edge of his control. Yet he stayed cold and clear, enduring, hurting, fighting.

Any battle is a succession of distinct conflicts, and the effect is magnified in sieges. A hundred metres down the line, warriors might be waiting in phalanx readiness, still yet to bloody their blades, knowing they must not break ranks and leave their position undefended. A hundred metres in the other direction, warriors are fighting for their lives; have been fighting for hours. Then the flow of war shifts. Reserve elements charge in to relieve exhausted defenders. Those that have been fighting for hours on end suddenly find themselves in a brief sphere of calm, able to retreat or brace for the next inevitable assault.

Even in the shield-to-shield phalanx warfare of Old Earth, men would wear themselves down to enervation within minutes. Those ancient battles that lasted hours were, in truth, divided into dozens of lesser skirmishes broken up by entrenchment, advance, retreat, relief, recovery. It had to be this way. The human body was at the mercy of mortal musculature. War in the first age of trenches and gunpowder weapons was a horrendously long game of brief strikes and charges, broken up by days – months – of waiting for the order to advance. The taking of a city still necessitated patrols, rides in armoured personnel carriers, returning to one's own lines for resupply, all transpiring over the course of weeks. The fighting was sporadic, not constant.

But on the Delphic Battlement, even the Astartes suffered. The press of bodies was all-consuming. Zephon saw nothing beyond the frenzy of overwhelming movement on all sides, at all angles. The threat of seizure was a constant in the muscles he had that were still flesh instead of Dark Age steel. The chron at the edge of his eye-lens display counted time in stuttering leaps that went in both directions. Just another thing that had ceased making any sense.

Thralls in Legion robes and silver breastplates were everywhere within the defenders' lines. They hunched and crouched and scrambled between their Blood Angels masters – some hauling away the dead, dragging corpses back out of the way for the sake of their lords' footing; others firing between the shoulders of the fighting legionaries, pouring las-fire into the faces of the Warmaster's human soldiers.

It seemed every atom around him was visible, vibrating in peaceless motion. He heard everything, everything, thousands of sounds adding up to an oceanic roar, its elements indivisible. A blade against a blade was a clash, a boltgun discharging was a rattling boom; but hundreds of thousands, all at once and over and over, became white noise without surcease. He smelled nothing but the burn-reek of charred armour and firing processes, a stink so thick it threatened to replace air. Each breath in tasted of fyceline. Each breath out tasted of the countless other chemicals used in the manufacture of annihilation. In the rare moments he saw anything past the warrior directly in front of him, it was always a momentary impression of Titans duelling in front of the battlement. They went at one another with sawblades and fists and hammers and short-range volleys of fire that occluded them in smoke before Zephon could discern which side either one fought for, let alone who might be winning.

And so it went.

The engines of Legio Ignatum repelled every charge made against the portcullises sealing the Delphic Archway. The ground of the wasteland was blended to ruination by the levels of firepower brought to bear, an expanse of hills and ravines through which the Warmaster's horde poured forward.

Princeps Shiva Makul of *Iracundos* did what she could to thin the numbers of infantry and armour, but their orders from the Great Angel were clear: Ignatum was there to kill Titans. The portcullis must stand.

They fought unsupported by infantry, and that was a dangerous way for Titans to wage war. It left them vulnerable, with several Ignatum god-machines already standing motionless, boarded by the warriors of the horde, their crews locked in fighting within the confines of their Titans' engineered bones.

Their principal advantage was the Delphic Battlement behind them, and the keep atop it, with its shield-bursting gun batteries. *Iracundos* had scored its first kill against a charging Reaver, an Interfector brawler stalk-striding ahead of its own maniple, either thirsting for glory or at the mercy of an unwise machine-spirit. With its void shields extinguished and its proud red-and-black heraldry bored through by gatling fire, the Interfector Reaver was three-quarters dead already. *Iracundos* hadn't even needed to open fire at range. By the time the brawler was up close, sparks were raining from her abused arm joints and she gushed oil and fluids from a dozen major wounds. The Ignatum Reaver strode forth to meet her opponent in front of the portcullis, stalking around to the rear where her plating was thinnest, and finishing her spinally with a volley of overcharged laser.

But the hunting got harder as the hours rolled on. Shiva saw *Gylgamesh* crumble when it was half-erased from existence by a volley of warp missiles. She saw *Optima Diktat* lose its brawl against another Warlord, gutted by the miserable slowness of her rival's chainfist. *Magna Excelsior* was brought down by the dogs of Audax, dragged from her feet by a net of ursus claws and overrun by exoplanar xenos – a description among the Mechanicus that was swiftly falling out of favour. Most crews were using 'Neverborn' to describe the things now. A few even named them daemons.

Iracundos held the line until her death, which came at the hands of the Warbringer *Glaivemaiden*. Shiva didn't see it coming; her Titan's demise was just one of the many that came at maximal range from coordinated fields of fire, when maniples would group up for a kill. The shell from *Glaivemaiden*'s quake cannon struck six point six-one seconds after the final layer of *Iracundos'* voids cracked out of existence, destroying the Reaver's head and a significant portion of its left shoulder superstructure. With the god-machine deprived of command crew, its stabilisers vented pressure, powered down, and went slack. The Titan's corpse toppled forward into the wasteland, where it settled with a crash and quietly burned, already half-buried in a crater carved out by enemy artillery.

Not that it would ever enter any Martian or Terran archive, but there was a lone survivor of this final fall. His name was Maestol Vurir, and he was a deacon-enginseer of middling rank within the Adeptus Mechanicus, as well as a lifelong servant and ally to the noble Legio Ignatum. He lived for almost another two hours, his legs crushed in the wreckage of *Iracundos*' annihilated insides. There he remained, in excruciating pain, praying to a Machine-God he'd never failed, beseeching the Omnissiah not to abandon him now.

For the final hundred and eight minutes of his life (between prayers, of course), Maestol tried in vain to move some of the debris off his legs, while it became harder and harder to breathe. He was unsure if he would expire from organ failure – when his augmented heart and lungs gave out under the strain of maintaining his broken form – or fluid loss from the blood and reagent lubricants he was leaking from his shattered legs.

Ultimately, it was neither. A chance spark from the Titan's failing electricals ignited a pool of spreading promethium, and he couldn't crawl away from the fire. It engulfed him, eating him along with the rest of *Iracundos*' insides. He wasn't limited to a skitarius' coded bleating, and possessed a voice that was mostly human, so he could still scream. Which, indeed, he did.

Arkhan Land's new leg was killing him. Not literally, but a person should be forgiven for their moments of hyperbole, provided they were validated by context. And Land, in the middle of a war between demigods, while limping on a bionic leg that was poorly integrated and increasingly refusing to obey him, was feeling extremely validated by context.

He had also learned a lesson he would have preferred to go his entire life without learning, and that was the primal horror that runs through your guts when your own lines break. Land had come to realise that even more frightening than open battle was the moment a deadlock, slipping into a defeat, risked becoming a retreat.

When a line holds, you can rely on the souls next to you, fighting as hard as you're fighting; and the soldiers behind you, ready to rush in and aid you when needed. Even in the worst of the chaos, there's a near-unconscious comfort in these things.

When a line breaks, you lose these tattered, precious reassurances. You can no longer rely on the men and women around you, if they're even alive at all. You're confronted with the fact that the enemy is stronger than you. You can lose. You can die. You *will* die if you hold your position and allow yourself to become surrounded. What do you do? Stand and die? Retreat and abandon the few survivors around you? Seeing you run, they run themselves, either out of the same prudence or the same cowardice, and the dissolution spreads. It's a train of consequences, each unfolding in inevitable succession as more defenders desert the unravelling line.

The Warmaster's forces broke through again and again, repelled at first by Blood Angels reserves, then by Custodian-led human units. How the Astartes in the front lines could even see what was happening was a mystery to Land. He focused on shooting between the warring Blood Angels, atomising World Eaters and Death Guard and who knew how many human soldiers in the colours of the Warmaster's regiments. When Zephon and the others stumbled on the mounds of bodies, he joined in with Eristes and the other thralls in dragging the corpses back for flamer teams to incinerate. Transacta-7Y1 had covered him without him needing to ask her. He was determined to take her with him, back to Mars, if they somehow survived.

Many of the bodies they dragged turned out to still be alive. That had been quite the unpleasant series of revelations; it surprised him every time they started thrashing. Some were well on their way to dying, others were hideously mutilated in the manner most unfortunate souls tend to become if they were foolish or zealous enough to go into battle against the Legiones Astartes. They groaned and flailed and cried out for help as Land dragged them back from the front lines. Plenty of them still had enough fight left in them to stab at him or try to shoot him; these he despatched with an atomic slug to the forehead, or he let the thralls' bayonets finish them off. A notable few were still aware enough of their surroundings to take heed of the incineration teams waiting at the battlement's rear, and these struggled or pleaded for mercy. Land dragged them to their burning deaths without even a proton's worth of guilt.

Sweat coated him. He was swaddled in the stink of his own body heat, dragging and shooting and – yes, let's be honest – cowering and running for hours on end. Along with the other humans, he was exhausted long before the Astartes even showed the first signs of tiring. When the order rang out for the first reserves to march in, Land had fallen in place, dropping from exhaustion. Spit ran from his bloody lips in stalactite strings. His muscles shivered with an exhaustion too profound to codify.

Unmoving, he let the reserves charge around him, and indeed over him, waiting for Transacta-7Y1 to help him up once their replacements had passed. Once he was back on his feet, they made their limping way back towards the rearward bunkers set up as respite stations. Zephon's thralls were with him, also granted reprieve. The wounded, in their droves, were carried along the Royal Ascension, through the open Eternity Gate, and into the Sanctum. Custodians and Sisters of Silence still guided scores of Imperial Army troops out from the Sanctum, ordering them to support sections of the embattled wall.

'We've been fighting forever,' said Land. His tone was one of exhausted wonder.

The thralls nodded, their faces matching those of all the soldiers falling back around them; displaying a kind of grim awe that they were still alive.

Transacta-7Y1, her facial expression obviously hidden by

her helmet, pointed out that it had not been forever. She gave him the precise elapsing of time instead.

'It's close enough, Tee,' Land sighed without rancour. 'Close enough to forever.'

Within the hour, they were back at the front line.

Above all of this soared the Lord of the Red Sands. He beat flayed wings as he hurled himself, again and again, at the Sanctum Imperialis below. Each attempt saw him thrown back into the sky, while the gods' laughter at his failure echoed in his ears.

Angron roared the words which would, in centuries to come, define his Legion. He bellowed that oath across the sky, with only the scarcest conception of what he was saying. Words repeated in the shouted voices of every living World Eater. Words taken by the ignorant defenders as the ravings of baresarks and killers.

Blood for the Blood God! Skulls for the Skull Throne!

He was the strongest. Instinctively, he knew it was so, the way a beast hunting in its domain knows it stands at the apex of all surrounding life. But his strength was what held him back. The weaker Neverborn were beginning to advance, pressing through seams in the unseeable shield. The Lord of the Red Sands could see them, these lesser things, advancing behind the human horde. But the strongest of them were still repelled with hateful force.

Hundreds of thousands of souls stood on the wall, fighting. He thirsted for their blood. He would wallow in it, he would pour fistfuls of their skulls down his throat, he would bathe in reaped life, if he could just breach the shield. If their father would just weaken enough…

+No, not if.+

Horus?

+Not if, brother. When.+

* * *

Inzar's frenzy was a careful thing. He fought in the front lines, but he fought cold, forcing World Eaters and Death Guard in front of him to face the most eager blades, while he focused on butchering downed Blood Angels. Beneath him, the battlement shivered without end. It was still firing into the wasteland, bellowing at the advancing horde, bringing down Titans and regiments and tanks not yet at the wall. Despite the overwhelming numbers the Warmaster's forces possessed, he suspected the taking of the Eternity Gate would be a protracted engagement, not the easy triumph many of his weaker-minded kindred were so earnestly howling about.

He had to keep his wits and resist the lure of losing himself in the battle. Inzar hadn't come this far to die in the final days.

This kind of war, the merciless kineticism of transhumans killing each other faster than the human eye could follow, was murder even on Astartes physiology. Inzar was a field commander in his Legion, and he knew his own limits as well as those of the Space Marine form. The prime virtue of the Astartes genetic template wasn't strength, but endurance. It was their capacity to endure that won wars, even against more numerous foes or technologically superior cultures.

And it meant nothing here. Both sides fought with the same speed, the same ferocity, the very same capacity to endure. It was no longer an advantage for either side, just an evening of the odds.

In the press of bodies, Inzar barely had room to move. He'd never been an artist with his crozius mace, but all skill became fiction, a surreal memory of other battles. Like everyone else, he was reduced to grappling and stabbing at enemies close enough to hear the raggedness of their breath through helmet vocalisers. Warriors were strangling each other in the grinding front line, gutting one another with daggers for want of room to swing axes and swords.

His primary and secondary hearts beat in twin flurries, forcing oxygenated blood towards overworked muscles. He was aware of them in his chest in a way he'd never been before: crude, pumping organs that sustained him. His breath sawed through the cage of his clenched teeth, and he heard the same bestial sound from every warrior nearby. These were the unwelcome sounds and sensations of mortality. His own death seemed a certainty, the only doubt was when the shell would strike, or the blade would fall.

The World Eaters wanted to fight. Of course they did. The Death Guard and Sons of Horus and Thousand Sons were almost as eager, if not quite so mindless about it. Even packs of sky-borne Night Lords were descending in shrieking covens, hurling themselves on Blood Angels blades with idiotic abandon.

It fell to Inzar, and the other Word Bearers stationed throughout the horde's ranks, to do what they could to let the humans run in first.

Fools like Kargos (and what a useful fool Bloodspitter was turning out to be) wanted to wage this war the old way, Legion against Legion, but those days were done. This was all far, far too important for the indulgence of moronic conceits like Legion pride.

The humans in the Warmaster's ranks, hundreds of soldiers and cultists and conscripts for every Astartes on either side, were the most dangerous element in all of this. Individually, they were nothing. The Blood Angels killed and killed and killed them; the World Eaters even killed them in their mass-frenzied state, butchering them from behind if they found humans between them and the Blood Angels. They were faceless things, their uniforms and home worlds irrelevant: a flood of souls without identity. The Blood Angels broke open their skulls and hammered them to the ground. Inzar saw the sons of Sanguinius delimbing them, disembowelling them, trampling them underfoot and crushing the life from them. But the flood of flesh never abated. Pulling one apart only conjured three more, three more men and women jabbing at the Blood Angels with bayonets and shrieking at them in variances of Gothic that Inzar couldn't parse in the clamour.

Their purpose wasn't to break through, of course. Their purpose was to die. These wretches scarcely dealt any casualties to the defenders, but they slowed them, wore them down. The very meat of the humans' bodies was a burden, clogging chainswords, weighing down limbs, breeding exhaustion in the loyalists by virtue of the amount of killing they were forced to perform. Inzar had grinned behind his mask of office the first time he'd seen one of the IX Legion borne down beneath the thrashing weight of several soldiers, the humans dragging at the warrior's arms and chest, slowing the Blood Angel enough for Kargos to split the defender's head open with his axe.

At first the dead littered the ground, then carpeted it, then layered it. Attackers and defenders staggered as they fought, mulching the dead beneath their boots, the Astartes ankle-deep in cadaverous wreckage. Footing on the rampart grew treacherous with the thousands of deaths, blood sluicing across the stone in a conjoined gush. Warriors were sloshing through it. A glittering crust of spent shells floated on this sanguine sea. Ejected ammunition fell upon the mounds of bodies, decorating the dead with jewellery of smoking, brassy cartridges.

It was slaughter unmatched. It was glorious. Inzar felt like singing a prayer to the teeming sky. He looked up, where the aurora borealis faces of his gods leered down at the devastation. They were the truth, and what could be more beautiful than the truth? Was the perception and telling of the truth not regarded as the highest virtue? Was truth not the very thing – the fundamental thing – all souls strived for?

This is the way the world ends. Not with a whimper, but in fire.

We have taken humanity's cradle and purified it, rendering it a beacon lit by the holy toil of the faithful.

Terra blazed in the endless night of space. The Pantheon had come as promised.

Soon, he promised his gods. *Soon.*

THIRTY

Lost in the world between worlds

Vulkan

The wraithbone statue shattered, fragments of its face and torso clattering across the ornate floor. These shards of blackened ivory steamed where they came to a rest. What remained of the statue, little more than a pair of slender alien shins in revoltingly elegant boots, also steamed from the stumps of its knees.

Vulkan turned in the silence of the spire-top chamber, but this time, he didn't raise his hammer. Five destroyed statues were monuments to the futility of that gesture.

On the other side of the chamber, Magnus stood unconcerned, looking over the Impossible City in what Vulkan presumed was the direction of the Imperial Dungeon. The immense figure spoke without bothering to regard him.

'Now is the moment that you ask, "Why these tricks, Magnus? Why not just face me?"'

Vulkan exhaled the breath he was going to use to speak those very words.

There was a smile in Magnus' voice as he continued, *'Destiny is merciless to its victims. Even now, you misunderstand this moment you inhabit. You hold your tongue, believing you choose not to speak the words I predicted. Yet you fail to see I gave my prediction only to prove I could render you silent. That is the power of prophecy. Its manipulative potency. You have no agency here, little dragon, all you do here is play out the part apportioned to you.'*

Finally, Magnus turned. His mother-of-pearl wings rippled, and Vulkan was momentarily put in mind of Sanguinius. Everything resplendent about the Angel was inwardly restrained; Sanguinius was a man almost ashamed of his ostentation and purity. Everything about this daemon-king was self-satisfied, charmed by its own capacity to preen.

'What now, Vulkan?' The daemon's face shifted from the one-eyed features of the brother Vulkan knew, to the cyclopean monstrousness of what his brother had become. Shifting, transmuting, always in flux.

'Now–'

'Let me tell you,' Magnus interrupted. *'Now you will say that you wish it had never come to this. That I had my chance with father's final offer, and I failed at the last step. I see all of this in your eyes, they tell the tale in accordance with fate. Now your knuckles will tighten on the haft of that toy you carry. See? Now you will step forward with a heavy heart, believing that you must put me down like a wounded animal. See? And through all of this, you will still believe you might actually succeed, that you can finish me before I break the Emperor's shield.'*

In the seconds that followed, as Vulkan advanced, Magnus' crimson features curdled with amusement.

'Now you are wondering if I am really here at all, or if you will just destroy yet another statue when you swing that hammer at me.'

But Vulkan shook his head. 'Can you hear the arrogance frothing from your lips, or does the creature in possession of your soul not even allow you that freedom?'

Magnus' laugh was a growl of a thing, deep in his throat. Vulkan risked another few steps closer.

'You were always a stultified creature, Vulkan. The dullest of all of us, defined by your paucity of imagination. I speak of destiny and agency, sharing with you my insights into Creation. You sling tawdry insults in the misguided belief you can wound me with them. I am wasting my time, aren't I? Expecting you to understand this is no different from expecting a rock to grasp the principles of poetry.'

Vulkan could feel the flow of energy in the air around him. The wispy, leaching sensation of Magnus' focus as the daemon pulled at the metaphysical threads of the Emperor's distant shield.

'You're stalling,' Vulkan said as he advanced. 'And you are a poor impersonation of Magnus the Red.'

The creature didn't stop smiling. *'I am Magnus the Red.'*

'You were,' Vulkan allowed. 'Now, you are his flaws and weaknesses, laid bare and swollen. My brother would never say these things. He would perhaps think them, when he was most blinded by his own halo. Magnus was wreathed in a cloak of his own pride, and he could be vain while imagining himself humble. I will concede that. But he would never speak as you speak. My brother Magnus was many things, but he was rarely malicious, and never petty. Before we end this, answer me one thing. Is there enough left of you in there, to regret the deal you've struck?'

He swung the hammer. Magnus was gone – if he'd ever been there at all. Vulkan could have pulled the blow, but to what end? He let it fall, pounding into the wraithbone wall, smashing a hole that looked out over the maddening aeldari city.

Then he turned again. Magnus was there, as Vulkan knew he would be. The daemon crouched in the centre of the chamber now, idly carving runic mandalas into the floor with its black claws.

'*Regret,*' said the daemon-king. Magnus ceased his scrawling, closing and opening his great talons. Vulkan heard the tendons flexing, the sound like the creaking sailworks of an old wooden ship. The oval eye in the middle of the daemon's face was half-lidded in some mild, inhuman rapture. '*I can create and destroy life through the manipulation of energies you cannot conceive. I am immortal, my enlightenment preserved for eternity. I can see through time. Regret has no place amidst this flow of endless revelation.*'

Once more, Vulkan approached the thing that had been his brother. There was little else he could do. If this was Magnus' game, he had to play it.

'Then there is not enough left of Magnus within you to regret this enslavement. A simple "No" would have sufficed.'

He stopped, several metres away, and Vulkan looked up at the daemon, twice his height. He saw something that might have been aggravation flicker across the monster's features.

'*You are an insect, Vulkan. A creature so utterly blind to your insignificance that you cannot begin to comprehend your infinite irrelevance in the Cosmic All.*'

'I am not here to argue with you, Magnus. I am here to kill you.'

'*You will never understand–*'

'Enough! Enough talk.' Vulkan ran for the daemon-king, hurling his weapon ahead of him. Surprise flashed across the creature's face, and for a moment he saw Magnus not as the preening daemon, but bent-backed with effort, chanting, weaving his claws through the air, conjuring arcane streams of light and sound. For the first time, Vulkan saw visible effort darkening Magnus' monstrous face.

Vulkan had time to think, *I see you now, I see what you're really doing,* before the vision was gone and the confident daemon lord retook its place.

Urdrakule never struck Magnus; it collided with a wall of solid air, spinning harmlessly away – Vulkan tore it from the air as he reached the daemon's towering form. He swung overhead, the joints of his armour straining in tune with his roar of effort.

The blow landed. Magnus shattered into shards of red glass, a spill of jagged rubies tinkling across the floor. Vulkan ignored them, swinging again at where his brother had been. Shards popped beneath his crushing boots, bursting in little puffs of dust, as he brought the hammer around.

He hit nothing. He was fighting scarlet smoke, breathing in its ashy scent, swinging and missing, swinging and missing. He closed his eyes, listened for the creak of wings, and brought the hammer around again.

The impact jarred him to his core, every bone in his body seeming to vibrate, but not for a moment did it stop him striking again, and again, and again. Sparks cascaded over both brothers as Vulkan beat against the kinetic barrier, each impact ringing with the mis-chimed resonance of a broken bell. The more he hammered the barrier, the more visible it became, first as a heat-mirage ripple, then as a bruised red. And behind that straining barrier, the daemon lord crouched and chanted.

Magnus bared his teeth, his face wretched with hate.

'I am done with you, little dragon.'

Vulkan swung, and the world exploded in light. He didn't strike wraithbone, nor daemonic corpus, nor the kinetic barrier of his brother's will. His blow hit nothing because there was nothing there.

* * *

Vulkan staggered out into open, searing air. After the chill of the webway, his first gasp went down his throat like boiling water. His second breath tasted of volcanic ash. His third tasted of home.

I am still in the webway. I am there, not here. I cannot be here.

He stood beneath stars so familiar it hurt his heart to look at them. There on the horizon, above a ground of lava-cracked black, was the spear of Mount Deathfire. He was on Nocturne. He was on his home world.

Vulkan's boots pounded on Nocturne's infertile earth, throwing up sprays of gravel as he sprinted. He cried out Magnus' name, to no avail. He swung at the empty air in case this was mere illusion, and once more he struck nothing at all.

'Magnus!' he called to the horizon, to the stars. 'Brother!'

His sprint brought him to a chasm, one of the many nameless scars in Nocturne's hide. The heat of his world's heart breathed up from the split in its surface.

I am not here. I am in the webway. My intention determines my journey.

Vulkan stepped forward. Then he was falling, falling from fire into ice, falling through cold and gritty air that carried the lingering chemical tang of phosphex.

He hit the ground hard, rolling, clattering to a halt. He lay upon a bed of corpses whose funeral shrouds were nothing more than the ceramite they'd been wearing when they were slain.

Vulkan hauled himself to his feet, bringing his hammer up. Around him was an ocean of green and gold Crusade-era armour... All of it rent open, revealing annihilated black flesh. He was standing in a desert of his dead sons.

Isstvan.

The webway. I am in the webway.

He swung the hammer down, aiming the blow between the bodies of two slain Salamanders. With three swings of

Urdrakule, he pounded through the ground, and under the earth lay a void. Not the dark of space, not the seething tides of the warp, but a true void, the empty edges of an illusion. It was there, just beneath the ground's thin crust.

He threw himself in, swinging his hammer before him.

The blow slammed into a thick iron wall, its impact malforming the metal. Vulkan pulled the weapon from the ruptured wall, turning... knowing at once where he was. This was a place he still visited in the knifing memories that made up his dreams. This was the warship *Nightfall*, deep in its industrial guts, inside the maze constructed by his brother Curze, lord of the VIII Legion.

He'd been kept prisoner here, tortured to the beat of Curze's mad whims. His skin crawled for a delirious moment; had he ever left this labyrinth prison, or had the whole war after Isstvan been nothing but the misfiring of his tortured mind?

No. The webway. I am in the webway.

He swung at the wall again, blasting it apart, then at the wall behind that one, sundering it in kind. There, again, lay the void. From somewhere within it, he could hear Magnus chanting words in a tongue that bore no bond to Imperial Gothic.

Vulkan charged into nothingness.

There was no tower, now. Vulkan emerged on a vast wraithbone bridge spanning an eternity of mist. He didn't know if the tower had ever been real, or one of Magnus' illusions, or the elemental symbolism of this alien realm. It didn't matter. He was here now.

And if this is another illusion?

No. This scene was so desperately lonely that it had to be real. The thing Magnus had become was capable of almost anything now, but pride ran through its veins and leaked from its pores. It would never willingly let itself be seen like this.

Magnus was on his knees. His head was lowered, incantations mumbling through his slack fangs, his one eye squeezed closed and leaking blood from its edges. He knelt in the middle of the bridge, clawed fingers shaking as they painted spells upon the air, writing them in slashes of diseased light. Streams of psychic force threaded out from the daemon's fingers, there and not there, connecting Magnus to his father through a bond Vulkan could never hope, nor want, to understand.

He advanced on the kneeling figure, making no attempt at stealth. His bootsteps sent humming, almost musical tremors through the wraithbone.

'This ends now, daemon.'

Magnus laughed at Vulkan's greeting, though it was a weak and weary effort.

'How bold you sound, throwing around a concept like "now" as if you have any grasp of its meaning. Do you imagine you've made great haste to get here, little dragon? Time gusts down these passages in random breaths, and you have been wandering lost for longer than you know. The Palatine sector is a burning memory. Already our forces lay siege to the Sanctum.'

For the first time, unease spiked Vulkan's tone. 'You lie.'

'Often, and with good reason.' Magnus' cracked teeth gleamed with saliva. *'But not here, and not now. Your precious defenders have been bleeding on that wall for a day and a night. Already the second dawn threatens to light the sky.'*

Vulkan took a breath. He regarded Magnus, here in the middle of never and nowhere, and tried not to think of the horrendous losses they must have sustained on the wall. An entire day with their backs to the Eternity Gate. That many hours, against inconceivable odds. Even some of Dorn's calculated predictions had seen the battlement falling swiftly on the first day.

Hope kindled. Despite that grievous span of time, they held the wall, and the Emperor's will still kept the Neverborn back.

To survive to face the second day meant the defenders had already worked miracles. Their defiance lifted his heart.

Vulkan laughed; Magnus bristled.

'Amused by your own failure, little dragon?'

'No, by yours.' Vulkan gestured to the misty un-place around them. 'I have only now realised what should have been obvious. You're the one who is lost. That is why you are here, doing your malignant work at this distance and not at the webway portal itself. You cannot reach it, can you?'

'I can work my will against father's, wheresoever I choose.'

'But you could attack father directly at the portal. You could force your way through and finish this. Instead, you lurk here, working your compromised magic.' Vulkan smiled, and it was no longer a question. 'You cannot find the portal to father's Throne Room.'

'This place will not let me find it.' The sorcerer's words had the bite of an unwelcome confession.

It was one of the few times in Vulkan's life that he knew something his brother Magnus did not. This late in the day, it was no comfort whatsoever.

'The webway reacts to intent. Your passage is determined by strength of focus and spirit. Malcador told me that.'

'Malcador is a fool.'

'Then why am I here, while you are lost?' Vulkan tilted his head, his red eyes devoid of mercy. 'You once shattered this realm as you tore your way through it. You know how to break it, but that does not make you its master. It defies you harder now, because you are in thrall to the powers this dimension was created to thwart.'

Magnus snarled at him. *'Let me tell you–'*

'You will say nothing I need to hear, and you know nothing I want to know. You are sentenced to death, Magnus. I will not let you bring down father's shield.'

Magnus stared at him, lips peeling back from mother-of-pearl teeth. Amusement lit his single swollen eye.

'Then you should have killed me hours ago.'

THIRTY-ONE

Blame

When the warning came, it came not from the Delphic Battlement but within the Sanctum. Refugees, wounded fighters and
the very last defenders filled the halls of the final fortress in
their thousands. Hanumarasi of the Hykanatoi was one of the
few Custodians still within the Sanctum, all too aware of how
his kinsmen's presence was spread mournfully thin. He moved
through chambers and corridors of pale stone and kintsugi
gold, every space that was once home to austere silence now
teeming with unwashed humanity. It hadn't taken long to get
used to the smell of festering wounds and deprivation.

Some of the civilian survivors still came to him as he
patrolled, asking for word from elsewhere in the Palace or
for aid he had no capacity to give. Some even pleaded with
him to take them to the Emperor, which was a request of
such breathtaking delusion, yet so perfectly understandable,
that he didn't know how to answer. Hanumarasi tried to be
gentle but emphatic in his refusals.

He made his way through the chambers in the hours before

dawn on the second day, ashamed by how the damage marking his armour was visible to the tired eyes of the Emperor's people. One of the unspoken codes of conduct for his kind was to present absolute Imperial invincibility before the Emperor's enemies and His subjects alike. The war had changed that, like it had upended and blighted everything else in the natural order. It shamed him to present anything less than the image of Imperial perfection, with these final survivors witnessing the war-torn truth of his auramite plate.

He entered the Red Iron Sacristy, where several hundred families were housed in the chamber that was home to the Grand Archive of Martian-Terran treaties. The Twin Kingdoms Pact was stored here – the document that swore a most binding union between the two worlds at the heart of the Imperium. Arrayed across the rest of the chamber were many individual life-oaths of great import, such as between the orders of the Legio Titanicus and the Emperor in His incarnation as the Martian Omnissiah. It was a place of precious banners dating back through the centuries of Long Night, of parchments stored in reinforced stasis displays, and digital records displayed as hololiths. All of it vital, all of it priceless – all of it now just detritus in the way of these frightened souls.

Hanumarasi's boots no longer echoed on the floor of off-world orange sandstone. The press of bodies generated a low-level hum of conversation loud enough to drown out his foot-steps, the same way it created a scent not entirely unlike a livestock stable.

'Golden lord, golden lord,' said a small voice.

Hanumarasi turned with a purr of active armour, inwardly ashamed once more of the subtle clicks in his warplate's joints – another sign of the wear and tear of battle. He looked down at the girl-child wanting his attention. She was a shabby thing, like all the others housed here. There was scarcely any

food left within the walls and water was tightly rationed by
adepts trained in the calculus of resources. None of the refugees had bathed the evidence of the war from their skin since
arriving, and some of them had been present for months.
They were fortunate not to have experienced any outbreaks
of plague.

'Yes, little one.' Hanumarasi had learned to soften his voice
when dealing with mortals. The low tone of Custodians' natural
voices tended to make humans uneasy, and it outright frightened most children.

Hanumarasi recognised this one. Upon arriving several
weeks before, she had asked where the Emperor's Throne
Room was. She had wanted to meet her king. Hanumarasi, not
a gifted liar, had naturally not wanted to tell her the Emperor's
Throne Room, deep in the Imperial Dungeon, was still many
kilometres from here, much of it reachable only through subterranean descent. Like many of Terra's native souls, she had
seen the Sanctum and presumed the fortress, itself the size of
a small town, was the Emperor's personal quarters.

The girl-child gazed up at him, wide-eyed. She had no such
question this morning.

'There is something strange, golden lord. Something my
family has found. You must see it.'

Hanumarasi tensed imperceptibly. His gaze, hidden from
the humans by his crested helm, flicked and tracked across
the chamber. A target lock slid over the refugees' faces, one
by one. He saw nothing untoward.

'What is it, little one?'

She drew her filthy robe around herself like a shawl and
moved towards where her family clustered by the far sandstone wall. The refugees of her bloodline likely had no idea
they were sheltering beneath the hanging banner of the Legio
Lysanda in its contrasting heraldry. Could these humans even

read? Would they care if they could? They had set up their lean-to and unpacked their meagre possessions wherever there was space. Near, Hanumarasi marked, one of the doors to a storage antechamber.

The Custodian moved past the child, his stride devouring the distance ahead of her tiny steps. He was midway through the chamber when the refugees began to close in on him, like beggars pleading for alms. The families knew better than to mob the Custodians like this, but emotion sometimes got the better of them, especially when they were new to the Sanctum.

He did what he always did: he activated his spear. He didn't raise it or threaten them with it, but the power field sheathing the blade shimmered with slow, oily lightning and breathed out its aggressive thrum. It always served to warn the humans back.

Not this time.

'Back,' he ordered them, no longer modulating his voice. Their pleading hands caressed his armour as he passed, and they were beginning to impede his passage. He could hear the scrape of their fingernails against the gold. 'Get *back*, all of you.'

It worked, barely, just enough for him to reach the family. The refugees trailed him, clustered around him, but he paid them no heed; his focus was drawn at once to the unlocked antechamber door. Flies swarmed through the cracks and joins in the white wood.

'Move,' he ordered the family. Wisely, they moved.

Hanumarasi kicked in the door, levelling his spear. Dozens of bodies, some still bleeding in their freshness, lay within the antechamber, butchered and piled upon the mosaic floor. The nude and slaughtered forms of over a hundred families.

Hanumarasi whirled, blade up and already speaking into the vox as the refugees of the Red Iron Sacristy leapt upon him. Two words was all it took, two words sent to every one of the Custodian Guard still alive within the Sanctum:

'They're inside.'

The Neverborn had drilled their way into the minds of the exhausted refugees, hollowing them out, skin-riding them... Finally butchering the ones that resisted possession. Now they sloughed the false flesh from their bones, revealing that they weren't people at all.

Hanumarasi's revelation was by no means unique to him. He was the first, but Custodians were making similar discoveries throughout the Sanctum's surface chambers. Across the Sanctum, daemons tore their way into reality – some breaching the veil by force, ripping through the last of the weakened Emperor's shield, others manipulating their way into physicality by changing the flesh and bones of a convenient puppet.

Sirens sounded throughout the final fortress. Neverborn feasting across the face of Terra, sensing the war's end at last, turned their heads towards the Sanctum Imperialis like pilgrims praying to a sacred cardinal point.

The Sigillite raised his eyes to the cavern ceiling. The laboratory, which trillions of Imperial citizens imagined to be a royal throne room cut out of a faerie tale, was a hive of frantic industry. Malcador stood at the prime chamber's edge, not far from the Silver Door. Like Vulkan days before, he'd found himself gazing upon the art engraved here upon the original Eternity Gate, and pondering its dubious resemblance to reality.

The last two centuries hadn't looked much like these glorious etchings, all things considered. Out of sight of even the loyalest eyes, the truth was rather more harried and desperate. Grand plans against insurmountable odds often were, and the Emperor's ambition was the grandest plan against the most insurmountable odds imaginable.

'They're inside.'

Malcador turned to regard Diocletian, the last tribune. The Custodian loomed over him, masking his features by slamming his helm into place.

'I know.' The old man took a breath. 'And we always knew it would come to this.'

Custodians and the last of the Sisters were spilling through the open door. Malcador could sense Diocletian's desperation to join them.

'Leave a token force here,' he told the warrior. 'Lead the rest up to the surface to defend the Sanctum. Cleanse the upper halls as best you can, and be ready to receive survivors from the Delphic Battlement. We will need every soul that can reach the Sanctum.'

He felt an unexpected shiver in his words as he added, 'When there is no longer any hope, you will seal the Eternity Gate. Those still outside…'

He cleared his throat. This was it, the enemy was at the door, and now the moment had come, the words would not.

'Sigillite?' Diocletian pressed.

'When there is no longer any hope, you will seal the Eternity Gate. That is all.'

But Diocletian hesitated, something Malcador had rarely seen any of the golden warriors do.

'How did the Neverborn get inside? Has the Ninth failed us on the wall? Has the Eighteenth failed us in the labyrinth?'

How could he answer those questions in a manner that would ever satisfy one of the Ten Thousand, the most loyal of the most loyal? They held all beings to standards no other being could reach. Least of all the primarchs – a pantheon of humanity's traits, magnified. No wonder the Legiones Custodes despised them all.

'Go, Dio. Die well.'

The golden warrior made the Fist of Unity, knuckles against his breast-plate.

'You too, old man.'

Arkhan Land ran.

When the call had come for the human forces to fall back, he'd grabbed a buckle on Shenkai's breastplate and started dragging. The tide of exoplanar xenos spilling over the rampart signalled the end of his brief career as a brave and dutiful soldier.

The last of Zephon's thralls had backed away from the creatures materialising on the rampart. He was fumbling to reload, speaking a stream of Aenokhian nonsense in his rising panic. Transacta-7Y1, while showing no outward sign of fear, had raised a hand to her visor, knocking it with her knuckles to crudely retune it into clarity.

'Don't look at them,' Land had snapped, still dragging on Shenkai's buckle. 'Both of you, stop looking at them! *Come on.*'

They came on. Three souls and a scampering psyber-monkey, joining a human flood retreating from the Delphic Battlement at a dead run.

The Royal Ascension was an avenue of staggering proportions, built for parades of Titans and hundreds of thousands of troops to present their banners before the grandeur of the Eternity Gate. For all the Imperium's relative youth (what was two centuries in terms of an empire, really?) statues of scholars, explorers and generals lined the Ascension in their hundreds all the way up the rising hill to the Sanctum. It was a living history rendered in bronze. Many of the icons represented Imperial scions that still lived.

Arkhan Land had a statue here. He hadn't ever seen it, and he didn't frankly care about being captured for posterity by something as banal as a statue. *Fame* was when people knew your name from a text or your face from a statue. People could be famous for being beautiful, or humorous, or simply wealthy, and that made fame worthless. *Renown* was when people owed whole swathes of their way of life to your deeds and discoveries. Arkhan Land cultivated renown.

To say he was exhausted in the hours before the second dawn would be to underplay the endless cramping of his muscles by an order of magnitude. He'd fought for what felt like every minute of the last day and night, through a physical exhaustion so profound it brought delirium. When it had been at its height during the night, he would sleep for the split seconds between blinking, to find the world had jumped a moment forward each time his eyes flicked back open. His throat was raw from gunsmoke and rock dust and shouting to be heard by those standing right next to him. His hands shook so badly with bone-deep fatigue that he could no longer aim – for hours now, he had been reduced to lifting his weapons in a vague direction, praying, and firing. Far more often, he'd been forced to rest and recover in the bunkers back from the crashing front lines, while two armies of transhumans tore each other to pieces a hundred metres away.

As he fled the wall now, his new leg (the useless bastard thing) kept giving out beneath him. The third time he stumbled, he went down in a rolling heap across the ascending steps of the Royal Ascension, tools and mementos scattering as they spilled. Transacta-7Y1 and Shenkai picked him up, supporting him between them. Other civilians and soldiers streamed past them, fleeing along the Royal Ascension towards the great ivory-and-gold structure of the Eternity Gate. Sapien scampered alongside his master, wide-eyed with worry. The artificimian had no conception of what was supposed to be happening, but the cogitator in its little skull doubted its current circumstance was an optimal situation for any life form to be in.

Panic like this, it had a smell. It had a *feel*. Land felt it around him, smelled it in the breath of those panting as they ran. Far past exhaustion and nothing like cowardice, it was a primal aura, something bestial, keyed only to survival.

Land didn't know if he'd failed to counter Zephon's earlier threat or not. He'd certainly tried to keep the Blood Angel's thralls alive, though only one-third of his wards were still with him now. In the never-ending shift of the front lines grinding together since dawn the day before, he'd lost track of Zephon and Anzarael within the first hour. Thousands of the IX Legion's thralls went through the same separations as the battle raged, fighting independently of their masters and supporting whichever Blood Angels they found themselves nearest. Finding single warriors, or even specific units in the ceramite carnage atop the rampart, was a ludicrous notion. All was in motion, everything was in flux.

Eristes had died yesterday in one of the early breakthroughs, when the Warmaster's horde spilled through a breakage in the line. A Custodian had led the counter-attack – Land never learned the warrior's name – the golden figure leading several hundred civilians and Imperial Army into the breach, preventing the Blood Angels from being surrounded. Slowly, at great cost in life, the horde was forced back to the wall, their beachhead destroyed, and the defenders' line reinforced.

When the humans had fallen back in the aftermath, their numbers grievously diminished by Sons of Horus chainblades, Land strained to haul the dead and wounded away... realising, as he hauled the second body, that he was dragging Eristes. The Martian's hands were red to the elbows with the thrall's blood. A chainsword had done its gouging work across the man's breastplate, biting into the body beneath. He was quite plainly, quite absolutely, dead.

Transacta-7Y1 had placed her clumsy metal hands over

Land's own and detached his grip from Eristes' bloody robes. She emitted a brief spurt of code.

Land had stared at the corpse, at the man's open eyes, feeling somehow betrayed. His reply was a stutter: 'But I was helping him.'

Transacta-7Y1 allowed that, yes, she understood this was the case; that yes, he had done his best; and that no, it wasn't his fault.

With precious little time for sentiment, Shafia and Shenkai carried the corpse to a team of incineration servitors at the rear of the wall. They were back within minutes, dry-eyed, weapons ready, already hollowed out from weariness.

Shafia had died as the first day slipped into night. Not that it was ever full dark, with the sky curdled by etheric phantasma, with the continual detonations of overloaded reactors, with the flare of discharging energy weapons, with the frequent eruptions of flame weaponry, and a thousand other incendiary reasons besides. Along the rampart it was usually bright enough to resemble eerie daylight.

The breakthrough that killed Shafia came with a surge of World Eaters jump-packing over the clashing front lines, the regiment ending its suicidal leap between dozens of reserve forces and the Blood Angels' second, third and fourth waves of warriors waiting to be called to the line. The World Eaters were cut down in their hundreds, but not before they turned their flame weapons on the human reserves and several ammunition caches, eager to lay down their lives for the sake of spreading fires behind the defenders' lines.

Whatever alchemical concoction sloshed in the tanks of their weapons, it behaved more savagely than any promethium mix Land had ever seen. The liquid fire leapt from soldier to soldier in a mockery of physics, moving as though possessing some feverish life, igniting bodies as soon as it touched them. Water aggravated the flames. Flame suppressant achieved nothing at all. Those afflicted burned down to statues of ash within seconds, frozen in their postures of final torment.

Shafia was one of those engulfed. Shenkai had cried 'Mother!' and unlimbered his handheld canister of flame suppressant, one of the tools on his belt webbing for use in the maintenance of Zephon's armour. Transacta-7Y1 had borne the thrall to the ground, preventing him from getting closer to the inferno in human form. Around them, the burning corrosion leapt and flashed between soldiers, thralls and skitarii. Even at a remove, the heat was fierce enough to blacken skin and ignite clothing.

Land was with them a moment later, slamming down what looked like a grenade centimetres from Shenkai's face. Instead of detonating, it emitted a tinnitus screech and projected a three-metre dome of wavering force. Fire pouring itself against the field dissipated in bright flashes, as all heat and kinetic energy touching the field was converted to light. Hundreds of people burned to death around them, several just out of arm's reach, while the three of them sheltered inside a bubble of muted sound and refracted light. The entire time, Land felt Shenkai's helpless quivering, though the younger man didn't cry out again. Blessedly, the shimmer of the dome obscured vision enough to deny him the sight of his mother's final incineration. Land considered that an unexpected but entirely welcome benefit.

By the time the last World Eater was slain, a museum of the ashen dead stood testament to XII Legion malice. When it was over, Land picked up the projector. The emitter was out of power, and he had no reasonable idea how to repair it.

'I found this in the Tomb of Enkar-Thune,' he said quietly. 'In Western Tharsis.'

Shenkai didn't care. The thrall had circled the ashen statue that had, a moment ago, been his mother. Shafia's features were preserved with wrenching clarity, her hands at the side of her head, her face twisted in a silent scream. She'd died trying to beat out the flames engulfing her hair. Arkhan Land wondered at the chemical properties of a killing fire capable of such preservation, and in a rare moment of guilt, felt uncomfortable for his curiosity.

Then the battlement shook yet again, and the thousands of ashen statues had crumbled in dismal unity. The survivors coughed through the morbid powder. Even hours later, Land could still taste it. It made him more than a little uncomfortable to know he was tasting people.

Now, as they fled the wall and made their stumbling way up the grand stairs of the Royal Ascension, Land made the mistake of looking back. He expected the sight over his shoulder to be the host of retreating human soldiery and the Blood Angels valiantly – albeit futilely – holding the rampart in the distance.

This was not the case.

'They've broken through,' he panted. His companions' replies were a breathless grunt and a dribble of code, respectively.

Behind them came the sounds of dying, in all the forms it took in this war. The machine whirr of Dreadnought joints. The crashing of bolters. The whine of chainswords and the guttural interruption when their teeth met meat. The sounds that defied description from creatures that defied reality. A cavalcade of noise, adding up to Terra's unique song.

Winged daemons swooped down and plucked unfortunate souls from the retreating tide, carrying them away to be devoured or dropped like living missiles upon those fleeing below. A soldier next to Shenkai was dragged up, his absence marked by a fading scream, and Land almost slowed down to take a shot at the abducting creature. He might've done it, a matter of instinct rather than any attempt at heroism, had

Transacta-7Y1 not hauled him roughly onward the moment she saw him hesitate.

The stolen man returned to them, albeit headless, dropped from above onto several nearby soldiers, knocking them to the ground. Had Land been a betting man, he would've wagered more than one limb or backbone snapped in that collision and tumble.

Deep in the retreating tide, the trio ran across the shaking expanse of marble that marked the halfway point of the Royal Ascension. The ululating murmur of anti-grav systems joined the roar of engines and monsters and everything else, as Land Speeders and jetbikes sliced overhead. The Blood Angels racing for the Sanctum. The World Eaters racing to get there first. No way to know, with the speed the things moved.

The trio fled between the legs of the Warmonger *Malax Meridius*, passing through the gum-stinging aura of its void shields and into its titanic shadow. To their left, its immense foot lifted with a tower's worth of screeching metal. It passed over them, shockingly loud, god-loud, the sound of a flight of gunships roaring overhead. It washed them in Titan life-heat and choked them with the stink of holy chrome. For a moment he struggled with a profoundly unpleasant nausea, falling again as he lost track of which way was up. Passing beneath the tower block legs of a walking cathedral tended to upset the senses.

Hundreds of Imperial Army soldiers already manned the rockcrete barricades ahead, those very last lines of defences before the Eternity Gate. They massed in firing lines, heeding the shouts of their surviving officers, or any survivor raising their voice loud enough to inspire compliance. More survivors from the wall filtered past and through these emplacements, running for the Sanctum.

Almost there, thought Land. A foolish thought, insipid in its obviousness. He'd spent his life rolling his eyes at people who gave voice to such banalities. Now here he was, thinking in them.

The Eternity Gate, in all its adamantium-and-ceramite-layered glory, rose for a kilometre and more above their heads. It was burnished orange by the first rays of anaemic dawn, and as they drew closer, it seemed almost to reach the tainted sky, where great clawed hands stirred the clouds, and–

Don't look up.

He stumbled again, and again Shenkai and Transacta-7Y1 were there to help him. His bionic leg sent shocks of red pain throbbing through his hips and spine with every step. He suspected the surgical seams of the crude graft (where meat met metal, if one wished to be blunt about it) were edging in the direction of infection.

Las-beams slashed past them, above them, ionising the air he breathed. It was like sprinting through spikes of angry light, knowing any one of them would kill you, and knowing you were just as dead if you stopped running.

They made it to the first barricade, collapsing for breath as Blood Angels and soldiers took up positions around them.

This is it, Land realised, with the same profoundly irritating banality. *This is it. Our backs are to the Gate.*

'You know,' he said as he caught his breath, 'I think we're about to die.'

Shenkai checked his boltgun and gave a mirthless smile. Transacta-7Y1, readying her latest scavenged rifle, allowed that, yes, termination did seem to be the likeliest event given current circumstances.

Sapien scampered into cover with them, his hackles raised, his scorpion tail bristling. His mechanical chittering didn't add anything particularly weighty to their conversation, but was nonetheless welcomed by all of them.

* * *

As he retreated, sheeted with the slime that passed for the Neverborn's blood, bitterness was thick in the back of Amit's throat. It tasted like unspat acid. Some small part of him, a too-human core, railed at the unfairness. They had held out for so long; already the second day dawned on a battle that had been predicted to end within mere hours. The Legion had done the impossible and it still wasn't enough.

What treachery had transpired in the Sanctum? How could the Neverborn manifest within its walls when surely every one of them blackened the sky and the wasteland and the wall itself out here?

As one of the few captains left alive after a day and a night on the wall, command of the piecemeal evacuation fell on his shoulders. Sanguinius' first and only command had been for him to assume the mantle with any other surviving officers.

'Where will you be, sire?'

'The Gate.' The Great Angel's voice over the vox was a ruined, weakened growl. *'I go to the Gate. We will hold it open for as long as we can. Be swift, Nassir.'*

Amit fell back, ringed by the last living warriors of his own Fifth Company. The Secutors had numbered a hundred and five souls before reaching Terra. At yesterday's dawn, he'd had fifty-eight warriors remaining. This morning, he was retreating with the last twelve of them by his side.

The division of the Legion's forces came down to necessity, and Amit coordinated it on the move with his Master of Signals, Ghallen, giving the warrior a stream of orders and decisions to relay onward. Ghallen's helmet and vambrace hololith generator were rigged with specialist interfaces to link with the Imperial vox-web, and to transcode available tactical data in input/output streams. The interference from the ash and dust, then from the warp staining the sky, had

diminished his role greatly in recent weeks, but he had the
range to disperse Amit's orders along the falling wall.

Those orders were stark in their simplicity. Half of the
Legion's units were to run for the Sanctum with all haste, to
lend aid to the Custodians calling from within. They would be
engaged along the way; specific units were assigned rearguard
action, doing what they could to slow the enemy advance
along the Royal Ascension.

Half would stay on the wall. Their orders were to stand and
die. The horde could no longer be held back, and the defenders would be overrun, but every sword and boltgun remaining
on the battlement bought time for the rest of the Legion to
reach the Sanctum.

Of the units and companies and captains he called upon to
remain, not one refused or hesitated. Chimes of order-receipt
and acknowledgement came back across the vox, along with
brief oaths to hold as long as they could, or to wish Amit and
the others well at the Sanctum. So nobly did several thousand
Blood Angels commit to their duty, ending in certain death.

Amit had wanted to stay. Ghallen had seen it in his captain's
eyes, and with the usual lack of formality that existed in the
Secutors, he'd told the survivors of their company to drag
Dominion Amit by force if he tried to waste his life here when
he was needed at the Gate. Falling back from the wall, the
Secutors had taken a Rhino, with Amit and Ghallen clinging
to the external handrails, still conveying orders as they watched
the unfolding retreat.

The Royal Ascension was one of the last untouched regions
of Terra. Within minutes of the withdrawal being sounded, it
was a battlefield like any other. Amit watched it sweep past
as their Rhino made its rattling way up the vehicle inclines
alongside the great steps. Already, the vanguard of the Warmaster's horde had breached the wall in vast numbers and

were beginning to swarm the Royal Ascension. All notion of a front line became illusory; clusters of warriors fought in embattled circles, warband against warband, pack on pack. The front line was a million front lines, wherever two warriors stood together with blades bared and refused to let the enemy pass.

For a moment, the bleak thought occurred that he could have just remained on the wall and died there. He was dead anyway. They all were. If the Blood Angels defended the Sanctum against the Neverborn, they would lose the wall to the Warmaster's horde. If they held the wall against the horde, they would lose the Sanctum to the Neverborn. If they did both, they would lose both.

Amit turned towards the great Gate. It towered above him in its monstrous splendour, and he spared a moment for the Emperor's graven image, depicted in triumph, a spear in hand as He looked down upon the surrendering foes of the Great Crusade.

For his part, Amit's recollections of the Great Crusade involved far more slaughtered cultures than surrendering ones, but he'd long since learned that the Imperium's artisans seemed disinclined to render the truth in their work.

Amit established a temporary command post at the first barricades, for what it was worth. He rallied the defenders and ordered the remnants of regiments onward up to the Gate. Every time he heard a Custodian speaking of daemonic intruders, or one of the Blood Angels left behind on the wall relaying how his force was surrounded, he felt the urge to leave here, to go backwards or to go forwards, to the wall or the Sanctum, and damn waiting here in this middle ground. How was it he was burdened with the responsibility for distributing thousands of other lives? He was a captain, not a general.

The battlement still held, even with all its breaches and the horde overrunning its rampart. It kept back the Warmaster's Titans, leaving them on the wrong side of the Sanctum's voids – and mercifully so, for the moment they got a War-lord through that wall, that would end the infantry defence of the Royal Ascension.

Amit had stopped tuning in to the Legio Ignatum vox-web. Let them die valiantly without him peering at their progress. Even at this distance, he could hear the duelling of god-machines in the wasteland beyond the wall.

Ghallen went down the line at the first barricade, dis-tributing ammunition to the Blood Angels filling out the masses of human defenders. Amit kept his focus pinned to the first wave of traitors on their way. Blood Angels and soldiers managing to stay ahead of the tide passed through the barricades; Amit ordered most of them on, keeping the least injured here, to reinforce the line.

'Hold them as long as you can,' he called down the line of sandbags and rockcrete barricades. 'Let them hit us. Keep them in place. Then start falling back in line order.'

A chorus of acknowledgements greeted this. As plans went, it at least had the virtue of simplicity. The horde was close enough now that the tanks on both sides began firing, ion-ising the air with streaks of headache red and migraine blue. The brightness of lascannons and volkites left searing trails across even transhuman retinas.

On a whim, he turned to look back at the Eternity Gate. His gaze lingered on the Emperor's image again, the monarch looking down upon the death of the Imperium. Everything was so clear, every detail crisp in the light of the weakling sun.

We who are about to die, salute you.

'Why are you smiling, sir?' Ghallen asked.

Amit turned back to the horde, his knuckles tightening on his weapons.

'Nothing. Something from another life.'

Kargos hunts and kills and carves and they are close now, they're so close, it's all about to end. They take the wall and then they're running. Then he's holding the side of a Land Raider. Tanks are making it through the breaches in the wall. Tanks. Warriors. Daemons. Trickles of everything, soon to be a tide. The road beneath them is white and long and leads to glory. These are the things he knows, and he can't recall ever knowing anything else. The Royal Ascension stretches ahead. Kargos will paint it with blood, blood, blood for the Blood God.

Ahead are the barricades. Beyond them, the Gate.

Bolters crash and volkite guns screech and Kargos leaps from the Land Raider over the rockcrete barrier. Blood Angels die and that's good, that's what Blood Angels do, they die when he cuts them and guts them and feels their blood washing his armour. He wears their shed life like medals, and he feels the God of War watching. This, too, is good.

Flesh Tearer, he thinks, and this thought is clear, clearer than all the others, so clear it feels almost as if it isn't his own.

Blood Angels get in his way and they die because they're slower than him, they die because they're fools, they die and their blood runs to honour a god they don't believe exists. They die and their souls are gone into the warp and the mouths of the god-things that wait there.

Even the ones praying to the God-Emperor, their meekness setting Kargos' teeth on edge, even their spirits leave their bodies and plunge not into the warm arms of their false god, but into the maws of daemons that laugh and gag and choke on the harvest of souls.

Flesh Tearer, he thinks. Flesh Tearer.

He turns, no longer trying to break through the line, trying instead to fight his way along it. More Blood Angels die. More humans die. Some of the Blood Angels try to hurt him and they do, they do hurt him, but pain is for mortals, pain is weakness leaving the body, pain is good, pain is pleasure because pain means war, and war means the flow of blood and the ripping of muscle from the bone.

Flesh Tearer. Again comes the feeling that it's not his thought, it's something from above, dropped inside his skull. Flesh Tearer. Flesh Tearer.

There are others with him, so many others, it's as if every being in the world is a World Eater at his side, or the red things with brass blades that pretend to be World Eaters, and Kargos runs, vaulting barricades and killing the defenders that cower there. A tide of his brothers rushes with him, and some are laughing, drunk on the promises made by the God of War and Woe; others are screaming or weeping with discharges of emotion poorly processed by broken brains.

The preacher is with him still, and the preacher speaks of the Sanctum like it's a temple, saying it will be the Cathedral of Lorgar, and Kargos has no time for this, no time for any of the preacher's canticles, it's more Colchisian groxshit.

Flesh Tearer.

And yes, he's close now, he kills a human with a fist to the woman's skull and he kills another with an elbow to the man's throat and another with Gorechild, *Khârn's axe, Khârn was his brother, Khârn was his captain, Khârn was the best of them and–*

'Flesh Tearer!'

–and Amit turns at the roar of his name. The world is red torment and all Kargos can see is Amit, but that's enough, that's all he needs to see right now.

His chain-brother's face is familiar but unfamiliar; his expression doesn't mean pain or sorrow, but it means something like both. It's an emotion Kargos no longer knows, but it's on Amit's face now and Kargos knows he is the cause.

Engines scream and Kargos knows that whine, it's the whine of jump turbines, and more Blood Angels come, everything is breaking apart and scattering. He kills Blood Angels because they are in the way, and his brothers kill other Blood Angels, and he demands the Flesh Tearer face him.

Amit fights, but not towards him or even really away from him. Amit fights and kills as if Kargos doesn't exist, as if the other battles matter more and Kargos roars again, screaming his chain-brother's name and title and he's so close now, so close, it doesn't matter if Amit dies from an axe in the back, so long as Amit's blood runs to the earth and his skull is chained to XII Legion ceramite. The Blood God wants the Flesh Tearer's soul, Kargos feels it, and the gladiator will give it to him.

Two World Eaters die by Kargos' side, not from blade or bolt but in swift dissolution, like deletion, and Kargos doesn't understand until he sees the old man with the archeotech gun. It flares again and the warrior to Inzar's right dissolves, shrieking a sound no Astartes should ever make, as if the Emperor's Children legionary finds sweetness in his eradication.

There are weaklings in the way between Kargos and Amit so they die, he cuts them down – one is a skitarius and Gorechild goes through the cables she has for guts, and another is a thrall of the IX and he stumps the young man with a cut that takes off the thrall's arm.

Inzar is with him, and one of the weaklings is a little thing of spindly limbs and false fur, and it leaps upon Inzar, jabbing at the joints of his armour with a barbed tail like a scorpion's sting, and Inzar clutches the thing's head in one hand and squeezes, and the machine parts and organic pieces of the thing's skull crunch through the preacher's fingers.

The old man with the gun of eradicating fire is screeching like a child because the skitarius and the thrall and the monkey-thing are dead or as good as dead, but it doesn't matter, none of it matters, *because he has killed his way to Amit, and their weapons lock, and they're face to face again, just like before.*

'Fall back.' Amit spits the words but not at Kargos, he's spitting at the humans, because yes, the Sanctum is fouled by the Neverborn and they need every gun and every blade to save themselves, not realising they're all already dead. 'Line order, fall back!'

Face to face with his chain-brother, Kargos spits words of his own. 'Sanguis extremis.'

Amit shows his fangs, just like in the pits. 'Don't tell me. Show me.'

Then it happens, as it always happens in the arena. Everything breaks apart, becoming a thousand red moments that, later, he will barely remember.

THIRTY-TWO

Loss

On that day, as Kargos fought hot, Amit fought cold.

Blood Angels and World Eaters murdered each other in packs around the two of them, but the wider war narrowed to the two gladiators and the weapons in their hands. Amit knew how Kargos fought better than Kargos himself. The Nails gave his chain-brother strength but stole his memory, while Amit remembered every beat, every second, of their time together in the pits.

For Kargos, as soon as the Butcher's Nails bit, every fight was against a stranger. He relied on strength and speed at the cost of experience – which always served him well, Amit had to concede. But even against opponents he'd duelled a hundred times before, Kargos was always fighting them for the first time.

Amit knew the angle of every blow and the strength Kargos threw behind it. He knew which ones to block, which ones to parry or deflect, which ones to evade by weaving aside or leaping back. Kargos' brutish new axe was a fresh consideration, but the World Eater used it the same way he used his last three chainaxes, and Amit had the measure of it within moments.

It went against Amit's own instincts to hold back, only blocking and weaving away. He wasn't built for bloodless battle. Muscle memory and centuries of warfare made it a trial not to lunge when he thought he saw an opening, but he knew Kargos' swiftness too well to play with the risk.

Already, Kargos was frothing at the mouth. Amit saw it in the half-face visible in his chain-brother's broken faceplate. Grunts became growls, became snarls, became roars, with each wild swing cutting nothing but air. Just like in the arena, Kargos craved contact – the shedding of blood, the impact of a fist against flesh. Without it, the Nails knifed into his mind, goading him on and punishing his failure.

Amit smashed aside a blow with his vambrace; leaned away from another arcing cut. He couldn't wear Kargos down, the Nails wouldn't allow it. The World Eater would erode down to nerveless bone before the pain engine in his head let him realise the limits of his body. Amit watched for the right moment, the balance point between his own weariness and Kargos' Nails-born frustration. If he waited too long, it wouldn't matter how frenzied and artless Kargos became. The Blood Angel's strength would always leach faster.

He cuts and he cuts and he's chopping air, and breath saws in and out of his open jaws, and the Flesh Tearer isn't fighting, he's not fighting, he's doing everything but fighting back. Kargos hears these grunts and these curses of wordless sound, and is it him, is it he who's snarling like a kicked wolf?

He cuts he cuts he cuts, again, again, and there's acid in his spit now, he can feel it infused there, milked from his Betcher's Gland, he can feel it warm on his chin as it runs from his roars. The Flesh Tearer is a ghost, a coward, he's not there, he's not there, and Gorechild thirsts, and he can feel the axe almost slipping from his grip in the thirst for blood, or the thirst for a new bearer, one who will not fail, and the Nails are pinching and biting and they–

Drill they drill they drill they drill into him, and Amit is laughing, and the Nails drill and they drill and the back of his brain must be bleeding by now, and–

Amit goes for the axe, no, not the axe, the chain, and they're grappling and Kargos is stronger, but Amit has the chain and–

He can't breathe. He can't pull his chained arm free. He's leashed by his own weapon chain, wearing it like a slave collar, and he can't breathe. That's fine, he is Astartes, he can survive without breath, but the bones and ligaments in his neck are clicking, and crunching, and it's the sound of branches breaking and–

And then he sees it. Kargos sees what's been behind Amit's eyes all this time. He sees what was inside his chain-brother's soul every time they stepped into the arena. He sees the predator under the perfection as Amit goes for his face, fangs like ivory knives. He feels his brother fasten down on his cheek, and bite, and throw his head back. There's the unreal ripping of wet leather, and blood sprays, and Amit spits out a mouthful of his own brother's face.

There's no pain, though Kargos knows that will come later, when the Nails retract; then there will be pain aplenty.

And there's no mockery in Amit's gaze, no laughter, not even any glory, there's just princely hate in those pale eyes, and flecks of Kargos' blood showing stark against the sclera. Then he does it again, he does it again, this time fastening his fangs on Kargos' nose and other cheek, and this time the ripping comes with the sound of grinding gravel. The Blood Angel takes bone and cartilage away with him.

And this time, Amit swallows. He swallows the flesh of his brother's face and he takes inside him the taste of his brother's blood. Kargos can feel the dawn air on naked bone, and he wonders even through the Nails, he wonders *how much of my face is left–*

And then there is a sound and a feeling in the same terrible second, a crunching snap, like a grind and a gunshot in the same instant, and Kargos flails because his spine is breaking, he lashes out blindly, fingers fumbling and finding Amit's belt knife and drawing it and ramming it back over his shoulder into his brother's chestplate. It scrapes and stabs and deflects from the ceramite until it catches a joint and slides inside and bites. Meat bleeds. Blood runs. Amit falls back.

He is free. Free. The pressure is gone and Kargos goes for his axe and he turns with a scream to finish this. He turns right into Amit's backhand blow and something breaks inside what's left of his face. Amit's fists are cracks of thunder, each one painting his senses with smears of pain that blind him, literally stealing his sight, and Kargos feels the joints of his jaw give with a dislocating crunch, and he feels the bone at the side of his skull crumple like tin, and he feels cold air and acid spit on his mutilated face.

Amit's blade drives into his guts and is torn back out before Kargos can even breathe. He staggers but he doesn't fall, though something has come undone inside him, he knows that, his legs are weak, and he raises Gorechild, swinging it, but Amit smashes the axe aside and sheaths his sword in Kargos' guts again, this time carving up before pulling out. Eye to eye, face to face, it is the most intimate moment of Kargos' life, a moment of intimacy without sensuality, the two of them joined by the impaling blade, and

Everything

Slows

Down.

'I told you,' Amit breathes, 'to eat shit, traitor.'

The Blood Angel moves away. Kargos doesn't give chase. His legs fail.

Time passes. Or seems to. Perhaps it does, perhaps it doesn't. The sounds of war are dim now. Kargos is on the ground. He looks up at Amit. His vision is halved, and he realises he's lost an eye. What remains of his sight is stained red.

The Nails no longer bite. It's like they've burned themselves out, burst in the back of his head, no longer able to spread their poison.

There will be a moment now. A profound moment of brotherhood. Their gazes will meet and they will acknowledge how far they've both come. They will share, unspeakably, all that has brought the two of them to this fated moment.

But there's no moment of beautiful fraternal reflection. Amit fights on, grappling with other World Eaters. Fighting the war instead of devoting everything to this single duel. Kargos watches him, burbling through the vocoder implant in his throat. Demanding that Amit acknowledge him. Yet Amit fights on.

And soon, Amit is gone. Boots clatter around him. Several thud into him. He can stand, he can, he just needs to gather his strength now the Nails have deserted him.

The World Eater turns his head, pain lightning-bolting down his abused spine. He stares into the pulped remains of the psyber-monkey, its skull crushed in Inzar's grip. Strange, ugly little thing.

He turns his broken head again. Above him is a churn of clashing bodies, their identities meaningless. Their blood rains on him in warm spatters.

'Inzar,' he tries to say. 'I can still beat him. Help me. Help me up.'

When the bodies break away, Inzar is there. Kargos lifts a hand, trying to rise, needing the preacher's aid.

But the preacher regards him through the eyes of his skullish helmet. He doesn't take Kargos' hand. He presses his boot down onto Kargos' chest.

'As pathetic as Khârn,' the Word Bearer muses. 'Able to butcher anyone on the planet except the one man you want to kill.'

'Brother,' Kargos tries to say. 'Help me up.'

Either he doesn't manage to say it or Inzar doesn't care. The Word Bearer lifts his foot away, turning to the towering Sanctum.

'So close now.'

'Inzar…'

'Wash my name from your tongue, weakling.'
'Preacher!'
But he's shouting at nothing and no one. Inzar is gone.
'Medic…' Kargos calls. 'Apothecary…'
And he starts laughing.

Land and the others ran, but they didn't get far. Only to the next barricade. The Imperial Army soldiers there were already falling back from the position, making for the third and fourth redoubts, closer and closer to the Gate.

Shenkai was white, losing the strength to hold his hand to the stump where his bicep ended. His robes were painted down one side, dark with lost blood. Blood still flowed between his weakening fingers, trickling far slower than its previous spurting gusto.

Land guided him to sit and crouched before the thrall, gripping the younger man's chin with dirty fingers. He forced Shenkai to meet his eyes.

'You're going into hypovolaemic shock,' he said. The thrall nodded, but Land could tell from his eyes the young man had no idea what Land was saying, or even who was saying it.

Transacta-7Y1 collapsed next to them both, screeching a spiel of wounded code.

Land thanked her, she was right, of course – and he went for the canister of armour cement hanging from the thrall's webbing.

'I'm going to cauterise the wound,' Land told the shaking thrall, 'then I'll… Look, just hold on, Shenkai, just hold on.'

He aimed his Dark Age pistol up at the sky, discharged it once on maximal settings, and a blast capable of atomising a Rhino launched upward. With a murmured 'sorry' he pressed the hissing barrel against the stump of Shenkai's arm. Flesh sizzled and Shenkai yelled, which Land took to be a wonderful sign, given current context.

'Almost done,' he promised. And then, because it wasn't the same thing but it was equally true, he added, 'We're almost there. We're almost at the Gate.'

He smeared armour cement on the cauterised stump, ending the last of the blood flow. Exhaling, he turned to Transacta-7Y1.

Tee was failing to hold in the biomechanical slug-cables that made up the ropy portions of her intestinal tract. Several loops of the stuff had already slipped free in their run from the first barricade. Blood, in interesting and sacred shades, was running from her vitals in uneven trickles. That World Eater. The one that screamed Amit's name. That World Eater had come close to killing her.

Land swore in particularly crude gutter Martian.

Transacta-7Y1 replied that she did not believe such an act was biologically possible. Then she allowed that she already knew this, and that she had been making a joke. She queried if he found the joke funny.

Land didn't smile. He looked over his shoulder, where fifty kinds of hell itself was making its way along the Ascension, held back by surrounded clusters of defenders.

Transacta-7Y1 informed him that, in her considered opinion, it made the most tactical sense to leave her and go.

'I'm not leaving you.' Arkhan Land had heard and read these words uttered by fools with symmetrically balanced features in various tales of fiction in the past, and always found them trite beyond comprehension. Now, as they left his mouth, he meant every syllable of them.

Transacta-7Y1 replied that he was compromising his already slender odds of survival, adding that she was dying, and Land expiring here with her wouldn't change that outcome. She was also in significant pain, but she neglected to include that. She didn't wish to add to his emotional unrest.

'When we first met,' Land said, 'you saved my life.'

Transacta-7Y1 allowed that, yes, this was true, and that he had been sufficiently pleasant company since then, thus she did not regret the deed.

'I'd name my firstborn after you,' he said to her, 'but I despise children.'

Transacta-7Y1 pointed out that he was also of extremely advanced years, far beyond optimal breeding age.

'Yes. That, too. But come on. We can make it. We can make it, Tee. I can fix you once I get a good look at you.'

He rose, awkwardly straining to lift the unconscious form of Shenkai. His bad leg gave way at once.

He couldn't do it. He probably couldn't even have supported Shenkai's weight in the prime of health – he was a stick-thin old man, and Shenkai was a muscled thrall who'd trained for war every day of his life. Nevertheless, Land tried again, and a third time when the second failed.

The Martian sagged down after the last attempt, groaning at the strain. 'Omnissiah,' he prayed, 'it's your most devout servant, Arkhan Land...'

A group of soldiers vaulted the barricade, all filthy, all catching their breath before the final sprint to the Gate.

'And my prayers are answered,' he said.

They regarded him with adrenal confusion.

'My name is Arkhan Land,' he told them, 'and I am a deeply important man. It's likely you have heard of me. I need you to help me carry my friends to the Sanctum.' He trailed off, then remembered. *'Please.'*

Two of them lifted Shenkai, and Land turned to Tee, grinning.

'Let's go, you stubborn skit. Just a little further.' Land's smile dimmed. 'Tee? Tee?'

Transacta-7Y1 didn't reply.

Quite why Land did what he did next, he was never entirely sure, and he would have denied it had he ever been asked about it. But he cradled her helmeted head in his hands and kissed the metal forehead. A radiological alarm deep in his robes gave a warning click.

A shadow fell over him, bringing the drone of power armour. He jerked around, scrambling for his pistol, raising it – only for a Blood Angel to knock it aside.

Zephon bore several new wounds that would most surely scar, and his face was sheened with blood. Land had never seen him look quite so destroyed by exhaustion and injury, even when they'd journeyed together into the Imperial webway. Frankly, he'd looked better carved open on a surgical slab.

A host of Blood Angels were touching down, landing before the Gate, falling back before the advancing horde.

'Go,' Zephon bade him. 'This is the end, Arkhan. Make for the Gate while there is still time.'

'Zephon.' He said the name with almost insane calm. Lascannon fire screamed overhead, turning the void shields briefly prismatic and making the air stink of dirty ozone.

'Arkhan,' the Blood Angel pressed. 'My friend. The Gate. Go, while you still can. We cannot hold them back much longer.'

'Zephon,' Land said again, with the same intensity.

For a moment, Land wasn't sure what to say. Then for the second time in a week – and only the second time in over sixty years of adult life – he burst into tears.

'Zephon, they killed my friend. And my monkey.'

THIRTY-THREE

Bane of the Ninth Bloodline

The Bane of the Ninth Bloodline took shape and substance from the angelic dead. Their flesh became its flesh, their armour its armour. All of that meat and ceramite was darkened and altered, but everything in the daemon's corporeal form was harvested from the charnel field of butchered Blood Angels. It was a crop that grew in abundance here.

Only the creature's weapons were pulled raw from the warp, appearing in its hands as the daemon closed its claws into fists. A whip. An axe. The former parched and ragged, the latter catching the light of the poisoned sunrise.

The Craven God's shield of will had kept the daemon and its kind away from the Sanctum, but the half-mortal puppet was close to success in the webway. For that, the thing called Magnus should be tolerated in its exaltation. Perhaps not praised, and never trusted, but tolerated.

The daemon took its first step upon the gold-veined marble of the Grand Processional, leading up to the Delphic Archway, and sounded its arrival to its lesser kindred. Once, this would have been a roar that cracked stone, a bellow ripe with pride. Now, it was far more bestial, a laboured howl that oscillated the clutch of muscles in its throat. The daemon had learned humility. It had been given no choice.

Its lessers fled its presence, their own connection to reality yet frail with the Craven God's aura so recently brought low. Far above, the Bane sensed one of the other exalted mortals – the Lord of the Red Sands – still flailing against the last vestiges of the False God's resistance. No matter. The creature needed no aid here from some half-mortal pretender. Beneath the daemon's tread, marble soured to granite, the veins of gold transmuting to blood in the alchemy of unreality.

Some of the mortals it passed cried out in worship. In past incarnations, this would have amused the beast, and in further distant manifestations, it would have flattered it. The daemon killed them now with careless gestures of destruction, in case their prayers were laced with mockery.

Manifesting here had taken a supreme effort of will, and etheric vapour still steamed from the daemon's skin. Behind it, in a spillage of warped afterbirth, came lesser shedders of blood, riding the brass-bodied rhinos born-forged in the War God's realm.

The daemon stretched its wings, feeling sinews crackle and crack. They felt unfamiliar and tight, which of course they were. This incarnation had never flown before, and the last time the creature was incarnated in the corporeal realm, it had lost a wing on the night it tasted deeply of shame.

It sounded again, beast-loud and beast-dumb, a predator's warning whine. The first sweep of its axe reduced three statues to rubble, an act of needless spite that nevertheless contained a seed of joy. This was the Sanctum of the Craven God. This was where everything would end, and before that end came, this was where the Bane of the Ninth Bloodline would feed.

There were yet angels upon the battlement, surviving in diminishing phalanxes against a host of daemons numerous enough to blacken the sky. Humans and angels beyond lined the Royal Ascension, ripe for bleeding. In every direction, false-godlings with bodies of metal fought each other: the things mortals named Titans.

Such a hunting ground.

With a shudder at the feel of corporeality cold on its steaming skin, the daemon turned towards the portcullis that held like clenched teeth in the maw of the Delphic Arch. It could clear the battlement with a dozen beats of its warp-wet wings, but they were still weak and stunted, the membranes thin, the veins not yet pumped with what served the creature for blood. It needed to slaughter its way back to its former strength.

The God of War wanted the IX Legion to bleed. He had despatched his shamed champion to see it done, and at the end of the hunt lay redemption.

Above all things, this daemon desired redemption.

The Warlord *Oberosa* staggered as the chainfist slid back out of her guts. Mechanical debris rained from her disembowelled superstructure, crushing the Warmaster's infantry swarming around her feet. She was dead, she knew she was dead, but her crew were still in control during her dying seconds. The two Reavers that had carved her apart stalked back in case she lashed out with the power fist on her remaining arm, but her command crew couldn't muster enough locomotive force for a final blow.

She vented her reactor and purged it of power in the same desperate exhalation, turning with brutal slowness and managing three steps towards the Delphic Arch before the motive light went out of her machine-spirit. The Warlord Titan fell with almost human weakness, her knees buckling first, her waist failing second. Her murderers circled her, the Reavers pouring fire into the cooling steel of her corpse, but her reactor was parched of power and refused to go nova. When *Oberosa* toppled the rest of the way, it was just enough. The Warlord's corpse crushed the infantry at the portcullis, blocking the passageway with a mound of dead metal. There it lay, another Ignatum body outside the wall: loyal unto death, and arguably beyond.

The Warhounds of Audax took over from the vox-screaming Reavers. *Hindarah* was among them, a maniple of half a dozen Ember Wolves pounding their harpoons into the wreckage and doing their best to haul it out of the way.

The last of the battlement's guns focused their fire on the Titans and troops closest to the arch. On sections of the wall overrun by the Warmaster's horde, warriors in the colours of the Traitor's Legions set explosives on the autoloaders feeding the battlement's guns, or sabotaged them with blockages using the bodies of the dead.

Ka'Bandha watched all of this with burning eyes. The desperation of mortals, the absolute futility of their scrabbling dramas. He went over one of the Warhounds with a crack of his wings, briefly irritated by the waspish buzz of the walker's suffering void shields.

The Bane charged, his form a blur of indifferent flame, heedless of what he incinerated on his charge to the portcullis. The daemon tore through them, his axe not slaved to mortal physics; the blade didn't cut metal, it rent reality. He tore a hole, ripped it wider, and crawled through. Infantry followed him, shrieking, praying, laughing. Pitiable, ignorable little things. They thought all of this was about them. What they wanted. What they *deserved*.

Tearing through the first of the portcullises brought the Bane into the arch beneath the Delphic Keep, where the automated defences above rinsed him with firepower from a hundred murder holes. In the forgotten mists of history, castle defences would have poured hot sand or boiling oil from similar openings. Here, heavy bolters and volkite cannons unloaded their anger, annihilating the infantry in the Bane's wake. The daemon cared nothing for this; he was already carving through to the third portcullis.

The daemon possessed no vox and knew nothing of the legionaries' plans. Their pleas for the Bane to rip open the portcullises wide enough for tanks and Titans to come through never reached his ears. Even if he'd heard their needs, in what mad existence would mortals expect Ka'Bandha to do their work for them? Let them bleed outside the walls if they were too weak to get in themselves. The Blood God cared not from whence the blood flowed. Theirs or their enemies', it was all the same.

Volkite beams raked the Bane's ectoplasmic flesh from above, and the blood-sweat on his skin ignited like promethium fuel. The daemon never slowed, never wavered in his hunger for the blood that would run on the other side of the barriers. When he broke through, crawling and clawing his way between lengths of twisted metal, he gave another roar that could have come from the throat of one of the long-dead tyrant lizards that once ruled over the primeval surface of Old Earth.

He was inside.

Ahead lay a marble avenue infested with tens of thousands of warring mortals, and at the very end stood the Gate. The daemon felt the pull of his god's anger, his god's need, as he gazed into the open Gate and saw the weaklings fleeing through it to cower in the Sanctum of the Craven God.

But between here and there, thousands of Angels fought amidst the throng, and their blood was promised to the God of War.

They started coming for the daemon now. Some from the

Royal Ascension, turning back to face the newest, largest threat; some from atop the wall, dropping down and attacking from behind. The creature sensed the efforts of smaller Titans and tanks doubling their efforts on the brutalised archway, and the zealous, righteous souls of Blood Angels descending upon him.

This time there was emotion in his cry when he sounded his presence to the turgid sky. There was rage in the sound, and resolve, but above all there was joy. Redemption was upon him.

Let it begin.

Orion had been dead for so long he could no longer recall what it felt like to be alive. He'd been cold for so long he could no longer remember what it meant to be warm.

Even the dead could tire. Orion was proof of that. His weariness was a matter of cognition, not a physical thing, but that didn't stop it aching in what remained of his flesh. An activated Dreadnought was supposed to go a matter of weeks at most without maintenance. Orion had been awake and fighting without maintenance for four months. He floated in the icy milk of his amniotic tank, the fluid desperately in need of purging and cleaning, feeling particulates and organic debris against his skin. He could feel clogs in several of his intravenous cables. The shell within which he was interred had been suffering input lag for weeks; either it was struggling to obey his mental impulses, or he was too worn down for a clean cognitive link. Whichever the case, the result was the same. Corpses were not clean things. He was slowly being poisoned by the toxins of his own filth.

None of his brethren saw this. They fought together on the Ascension side of the portcullis, guarding the Delphic Archway from the ground, and they saw the Contemptor Dreadnought stand with one foot on a mound of the traitorous dead, laying waste to the Neverborn with its Kheres assault cannons. They heard the artificial thunder of its battle cries, a simulated boom only loosely reminiscent of Orion's own voice. They saw and heard nothing of the revenant inside, curled foetal in its dirty fluid, its mouth moving wordlessly as its thoughts were translated to motion and vocalisation. He was among his brothers yet separated from them, here in the filthy cold of his false womb.

The corpse twitched. Its lips moved.

'For the Angel and the Emperor!' the Dreadnought called. It turned, panning with its cannons, the fire of muzzle flares lighting up its armoured shell. In this cluster, just over two hundred Blood Angels still fought, forming a shrinking circle against the Neverborn. The Dreadnought's whirring guns cleaved through the daemons' ichorous flesh, cutting them down, bursting them open, breaking them apart.

Whatever had gone wrong within the Sanctum, it was getting worse. The Neverborn pouring over the wall were growing, not only in strength but in size. It was impossible to follow even a fraction of what was taking place. Shadowy things sliced the air overhead. The ground shook, sometimes hard enough to throw the defenders from their feet. Creatures defying description, some defying even the attempt to look at them, manifested and vanished and reappeared and cavorted and fought and killed – and sometimes, but never often enough, they died. Every few seconds, another blade crashed against his shell. The warriors at his side killed most of the daemons bearing these blades, though more and more he had to kill them himself with a backhand from a cannon or a stamp of his immense foot.

Feedback pulses reached the cadaver as a throb in the place where its hands used to be. The Dreadnought stepped back,

wading through the dead, moving to the centre of the Blood
Angels' circle. A clutch of thralls and cyborg servants still held
out within the regiment's defensive ring.

The corpse twitched. Its lips moved.

'Reload,' the war machine ordered, as he brought himself
to one knee with a protest of wearing-down joints.

They dragged ammo hoppers towards him and went to work.
There was the moment of conflicting freedom and vulnerability
as the empty canisters were unbound from his guns, then the
reassuring weight of their replacements crunching into place. The
seconds passed in excruciating slowness with the noise of his
brothers fighting and dying echoing in his damaged aural receptors. With his sensors failing, all sound was ghostly and indistinct
through the amniotic fluid and the muffling iron of his shell.

One of the thralls banged a fist against his armour plating.
The corpse twitched. The Dreadnought rose.

Orion didn't feel immortal. Titan crews told tales of how
it felt to embody the god-machines they piloted – how they
felt the immense metal superstructures as their own flesh and
blood. Orion felt no such connection to his shell. He was a
corpse in a cold coffin. The Kheres cannons weren't his arms.
The shell wasn't his body. What emerged from the vox-system
in the shell was his emotion translated into words through a
machine-spirit; accurate but imperfect. His experience of the
world was entirely untactile. He was the living-dead core of a
war machine that killed when he told it to kill.

The corpse twitched. Its lips moved.

'We are the wrath of Angels!' cried the Dreadnought from
its vox-caster. 'We are death to the treacherous!' He strode forward, reinforcing the outer ring where the line was bending
back, opening up with both cannons. They cycled live, warm-
ing up with twin metallic whines, then chattered with recoil
as they liquefied the Neverborn.

The line was breaking. The Neverborn cut into the defensive ring, the first of them making it to the groups of thralls and servitors in the middle. Orion turned, his cannons reducing the daemons to etheric mince. He strode forward, heedless of their blades, his iron feet grinding through warp slush that blackened the red of his shell.

The ground shook again, hard enough that the compensators in his joints momentarily jammed. The corpse thrashed in its amniotic murk, its mouth opening and closing, struggling to discern anything through its mental heads-up display. He could see/sense the enemy everywhere, too many to fight, beginning to swarm his shell. Each shiver of the Royal Ascension seemed to breed more of the things.

Brothers, he thought. *Brothers, to me.* The words lodged somewhere between his mind and the vox-caster, so all that emerged was a furious snarl.

They came for him, several of his kindred carving the beasts off his shell and granting him enough time to stabilise himself. Gratitude flooded him, the strongest emotion he'd felt in days.

The corpse twitched. Its lips moved.

'I am grateful,' the Dreadnought said for him, but there was no respite – even as the shell threw off the last of his attackers, he was turning to open up on the next foes.

Inexorably, they were pushed inwards, the defensive ring shrinking with each lost life. They shrank against their reserve ammunition and weapon caches, as the vox crackled, a steady stream of reports from other clusters in the Stand and Die forces.

Orion could see/sense through the portcullis, where Ignatum's engines were clustered outside the wall, holding the line against the Warmaster's own god-machines. His vision was a multilayered heads-up display blending pict-lenses, echolocation and auspex scan pulses transmitted to his mind's eye, and it flared with impression cascades each time a Titan died in the wasteland.

It flared brightest of all as something struck the portcullis from the other side. Something that had no right being there, something carving its way through as its skin erupted with unnatural fire.

Orion had fought on Signus Prime. He was almost a century dead by the time of that campaign, interred within this coffin and awakened only rarely between battles, but he'd been on the surface of Signus Prime when the Legion learned the first grievous truths about Horus' war.

He knew what he was seeing when the axe tore through the portcullis, and he recognised the daemon that burst through in its wake. The name ripped across the vox in amazement, in warning, in defiance, and in the voices of hundreds of warriors.

'Ka'Bandha,' the Dreadnought shell vox-casted, following Orion's unspoken thought. The corpse twitched. The war machine raised its guns and started firing.

He was the first Blood Angel to die to the daemon's axe. It struck him with enough force to shatter his shell and send the Dreadnought crashing across the ground of the Royal Ascension. When the shell came to a rest, bleeding oil and artificial womb fluid, cracks in the armour revealed the corpse within. Without the life support systems of its destroyed coffin, the mutilated corpse flailed helplessly, feeling the touch of the open air like acid on its skin.

Orion took almost a minute to truly die, staring up at the sky with his own eyes for the first time in almost a century, choking on air he was no longer used to breathing. His death was technically a stillbirth, as he died while being born, thrown halfway out of his synthetic coffin-womb. Such are the wonders of Imperial technology.

* * *

The daemon drank each life he ended. Souls swirled around his head; a halo visible to the others of his kind, a crown to inspire jealousy. With each fall of his axe, the daemon reaped angelic life, feeling his corpus swell with returning strength.

The cream of Blood Angels' heroism thrashed in his aura, their souls disintegrating to become part of him. As their identities crumbled, the Bane felt the memories filling out the hollows of his essence. He remembered wars against aliens he'd never fought. He remembered glories he'd never earned. He was flushed – bloated, even – with the righteous anger of humanity's living weapons. Step by step, Ka'Bandha avenged himself on the Legion that had seen him slain several corporeal years before. He craved their lives for his feeding frenzy. He could not take the Gate without building his strength.

He crushed angels between his fingers, squeezing them until pulped meat ran through the cracks of their ceramite. He ground the wounded ones beneath his hooves as they spent their last seconds of life hoping he could be killed with bolter fire. He killed with every step, not content to merely swallow souls; devouring angels whole or in pieces if they were moronically brave enough to come within reach. Several were wise enough to fall back, only for the daemon's whip to lash them in coils and pull them within reach of eager, curling claws.

His wings thickened, grew stronger. His claws hardened, no longer feeling as though they might crack at the first rake of his talons. He licked blood from his palm and fingers, tasting the final desperation of the last warrior he'd killed. Armand was the mortal's name. Sixty years of valiant service, not only to mankind's ignorant empire but to the Blood God that every warrior secretly served.

How could they not know it? Every drop of blood shed fed the Father of War. Here, of all places, all they had to do was look up and see the faces, the teeth, the smiles in the seething sky, horizon to horizon. Everything they did here fed the Pantheon. Even if they won, they would lose.

Later, there would be tales told of the Battle for the Sanctum Imperialis, and in the way of such stories they would be an uneasy mix of truth and lies.

Zephon would hear many of these tales, in a time when memories of their father were all the Ninth Bloodline possessed. He would listen to the tales of how the Great Angel fought with his back to the Eternity Gate, and he would know which parts were truth and which were myth fuelled by idealism, or manipulations driven by the speaker's agenda. Only rarely did he lend his voice to affirm or deny, no matter which way the stories went. Far more often, he would listen patiently and commit these newest tellings and mistellings to memory, then when the time came, he would retire to his stasis-crypt aboard the warship *Invictrix*.

A sleeper is not supposed to dream in stasis, but in this time yet to come, in the years after the war, Zephon always dreamed. In his visions, the tales he heard would mesh with his true memories, creating tales that danced along the border between fact and fiction. Upon rising, he would cast off these unwelcome dream-echoes, but it became more difficult as the years wound on.

The only time Zephon would disagree with a speaker was if they said Sanguinius had waited. He heard this often – between the tales of the Great Angel defying the entirety of the Warmaster's horde alone, which were glorious but equally impossible and fantastical – and these were the times he would say, in his gentle tones, that the speaker was wrong.

He would lean forward with a purr of black armour, and he would say no, the Great Angel did not stand with his back to the Gate and watch as the Bane of the Ninth Bloodline tore its way along the Royal Ascension.

In response, the speakers would inevitably become listeners, keen to know what happened through the eyes of one who fought at the Great Angel's side. Zephon would defer to let another speak if they knew the truth as he knew it, and only on the rarest occasions would he set the record straight himself.

What, the listeners would ask, really happened?

So Zephon would tell them.

'The duel was swift. That much of the old stories is true. It lasted scarcely five blows between man and daemon. But the creature you speak of was not there for our father. He is not named the Bane of the Great Angel, he is the Bane of the Ninth Bloodline. He was there for us.'

Zephon fell back, throwing aside his empty pistol and scavenging a boltgun from the hands of a fallen brother. He risked a look back over his shoulder, seeing Arkhan Land hobbling into the Sanctum, part of a stream of wounded soldiers and militia. Turning back to the Ascension, he opened fire over the heads of his retreating brethren, cutting into the tide of World Eaters on their heels.

Hundreds of Blood Angels manned the barricades outside the Gate, funnelling survivors through into the Sanctum. The vox was a ceaseless spill of overlapping voices; those inside reporting on entire reaches of the Sanctum's surface overrun; those outside repeating the same name, the same name Zephon had read in all the archival data of Signus Prime. He hadn't been there. He'd been on Terra, in his crippled exile. What little pict-data there was, was hazy with etheric interference. Winged silhouettes. Fragments of audio, replaying snarled threats. The sound of great wings beating. The kinds of fragments that, later, make legends.

Nevertheless, he recognised the daemon as he saw it massacring its way along the avenue. It hunted the warring

Blood Angels, and they were the ones to die beneath its falling axe. Humans fled its presence, ignored by the creature, dragged down instead by the howling beast-things in the daemon's wake.

The Custodians demanded the Eternity Gate's closure, and Zephon had the rank to neither agree nor oppose them. He heard Diocletian's voice among those ordering the sealing of the Gate, and for a moment he was back in the webway, marching with Land and Dio and the Custodians, fighting against hordes of Neverborn in the fall of Magnus' Folly.

'No,' the Great Angel said at his side. Sanguinius slashed the air, flicking daemonic blood from his blade. He didn't address Zephon alone, he spoke to every Blood Angel in earshot and every Custodian within vox range. 'Hold the Gate open as long as you can. I will deal with this.'

With that promise, Sanguinius launched skyward.

Ceramite crumpled between his teeth, broken up and ground down enough to swallow. The taste of IX Legion meat spiced each chunk of armoured flesh. Every death was the murder of uncountable paths: a warrior that would not rise to primacy in the future, a legionary that would kill no more of the gods' children, an officer that would never become a hero. This served the Pantheon in their brief and jagged unity, but these fateful severances were of no concern to Ka'Bandha. The daemon harvested the Blood Angels' souls and shed their blood as the currency of atonement.

The courts of the Four Gods took much of their substance from ancient human aristocracies. After Signus Prime, Ka'Bandha had crawled, bleeding, before the Skull Throne, there to endure the War God's laughter. He could have suffered through the mockery, marking the names of his kindred that laughed loudest in their creator's shadow, and adding them to the butcher's bill once this time of shame had passed. Every sneer and smirk would motivate him.

But Ka'Bandha had not been ready for the War God's disgust. The Lord of Blood had not derided him like the lesser creatures of the court, nor punished him in a rage, as had happened to the Wingless One, the exile Skarbrand, for the moronic sin of taking up his axe against the Blood God himself. Khorne, armoured in runic plate and as tall as the chain-wrapped sky, had regarded his beaten champion, who brought the stink of failure into this sacred realm in the warp's deepest reaches.

No punishment. No mockery. Ka'Bandha prostrated his ruined form before the Skull Throne, feeling the eyes of his former underlings upon him like the itching of vermin. There before courtiers in the shapes of a thousand beasts and monsters, the Blood God dismissed his failed templar with a flick of armoured knuckles.

Reality melted around him, and when it took shape once more, he was far from the Court of the Brass Lord.

The rage that had sustained him and formed so much of his identity was cold and slow to rekindle. He hid from his former lessers in the farthest reaches of the Blood God's realm, at the edges where shadow and unshaped warp became one. In the Unformed Wastes, he survived on the pathetic souls of ignoble ends and deaths devoid of consequence. He could not remake himself without the War God's favour. He was without weapons, his armour ruptured, his wings too mutilated to soar. Hiding from his own kind made a sick kind of animal sense.

Sometimes they hunted him. Packs of them tore through the Un-formed Wastes, his former equals goading on packs of their weaker kindred. Ka'Bandha would cower in the memory ruins of forgotten temple-cities, cringing from pursuit and learning the taste of humility. And with that came a new weapon, one previously denied to a creature that relied wholly on the strength of his rage. Ka'Bandha learned to be cunning.

He hunted the hunters. At first, he moved through the memories of dead civilisations and picked off the weakest of his kindred. Devouring his lessers would once have been as shameful as a human fighting a stray dog for a meatless bone, but he was so weakened by his destruction on Signus Prime that even a vulture's portion was enough to restore him by degrees.

A timeless time passed, in a realm where time is just a story told by creatures that cannot understand it. Ka'Bandha nurtured the dregs of his strength and gathered the weapons dropped by his prey. This slow rejuvenation became the entirety of his existence.

He made the long journey alone back to his creator's court, always careful to move unseen at the edges and dark places of Khorne's war-torn realm. His lessers and former equals – many now his greaters, in truth – jeered and threatened as he stood before the throne where he had once served as champion. His armour that day was a patchwork of stolen plate from the other daemons he'd killed, and though they were miserable trophies, he cast down the blades and skulls he'd taken from those that had hunted him in the Unformed Wastes. He came to the throne not crawling in defeat, but with a hunter's humility burned into his heart.

The daemon did not expect another chance, nor plead for one. He demanded one.

'I have swallowed failure and learned its bitterness. Now let me redeem myself or destroy me where I stand, for I have eaten enough shame to last an eternity.'

The Blood God had listened and set him a task, as mortal kings once did for their champion knights.

Five hundred souls.

'Five hundred souls from the bloodline that shamed you.'

That was no test. He could achieve that in a day. In an hour, if his strength returned swiftly enough. Malicious hope flared in the daemon's core.

'Five hundred souls,' the War God continued, *'from the bloodline that shamed you, harvested in the presence of the Angel of Blood.'*

The daemon dined on their bodies and drank their blood like a glutton gorging on wine, ingesting the stories of their lives, leaching the strength of their deaths. It wasn't long before even the Blood Angels fled, falling back towards the Gate or crawling into their battle tanks in a bid to find some way to fight back. They were slow, far too slow. Ka'Bandha was war given form. Those that ran, he leapt upon or pulled back with cracks of his whip. Those that remained died where they stood.

He heard them calling for their gene-sire, and what a sweet sound their controlled panic made. These transhuman pretenders to immortality, eloquently begging for the aid of their angelic prince… Ka'Bandha cut them down mid-plea, feeling their pain spiced with desperation as their souls meshed with his essence.

The daemon did not count lives as a mortal would count; he simply knew. He felt the tally of souls in his essence, each one becoming part of his corpus as it was torn from the flesh and freed for the warp to claim. Swollen to his previous power, the creature never slowed, never ceased. When his prey retreated, he gave chase; he lashed them down; he cleaved the earth with his axe, pouring his wrath into the ground to swallow groups of earthbound angels. Within corporeal minutes after manifesting, the creature was close. He could feel the eyes of his creator above, and the zealous, jealous hate of his blood-letting lessers.

The Angel landed before him, wings spread in artistic inti-
midation, pale features composed in warlike serenity. That
serenity was almost believable but for the hate that burned
in those beautiful eyes. Ka'Bandha was immune to the primarch's masquerade of perfection. He knew the fear of failure
that ran through his foe's bloodstream, and he'd breathed in
the Angel's hatred before.

Their presences exerted a pull of gravity, the battle coalescing
around them. The Blood Angels coming for the daemon lord
were cut apart and dragged down by red-skinned children
of Khorne. The daemons foolish enough to run at the Angel
were destroyed by the phalanx of Astartes forming around
their primarch.

'Daemon,' Sanguinius said with almost disbelieving soft-
ness. 'Are you so eager to die a second time?'

To the daemon's way of seeing the world, in smears of life
force and promises of running blood, the Angel looked burdened by weariness. He could scent the exhaustion burning off
the Angel's sweating skin. Ka'Bandha smiled, his own unease
dissipating. His tongue slopped from his parted jaws and polished the cracked obsidian of his teeth. Slaver hung in ropes
from his maw.

'You look tired, little Angel of the Craven God.'

It began on the ground. Angel and daemon came together,
blade on blade, beating their wings for balance in opposition.

'I killed you once,' the Angel snarled into the daemon's
inhuman visage.

Ka'Bandha's answer was to clench the muscles of his gullet
and craw, bringing up a steaming flood from his replenished
guts. Laughing, the daemon vomited the lifeblood of Sanguinius' slain sons into their father's face. The Angel endured the
pain and the shame without retreat, which only delighted
the daemon more.

'I will kill you again,' the Ninth Primarch swore through the effort of matching the daemon's strength. Blood hissed and steamed on his armour and face. It trickled into the lines of his lips.

Ka'Bandha bared his teeth, fury melting back, replaced by a mocking grin. The creature had expected these words. Now they were spoken, he welcomed them.

'In your arrogance, you still believe this is about you and me.' The daemon barked a laugh, bloody saliva spraying from his jaws to decorate the Angel's already bloody features. *'That,* **O purest one,** *is your father's vanity within you.'*

The daemon was ungifted at reading human expression, but something like pain flickered on the Angel's face – and that, too, was beautiful.

Ka'Bandha drew his gargoyle head back, brazenly readying for a headbutt. The Angel launched backwards, just as the daemon desired, and Ka'Bandha stole those precious seconds of freedom to turn and sweep his great axe through the warring Blood Angels and Neverborn nearby, butchering swathes of both. Strength flowed through him with a cramping sting, and the creature turned in time to catch the Angel's blade against the flat of his axe. Again, they came face to face.

'I am not here for you.' The daemon's mouth wasn't made for human language, and his fangs were aligned for the aesthetics of cruelty, not set by evolution. *'You are nothing. A flicker in the fires of time. A pawn with pretty wings, calling itself a king.'*

Sanguinius' eyes were tight, half-closed with the strain. Words were almost beyond him, every vein and tendon thickly visible. Ka'Bandha's blood-coated throat was already hoarse with the effort of human speech, but more words bubbled up and forth through a knife-fang smile.

'You taught me patience, Angel of the Craven God. You taught me my place. I am the beast that will feast on your sons in the

centuries to come. I am the cancer that will eat away at your lineage, until the last man with your blood in his veins is dust in Baalfora's wind.'

Fire from the burning avenue reflected along the length of the Angel's blade.

'I will destroy you, daemon, every time you crawl from the prison of hell.'

Ka'Bandha, teeth clenched with effort, spoke with his breath reeking of Astartes blood. Insidious sensuality flavoured his tone.

'You won't be around to defend your children forever.'

Sanguinius paled beneath the war-grime darkening his features, and Ka'Bandha roared, hurling the Angel back. Sanguinius twisted in the air, avoiding the swing of the axe but not the lash of the whip. It barely struck, coiling around one wing, but it was more than enough for the daemon's need. Ka'Bandha dragged on the leash, pulling the primarch from the air and back down to the broken marble. Sanguinius struck with inhuman grace, already weaving to slice at the entangling lash.

Ka'Bandha cared not. He abandoned the whip, leaping and beating his wings, making for the centre of the Royal Ascension where the Blood Angels clustered at their thickest. World Eaters and the Warmaster's other half-mortals cried their blessings up at him. As if their benedictions mattered at all to a being such as he, in a moment such as this.

He landed amidst dozens of red-clad Blood Angels, reaving them from life with swings of his axe, sounding his carnosaur roar as he devoured their souls and stories. Names and faces and memories not his own saturated him, threatening his senses; still the creature killed, using every precious second.

A few more... The failed champion's thoughts were a storm of uneasy, unsettled psyches. *A few more...*

Twice more, the Angel was upon him, cutting and hacking. Twice more, the daemon managed to break free, battering the primarch aside or hurling him away.

Ka'Bandha fled again, taking flight, and this time the Angel was on him in the air. The two of them crashed to the earth scarcely two seconds after leaving it, the slender golden figure rolling atop the daemonic giant, raising his sword, plunging it down.

The daemon pounded the Angel aside with the flat of his axe, desperation sinking into his essence now. This was faster than their battles on Signus Prime, devoid of posturing and skill, reduced to the clumsy viciousness of a brawl. He rose, bellowing, roaring for opponents, launching himself at the closest Blood Angels and rending them limb from limb. Their bolters spat up at him, their swords cut into him, and they died making that display of futile wrath.

The Angel struck him again, this time with enough force to throw him from his hooved feet. The primarch was a hunting hawk, all wings and cutting edges, thrashing against the daemon as it fought to get free. Ka'Bandha shielded his face with his free arm a moment too late; he snarled at the crash of the silver blade laying open his face to the bone, stealing one of his eyes. It didn't hurt as mortals feel pain, but shame and rage burned in their own ways, just as fiercely.

Ka'Bandha reached blindly with one arm, raw fortune letting him close his fist around one of the Angel's legs. He cracked the primarch like a whip, smashing him into one of the statues lining the Ascension, not turning to see how wounded the Angel was, not caring beyond the fact he was free. He could slaughter a few more of the Angel's miserable children and make for the open Gate… The God of War would reward him, restore him to favour…

He beat his wings, gaining the sky, hurling his axe at the

incarnadine form of a Legion Fellblade. The weapon cut through to the tank's core, detonating it in a plume of fire that smoked with fresh souls.

Just a few more...

The daemon weaved aside from the irrelevant slashing of lascannon beams and rockets going wide. Unarmed but for his claws, he dived towards the Blood Angels closest to the Gate. His claws would be more than enough.

Zephon was one of those hurled aside in a tide of crashing ceramite, as Blood Angels were thrown from the daemon's path. Its bleeding wings were a tattered banner, proclaiming its march to the Eternity Gate. Talons the length of spears raked through red armour and tore open the precious meat beneath. Every soul torn free quickened the creature, hastening its charge. It wanted the Gate, and it wanted the blood of the Gate's defenders. The beast refused to fight the Angel in the air, where Sanguinius held every advantage of agility.

They ran at it with swords that broke upon the beast's skin and fired weapons that vultured away chunks of its corpus without slowing the creature at all. It clawed and carved and clutched and twisted. Ceramite gave and blood ran. Never once in its killing fury did the creature's eyes leave the guardians of the Gate. The deeds and doings of tanks and Titans and primarchs were meaningless. This was its last chance.

Zephon held his blade two-handed, ramming it through the creature's calf. It was like forcing a sword into bedrock, and the generator in the hilt backlashed, sparking out and failing in his grip. In the space of two seconds, Zephon drove the sword home, failed to wound the creature, and was smashed aside by the slap of one vast wing. He rolled across the Ascension's final plateau stair, close to the edge. One of his eye-lenses was smashed. His retinal display screeched with warnings of suit rupture and wounded muscles. As if he couldn't feel it already.

He pulled himself to his feet, reaching for his fallen blade on the marble nearby, ready to throw himself uselessly against the creature again with the rest of his brothers.

Sanguinius was a bolt of gold and silver, harrying the daemon from above. The creature tried to ignore the Angel, then to batter the primarch aside, then – failing, enduring the wounds weaved by the Angel's blade – the daemon was forced to slow in its charge, venting its pain and frustration in another roar.

It clawed for the primarch, not to maul the Angel but to bring him to earth. On the third grasp, the daemon managed it, dragging Sanguinius from the sky and throwing him to the cracked marble beneath its feet. Zephon had never seen two creatures of such immense dignity and power reduced to such frenzied brawling. They rolled together across the Ascension's plateau of priceless off-world stone, raking at one another's eyes and driving their fists into armoured bodies.

Each time the Angel pulled free, the daemon dragged him back into the brawl. When the daemon surged back up, the Angel was upon it a half-breath later; a white-winged shrike, circling the creature and raining silver blows. Ka'Bandha's roars became howls, then bestial detonations of anger and pain.

The daemon had lost an eye; Zephon saw the Great Angel pulp it in his fist and hurl the resulting sludge aside. When Zephon ran in with several of his brothers, Sanguinius ordered them away in a strained voice over the vox.

'The World Eaters,' hissed the primarch. 'Hold them back.'

The daemon and the Angel clutched each other by the throat: the former to choke the life from the other, the latter using his grip only to smash the back of his foe's head against the marble ground. Sanguinius, dark with strangulation, with strings of spit hanging from his teeth, wrenched the daemon's head up and down, again, again, again, first cracking the marble with the anvil of Ka'Bandha's skull, then breaking it. The stone broke, while the beast's head refused to; nevertheless, it was enough. The creature's claws went slack for long enough that the Angel broke free. Zephon saw his sire launch into the sky.

The daemon was either unable to ignore this foe, or too wounded and blood-frenzied to let it go. With a spray of stinking blood from its wounded wings, Ka'Bandha gave chase.

Later, it would regret this.

Later, it would realise it poisoned its final chance at its fading victory the moment it abandoned its hunt for the souls of the Ninth Bloodline, when it allowed rage and fear to shroud its vision.

Later, it would be too late to matter.

Zephon was free for long enough to witness the brawl's end. He saw Sanguinius descending as the daemon rose. The primarch had drawn both spear and sword, and the Angel hurled the lance with a cry of effort. The spear took the daemon in the chest, penetrating armour and corpus, sinking home as if it belonged there. A thunderous cheer rose from the warriors on the ground, Zephon's voice among them.

The daemon's next roar was wholly bestial, a cry of vented frustration. Wounded in truth, it struggled to climb, feverish, almost fearful in its need to catch its tormentor.

Sanguinius gave the wounded beast what it desired. Zephon watched his primarch close the distance, white wings sleek to his back. The Angel took the creature as it was gaining strength in its climb, rolling aside from the daemon's reaching claws and striking from behind with the force of the Emperor's own wrath.

He hit it between the wings, his sword hilting in the creature's spine, shattering its back and bursting from Ka'Bandha's breastplate. The blade's point hissed with the smoke of stolen souls leaking from the wound, and the daemon hung in the air a moment more in defiance of mortal law. It gagged, and a sludge of undigested spirits sluiced from its open jaws.

Ka'Bandha dropped, the creature crashing against the Sanctum wall and leaving a smear of daemonic blood as it fell. Its wings no longer beat. Its limbs were dead. Sanguinius followed the body down in a dive, gripping the daemon by the back of the neck and the hilt of his sword impaled in its spine.

He could have let the creature fall. Zephon would always think that in the days, the years, the decades that followed, when he wore black and fought for an Imperium he no longer understood. Sanguinius could have let the daemon fall, striking the earth before the Eternity Gate.

But the Angel screamed, the sound as invested with rage as any sound that ever left the daemon's throat, and he hurled the dying monster out across the Royal Ascension. It crashed amidst the advancing horde and rolled bonelessly down the marble stairs. A monument to the failure of naked fury.

Zephon's last sight of Ka'Bandha was as packs of lesser daemonkind swarmed over the body, doing their carrion work. There was no comfort in that, no vindication. It echoed too closely to the IX Legion's old rituals. He wanted to acknowledge no kinship between his kind and theirs.

Sanguinius landed before the Eternity Gate, weakness forcing him to one knee. Platinum hair, streaked with blood, curtained over his features. His heart beat out of time in his chest, too hard, too fast, too weak, too slow. He felt every hour of the war. Too much of it, thickening his blood, filling his head.

They needed him to be everywhere, to do everything. He'd tried, he'd done all he could, hour after hour, day after day,

week after week. It was never enough. They always needed
more. All he'd wanted was to give it to them.

The horde saw him falter, and it surged for the Gate. They
heaved forward with one voice, as one tide.

The closest Blood Angels rallied to him, ringing him in
ceramite, offering their flesh as a shield to purchase the time
their sire needed to rise once more. He heard them fighting,
dying, selling their lives to lengthen his. Sanguinius clawed
for his dropped sword, rising, joining the fight on the ground
as he stretched the quivering lock of muscle cramps from his
bloodstained wings.

Behind him, without his order, the Eternity Gate began to
rumble closed. The doors drew towards him, folding closed
on tracks that had never been tested. The vox was alive with
the calls of struggling Custodians, demanding he fall back
within the Sanctum, pleading with him to aid in the purge
of the final fortress.

The Emperor needed him, they said.

The Gate had to be sealed.

Inside the Sanctum, they were being overrun.

He heard Diocletian's voice above the others, the last tribune ordering Sanguinius inside as if the primarch were a line
soldier and not the Emperor's own son.

Sanguinius stared at the battle raging along the Royal Ascension – thousands of his sons still embattled on the marble
stairs; thousands more still engaged on the Delphic Battlement. Humans of the Imperial Army. Titans of Legio Ignatum.
His own Blood Angels. Tens of thousands of them would
remain out here. So few had yet reached the Sanctum, yet the
ground quaked with the Eternity Gate's closing mechanisms,
making the decision for him.

World Eaters bayed and howled and died at his feet for
the sin of thinking they could end him. Neverborn burst

and disintegrated under his blade. The Gate ground on, a twin doorway the size of a hab-tower tectonically scraping towards closure. The engines responsible for its sealing had never needed to function before.

Sanguinius fell back. First only a single step, then a second – a fighting withdrawal that brought him into the shadows of the sealing Gate. The Blood Angels at his side fell back with him, leaving only when he commanded them to run, to reinforce the others fighting the Neverborn within.

'It's over,' he breathed. This was the way the world ended, with the crash of a closing door.

He stood in the deepening shadows, watching the foe in their thousands running for the Gate. Too late, all of them too late.

A Titan, a lone Warhound, rattled along the Royal Ascension, its jagged gait screaming evidence of overworked stabilisers, and its gushing vents promising a reactor detonation without swift control. The Titan crushed warriors of both sides beneath its canine tread, heedless in its headlong run. It hunched lower, bearing down as it lurched its sprinting way up the parade stairs.

Its armour plating was cast in the black and mottled crimson of the Legio Audax. On its carapace was the name *Hindarah*. That was the moment Sanguinius realised why it was running.

The Warhound stopped short of the Gate, hammered its stabilisers down into its joints, and fired its ursus claw.

The harpoon struck the Eternity Gate with the tolling of a funeral bell. It hit true, drilling through the layered armour, impaling the Emperor's carved image. When the chain slashed taut, it did so with the sound of Ka'Bandha's whip, and the Warhound began to back away.

The Gate's left door buckled, closing slower than its counter-part on the right. The Warhound dragged, straining at the

end of its leash. Around its ankles, the charging horde cried
in triumph.

The Angel rose on tattered wings – he would cut the chain;
there is time, there is still time – only to hear the thunderclap
pound of more harpoons hammering home in quick succession. The jackals of Audax came together in a pack, a full
maniple, their spears lanced into the same door. They dragged
back in ugly, lupine harmony, each chain cracking taut.

The Gate slowed.

Stopped.

Five chains. He could break five chains. He…

…lifted his pale eyes, seeing a flaming star fall from the
warp-locked sky. A star with wings, that bellowed his name
in his brother's voice.

THIRTY-FOUR

These last seconds of life

Vulkan

He lay on the wraithbone bridge, riven by the pain of his broken back, his head turned to where his hammer had fallen. His hand still gripped the haft, though the weapon was a dozen metres away. The severed wrist painted the ground with a trickle of red.

Vulkan had died before. The pain of it was a familiar thing, never welcome but nothing to fear. The diminishment, though – the sense of self retreating down a darkening hallway, dissolving the edges of memory...

Yes. He would always dread that.

'A *valiant effort*,' said the daemon. He rippled his wings, peacock-proud of his capacity for fratricide.

Vulkan's heart slowed. His breathing slowed with it, coming shallower, harder to pull in, strangely even harder to force out. He thought he'd closed his eyes, but the darkness was simply the epilogue of an oxygen-starved brain.

Magnus said more, but Vulkan was too far gone to hear anything but a stream of syllables, bleached of meaning.

Then there was nothing.

He hit the wraithbone hard enough to crack his skull, feeling a line of searing red split its way down his face. On trembling limbs, he rose again, using his hammer as a crutch. Blood burst from his broken jaw, a slurry of life that he vomited onto the bridge. He was certain, without touching his head, that his face was laid open to the bone. The chill of the air was ice itself.

Further down the bridge, Magnus was breathing heavily, the sound punctuated by snarls.

'Amusing,' the daemon lord growled, sounding anything but amused.

Vulkan took three shambling steps, swinging his hammer. He never even came close. Magnus beat his wings with a thunderclap of force, the brutal rush of air hurling Vulkan to the ground again.

He couldn't reach his hammer. He started crawling towards it, knowing he wouldn't make it, knowing there was no choice but to try.

The crescent-shaped *Blade of Ahn-Nunurta* came down between his shoulders, lancing through him with an indescribable crack. He couldn't breathe, couldn't move, though he kept trying to do both. Vulkan raked his fingers against the ground, trying to crawl away from the weapon that nailed him to the wraithbone floor.

There was greyness. Then there was black. And then the world turned.

Vulkan dropped his bloodstained hammer. The slime that served Magnus for blood cooked in the weapon's power field, bubbling away to steam. It had the reek of something that had died long ago and somehow kept moving.

This is what's inside you, Vulkan thought, staring at his brother. *This stink. This foulness. How can you not sense it?*

The daemon held a taloned claw to his chest, where the hammer blow had blackened the creature's crimson skin. Saliva the colour and consistency of swamp water hung in strings from his maw. In his one eye was a glare of aggravation, milking over the last of Magnus' amusement.

Unable to stand any longer, Vulkan went to his knees. The wounds woven upon him were a masterpiece of muscle severance. He collapsed, unstrung, bleeding across the wraithbone, staining it pink.

Magnus appeared above him. Some of the daemon's marshy saliva spattered into his open eyes. He brought up more blood but couldn't turn his head to cough it away and clear his mouth; instead, he started drowning in it.

Up came the Crimson King's avian foot. Vulkan saw the writhing of miniscule warp parasites, wormy things feasting between the daemon's webbed, clawed toes.

Then the talons came down, and then there was nothing.

Vulkan staggered backwards. His lacerated skin shone with blood and effort, and the hand pressed to his throat was a futile attempt to stem the gore sheeting down his breastplate.

Magnus snarled at him, bestial with infuriation, his one eye shot through with swollen capillaries. For a creature that had no cause to breathe, Magnus was labouring, his chest working with the force of a bellows, his scarlet skin diamonded with sweat. Fluid ran from ruptures in his corpus, glistening leakages of the psycho-organic plasma that ran through his veins.

'*Enough,*' the daemon cried. '*Enough.*'

Vulkan's strength deserted him with the flood of red from his throat. Magnus was suddenly taller, and it took him a moment to realise he'd fallen to his knees. Awareness was receding swiftly, this time.

'Enough, brother,' the daemon hissed. On that final syllable, the world darkened, and then there was nothing.

Magnus backed away, spitting something in Tizcan Prosperine, a sibilant mantra that could have been a spell as easily as a curse. The daemon spread fresh mutation through the wraithbone underfoot, the ancient material flowering with violet crystals that cracked in turn, disgorging clusters of unnatural insects. They died as slushy paste beneath Vulkan's boots as he advanced.

'I see him behind you,' Magnus accused. *'I see him composing the concerto of your resurrective immortality.'*

Vulkan said nothing, had no chance to say anything. Every cell in his body ignited in the same moment, the properties of his genetic data mutated into flammability. He took five more steps, each one slower than the last – a walking inferno of supernatural white fire. On the sixth step he fell, coming apart, crumbling in flame.

It was among the most painful deaths he'd yet known, and though he didn't cry out, this was as much due to the incineration of his lungs and vocal cords as it was down to his superhuman resolve.

The blackness came at last. Blessedly, finally, there was nothing.

He watched the sorcerer emerge from the mist, watched the way Magnus landed on the bridge with a frenzied resignation that stank like panic. The daemon was bleeding, his flesh discoloured from damage that seemed slower to regenerate each time.

Every time Magnus took flight, he'd vanish into the webway's mist – and reappear a moment later, screaming in frustration.

Again and again and again, the creature launched itself into the fog only to emerge from the mist back above the bridge.

Now he landed, eyeing the hammer in his brother's hands with new caution.

Vulkan charged at the wounded monster, battering Magnus' khopesh aside, bringing the dragon's-head hammer down on the daemon's thigh. Corpus-flesh shattered in a way true flesh never could, and the creature retreated with a sound close to a goatish bray. Vulkan heard pain in the cry, and more: he heard anguish.

The unseen coils of energy reaching from here to the Emperor's Throne Room thrashed as they eroded and thinned. Vulkan felt it in the air, that dissipation of focus.

Hunched now, slavering, Magnus regarded him with naked hate.

'Ask yourself, my brother. Ask yourself why we've chosen to oppose you. Ask yourself why we let the galaxy burn.'

In silence, Vulkan kept advancing.

The daemon's growl was rife with exhausted torment. His words lacked even the strength of the hate in his stare. *'How many times must I destroy you?'*

From his expression, Vulkan saw he expected no answer even as he craved one. He kept silent, taking those last steps. Wondering how it would happen this time.

Magnus denied his brother breath, turning the air in Vulkan's lungs to amber. A second incantation sealed Vulkan's lips together with a weave of fleshcrafting sorcery.

The sorcerer watched his brother asphyxiate on the wraithbone bridge, and once the struggles had ceased, he backed away from the body.

For Vulkan, after the last minutes of strangling red, there was pulsing black, and then nothing at all.

* * *

Magnus retreated, holding his broken blade as if reluctant to cast it aside.

'*Father's plan would never have worked. Even you must see that, walking in this world between worlds.*'

'Save your breath. This is your execution, Magnus, not your trial.'

Vulkan charged – and froze. His joints refused to obey him. He stood still, not tense, merely motionless: held in a stasis so absolute he couldn't feel his heartbeat, or the hammer in his hand. All sensory flow between his mind and body was severed.

Magnus, looking weary beyond reckoning, stalked forward with his broken blade. He swung; Vulkan's body fell one way, his head another.

Magnus howled, retreating, shielding his broken face with one great arm, and raising a kinetic barrier with his other hand outstretched. He no longer hissed defiance, but it was written starkly across his mutilated features. One side of the daemon's skull – or whatever passed for bone structure inside his corpus – was malformed from the last impact of Vulkan's hammer. A blow that would have destroyed a Land Raider had only caved in part of the Crimson King's head.

'*You do not know,*' Magnus breathed, '*why you fight.*'

Vulkan ran in, swinging, grunting with the effort. On the eleventh blow, he felt the kine-barrier waver, softening against the incoming impacts. On the nineteenth, it burst with an expulsion of force that bred more cracks across the wraith-bone bridge. At the last moment, Magnus turned the hammer aside with a desperate telekinetic shove.

'*You do not even understand what you're fighting for.*'

Vulkan was relentless, forcing the daemon back, endlessly back, making him expend energy in pushing each blow aside.

Every swing was deflected at the last moment by telekinetic pressure; the last one coming closest, snapping one of the ornate tusks from the daemon's chestplate.

Magnus screamed, his etheric form swelling, and with a bellow of concussive force, he hurled his brother from the bridge, throwing him out into the empty mist. Magnus' laughter, ragged and forced, receded as Vulkan fell.

There was a seamless, windless eternity of golden fog. Then darkness. Then nothing.

Incineration.

Decapitation.

Suffocation.

Exsanguination.

Electrocution.

Dissolution.

Evisceration.

Transmutation.

Uncontrolled genetic blooming, saturating him with cancers lethal enough to kill within seconds.

There was pain each time, pain enough to drive a mortal beyond the boundaries of reason; pain enough to render even an immortal mad. And there were times – years – over the course of his life, that Vulkan's thoughts had become a fragile composition at risk of breaking apart at the slightest provocation. The gift bestowed upon him wasn't gentle on his mind. But he was born to endure. He was built – consciously or by whatever winds of fate breathed into the process – to endure what no others could.

There was always pain. Then blackness. Then nothing.

And after the nothing, there was a wraithbone bridge, a duty to a distant father, and a hammer in his hands.

* * *

Magnus was down on one knee, his wings broken, his face a cracked portrait.

'*No more, Vulkan.*' He dribbled the words through a crushed jaw. '*No more.*'

Vulkan circled the downed creature, red eyes narrowed for even the merest movement. The daemonic blood on his hammer steamed with the smell of a funeral pyre. He didn't trust his brother's vulnerability, and he saw his caution reflected at him in Magnus' blood-webbed eye.

'I sense the energies you have wrought,' said Vulkan. 'Thinner, weaker, but still curling in the air around us. You are still attacking father.'

He expected Magnus to laugh. Instead, the sorcerer sighed.

'*You deal with forces you do not comprehend. Killing me may let the Emperor breathe easier, but it will not free Him from the Golden Throne.*'

Vulkan's tone was ice and iron. 'Nevertheless, you die.'

'*So finish it.*' Magnus hunched over, lowering his head for the executioner's blow. '*Save the Emperor. Let ignorance triumph over truth.*'

Vulkan hesitated.

'*Can you afford to wait any longer, little dragon?*' Magnus slowly raised his head, and in his gaze was the mockery Vulkan had been expecting. '*Where is your urgency now? Where is all that* righteousness?'

Knowing it was a trap, knowing he had no choice but to spring it, Vulkan raised his hammer. As it fell, the world turned.

It wasn't blackness, this time. He saw planets turning in the deep night, beautiful no matter their colours or surface conditions, beautiful for their infinite complexity. Vulkan never looked at a planet and saw territory, cities or resources. He saw a geological jewel, a sphere formed by astrophysical law and the geo-mathematical processes that bound it all together. Each world was unique, shaped just so. He believed there was beauty in that.

He drifted through space, descending to one world until it was a plateau beneath him of hazy blue atmosphere and immense wilderness. He knew it at once.

'Prospero,' said Magnus, by his side.

His brother wasn't a daemon. Magnus was the man he'd been long ago: red of skin, darkened further by the sun, clad in a toga of white silk. He smelled of ink, fine parchment and lies.

'I thought we could speak,' the sorcerer said. 'One last time.'

Vulkan tensed, preparing to–

'No, brother.' Magnus showed his pale red palms, bare of any weapon. 'No time is passing. In the Labyrinth of the Old Ones, our hands are around each other's throats, with death yet to be decided. Here, we exist between heartbeats.'

Vulkan stared into his brother's remaining eye. 'I believe you,' he said.

Magnus gave a tired smile. 'It has been a long time since I heard those words.'

Prospero turned beneath them. Vulkan gazed at the wild lands of the vast Pangean continent, and the distant silver pinprick of Tizca, the world's only city.

'Speak, then.'

'And you will listen?'

Vulkan nodded.

'Very well. This is what I would have you understand, brother. The Imperium is the lie we tell ourselves, to make sense of a reality we fear to face. We tell each other that it is necessary. That we do what must be done. That whatever might replace it would be worse. But look at all we do not say. Father is a tyrant, and you, out of all of us, should have seen that first. The Imperium is built on the lies of a would-be god and the violence of His crusade. What benevolent monarch instigates a crusade?

'Under the Emperor, we have perpetuated a holy war that has sucked worlds dry of resources and cost billions upon billions of lives. We have spent life like meaningless currency, all because one man said we must. How many cultures have we annihilated, Vulkan? How many have we assimilated and robbed of their vitality, replacing innovation with conformity? How much knowledge have we destroyed because father decided no one was allowed to learn it?'

Vulkan considered this. The planet rolled on, sedate and slow despite its relative astronomical speed. He realised he wasn't wounded here. He wore his armour, but it was pristine, not the scraps of torn ceramite left to him on the bridge.

'This is how it got to you, isn't it?' Vulkan knew the answer even as he asked the question. 'The creature that gouged its way inside your soul and laid its eggs there. The thing that pulls on your strings. Did it promise you knowledge? Did it paint the Emperor as the death of enlightenment?'

Magnus' expression answered for him. Long red hair fell to frame his face, and the sorcerer brushed it back from his cheeks.

'The Imperial Truth is a lie. The empire we built cannot be reformed, only overthrown. From violence it was born, and in violence it must end. Don't you see? Once the board is swept clean, we can start again with our eyes open, aware of the truths of the universe.'

'You make this sound like a principled stand,' said Vulkan. 'As if all you have done, all Horus has done, could ever be justified.'

Magnus turned to him sharply. 'I? What do I have to justify?

Each time I was attacked, I defended myself. Each time they tried to silence me, I made sure to speak out. The Imperium lavished punishments upon my Legion, draping its hypocrisy over us as a funeral shroud. We fought back.'

Vulkan met Magnus' gaze, seeing the ironclad surety there. This was futile, he knew it, yet the words came forth anyway.

'Look at the horrors your side has unleashed upon Terra. The massacres, the mutations. Magnus, you are taking part in the extinction of your species… You cannot truly think you have done nothing wrong. Even you, brother. Even you, in your arrogance, cannot believe this is justified.'

'Necessity justifies all. And this is necessary. Without this primeval force, without this *Chaos*, there will be stagnation. Ignorance instead of illumination. Existence instead of life. I did not write the laws of our universe, brother. I take no joy in the truth of reality. But I won't hide from it.'

Vulkan looked at him as if he spoke in another tongue. 'Necessary, you say.' Magnus nodded, and Vulkan continued, 'Necessary according to whom? The alien god that exalted you and now demands you commit genocide?'

Magnus clenched his teeth, and the world turned…

…but not far. It turned to reveal Tizca, City of Light, metropolis of white pyramids and silver spires. The city was aflame beneath them, burning from the raining hellfire of an Imperial fleet. The golden vessels of the Emperor's chosen. The sleek black hunting ships of the Silent Sisters. The many, many warships in the storm-cloud grey of the Space Wolves.

'The Razing of Prospero.' There was murder in Magnus' eye. Murder and sorrow. 'Bear witness to our brother Russ, bringing death to my home world and all its people. Tell me, Vulkan, would you have reacted with temperance to this, had it been the destruction of Nocturne?'

Vulkan didn't need to stare at the orbital bombardment. He'd read the reports, he'd seen the picts and the footage and spoken to many of the Custodians that took part in the ground assault. Nothing unfolding here was a revelation he wished to experience twice.

'Russ was lied to by Horus, deceived into attacking.'

'I know. It changes nothing.'

'But it should. You, who value truth so highly, willingly align yourself with the one that engineered Prospero's death. And when the Space Wolves fleet arrived in your sky, what did you do, Magnus? Did you try to enlighten Russ? Did you use your power to prevent the assault? Or did your belief in your own persecution leave you assuming the worst of the Emperor's intentions? All witness accounts say you languished in your tower, welcoming the destruction as your penance, until you decided to fight in the final hours, when it was far too late to stop the massacre.'

Vulkan gestured to the destruction raining from the upper atmosphere: lance strikes, drop pods, the slower trails of gunships making their descent. 'Why would the Emperor order you and your entire Legion dead? Did you not stop to wonder at the scale of this misunderstanding?'

Magnus laughed at the questions, the sound wet and bitter. He gestured away from the burning city, and the world turned, falling away.

They were in the webway again, but no longer upon the lost bridge. They drifted through the oval tunnels, following angles that hurt the human eye. Always ahead of them, an avatar of fire blazed through the tunnels, shattering the wraithbone membranes without heed, blind and deaf to the horde of daemons surging into the webway in its wake.

'I did this,' said Magnus. 'I thought He wished to punish me for ruining His Great Work.' For a moment, Magnus paused, gazing at the host of Neverborn darkening the tunnels, as if seeing them for the first time.

'But how was I to know? He refused to tell me of His grand plan. If He had told me...'

Vulkan resisted the urge to spit at the sudden foul taste on his tongue. 'Again, you see the worst in all others, absolving yourself of blame. Why did you need to know of the Great Work? You were warned not to toy with the warp. We all were. But you couldn't resist. You believed that you knew more, that you knew best. And why is it that you alone lament being kept unapprised of father's plans? Why is Sanguinius not enraged that he never knew of the Webway Project? Why am I not enraged that I was kept ignorant of it? Why did *you* need to know?'

Magnus' eye gleamed with the reflection of the burning icon ahead. His former self, years before, racing to warn the Emperor of Horus' betrayal. Reducing the webway to unsanctified rubble with his passing.

'Had I known the truth, I would never have... done what I did. Father should have told me.'

Vulkan laughed, unable to believe what he was hearing. 'How could father have predicted you would defy His one command? Not only did you use the warp against His orders, you fuelled your psychic warning with human sacrifice. How could any of us have known you were capable of such barbarity?'

Magnus exhaled slowly, his hands clutching the folds of his toga. He spoke a word of power, and the world turned.

They were in the Throne Room. The blazing avatar had incarnated before the scientists and techno-magicians of the Emperor's secret work. It had forced the webway portal open, making it radiate wounded light. Already, it grew dark with the silhouettes of daemons as they drew near.

The Custodians present – precious few of them, for how could they have anticipated the sudden death of the Emperor's dream? – opened fire on the image of ghostly flame. It ignored their paltry defiance, and it ignored the explosions its arrival had birthed across the great laboratory. It hovered before the Emperor, like some spectre of religious revelation from the ancient tomes, when such things were believed by credulous men.

'I had to warn Him,' said Magnus, watching the scene.

'No,' Vulkan said gently. 'You *believed* you had to warn Him. You believed as you always believe – that you knew best, that you had to act, that you alone knew what had to be done. And never once did you think, through all this destruction, that there was something deceiving you.'

The sorcerer glared at him. 'Why do you speak to me as if I were a lowly pawn in this game of regicide? The Warmaster and the Emperor both know I am the most valuable piece on the board.'

Vulkan was unmoved by the sorcerer's words, and by the cataclysm playing out before him. His tone was patient, as it had been in the days before the war.

'Vanity is what leads you, Magnus. You choke on arrogance, unable to see you are the architect of your own downfall. All the others, all of Horus' broken monsters, at least they can see the bars of their cages. Even Horus, driven out of his mind to serve as a hive for the Pantheon, knows in his soul's core that he has lost control. You are the only one that still believes he is free.'

In silence, Magnus shook his head. The world turned with the motion.

They remained in the Throne Room, but the great machines were overloaded and black, slain by esoteric forces, and the industry of the laboratory was replaced by the militancy of a garrison presence. It was no longer a place of vision – it was a barracks. And it was closer to Now. This was how the Throne Room had looked when Vulkan had last been here.

Vulkan and Magnus were present at this point in the recent past, as well as drifting through it in their current incarnations. They watched themselves at the foot of the Golden Throne: Vulkan implacable but for the regret lining his features; Magnus manifest as a being of light, shimmering in and out of the layers of reality perceptible to the human eye.

'Here,' said the Magnus of Now, watching the Magnus of Then. 'Here is where I made my choice. You saw the Emperor make His final offer to me. You heard Him promise me a new Legion, if I would only forsake Horus and come back to you all. A matter of mere weeks ago, brother. Will you tell me you've forgotten it?'

Vulkan sighed. He seemed suddenly weary.

'That is not what transpired here, Magnus. The last unstained shard of your soul burst into the Throne Room and begged to be saved. With a heavy heart, father refused you. That is what I saw. That is what happened.'

Magnus' laughter was blunt, practically a derisive bark. 'And you say I'm the one who has been deceived?'

Vulkan was too tired to rise to the bait. He met derision with solemnity.

'This thing that runs through you, this chaotic force you proclaim as freedom, is not a disease to be caught on contact. It is the layer of emotion behind reality, a poison that has achieved near sentience. It makes its prey into willing victims in their own damnation. You are riven by it, Magnus. Hollowed out by it.

'And it was already in your Legion, in your sons' blood and genetic code, in the form of the Flesh Change. And when you

dealt with the Pantheon, believing you had cured your children, all you really achieved was a deepening of the taint,
hiding it from sight, delaying the inevitable. This thing, this
force, cannot be *cured*, Magnus. You cannot pray it away once
the rot sets in. Once you are on the Path… your fate is sealed.'

'Wait, Vulkan. Wait. How can this be? How do you know
all of this?'

In the silence that reigned in the wake of those words,
the Throne Room began to fade. Golden mist hazed its way
around them, revealing patches of wraithbone architecture.

Vulkan was relentless, his voice growing firmer. 'How could
the Emperor ever trust you now? Why would He offer you a
new Legion, let alone a place at His side? You dreamed up
your own redemption, just to give yourself something to rage
against. Because you need to feel as though you are the one
choosing, not having the choices made for you. The creature
that exalted you will never let you see the chains that bind
you to its will.'

The mist was everywhere, thickening. Magnus felt the change
upon him, and beneath the sensation of power was a *pull*, a
wrenching, the sensation of a trillion filaments woven into
the cells of his body, dragging at him.

'How…?' Magnus asked, barely above a breath. Where the
mist touched him, his flesh was darkening, swelling. The shadows of ragged wings loomed above his shoulders. 'How do
you know all of this?'

Vulkan remained in place, saying nothing, doing nothing.

'Who are you?' demanded Magnus.

The world turned, and this time it wasn't moved by Magnus'
will.

The first strike of the hammer pounded Magnus to the wraithbone ground, a magma flow of ectoplasm running from his

riven skull. The second cracked the bones of one wing, splintering the spine and shoulder blade beneath. The third eradicated the daemon's right hand, rendering it into dissolving paste.

Breathless, standing over the paralysed remnant of his mutated brother, Vulkan raised his hammer. In the same moment, Magnus somehow lifted his head. The sorcerer stared past Vulkan, over his executioner's shoulder. Either he saw nothing, or he saw without the use of his eye, which was a burst fruit of a thing, turned to leaking pulp in its shattered socket.

'Wait,' the daemon wheezed, the word ruined by the graveyard of his teeth. 'Father. Wait.'

Father is far from here, Vulkan almost said, wondering what visions were conjured in his brother's dying mind. But he saw the fear on Magnus' face, imprinted with the lines of regret. It was enough to make him hesitate.

I don't have to do this.

But he did. Not just because it would free the Emperor from the sorcerer's assault, not just because thousands were dying in front of the Eternity Gate, but because this was how the Archenemy drilled inside a heart and soul. The creatures sank their tendrils into a person's hesitations, cracking them open to become doubts. They caressed along the edges of someone's virtues, heightening them, souring them into flaws.

They would do the same with Vulkan's mercy. Mercy was how the Pantheon would welcome him, and how he would begin to do their will. He would trust someone that breathed deceit. He would spare the life of a man that must die.

And he would feel righteous, as his nine traitorous brothers felt righteous, deaf to the laughter of the gods as he moved to their etheric melodies. Like his brothers, he would believe it was his own virtue guiding his hand.

'I see now,' the blind daemon whispered. 'Forgive me...'

+He lies.+ The Emperor's voice was ice behind Vulkan's eyes. It ground into his temples from the inside, seeking a way out of his skull. +He lies even to himself. It is all he can do now. Finish it.+

Magnus grunted as if overhearing the words. His contrition soured, becoming spite. As his expression darkened, the Emperor's tone struck Vulkan's mind with the force of a storm's wind.

+THEY PREY UPON YOUR MERCY – HE GATHERS HIS STRENGTH – KILL HIM+

The two brothers moved in opposing harmony, perfect-motion reflections of one another. Vulkan dealt the executioner's blow, and in the same moment, Magnus dealt his.

Vulkan couldn't be killed. That left only one recourse.

It started with a pattern. A twinned helix of genetic code, the equation at the core of every mortal's existence. Even with his eye destroyed, Magnus could see this calculation written through his brother's blood. Signifiers of their father's arcane science were flowing through Vulkan's veins.

He followed the calculations, the process metaphysically no different from reading the notes of a song from the page and hearing its melody in the mind. Once he could make out the flow of these blood mathematics, he followed them along their temporal axis. A journey through time, seeing cell degradation and replenishment; sensing through atmospheric and environmental shift all the places his brother had been, then branching outward, a horizon-wide view of the souls Vulkan had met, the deeds he'd performed, the worlds on which he'd walked... Learning the permutations of the code, the answers at the ends of its inevitable questions.

He had seen enough. The sorcerer pulled back, plunging again into the core of the code, feeling the currents of life flowing through his brother's body. He closed the jaws of his reaching mind around the strands of this secret pattern, clutching not the code itself but the skeins it wove. Blood mathematics. Genetics. The processes of life. The harder he held to it, the deeper his touch went, down to the level of molecules, to protons and neutrons, to atoms.

For one moment, his mind was entirely scattered throughout Vulkan's flesh, diluted through the avenues of his bloodstream. It was enough. It would work. If Magnus could not kill him, he would unmake him.

The sorcerer severed the code's strands. He pulled at the calculations, unsolving them. He unravelled the strings and skeins of the blood mathematics – a literal unmaking at the molecular level, the sundering of Vulkan's very atoms.

Physically, Vulkan came apart at the biological seams. His black skin ruptured with holes that siphoned light. These bloodless ruptures spread through his bones, his organs, his armour. What remained of his skin ignited, then blew away an instant later as ash in the webway's sourceless breeze. A partially articulated skeleton, bound together by disintegrating tendons, staggered back as its eyeballs caught fire.

Magnus haemorrhaged power. He poured himself into the process, diluting his essence across the sine wave of his brother's existence. When the dissolving skeleton stumbled, he felt a laugh wheeze through his own ruined mouth. The process was imperfect – it could only be imperfect, devoid of ritual structure and born out of frantic will – but it was working. A testament to his might, and to the choices made to reach this point.

This sense of exultant pride was his second to last thought. Pride in himself, in what he was capable of: unweaving his brother's existence, rewriting reality to obey his desires.

And yet, he couldn't understand how the man in front of

him could still be on his feet. He couldn't believe this flayed, immolated thing, being erased from existence, endured all this and still swung its hammer. He couldn't lose here, he couldn't die, he couldn't–

And then there was silence. A stillness descended across the webway, as sensory and real as the golden mist.

The thing that had been Vulkan stood motionless in the sudden quiet. It held onto its hammer for a moment longer; with its skinless grip fused to the weapon's haft, it had no choice but to keep it in its clutches. The joints of its elbows gave out with straining creaks, lengthening on strings of melted tendons, then breaking apart. Only then did the hammer drop to the wraithbone floor, along with the primarch's forearms.

The corpse of Vulkan fell to its knees beside the headless body of Magnus the Red. There they rested, at the heart of Magnus' Folly, humanity in microcosm: a study in fratricide.

The skeletal corpse's final breath whistled out through charred teeth.

There was silence. Then darkness. Then nothing at all.

Later, a figure walked alone through the aeldari necropolis, passing beneath the spired monuments to the failure of two species' attempts to tame the webway. It moved with a care for its wounds, sometimes shambling but never stopping. It looked more like a skeleton than a man, its blackened bones bare to the golden mist. It was either dead but alive, or alive but dead – the effect was the same, no matter which way an observer came down on the philosophical divide.

The living dead thing would have to fight its way back. It knew this. It was ready.

The sound of the figure's passage was iron grinding against wraithbone. Behind it, in a fleshless grip, it dragged a hammer.

THIRTY-FIVE

The Eternity Gate

The Angel and the daemon meet in the air, beneath a sky the colour of blood, drawing breaths that taste of murder. The first impact of blade against blade is a metallic thundercrack while their sons wage war below, fighting and dying in the shadows of their fathers' wings.

The Lord of the Red Sands swings and the black blade shrieks, its steel fattened on souls, but the Angel is gone, twisting away, soaring higher. Angron beats his wings, giving chase, enraged at his own cumbersome strength. It's like fighting a shadow. Each time he closes on Sanguinius, the Angel rolls aside or furls his wings and drops away. Each missed swing of his sword, each failed grasp with his talons, resonates inside Angron's skull with a splash of acid. The Nails bite to give him strength, this is so, but they also bite to punish him. Now more than ever, the Nails bite with the sound of Horus' urgent command, begging for the Angel's death.

Angron – what little is left of Angron now that his soul has been transmogrified into the flesh-matter of an ethereal god – has never heard Horus beg before. The weakness in the Warmaster's voice makes him shudder with revulsion.

Sanguinius dives low, swooping towards the ground, and Angron follows. Volkite beams stab up at them both, lancing the sky. They fly through detonations that blacken the Angel's armour and darken his wings; explosions that do nothing but tighten the daemon's hold on incarnation. Every death taking place upon this planet, every life ending beneath them, strengthens Angron and seals his wounds.

Closer, he comes. Closer. He can smell the sweat on his brother's skin. He can hear the drumbeat of his brother's blood. He can smell the sweetness of the Angel's wounds.

Sanguinius senses it. The Angel veers away with a grace Angron cannot hope to match; a spread of feathered wings arrests his dive and a slash of straight silver rips across the daemon's face. There is no pain. Most of his face has been cut from his skull but there is no pain. He experiences pain the way others might feel grief, or trauma, or frustration: to him it is a helplessness, a wound within. It is something that cannot be tolerated, something that can only be overcome with the running of enemy blood. He's blind, his face broken by the silver sword, and without the organic receptors to process injury, it's the weakness that hurts.

His eyes regenerate as he thrashes blindly with his blade. He can see again, dull and dim for another few moments, then with a clarity that defeats the ash and the dust swirling in the air. He doesn't see as a human sees. Angron sees the fire of souls, and his brother's flares brightest of all.

When they meet again, it's in a killing embrace. The Lord of the Red Sands tears the Angel from the sky, clutching his golden brother in his great claws, bearing Sanguinius down. They fall, and fall, and fall, and crash through the glassaic dome of the Martian temple atop the Warmonger Titan Malax Meridius. They strike the floor in a roll that would break any mortal bones, their tumbling bodies obliterating the mosaic rendering of the Opus Machina, sacred icon of the Adeptus Mechanicus and the Martian Mechanicum alike.

This is a sacrilege neither brother notices. Tech-priests and menials flee the duelling demigods. Neither of them notices that, either.

Angron gets a clawed hand around the Angel's head. He beats Sanguinius' skull against the floor once, twice, thrice, and cracks web out along the tiles in stone-splitting veins; a fourth time, a fifth–

There is weakness, then. Perhaps it should be pain, as well, but it is most definitely weakness; Angron's grip slackens, his arm dissolves, literally it dissolves from the shoulder down, and the Lord of the Red Sands is thrown back as the Angel rises. In Sanguinius' hands is a pistol, and the dregs of Angron's sentience recognise this as the melta-weapon infernus: a one-use thing of incineration. The Angel casts it aside and takes wing – diving right at the daemon, leading with his sword. Angron raises his own blade, feeling the flow of the incoming blows like promises whispered in warning, and he catches each of the Angel's thrusts before they can impact against him.

Metal grinds. Sparks spray, arcing out from the meeting blades, hypnotic in their falling beauty. For a moment, just a moment, he is on the Plains of Desh'ra'zhen, camping rough beneath the pale moon, watching fireflies play above the banked campfires of his freed-slave army. How peaceful that night had been, even with the Nails knuckling into the back of his brain; how peaceful that one night was before the Emperor tore him away from his real brothers and sisters – the siblings of his heart and not of manufactured blood – leaving them to fight alone, leaving them to die, leaving him to face this unwanted life and–

Sanguinius impales him. A lance of ice runs through where his heart should be. The two brothers are face to face; one of them a visage of bloodied human perfection, the other a construct of absolute inhumanity, rage made manifest.

As close as they are, despite the changes to Angron's vision, he sees the tiredness etched on the Angel's features. The faint cuts and scratches that the Battle for Terra has written onto Sanguinius' flesh, indelibly marking him. This war has rendered the perfect imperfect.

'Die,' Sanguinius tells him, with the gentleness of giving a great gift. 'I free you from this torment.'

Angron's lips peel back in the memory of a smile. He tries to speak. Speaking is difficult, not because he is dying but because he is no longer a creature for whom speaking is a natural or necessary process. Speech is an echo from a lost life – the Lord of the Red Sands expresses himself in slavering roars and the death of his foes.

Sanguinius sees this. Sees the way Angron's face twists, trying to remember how to form words. Sees that the daemon is not dying.

The Lord of the Red Sands moves, but the Angel is faster. Sanguinius tears the blade free and leaps upward, taking to the sky. Bleeding, laughing, the daemon follows.

They swoop between the temple towers that rise from the back of Malax Meridius. They break away, into open sky. Sanguinius is slower in the open, but he is built for this; he is graceful and experienced and born for aerial warfare. Angron has the unreal strength of daemonic muscle, but he is a gargoyle chasing a hawk. Sanguinius weaves and soars and dives out of his clutches, and–

+Kill him.+

Horus, inside the daemon's mind. The words are bloated by the Pantheon, ripe with the borrowed power of the gods. Behind those words is the promise of pain, true pain, Nails-pain. The Lord of the Red Sands beats his wings harder, his sword leaving a trailing wake of screaming souls: the dead of Terra, singing their song.

They race low to the ground, hardly an arm's reach above the heads of their warring sons, fast enough that their armies are an indistinct blur. Angron swings the black blade. He gouges earth, he sends Blood Angels and World Eaters tumbling across the ground, their bodies destroyed, their souls spilling into the warp's million waiting maws.

Without warning, Sanguinius climbs, soars.

+This is your chance. What you were born and reborn for.+

The Lord of the Red Sands ignores Horus' puling. He senses Sanguinius tiring and sees it in the flicker of his soulfire. His brother's spirit ripples with the desperate sweetness of exhaustion. The war… the battlement… the Bane of the Ninth Bloodline… Yes, the Angel's strength is running dry.

The daemon gathers speed, flying into the polluted wind, while anti-air fire stitches the air around him. Sanguinius weaves aside from the blinding slashes of lascannon beams, rolls away from the juddering passage of a Legion Stormbird. Angron, far less manoeuvrable, crashes into it – goes through it – tastes the flavour of those doomed souls as their craft comes apart around them.

It is nothing to him, the expenditure of a breath's worth of effort. Behind him, the Stormbird falls from the sky, its hull aflame and cleaved in two. The largest piece of its structure will tumble against the side of the Sanctum Imperialis, detonating against the thickest void shields ever created. Wreckage will rain upon the warriors of both sides. Angron knows none of this, will never know it.

+Do not fail me, Angron.+

The babbling of a frightened creature, speaking as though it were in control. The Lord of the Red Sands pays it no heed.

They dive through the death-cloud of a falling Titan, into black smoke and the white fire of plasma. The billowing smoke cannot hide the light of the Angel's soul. Angron is close, close, close enough that he parts his jaws to reveal uneven rows of mismatched teeth that jut up from bleeding gums. As they circle in this burning, choking sphere that only burns and chokes one of them, the daemon gives a draconic roar. The sound is exultant and instinctive, it is unfiltered emotion, and it reeks more of triumph than rage.

Angron's mouth is still open when the spear, hurled from the Angel's left hand, strikes. It shatters most of the daemon's teeth, severs his tongue at the throat-root, and punches through the back of his head. With the cervical segments of his spine reduced to ectoplasmic chunks, Angron falls – boneless, stunned – from the sky.

The Angel twists in the smoke and follows his brother down.

Angron hits the Royal Ascension with cratering force at the heart of the two warring Legions. His impact kills almost a hundred warriors on both sides, but this is another concern outside the shreds of his sentience. The surviving World Eaters cheer him through the dust, they bay at him like loyal hounds, but he knows nothing outside his own fury.

He claws at the spear, he roars around its impaling length; in these helpless seconds he's beast-stupid in sound and action, thrashing in the dirt. The lance comes free, slick with ichor pretending to be blood, gobbets of daemonic flesh sizzling on its silver surface. Already, the daemon is reforming, reknitting, sustained by whatever metaphysical processes fuel his existence. The Lord of the Red Sands throws the weapon away in time to meet its wielder. The Angel descends with a silence that stinks of false righteousness – as though he were a creature too enlightened to feel rage.

The brothers collide in the crater they made. Around them, the battle for the Eternity Gate rages. The World Eaters are coming – the World Eaters and the Life Takers and the Blood Letters – Sanguinius senses them draw near, hears their howling; Angron sees this awareness dawn in his brother's eyes. Sanguinius hacks and hacks and hacks as the snarls of chainaxes and daemon-blades grow louder. It isn't enough. The Angel launches away, a crack of his wings carrying him upward.

The Lord of the Red Sands knows he can't catch Sanguinius in the sky. He scrambles for the fallen spear, draws it back, and this time, there is no chase. This time, Angron is ready.

He throws the spear, still slathered in ichor from when he tore it out of his own throat. The second he casts it, it rips through the air with a concussive drumbeat, breaking the sound barrier.

The Angel rolls aside with the grace of the sky-born, dodging this streak of bladed intent. No, Angron sees; not dodging. Faster than the human eye can follow, the Angel has caught his spear as it passed, rolled with the momentum, and now he casts it back to the ground with a cry of effort.

Angron will catch it, this twig of a thing, and–

He clutches nothing but air and the force of a meteor hits him in the chest, throwing him down, pinning him to the warp-stained ground. For several unreal seconds, the Lord of the Red Sands is impaled in place, speared through the chest. There is no pain, only humiliation.

He frees himself in time to see Sanguinius ascending. Leaving him behind. His wounds close, but slower, slower, slower than before. The Nails bite harder, despising his weakness.

Angron turns his back on his brother, seeking the lesser Blood Angels in Legion red. He wades through them, ending them, sending their bodies flying back, with heaving swings of his soul-thirsty sword.

If he cannot catch the Angel, he will lure the Angel back to him. He learned this from the Bane.

It takes no time at all. Angron has scarcely begun to shed blood before he hears the descending beat of angelic wings. The Lord of the Red Sands wipes the writhing bodies of dying Blood Angels from where they're spitted upon his blade, and turns to meet his brother once more. Bolt-shells impact against him. Chainswords carve into the un-meat of his legs. He ignores this, the pitiful defiance of his nephews with their bolters and chainswords. He will kill them and devour them and offer up their skulls to the Skull Throne, yes, but now, first, the Angel must die.

The brothers go at one another, sword to sword. They are a blur to the mortals around them, so swift are the clashes of their blades that their swords sing a single extended note, a lasting ring without crescendo or diminuendo. It is beautiful, that ululating chime. A masterpiece of broken physics.

But only one of them is immortal. Sanguinius, failed by mortal muscle, weakened by the war, begins to slow. His thrusts become *deflections; his hacks shift to parries. He gives ground, at first by centimetres, then with greater steps. Through eyes tense with effort, he sees that he's being driven back towards the violated Eternity Gate.*

The Lord of the Red Sands sees it dawn on the Angel's face, how the longer they fight, the weaker only one of them becomes. In the searing thresh that passes for Angron's mind, he knows it will come, any moment now, when desperation will force his brother's hand.

Blades clash. They clash. They clash and clash and clash and then...

Angron lets the silver sword run through him, taking it inside his daemonic corpus as a sacrifice. He uses the blow, feeding off the pain and craving the damage because it lets him get closer. Ooze bubbles through the cage of his teeth, the ectoplasm that animates him running from his body in a flow of lifeblood, but no matter, it's worth it. A taloned hand snaps around the Angel's throat. The other thrusts forward with his blade.

Deep in Ultima Segmentum, there was a planet that was not, in truth, a planet. A sphere of debris coalesced to form a planetary crust, but the world's deeper layers were saturated in a metanatural churn of etheric energy. This broken bauble in the shape of a world was called Sarum. It was liberated during the Great Crusade by the Eaters of Worlds, and it had supplied the bulk of that Legion's arms and armour ever since its bloodstained saviours left in liberation.

The most accurate description of Sarum would be to say it was a prison in the shape of a planet. Inside its core was bound a daemon of immense strength and cunning, the source of Sarum's hollowed-out corruption. Lesser reflections of this abomination – shards, if you will; children, if you prefer – spread themselves across the planet, bound in secret by the Mechanicum at the hearts of their subterranean forge-cities.

Several years ago, a flicker of time in the grand scheme of things, a blade was forged within the hallowed underground halls of the Saekorax Foundry. Laced with techno-ritualistic runes that bound a coven of warring daemons within its edge, the sword was shaped to be a blight on the physical universe, the blackened metal of its blade at odds with all corporeality. Like the strongest of the Neverborn's trillion conjured breeds, it destabilised the world around its presence, growing stronger with each soul it swallowed. Finishing it cost the lives of several artisans, devouring them in the process of its construction, and after it left the forge-fires, according to ritual law, it was quenched in the blood of several hundred slaves. These slaves were captives of the Great Crusade's expeditionary fleets, shuttled back to Sarum on the secret orders of high-ranking elements within the priesthood of Mars.

This length of ensorcelled brass was known as *Vuragh'th* in the bio-mechanical tongue of Sarum: the Black Blade. It was the Mechanicum's gift to Angron upon his ascension to immortality, simultaneously honouring his triumph at the end of the Path, and further heightening his place upon it. By the time the two primarchs faced one another at the Eternity Gate, it had tasted the blood of over a million Terran souls. It had slain innocents and soldiers, adults and children, humans and Astartes – the sword, like its wielder and like the god that owned its wielder's soul, cared not from whence the blood flowed.

With every drop of blood melted into its metal length, with every soul pulled in by the creatures thirsting inside the blade, its acidic effect on reality grew fiercer. The weapon was now almost as toxic as the creature that carried it, with a similar exertion of mutation and hostility on reality.

The Black Blade's makers would have rejoiced, albeit in the

ways of their austere and murderous rituals, to know their creation would one day taste the blood of the Great Angel.

Sanguinius jerks as the sword slides, with miserable slowness, into his guts. His perfect features darken with pain, and the Lord of the Red Sands feeds on that sight, feeds on the Angel's baring of teeth, feeds on the stink of Sanguinius' rich, running blood. The sensation is narcotic, intoxicatingly pure. Even the God of War, in whose shadow Angron stands, bays with pleasure at the shedding of this being's blood.

Angron's grip tightens on the Angel's throat. He thrusts the blade deeper, growling at the fresh flow of blood that bursts from his brother's mouth. Sanguinius' mouth works, but at first no words come forth. All he manages to breathe out is his brother's name.

'Brother…'

It is a struggle for Angron to speak, but a lifetime of bitterness is dredged with the agony in his brother's beautiful eyes. He sinks the blade deeper into the Angel's body, hilting it in his brother's guts, and draws Sanguinius in until they're face to face. He's close enough to smell the blood on his brother's breath. He's close enough for it to spatter against his face.

'Angron…'

No sound in life has ever been sweeter than his flawless, beloved, exemplar brother hissing his name in strangulation. Angron's jaws are poorly shaped for human speech, but the Lord of the Red Sands forces the words from his maw.

'Hark, the dying Angel sings.'

Sanguinius reaches for him with weak and clawless hands. It's pathetic. The performance of a weakling. The Lord of the Red Sands doesn't need to breathe; he cares nothing if his brother's hands find their way around his throat.

But the sweetness is fading. The adrenal rush drains away. Is this truly how the Angel dies? Is this all the fight Sanguinius has left in his celebrated form?

+Angron!+

Horus. The Warmaster, the coward, in orbit. The Lord of the Red Sands hears the voice break through his ecstatic haze, and senses Horus has been seeking to reach his blood-soaked mind for some time. There is derision in the Warmaster's presence, but above all, there is fear.

+Release him! Release him, he is–+

Sanguinius' reaching hands close on a fistful of the cranial cables that crown Angron's head. The Angel grips the technological dread-locks that form the external regulators of the Butcher's Nails, and the beast that Angron has become realises, too late, much too late – the Angel has played the same gambit, risking a blade, welcoming it, to get close.

+Kill him, before–+

The words cease to exist, replaced by pain. Real pain, a thing he thought he was incapable of experiencing, now stunning in its unfamiliar savagery.

The Lord of the Red Sands gives a roar loud enough that the Sanctum's void shields shimmer with a mirage's ripple. He tears his blade from his brother's body, grappling, hurling, but the Angel remains. White wings batter at the daemon's face and defeat the raking of his claws. He abandons his own blade to scratch and scrape at the Angel. He tears away shards of golden armour. Wings bleed. Feathers rain. Never once does Sanguinius make a sound.

Angron cries out, a cry flavoured by something other than rage for the first time since his exaltation. Agony lightning-bolts through his head, fire and ice, ice and fire, a sensation he no longer has the mind to understand but that will destroy him whether he under-stands it or not. He launches upward, beating his ungainly wings, striving for the sky. Turning and tumbling, seeking to dislodge the straining Angel.

On the battlefield below, the Legions duel in the rain of their primarchs' blood. The Lord of the Red Sands – Angron, I remember,

I remember now, I am Angron – *feels his skull creaking, stretching; then a crack, a crack that paints the back of his eyes with acid; it's the cracking of a slowly breaking window, the crack of a skull under a tank's treads.*

He hears his brother now: Sanguinius' ragged hisses of breath, coming in time to the scrape of his gauntlet against the pain engine's mechanical tendrils. Their eyes meet, and there is no mercy in the Angel's pale gaze. Sanguinius is lost to the passions he has always resisted. The Lord of the Red Sands sees it in the pinpricks of his brother's pupils, in the ivory grind of his brother's fangs. The Angel has lost himself to blood-need, and veins show starkly blue on his cheeks. This is wrath. This is the Angel unleashed.

It is an anger so absolute, Angron feels the bite of another forgotten emotion: jealousy. What he sees in the Angel's eyes is no bitter fury at a life of mistreatment, or rage goaded by the will of a god that only rewards slaughter. It feeds the God of War, as all bloodshed does, but it is not born of him.

It is the Angel's own fury, in worship of nothing but justice. How beautiful that is. How naïve. How pure.

This is the daemon's last cohesive thought. Fuelled by animal panic as much as sentient rage, Angron's frantic clawing does nothing to throw Sanguinius clear. The brothers fall together, the daemon's strength lost to convulsive thrashing, the Angel's ripped and bloodstained wings unable to keep them both aloft.

The dreadlock-cables are fastened deep in the meat of the monster's mind. They are not attached to the brain, they are part of it, tendrilling their way through the pain engine that replaced and so poorly simulated entire sections of the Twelfth Primarch's cerebellum, thalamus and hypothalamus. The Butcher's Nails are woven throughout his brainstem, hammered in to bind them to the spinal column and central nervous system. It is a process almost admirable in its barbaric effectiveness, one reproduced with malignant perfection in his exaltation from a mortal to an immortal.

From behind the veil, Angron hears laughter. A god, laughing at him, because it cares not from whence the blood flows. The death of the Lord of the Red Sands is as pleasing to this divinity as the death of any other champion.

Warpfire flares from the cracks in the beast's deforming skull. The cracks become crunches, each one a conflagration that sweeps from the filaments behind Angron's eyes to the spikes of his spine. There is the feeling of violation, a deep and slick wrongness as something is taken from him, pulled from the root of his mind.

He screams then, and he does something he has never done – in neither his mortal nor immortal lives. His roar of pained rage is coloured by a sound so shameful he will spend the rest of eternity refusing to believe it happened. The sound is a word, and the word is a plea. He begs.

'No,' the beast grunts to his brother.

This moment will never enter the legends of either Legion. The primarchs are high above the battlefield, and the few sons able to watch their fathers are too far away to know what passes between them. Only Sanguinius hears Angron's last word, and it is an intimacy he will take to his grave.

The ground rises with disorientating speed. It's now or never.

As they free fall together, the Angel gives a final wrenching pull on the serpents of barbarian metal. The daemon's head bursts. It's a detonation, a release of internal pressure like pus from a squeezed cyst: the lion's share of Angron's brain comes free in a spray of fire and acid blood. The daemon's wings beat once more, just a shiver, a thing of reflex.

His claws slacken. All struggles cease.

Sanguinius throws himself free of the falling corpse, spreading his wounded wings, first for stability, then for altitude. Beneath him, the daemon strikes the avenue of stairs, shaking the Royal Ascension and stealing what little reason remains to the gladiator-warriors of the XII Legion.

A twinned cry rises to where he beats his wings above the battle-field. The Blood Angels fight with renewed hope, seeing their father victorious, the slayer of daemons. The World Eaters, wracked by the psychic backlash of their slain sire, see the Emperor's Angel haloed by the rising red sun.

Inzar was close to the top of the Ascension, surrounded by World Eaters and deep in the shadow of the Sanctum, when the body struck the earth.

The corpse of the Lord of the Red Sands crashed upon the stairs leading to the Eternity Gate, breaking open on the steps of marble and gold. The earth quaked with the impact, and in its wake the Chaplain heard a colossal cry rise from the throat of every living World Eater. This lamentation wasn't wholly physical, but something blasphemous he felt in the creases of his mind.

Demigods should not die, he thought as that awful cry rose to the haloed angel above them.

Inzar's breathing was uneven, hastened by adrenaline but weighed with fatigue. He felt the ache of wounds he couldn't remember suffering; the hundreds of incidental cuts and stabs that took place in the grinding of battle lines. Warriors of the myriad Legions clashed everywhere around them in rabid packs, all cohesion lost, but always the Warmaster's tide had pressed forward. Until now.

He looked ahead, past the dead-whale grotesquery of Angron's smashed corpse, to where the Gate still stood open. Beyond that open portal lay victory. Wounded squads of Blood Angels were still falling back through the doors, firing at the advancing horde.

'Forward!' Inzar cried. 'Forward, for the Pantheon! Death to the False Emperor!' He levelled his crozius at the Eternity Gate and sought to urge the blood-maddened warriors around him onward through force of will and prayer. The Colchisian tattoos across his face started weeping blood.

'Preacher,' one of the nearby World Eaters grunted. Frantic now, desperate for any ally, Inzar turned to him. He didn't know the warrior. He was just one of thousands in the stalled tide.

The Chaplain met the man's eyes, not unlike the meeting of gazes that took place in the sky between two demigod brothers only minutes before. For the first time, Inzar learned what it was to have the bloodshot glare of Nails-madness turned upon him. In that stare he saw not just the absence of reason, but the death of it.

'Kill,' the warrior snarled, his vocal cords thick with blood, mucus, or both.

'Come with me, we can still rally the others and–'

'Maim.' The World Eater's gaze was bare of comprehension.

'I am Inzar of the Seventeenth Legion. Hear me and heed me. Rise, and we can end this. We are so *close*…'

The World Eater seemed to understand. He reached out a hand, as if to make an oath. Inzar took it.

'Burn.'

The World Eater pulled on the preacher's hand as he brought the axe up, chain teeth revving. There was no resistance, the chainaxe went through the joint like it went through bone, and it went through bone like water.

Inzar staggered back, his arm amputated at the elbow, and crashed into another warrior behind him. He had a fraction of a second to see the Death Guard he'd backed into, going down beneath the hacking axe of another World Eater. It was a scene repeated in woeful plenitude wherever Inzar turned. The World Eaters were falling upon their own allies, howling, cutting, killing.

Blood for the Blood God.

Kill. Maim. Burn.

Skulls for the Skull Throne.

The World Eater forced him back, stumbling over the slain. Inzar fought one-armed, swinging his crozius, facing a foe that moved so swiftly he could only process what the warrior was doing after it was done. The legionary didn't dodge or defend, he chopped at the haft of the crozius, severing it, and on the backswing he relieved the Word Bearer of his other arm, ending it at the shoulder.

The next swing went into Inzar's stomach, liquefying his intestines in a roar of chain teeth. The next cleaved down into Inzar's breastplate, the teeth churning with exquisite brutality, chewing through the layers of ceramite, muscle, bone and organ meat. Inzar's retinal display went red with the gush of blood he vomited into his helmet.

Combat narcotics and meditative focus couldn't deaden the excruciation of insides ground into mince, but the pain was secondary to the insane clarity that gripped him. The more he was carved apart, the colder and clearer everything became.

He thought, against the reality of what was happening: *Wait, do not do this.*

Then, a moment later: *We can still win. We can… still…*

Through red-stained vision, greying at the edges, he saw the World Eater towering above him.

Have I fallen? Inzar wondered. *Am I on my back?*

More of them drew in, clawing at each other, lost to madness in the aftermath of their primarch's death. One of them was convulsing hard enough that his weapon chain rattled against his warplate. He was the one to look down at the fallen Word Bearer, and he grinned with blood-streaked metal teeth. Inzar saw the axe's teeth cycling, cycling, and descending.

He heard the gods laughing as he died, and for the first time, there was no comfort in the sound. They were laughing at him. They'd always been laughing at him.

* * *

Lotara Sarrin bore mute witness as the vox-web and its attuned hololiths erupted in impossibilities. The *Conqueror*'s command deck hadn't seen this level of activity in months, with officers and ratings moving to consoles that came back to flawed life.

She moved from station to station, watching footage from the surface that couldn't be real, hearing reports in panicked voices she could barely understand.

'Someone get me a clear report of what's going on down there.' Lotara was revolted at her own shaking tone. 'Helm, negative barriers and roll us to Earthrise.'

The ship obeyed slowly. The armoured shutters protecting the bridge's gigantic windows withdrew, immediately admitting the warp's seething un-light. Rolling back the barriers changed nothing; the surface was hidden in the warp's tides, leaving them relying on hololiths.

'Any word?' she called across the deck. The surviving bridge crew were absorbed in their tasks, trying to make sense of what they were seeing themselves. She cursed the loss of her executive officer and practically everyone else of worthy rank.

A wave of nausea washed over her. She was getting angry, and her malnourished frame was punishing her for it. When had she last eaten? Or last tasted pure water? Throne, how many times had she asked herself those questions since reaching Terra?

Lotara rubbed gummy eyes and tried to refocus. Slowly, she made her way to her throne, turning away at the last moment with a dry heave. Like the rest of the bridge, it was matted with a rime of bloody matter, and glancing at it made her eyes ache, fit to burst. She lowered herself to the deck instead, sitting on the stairs of her raised dais. The only way she could still her trembling hands was by bunching them into fists and pressing her knuckles to the grimy iron floor.

The hololithic displays kept coming, spooling out images

with only the scarcest sense from the shouted reports. Lotara watched, piecing it together where she could. Her eyes were wide pools, reflecting the scrolling hololithic words.

Angron was dead.

Sanguinius had torn the crown from Angron's head and cast the Twelfth Primarch's body down the steps of the Sanctum. That alone was madness to countenance. She'd never have believed it without the scratchy pict-footage from helmet feeds, showing Angron's immense form crashing to earth and rupturing open.

The World Eaters had lost the last of their senses, baresark beyond sentience with the death of their father. Report after report cited the World Eaters turning on their own side, and on each other, in mindless butchery. The reports of Angron's humiliating death came not from the Legion, but from the human elements in Sanctum Imperialis Palatine, somehow still unslaughtered.

Other hololiths showed warriors of the Thousand Sons Legion undergoing... changes. Thousands of them were suffering rapid onset of mutation, flesh bursting from their armour, sending them into frenzies of psychic violence. The world was turning to stone and glass and meat around these unfortunates – at first, no one knew why. Was this the Sigillite's work? The wrath of the Emperor? The displeasure of the gods?

No, she knew, though she couldn't say how she knew. It was purely that nothing else made sense. *Magnus is dead, too.*

Lotara's attempts to reach any World Eaters officers on the ground met with abject failure. She got screams, she got static, she got howls that suggested a kind of pain she never wanted to know.

Lotara stopped trying. She watched the hololiths with their carnivals of massacre and mutation.

Two primarchs dead.

Two Legions lost to madness in the same moment.

Only one World Eater remained calm. Khârn, kneeling at Lotara's side, wordlessly watched Terra burn on the oculus. He had no interest in the hololiths beaming above the crew consoles. He was wholly unmoved by the crackling reports. He just watched the world slowly turn, slowly burn.

When a link to the surface came, it was riven by distortion. Lotara stared at the image resolving on the oculus. The thing she was speaking with was a legless amalgamation of three people, fused to the floor and sides of its cockpit with arches of bone and pulsing red flesh. Its arms were stalks and cables, forming power feeds to various machinery. It looked at her with six eyes, and answered her with three mouths, none of which were remotely human anymore. Strain coloured the creature's words, effort clear in its voices.

'This is Princeps Ulienne Grune of Audax. I command Hinda-rah. *Angron is dead. The assault is failing. We cannot keep the Gate open without immediate reinforcement.'*

Most of the creature was dead. Entire portions of its amal-gamated body were necrotic, mottled with the onset of rot. The way it was attached to its surroundings seemed to be sustain-ing it somehow, but not enough to keep all its extremities alive. Four of its six eyes looked milky, at best blind, more likely decaying. The feed wasn't clear enough to be sure.

'Sacred hell,' Lotara said under her breath.

'The Angel…' it said, and its voices drained away into a groan of effort. The thing's three tongues, two of which were black and sporting what looked like puncture holes from care-less fangs, briefly licked across the lower half of its face. *'We cannot–'*

The oculus went black. The command deck's lights, already dull with power drainage, glowed a sudden emergency red. It had been so long since the ship went to battle stations that it took the malnourished crew several seconds to realise and react.

'Voids to full!' Lotara called, but several officers were already working at it, lighting the generators from minimal layering to active shielding. When the ship shivered, it was with incoming fire splashing against her voids, not the deeper rumbles of impact damage. 'Who the hell is firing on us?'

Lotara rose to her feet before her throne, feeling more like herself than she had in months. Her mind was beginning to pick up speed again. *Betrayal*, she thought. *Someone in the fleet is firing upon us, and someone in the fleet is going to die.*

'Helm, bring us out of geostationary orbit and summon the rostered escort squadron to our side. Kindle the auxiliary reactors and run out the guns. Whoever is firing at us is about to regret it.'

One of the ratings by the Master of Vox station held a hand to his cabled earpiece. 'Speak,' Lotara commanded him.

'The whole fleet is under attack,' he called, looking past Lotara.

'Address me,' she ordered, 'not my throne.'

The officer's eyes unfocused as he processed the conflicting voices of several dozen officers aboard several dozen vessels.

'The attack isn't coming from another ship. It's coming from the surface. A sustained cannonade against the entire fleet.'

Lotara's blood ran cold. There was only one installation on the surface capable of...

'Pull us out of range. Shield us with our secondary squadrons, and open a channel to the *Vengeful Spirit*.'

The *Conqueror* juddered around them, its engines forcing a slow rise. The void shield trembles kept coming.

'The flagship is holding position in the upper atmosphere.' The console officer paused. 'And... its shields are down.'

Lotara turned to the man. *'What?'*

'The flagship's shields are down.'

'Minimal layering?'

'No.' He was addressing her throne again instead of her. 'They're entirely lowered.'

The oculus flared to life again in a blizzard of harsh static. It resolved partway, showing the silhouette of the *Vengeful Spirit*. Vessels of all classes around it were rolling, pockmarked with barrage damage, pulling up out of their bombardment positions to escape the firestorm lancing up from the surface. The flagship alone held its place. It was untouched. Ships in close formation were igniting, burning as they strove to fly free, but the *Vengeful Spirit* remained, impossibly unharmed.

'Incoming signal,' called the rating assuming Master of Vox duties.

The central hololithic table powered up again, projecting the stern image of a Legion warrior wearing the white of Jaghatai Khan's White Scars. His revolving image painted every upturned face a flickering blue.

'I am Shibhan Khan of the Fifth Legion, honoured to currently hold the mantle of regent-commander of the Lion's Gate space port. I address this message to the fleet of treasonous dogs laying claim to the skies of Terra. You will find Lion's Gate's surface-to-orbit defences are once again operational. Message ends.'

The hololith vanished. He was gone. Lotara almost laughed; Blood of the Emperor, but she admired his attitude.

Exhilarated now, she turned to retake her throne for the first time in weeks. Lotara approached the great seat of twisted metal, and froze.

'Don't look,' Khârn told her. He was still unarmed, his armour ruined by the blows that had killed him.

But she'd already looked. Now she couldn't look away.

There was a murderous thing sitting in her throne: a thing

with shining black eyes and malevolent flesh, as if some perverse whim had granted a loosely human form to the ship
itself. The thing in her throne wore her uniform, with her Red
Hand symbol on its slender chest. Its hair was a ratty snarl
of greying black, its mouth was a split-lipped slit housing an
arsenal of saw-teeth. It was captivating in the way apex pred-
ators were captivating. It radiated that same lethality.

And it was joined to the throne. From the immersion of
its limbs in the dark metal chair, it had been joined here
for months. Its unpleasantly human head swung left, then
right, the slits of its nose flexing as it sniffed the air, brazen
as any beast.

It looked hungry. It looked vampiric.

'It is Lotara Sarrin,' said Khârn.

Lotara backed away from the thing. It paid her no heed,
its lidless eyes blinking with wet flickers of blood-soaked
membranes. Claws the length of knives *clickety-clicked* on the
arms of the metal throne.

'Signal the *Vengeful Spirit*,' said the thing in Lotara Sarrin's
throne, in a rasping approximation of Lotara Sarrin's voice.
'Inform the Warmaster, we stand ready.'

The crew obeyed the thing at once, showing no fear, only
weary obedience.

She remembered the Warmaster's words, days before. *You
are not Lotara Sarrin.*

Lotara turned to Khârn, saying it because she had to say it,
not necessarily because she believed it.

'That's not… me. *I* am Lotara Sarrin.'

'You are a wraith,' said the throne-bound huntress. Her
voice was pitched snake-low, sibilant, not without sympathy.
'You are the *Conqueror*'s memory of Lotara Sarrin. You are the
machine-spirit's echo of what once was, given false life along
with the other ghosts that walk the halls of my ship.'

'*I am Lotara Sarrin,*' Lotara said again, her firmer tone only making her sound more desperate.

'You are not even the first of my spectres,' the huntress promised, and sincerity gleamed in her black eyes. 'The *Conqueror* conjures you along with the others, over and over. It brings back the dead that it remembers, and the living that have now changed. The crew is plagued by their former incarnations. These hauntings are just one of the ship's many madnesses as it awakens here in the warp. I was polite to the first few of you. I try to ignore you now. It upsets you when you learn the truth.'

'I am Lotara Sarrin,' she said one more time, the words breathless, escaping her lips as vapour.

'Do you know what I think you really are?' The huntress tilted her head, considering the ghost before her. 'You are my weakness, cut from me. You are my amputated doubts, echoing through my ship. You are the part of me that wanted to run from the *Conqueror.*'

I am Lotara Sarrin, she thought, finding she couldn't give voice to the fading claim.

The wraith was growing faint now. Lotara ignored it as she reclined in her filthy throne. There would be another one, and doubtless soon, drifting its deluded way down the ship's haunted hallways. It, too, would exert minor control over the ship's systems, thinking itself mistress of the *Conqueror.*

'Incoming message,' called her Master of Vox. 'Text only, pulse-beamed from an extra-solar location. The fleet has intercepted it from reaching Terra.'

Lotara welcomed the contact with a flicker of her talons. A message from beyond the Sol System? Today was shaping up to be a day of significant goings-on.

She brought up the message on the gore-crusted screen built into the arm of her throne, and ran her black orb eyes over

the words. Quite unintentionally, her bloody lips peeled back
from the ivory daggers she had for teeth.

'Who knew the Lord of the Thirteenth Legion could be
so sentimental?' She breathed the words through strings of
blood-pinked saliva. 'Keep blocking the signal. Don't let it
reach the surface.'

*Sanguinius lands with his back to the Eternity Gate. He has passed
beyond all of exhaustion's miseries and burned through the reserves
of his body. He has accrued wounds incidental and grievous, layering them upon each other month after month, leaving him a
patchwork revenant beneath armour of broken gold.*

*Two of his sons come to him, bearing his fallen sword and his
golden spear. To Sanguinius' shame, in his pain, he does not recognise them by the sigils on their armour. He thanks them nonetheless,
accepting the blade* Encarmine. *For now, he forgoes the spear.*

*Whatever malefaction was in the flames that erupted from
Angron's skull, Sanguinius' hand is a seared ruin. His fingers
curl in the charred shell of his gauntlet, but the flexion is tight
and the ligaments weak. This is far from the worst of his wounds,
but he cannot confront the truly grievous one yet. He can only feel
it, spreading through his bloodstream like burning venom, crystal-
ising in his joints, making it harder to breathe. His brother would
never use venom. This is something else, something worse.*

*He still carries Angron's crown, the Butcher's Nails. The bio-
etheric matter in Sanguinius' fist is a wretched squid of wet steel.
It trails lesser cords and shards of spinal bone like trophy ribbons.
He turns the parasite engine over – the cause of such grief, such
strife – and sees the last flickers of tainted electrical signals sparking along the vascular cables. Hanging from razor wire strings are
his brother's bloodstained eyes.*

*Sanguinius casts a final look over the Warmaster's horde – the
beasts still charging closer, the World Eaters lost in butchering each*

other, the Titans gearing up to fire upon their own side if it gives them even a whisper's chance of hitting him. They vent their rage on the Sanctum's voids, doing nothing but painting the air around the Eternity Gate with prismatics and fractals.

The Royal Ascension is warping, shifting with great cracks of mutating marble. The statues lining the avenue twist to become icons of sin. The ground splits and blackens at its burning edges, and the army of humanity's afterlife claws its way from the underworld. The gods are here. Real or not, they are here.

'The Gate,' the Custodians and his own sons cry at him. 'Seal the Gate, seal the Gate.' They fight and die all around him, some close enough to touch, some cut down here in the eleventh hour, some shedding blood in this last, desperate retreat. Those that pass into the shadows of the Sanctum will live, for now. Those that remain outside...

So many are yet too far to make it back, dying by degrees lower down on the platformed steps of the Royal Ascension. They fight on, encircled. Doomed. It breaks his heart to see such valour, and to know he must turn his back on it.

'Sire!' one of his sons calls, in the flood of retreating warriors. It is the Bringer of Sorrow, the one who exiled himself to Terra in shame, fighting at the side of the Flesh Tearer. Two sons that failed him in better times, making him proud now all is almost lost. He loves them as he loves all his Legion; and though he would never give it voice, his heart always goes out most to the disappointments, the ones that struggle to reach the perfection the others take for granted.

'Sire!' Zephon calls as he fights at his brother's side, in his father's shadow. Despair twists his familiar features. 'The Gate!'

Wings flex – no longer white; they're scorched, featherless in places, raked bloody in others – and Sanguinius launches upward, sword in one hand, the Butcher's Nails in the other. One by one he severs the chains: some snap in a single blow, others take a second hack to cleave through, but Audax iron gives way against the fall of the primarch's blade.

Freed, the Gate's engines grind again. The last Blood Angels that will make it through do so at a dead run. Not all of them make it. Some choose to turn, to fight, to buy a last few seconds for their brothers. Sanguinius lands between the closing doors. For a moment, he does not know which way he will walk – back into the Sanctum, or back out into the battle with those who have chosen to remain as rearguard and fight, to the end, and the death. He knows what he wants to do, but he knows what he must do.

The Emperor's Angel throws the wreckage of his brother's brain to the ground and crushes it beneath his boot. Then he turns his back on the war outside, and the Eternity Gate seals behind him with a crash that cuts him to his core.

The past is on one side of that sound. Fate is on the other.

EPILOGUE

A voice in the black

Sanguinius.

What transpires on the surface of the Throneworld, I cannot say.
What horrors you have endured, I cannot imagine.

All I know for certain is this: I am mere days from the system's
edge, and within a solar week, I will be in the skies above Terra.

With me I bring the entire might of the Thirteenth Legion, and
I am not alone; word has reached me from Russ and the Lion, at
the vanguard of the Sixth and the First. Our numbers are enough to
cleanse the heavens and tear the world from the Arch-traitor's grip.

Hold on to hope, brother. That is all I ask. Can you give me
that? Can you stand your ground for these last, ultimate hours?
Those elusive twins, Victory and Vengeance, are coming. This war
ends the moment I reach Terra.

Hold, in the name of the Emperor and the Imperium we have
built together.

I will be with you soon.

ACKNOWLEDGEMENTS

There's a lot of gratitude to go around on this one.

Prime thanks goes to the Besiegers: John, Guy, Gav, Chris and Dan, who I'll miss dearly now we're putting this beast to rest. Sincerest thanks to all of them for their encouragement and their patience with the eternal email chains, the double-checking, the reassurances, the ideas, and the streams of consciousness. That includes some extensive chatter with GMac, out there on his conquest of The Americas.

It'd be remiss of me not to especially thank Dan, here. Partly for the many 5am Skype calls we shared to plan Books 7 and 8 in their dark symbiosis, but mostly for his tireless efforts on the personal side of things. You know what I'm talking about here, Dan. Thank you.

Also some thanks on the side (but no less sincere for that fact) to Jacob for destroying his hands by writing down every word we said in the eight million Siege of Terra meetings.

Thanks to Dr. Daniel Smith, J. Wood and Richard Fletcher for their 'Okay, so the geology at work here...' when it came to annihilating Terra. A similar degree of gratitude to the consultants (especially G. Clarke) who helped me with the specifics of artillery, architecture, and meteorology.

An effusive *Ta, Mate* to Robb Dunphy for his desktop remote-connecting one fine day, managing to save a significant chunk of the book from the jaws of accidental deletion.

Thanks to Alfabusa for his insight and emotional support. Dude, you're lovely. I owe you. On a similar note, thanks to Chris Metzen and Toby O'Hara for always being there when it came to late-night mental health talk.

Thanks to Henry Cavill for saying something nice at the right moment, though I may never forgive him for not replying to my (admittedly extremely awkward) DM.

Thank you to Kate Hamer (WarHamer 40Kate) and Hannah Hughes for basically every word they said over the course of writing this novel.

Thanks to Neil Roberts for the amazing cover (one of your absolute best, N), and to Francesca Baerald for the breath-taking map.

And an extra special thanks to my editor, Nick Kyme, for all the usual reasons plus about fifty new ones. Professionally and personally, I owe you too much to mention on this list. We got there in the end, mate.

Last but never least, thank you to the readers for your patience and enthusiasm.

A portion of this book's proceeds will go to Cancer Research UK and Ellie's Retreat: a charity in Northern Ireland for H-ABC research and the affected, bereaved families.

ABOUT THE AUTHOR

Aaron Dembski-Bowden is the *New York Times* bestselling author of the Horus Heresy novels *Echoes of Eternity*, *The Master of Mankind*, *Betrayer* and *The First Heretic*, as well as the novellas *Aurelian* and *Prince of Crows* and the audio drama *Butcher's Nails*, for the same series. He has also written the Warhammer 40,000 novels *Spear of the Emperor* and *Ragnar Blackmane*, the popular Night Lords series, the Space Marine Battles book *Armageddon*, the novels *The Talon of Horus* and *Black Legion*, the Grey Knights novel *The Emperor's Gift* and numerous short stories. He lives and works in Northern Ireland.

YOUR
NEXT READ

DARK IMPERIUM
by Guy Haley

The first phase of the Indomitus Crusade is over, and the conquering primarch, Roboute Guilliman, sets his sights on home. The hordes of his traitorous brother, Mortarion, march on Ultramar, and only Guilliman can hope to thwart their schemes with his Primaris Space Marine armies.